CRACK IN THE CODE!

© 2021 Mojang AB. All Rights Reserved. Minecraft, the MINECRAFT logo and the MOJANG STUDIOS logo are trademarks of the Microsoft group of companies.

Published in the United States by Random House Children's Books, a division of Penguin Random House LLC, 1745 Broadway, New York, NY 10019, and in Canada by Penguin Random House Canada Limited, Toronto. Random House and the colophon are registered trademarks of Penguin Random House LLC.

rhcbooks.com
minecraft.net

Library of Congress Cataloging-in-Publication Data is available upon request.
ISBN 978-0-593-37298-2 (trade)
ISBN 978-0-593-37299-9 (library binding) — ISBN 978-0-593-37300-2 (ebook)

Cover design by Diane Choi

Printed in the United States of America
11

CRACK IN THE CODE!

By Nick Eliopulos
Illustrated by Alan Batson and Chris Hill

Random House New York

MORGAN

HARPER

PO

JODI

THEO

PROLOGUE

Theo Grayson stood alone in the Overworld.

He wasn't supposed to be here by himself. It was one of his friends' most important rules. **Nobody went into Minecraft alone.**

There were monsters out there, after all. And he and his friends had souped-up goggles that let them actually enter the game for real. And that meant the monsters, the danger—and the *unknown*—were real.

But today, curiosity had its hooks in him. He was here looking for something. Something new. **Something . . . unusual.**

Theo saw all the most common mobs of Minecraft. He saw chickens and sheep. He saw pigs and cows.

And then he saw something colorful out of the corner of his eye.

Theo's digital avatar didn't have a heartbeat, but he felt like his pulse was racing. His avatar didn't have lungs, but he felt like he was holding his breath. He spun around and looked to the sky.

There, fluttering in the air, was a single butterfly.

"I've done it," Theo said out loud, even though he was alone. **"I'VE CREATED A NEW MOB!"**

He hoped his friends would be impressed. He hoped they wouldn't be mad—even though he had broken a second rule that day.

He wasn't supposed to mess with the code.

But that was one rule he didn't agree with.

He was just doing a little modding.

What was the worst that could happen?

Chapter 1

THE MORE THINGS CHANGE, THE MORE THEY ... NO. WAIT. THIS IS GOING TO BE TOTALLY DIFFERENT.

Theo arrived early at Woodsword Middle School. For once, he was eager to start the day.

After all, he had news to share with his friends. Big news.

Big **Minecraft**-related news.

Theo was the newest member of an unofficial Minecraft club. On most days, the club met after school in Woodsword's computer lab, where they played Minecraft together on a shared server.

But Theo couldn't wait until after school. **He needed to**

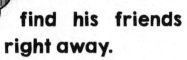

find his friends right away.

He hurried to the large oak tree where the group sometimes gathered before school. Today, only one figure stood beneath the tree. She wore a fedora and dark sunglasses. Despite the disguise, Theo recognized Jodi Mercado immediately.

"Hi, Jodi," he said. "Do you have a minute?"

"Jodi? Who's Jodi?" said Jodi. **"I'm Agent J. I don't know any Jodi!"**

"Oh," said Theo. "My mistake." What could he do but play along?

After a few moments of uncomfortable silence, Agent J lowered her sunglasses and whispered, "Just kidding, it's me. Jodi! But be cool—**I'm on a deep-cover surveillance mission."**

She leaned against the tree trunk and peered around it. Theo peeked, too but he didn't see anything of interest. A few students had gathered on the lawn. Safety patrols watched over the crosswalk. The public library stood across the street.

"What are we looking at, uh, Agent J?" Theo asked.

"Doc took a bunch of equipment into the library precisely"—Jodi glanced her watch—"four minutes and forty-two seconds ago. *High-tech* equipment."

"Is that unusual?" Theo asked. "Doc" was **Dr. Culpepper, their science teacher.** Theo knew she liked to tinker with technology . . . and that her tinkering often caused trouble. Her inventions and upgrades had a way of turning out not quite the way she planned.

"Everything Doc *does* is unusual," Jodi answered. "Maybe moving that equipment is harmless. Maybe it's nothing!"

"Yeah," said Theo. "You're probably—"

"Then again, *maybe* she's replacing the local librarians with cyborgs. **Once the cyborgs are in charge of the library, they'll control all the information.** And once they control the information, they'll control the world. Just think of the overdue fees they'll charge, Theo! Those fees will be astronomical!"

"Sure," Theo said. "Maybe that's it. Or maybe she's just donating old equipment. Or upgrading their air-conditioning. Or—"

"Hold that thought!" said Jodi, interrupting him. **"There she is."**

Theo looked again, and he saw that Jodi was right. Doc was in the crosswalk, heading back onto school property.

"I need to follow her. Sorry, Theo."

Theo shrugged. "Do what you have to do. But where's everybody else?"

"Dunno," said Jodi as she ducked behind a nearby bush. "I think Po is in the gym this morning. Check there!"

Po Chen was in the gymnasium, just like Jodi had said. As Theo watched, Po sped across the basketball court, turned his wheelchair on a dime, lined up a shot, and sent the ball sailing toward the basket. *Swish!* It was nothing but net.

Theo didn't know much about sports, but

it was easy to see why Po was a star player. Woodsword's basketball team was a mixed ability team, which meant that every player used a wheelchair during games, even though some of them didn't use wheelchairs in everyday life. It took a lot of practice—and somehow Po still had time for other extracurriculars, too. Including the after-school Minecraft club.

Theo thought that waking up early to practice sports *before* school sounded like way too much work. He could barely get out of bed in time for breakfast. **He yawned and almost got hit by a stray basketball!**

"Sorry, Theo!" said Po as he wheeled to the edge of the court. "That was a terrible pass. I almost turned basketball into dodgeball!"

"**No problem,**" said Theo. He retrieved the ball from beneath the bleachers. "I wanted to talk to you anyway," he said, handing Po the ball and lowering his voice. **"About Minecraft, and—the Evoker King."**

Po's jaw dropped. That had gotten his attention.

"Hurry up, Po!" said a teammate.

"Get back here!" said another. "You obviously need the practice."

"Ooh, burn!" said Po, smiling. "I'll show you who needs practice!" He turned back to Theo. "Sorry, man. Can it wait?"

"Sure," said Theo, frowning a little. "Do you know where the others are?"

"I know Harper had something to do in the science lab. Look for her there!"

Harper Houston was right in the middle of an extra-credit experiment. That was how she liked to use her morning time. With a pipette, she dripped liquid into a beaker, drop by drop. She spied Theo out of the corner of her eye.

"Sorry, Theo," said Harper. "I can't talk right this second. **If I lose my concentration here** even a little, the results could be . . ."

"Explosive?" Theo asked with a little too much enthusiasm. His favorite science projects involved rockets and volcanos and soda geysers.

"Well, no," said Harper. "I'm not working on anything dangerous. But if I get the measurements wrong, **it could make this whole wing of the school smell like skunk!** And nobody needs that right now."

Theo took a step back. "You've convinced me," he said. "I definitely won't distract you . . . with my news about the artificial intelligence who's been living in our Minecraft game."

Harper's eyes went wide behind her protective goggles. "Theo, you rascal! If anything can distract me, it's that. And you know it!"

He did know it. Harper was one of the smartest people Theo knew . . . and one of the most curious. She idolized Doc, loved science, and cared deeply about conservation and ecology.

She also had a great mind for Minecraft. Harper seemed to have every crafting formula and potion recipe committed to memory. Of *course* she would be interested in news about the artificial intelligence they called the Evoker King.

But Theo really didn't want to be responsible for stinking up the school first thing in the morning.

"Sorry, sorry," he said, grinning. "I'll fill you in later. **I'm going to try to find Morgan before the bell rings.**"

"Check the cafetorium," Harper said. "I think he had studying to do."

Morgan Mercado didn't even look up from his textbook when Theo approached his table.

"Not now, Theo," Morgan said. "I'm sorry, but I've got a test that I am *not* prepared for."

"No problem," Theo said. But he couldn't keep the disappointment out of his voice. **This was not how he'd imagined the morning going.** How were all of his friends this busy so early in the day?

Morgan seemed to realize Theo was hurt. He sighed and looked up from his book. "Is it something important?"

"Sort of," Theo  said. **"It's about the Evoker King, but I can tell you later."**

Morgan slammed his book shut and leaned forward. "Why didn't you say so in the first place?" he asked.

Theo grinned. He should have realized: Morgan *always* had time for Minecraft.

"I've been studying the code," Theo said. "And learning everything I can about mods. You know what those are, right?"

"Sort of," Morgan said. **"I know 'mod' is short for 'modification,' and 'modification' means 'change.' That's what you call it when someone makes changes to a game's code."**

"You're mostly right," said Theo. "Only, a mod

doesn't make changes to the *actual game code*. It's more like it puts extra code on top of the game code. Minecraft mods will do things like create new blocks or weapons or gems. They don't technically mess with how the game works. But they can make the game different in little ways."

Morgan nodded. **The Minecraft version that he and his friends had been playing was more than a little different.** It was uniquely weird. That was because Doc had used the school computers to experiment with virtual reality and artificial intelligence. So when Theo, Morgan, and the others played Minecraft . . . they played from *inside* the game. **Their minds were transported to a living, breathing world that was wondrous . . . but it also gave Survival Mode a totally new meaning!**

And they weren't alone in that world— artificial intelligence lived inside the game. He called himself the Evoker King. He had been their enemy, then their friend . . . and now he was in need of a rescue.

For reasons none of them understood, the Evoker King had turned to stone. He was a lifeless statue: Unmoving. Unfeeling. Unthinking.

It was a problem that Theo was determined to solve.

"Have you been trying to help the Evoker King?" Morgan asked. "Is that why you're learning about mods?"

"Yeah, exactly." Theo nodded. "Mods are how Doc affected the game. **That means it's a mod that gave the Evoker King access to Minecraft in the first place.** So I've been making my own mods. I've been practicing. *Experimenting.* So that I can figure out what went wrong with the Evoker King. So that I can fix him!"

He waited for Morgan to crack a smile. But Morgan looked deeply serious. "I don't know if this is a good idea, Theo," he said at last. "Messing with that stuff sounds risky. What if you make the problem worse?"

Theo wasn't sure what to say to that. He had thought Morgan would be thrilled with his idea.

"We should talk about this later," Morgan said. "I really do have to study."

"Okay," said Theo.

"And, Theo," said Morgan. **"Don't go messing with anything before we talk. Don't make any new mods, and don't make any changes to old ones.** Okay? This should be a team discussion."

"Yeah. Right," said Theo. "Of course. Team discussion."

But Theo knew it was too late for that. He'd created several mods already. And he'd started

tinkering with Doc's code. **He had done it without telling anybody what he was doing.** Morgan wasn't going to be happy.

Theo decided not to say anything more. He hoped his blushing didn't give him away. But luckily, Morgan had already turned back to his book.

Later in the day, Theo met up with the others. They gathered outside the computer lab, as they did most days.

After school was *their* time. To play Minecraft together. To share adventures and build great things.

But this was not a day like any other.

Morgan threw open the doors of the computer lab . . . and they all gasped at what they saw.

"**What in the world happened?!**" said Po.

In unison, Harper and Jodi said, "**The computers . . .**"

"**They're gone!**" Theo finished.

Chapter 2

NOT IN MY COMPUTER LAB, BUTTERFLY ... IF THAT IS YOUR REAL NAME!

Morgan was stunned. He couldn't speak. He couldn't move. **He felt like his brain couldn't process what his eyes were seeing.**

The computer lab was his favorite place. It was like a clubhouse—the one spot where he could forget about homework and chores and just spend time with his friends, gaming, laughing, sharing Minecraft adventures.

And now **the computer lab was gone**—replaced by some sort of indoor jungle. Bright green leaves were everywhere, and the air was warm and wet. A rain forest might as well have sprouted up in the middle of the classroom!

Were they in the wrong room? Were they at the wrong school? Were they on the wrong *planet*? Just what was going on here?

"Where did all these plants come from?" asked Jodi. She craned her neck for a better look and twirled in a slow circle.

"Well, they're potted plants," said Harper. She pushed a leaf aside for a better view. "They didn't just grow out of the ground. So someone brought them here."

"Did they bring the cocoons, too?" asked Po.

"Cocoons?" echoed Jodi. "Where?"

Po wheeled over to one of the plants and pointed out a small cocoon. Then another, and another. Now that Morgan knew what to look for, he saw them everywhere! They were hanging from leaves and light fixtures and windowsills.

"They're butterfly cocoons," said Harper. "From several different species, I think."

"This has to be Doc's latest mad-science experiment!" said Jodi.

"I knew we would be learning about butterflies in class this week," said Theo. "But this is overkill, even for Doc." Fascinated, he stuck out a finger to poke a cocoon.

"Careful!" said Harper. "They're fragile."

Theo poked the cocoon anyway. "You know, there are thousands of species of moths and

butterflies in the world. I don't think there'd be so many if they were *that* delicate."

Normally, Morgan would tell Theo to cut it out. But he was still reeling with shock. "I don't understand this at all," he said. He dropped to a sitting position, right on the ground, and put his head in his hands. **"Where did all the computers go?"**

Jodi snapped her fingers. "The public library!" she said. "This morning, I saw Doc taking equipment over there. She must have relocated the computers."

"Including the server we use to play Minecraft," said Theo. **"And the VR goggles—they're gone, too."**

"We should go across the street and see for

ourselves," said Po. "We can go right now!"

Morgan felt a little better now that he knew where the computers had gone. He sometimes teased his sister when she acted like a spy, but she *was* good at noticing things that other people missed. "Jodi and I should call our parents first," he said. "We need permission to leave school grounds."

Harper took out her smartphone. She was the only one of them who had one. "We can all take turns calling our parents," she said, handing the phone to Morgan first. "But hurry. I want answers as soon as possible!"

Morgan agreed with that, one hundred percent.

Excalibur County Library and Media Center was a large concrete building right across the street from Woodsword Middle School. Morgan had come here with his family almost every weekend when he was younger. They would go to story times and puppet shows and leave with stacks of picture books.

And no visit to the library was complete without a quick stop at the statue out front. It was Morgan's favorite kind of statue—one you were

allowed to touch! It was a model of a sword in a stone, just like the famous Excalibur of Arthurian legend. Because of the statue, and because Excalibur County Library and Media Center was such a mouthful, kids had always just called the place **Stonesword Library.**

Morgan touched the statue for good luck as he walked past.

As soon as they stepped inside, they saw two familiar figures standing in the lobby.

Ms. Minerva, their homeroom teacher, was talking with their science teacher, Dr. Culpepper. They were Morgan's favorite teachers, but they didn't always see eye to eye. In fact, Morgan quickly realized, they were having an argument right now.

"Absolutely not, Doc!" said Ms. Minerva. "Not here. **The library is my happy place!**"

"I only want to make it happier!" said Doc. "Don't be so afraid of progress, Minerva."

Morgan desperately wanted to run up and ask Doc what was going on with the computer lab. Ms. Minerva might know, too. She was the only adult who knew all about the Evoker King, and **she had even helped them on some of their Minecraft adventures.** For a grown-up, she was a whiz at gathering resources.

But Morgan knew better than to interrupt when adults were in the middle of whatever it was that adults found to get so upset about.

"You've already turned Woodsword into your own personal high-tech wonderland," Ms. Minerva

said to Doc. "The lockers
are secured with biometric locks,
the overhead lights are controlled by
whistling, **and the coffee maker
chats about the weather while it
brews.**" Ms. Minerva rubbed her temples. "And
the coffee isn't even very good!"

"Those are all wonderful innovations," Doc
argued. **"I refuse to apologize for making
Woodsword the most technologically
advanced school in the district.** And I
certainly won't apologize about the coffee. Coffee
always tastes terrible, and you drink too much
of it. How many cups did you have today?" Doc
leaned forward and sniffed loudly. "I smell at least

five cups on your breath."

Ms. Minerva gasped. **"How dare you?!"**

Beside Morgan, Theo chuckled. "Wow, this is entertaining," he said. "I should have brought some popcorn."

Morgan didn't think it was funny, though. Watching the teachers argue made him feel anxious.

"You forgot to sign in," said a voice. Morgan turned to see a man holding a clipboard. He was an adult, but obviously younger than the teachers. He wore colorful sneakers that matched his necktie.

For a moment, Morgan worried that they were in trouble. But the man smiled as he handed Morgan the clipboard. "You're Woodsword students, right? Just sign in here, and then you're free to explore."

"Thanks," Morgan said, signing his name to the sheet. **"I've never been here without my parents."**

"And we haven't been here at all in at least a year," said Jodi. "We mostly use the school library these days."

The man's eyes went wide. "Then you'll need the

tour. A lot has changed here in the last year." **He took the clipboard back when they'd all signed it, and he shook it gently.** "*This* will have to change next. I mean, a sign-in sheet for the computer room on a clipboard just feels so old-fashioned, don't you agree? Hopefully Doc can help us with that."

"Does Doc work here?" asked Harper.

"Not officially," said the librarian. "But she's helping us upgrade some of our equipment."

Morgan snuck a look at Doc. She and Ms. Minerva were still in the lobby, waving their arms in the air as they talked loudly.

"Someone should probably shush them," said the man. "But I'm not that kind of librarian."
He smiled. **"My name is Mr. Malory.** I'm the new media specialist. Let me show you around."

Mr. Malory took them on a brief tour. Morgan thought he knew what to expect—books, and a lot of them. But there were also vinyl records, DVDs, and even video games!

Harper ran ahead to look at a bulky electronic object. "Is this a 3D printer?" she asked.

"It is!" said Mr. Malory. "You'll be using it for some of your STEM projects this year. And look over here." He pointed through a large window, into a room where a teenager with a VR helmet sat at a computer with a steering wheel attached to it. "This is our driver's education room. We only have one device so far, but I hope to expand it."

Po made a high-pitched sound of pure joy. **"VR can teach me how to drive? Sign me up!"**

Mr. Malory chuckled. "Not until you're older, I'm afraid. That room is strictly for teens."

Jodi grinned at Po. "By the time we're teenagers, they'll probably be able to beam the driver's manual directly into our brains."

"You might be right," said Mr. Malory. **"Technology is changing at a rapid pace.** And educators like me need to keep up with those changes."

"I couldn't have said it better myself," said a familiar voice. Doc approached the group, grinning from ear to ear. "Mr. Malory and I are going to bring this building into the twenty-first century!"

"There's nothing wrong with this place as it is," said Ms. Minerva, who trailed behind Doc. "And there isn't enough space to make all the changes you want to make."

"There will be plenty of room if we digitize more of the books," said Doc. She waved an electronic tablet under Ms. Minerva's nose. **"I have a whole library's worth of books on this tiny device!** There's no reason to have shelves and shelves of books taking up space."

"There is every reason in the world to make room for books," said Ms. Minerva. *"Especially* in a library." She closed her eyes and took a big, deep breath. "For one thing, a library should smell like books. I love that smell. Don't you?"

Doc took a sniff of the air . . . and promptly sneezed into her sleeve. "I'm allergic to dust," she said.

Mr. Malory stepped forward. "Don't worry, Ms. Minerva," he said. **"The books aren't going anywhere."**

Ms. Minerva nodded. "That's all I wanted to

hear. I know I can trust you to keep Stonesword special." She turned to the kids. "Mr. Malory here was my student not too many years ago. I had a feeling he would grow up to be a librarian."

Mr. Malory cleared his throat. "Technically, I'm a media specialist."

Ms. Minerva grinned at the kids. "I've always preferred to be called a 'librarian,' personally."

Morgan grinned back. When Ms. Minerva played Minecraft, she wore a modified villager skin and called herself the Librarian.

"That reminds me. I think I know which technological innovation these students are looking for," said Ms. Minerva. And she pulled a familiar VR headset from her duffel bag.

Morgan felt a rush of relief. **That VR headset wasn't just an average piece of equipment.** Doc had upgraded it with cutting-edge technology. **There were**

only six of them in the entire world!

"I'm so glad to see this," Morgan said, taking the headset as soon as Ms. Minerva offered it to him.

"I almost forgot in all the excitement," said Jodi. **"But what exactly happened to the computer lab?"**

Ms. Minerva raised an eyebrow and looked at Doc. "Yes, Doc," she said. "Why don't you fill us in?"

"Okay, so, technically, that's my fault," said Doc. "I left the lid off a terrarium over the weekend."

"Right," said Po, tapping his chin. "The terrarium. It all makes sense now." He leaned over to Harper and whispered, **"What's a terrarium?"**

"It's like an aquarium," Harper said. "But without the water."

"Right you are," said Doc. "And this particular terrarium was full of caterpillars. The little things escaped and got *everywhere*."

"Doc didn't want to disturb the caterpillars—especially when they started spinning their cocoons," said Mr. Malory. "So she asked if she could move the computers here. Now Woodsword has its very own butterfly sanctuary, and **Stonesword will be hosting a few of Doc's classes and after-school activities."**

"I hope you know what you're in for," said Ms. Minerva. "Doc is brilliant. But chaos follows wherever she goes."

"That's unkind, Minerva," said Doc. "You shouldn't say such things in front of Mr. Malory."

"It's the truth!" said Ms. Minerva. "Or did you miss the morning announcements today, when your AI newscaster gave advice on how to make bigger, wetter spitballs?"

"It's news the kids care about!" Doc replied defensively.

"I can't listen to any more of this," said Ms. Minerva. **She handed the duffel bag of headsets to Morgan and stormed out.** "I need a *real* cup of coffee."

"We're not done . . . discussing!" said Doc, running after her.

Mr. Malory sighed.

"Maybe I should have shushed them after all,"

he said with a mischievous grin.

"**They disagree a lot,**" said Jodi. "But that felt especially intense."

Morgan gripped his headset to his chest. "Mr. Malory?" he asked. "Are we allowed to use the computers from the Woodsword computer lab?"

"Of course," said the media specialist. "Doc has everything set up and ready to go."

Morgan breathed a sigh of relief. **It felt like everything around him was changing faster than he could handle.**

But there was one place they could go where everything made sense: **Minecraft!**

Chapter 3

THAT FEELING WHEN A PRETTY GOOD PLAN GOES TERRIBLY, TERRIBLY WRONG . . .

Jodi always felt a thrill when she opened her eyes and saw Minecraft's Overworld spread out before her in glorious 3D. It was a just as real as the real world—a virtual space that she could *touch*.

But there was a twinge of disappointment this time, too. Because she saw the rolling hills, blocky trees, swaying flowers, and shining square of sun . . . but she didn't see her friend Ash.

Ash Kapoor was an important part of their Minecraft squad. She was a scout, a natural leader, and a good listener. Things hadn't been quite the same since she'd moved away.

They kept in touch. Ash had even taken the

sixth headset with her so she could join them in the game world from time to time. But they'd had a hard time making that happen. Ash was busy in her new home, and her school wasn't on the same schedule as Woodsword.

Jodi missed her friend.

"What's that over there?" Harper asked. "Is that a camel?"

"You'd better get your vision checked, Harper," Po said, teasing. "I'm not a camel. I'm a butterfly!"

Po liked to change his avatar's skin every few days. Today, in honor of the cocoons in the old computer lab, he was trying out a butterfly skin.

But Harper hadn't been talking about Po. "Not

you," she said. "Up there, on the hill. Look!"

Jodi turned to see what Harper had spotted. **It was a huge, animal-shaped concrete sculpture atop the nearest hill.** A small stream of water fell from its mouth to form a river in the grass. Jodi recognized Ash's handiwork immediately.

"IT'S A LLAMA," Jodi said, smiling. "It's even sort of spitting like a llama, see?"

"It looks more like it's drooling," said Po.

"Still, it's pretty cool," said Morgan. "Ash must have made that." He turned to Jodi. "It's her way of saying hi to you, Jodi. She knows how much you love llamas."

Jodi's heart swelled. It was the best sorry-I-missed-you present she could imagine.

Theo, on the other hand, was too occupied with Evoker King to even look at the statue. "I can't believe it," he said glumly. "The Evoker King is *still* solid stone."

Jodi looked the Evoker King over from top to bottom. Theo was right. The King hadn't changed at all. He hadn't moved an inch since the day he'd turned to stone. They were no closer to understanding what had happened to him, or why.

"WELL, HE HAS TO CHANGE BACK EVENTUALLY," said Po. "Doesn't he?"

Harper shrugged her blocky shoulders. "It's impossible to say. We just don't have enough data."

"Well, we can't stay here much longer," said Morgan. "We've been in this spot for ages, hoping that whatever happened to E.K. is temporary."

Po realized that Morgan was right. **They'd been spawning in the same area for a while, afraid of leaving the Evoker King behind.** Of course, they'd still had plenty of fun. Po got to try out new skins and role-play different characters. Jodi got to make sculptures. Harper was happy as long as they had materials to mine, and Morgan was happy as long as there were hostile mobs to fight.

The monstrous mobs were endless. They always appeared when the sun went down. But Po and his friends were having a harder time finding good materials in the caverns below their feet. They had mined most of the good stuff. All that was left in the area was stone and dirt.

"I think it's time to go," said Harper. "If we want to gather new resources, we need to move on."

Jodi's jaw dropped. **"BUT WE CAN'T LEAVE HIM!"** she said. "We had *just* convinced him to be our friend. How would he feel if he woke up and realized we had abandoned him?"

Harper rubbed her chin. "Okay. So what if we take him with us?" she suggested.

Po made a show of trying to push the Evoker King over. **"HE'S REALLY HEAVY,"** he said.

"Hm." Theo squinted. "Stuff in Minecraft doesn't really have *weight,* though. So how can he be heavy?" He poked the statue. "I think it's more likely that he's fixed in place. He's part of the scenery now. But maybe we could move him . . ."

"**WITH A SILK TOUCH TOOL!**" said Morgan.

"What's that?" asked Jodi.

"It's an enchantment," her brother answered in his geeking-out voice. "If you enchant a tool with Silk Touch, you can remove a fixed item without breaking it. **YOU SORT OF JUST . . . KNOCK IT LOOSE.**" He turned to Harper and Po. "What do you two think?"

"I think it's worth a try," said Harper.

"The Evoker King should fly free," Po said, dramatically fluttering his digital wings. "Like me!"

Morgan rolled his square eyes at Po's butterfly voice, but Jodi giggled.

"So we'll craft a Silk Touch pickaxe so we can move him," said Theo. "Then we can put him on a mine cart, lay down some rails, and take him to our next base of operations."

"I like it!" said Jodi. "Good plan, Theo."

Theo smiled brightly. "Thanks."

"We should have everything we need for the enchantment," said Harper. She ran into the small building where they kept their beds and their chests full of resources. **They called it the Shack.** When she came back, she set an enchanting table down on the grass and held out a shining blue rock. "I was hoping we'd find a good use for this lapis lazuli."

"Ooh, pretty," said Jodi.

"Pretty . . . and powerful," said Harper. **"LAPIS LAZULI CAN PROVIDE THE ENERGY NEEDED FOR AN ENCHANTMENT."**

Morgan set a smelter next to the enchanting table. "We've mined a lot of iron ore lately," he said. "We should smelt it all into ingots. We'll need those for the mine cart and rails."

"I'll go get the ore," Po said, fluttering into the Shack.

"And I'll provide the pickaxe," said Theo. He held out an iron tool. "Here you go, Harper. Go ahead and work your magic."

It only took a moment. Harper fed the blue lapis to the enchanting table. **There was a burst**

of light, and Theo's pickaxe shone with the power of the enchantment.

"I guess I'll do the honors," Theo said. He approached the Evoker King. He gripped his pickaxe, lifted it above his head . . . and swung.

Where the pickaxe struck the stone, **a crack appeared.**

"Stop!" said Morgan.

"That doesn't look good," said Jodi.

Theo took a step back. His eyes were fixed on the Evoker King, and on the small crack in his stony skin.

As they watched, **that crack began to grow.** And glow . . .

Chapter 4

DON'T BUILD WALLS BETWEEN YOU AND YOUR FRIENDS. DO BUILD WALLS BETWEEN YOU AND HOSTILE MOBS OF UNKNOWN ORIGIN.

Po stepped out of the Shack in time to see the Evoker King splitting apart.

Po was usually quick with a joke. He didn't take many things seriously. **Even when Minecraft got scary, he usually remembered that it was a game.**

But this wasn't funny. What if the Evoker King crumbled to dust before their very eyes? What if their new friend was just . . . shattered?

Broken?

Destroyed?

Po had to do something!

He crossed the grass in a hurry. Then he

wrapped his arms around the Evoker King's stony surface. Maybe if he squeezed tightly enough, he could hold him together.

Maybe not.

There was a great flash of light and a sound like breaking pottery. Po flew backward—wings and all—and crashed into his friends. They tumbled to the ground in a heap.

When Po lifted his head off the ground, the air was thick with curls of smoke and something bright and colorful, flickering and flitting. **Butterflies?** There weren't supposed to be butterflies in Minecraft, but Po could swear he saw them fluttering through the smoke.

Maybe he just had butterflies on the brain.

He strained his eyes. Just barely, he could see something else moving in the smoke. Something much bigger than a butterfly . . .

"Is . . . is that you, **E.K.?**" he asked.

There was no answer except a low growl.

"That sure didn't sound like him," said Morgan.

Po still couldn't make out many details through the smoke and dust. **Was that . . . a wing? A huge rocky fist? A pig snout?**

Something was very, very wrong here.

Po started laying down a row of blocks. Stone, dirt, brick—anything and everything he had in his inventory.

"WALL. NOW!" he shouted.

Harper quickly joined him. They didn't stop until there was a low wall between them and . . .

whatever was out there.

"What did you see?" asked Morgan. Po just hushed him.

They all waited in silence for a long minute.

They heard grunting and growling and a series of wet snorts. Then they heard flapping wings and trudging feet. All the sounds began to get farther away. Finally, there was silence. Po waited another minute before he poked his head above the wall.

There was nothing there. Just a crater where the Evoker King had once stood.

"What in the world was *that*?!" Jodi cried,

leaving the safety of the wall to peer into the crater.

"That shouldn't have been possible," said Harper. **"I GOT THE ENCHANTMENT RIGHT ... I KNOW I DID."**

"Maybe someone else should take this thing," Theo said, setting down the glowing pickaxe. "I feel sick."

"I don't understand what happened," Po said. He looked around. "Did the Evoker King just explode? Is he . . . gone? Forever?"

"Maybe not," said Jodi. **"LOOK OVER HERE. FOOTPRINTS!"**

Po saw what she meant. There was a line of little squares leading away from the crater, across the grass, and into the nearby forest. Those squares looked like small, blocky footsteps.

Morgan seemed suspicious. "Since when are there footprints in Minecraft?"

"Well, I can explain that one, at least," Theo said. He snuck a guilty look at Morgan. "It's a mod."

"DOC MADE A FOOTPRINT MOD?" said Po. "Why haven't we noticed it before now?"

"It's not one of Doc's," Theo said. **"IT'S ONE OF MINE."**

Morgan frowned. "I thought I told you not to add any new mods," he said.

"But I did this before you said that," Theo said quickly. "And this mod is harmless. And helpful!" He smiled. "I did it for Ash. This way, if we ever leave our Shack without her, she can just follow our footprints to find us."

"Sure," said Morgan. "But what else might follow our footprints? What if this mod leads monsters right to us?"

Theo's smile evaporated. "I don't think that will happen."

"You don't *think* so," said Morgan. "But that's the point. You aren't sure. You're being reckless!"

"Morgan," said Jodi. "Don't be mean."

"I'm not being mean!" Morgan argued. "Unlike Theo, *I'm* being a team player. When you're on a team, you talk about this stuff before you do it." He turned to face Theo. "Okay, Theo? **YOU CAN'T JUST DO WHATEVER YOU WANT TO DO, BECAUSE IT AFFECTS US ALL.**"

Theo looked like he wanted to shrink away into nothing. The blocky shoulders of his avatar

drooped. "Sorry, Morgan," he said. "I'll be more careful in the future."

That seemed good enough for Morgan. He let the conversation end there.

But Po couldn't help wondering about something. Theo had said, **"IT'S ONE OF MINE."**

One of them?

Did that mean Theo had installed more mods?

Was their game of Minecraft about to get even stranger?

Chapter 5

JOIN THE DEFENSIVE CIRCLE TODAY! YOU'LL BE GLAD YOU DID.

Harper led the way into the forest. She let the footprints guide her.

"Evoker King?" cried Jodi, creeping along behind her. "ARE YOU OUT HERE, EVOKER KING?"

"Man, that name is a mouthful," said Po. "When we find him, we should really suggest something a little easier. Like Bob!"

"I don't think we should be shouting *anything* right now," said Morgan. "It's dark under these trees. Something dangerous could spawn here."

"We might be *following* something dangerous," Harper added. "If these are the Evoker King's tracks . . . **IF HE SURVIVED WHATEVER HAPPENED BACK THERE . . .** why would he have come this way? Why avoid us?"

"Yeah. Hope for the best," Theo said. He pulled a splash potion from his inventory. "But be prepared for anything."

Harper certainly hoped they would find the Evoker King. **He was an AI so advanced that he had emotions and he loved Minecraft as much as Harper and her friends did!** Her mind reeled thinking about how much they could learn from him, if only they got the chance.

As they walked on, Harper noticed something strange. A block of wood was missing from a nearby tree's trunk. A minute later, she saw the missing block of wood on the ground ahead. Based on the footprints, whoever they were following had moved that block of wood.

And now she saw similar signs all along the path: **A block of dirt missing from the ground.** A block of spruce wood stuck onto an oak tree. The signs appeared completely random.

While she wondered about that, Harper spotted a butterfly flitting between the trees. It took her a moment to realize—**there were no butterflies in Minecraft.**

She looked back at where it had been. There was nothing there.

Maybe Po was right. Maybe she needed to get her eyes checked.

The trees parted, revealing a clearing in the forest. Clouds had moved in to cover the square sun, making the light dim, but Harper could see a figure standing on the far side of the clearing. **It was tall and blocky, and it seemed to be stacking blocks.**

"I think that's him," Jodi said.

"It looks like him," Harper agreed. She felt a rush of hope, and cried out, **"EVOKER KING! HELLO? OVER HERE!"**

The figure paused at the sound of her voice. It turned to look at them.

"That's not the Evoker King," said Morgan. "That's an enderman. Harper, don't look!"

Too late. Harper turned her head, but the enderman had seen her staring.

And endermen *hated* to be stared at.

The mob emitted a low, terrifying shriek. Harper risked taking another look—but it was gone.

"IT'S TELEPORTING!" she said, and as soon as the warning left her mouth, the enderman appeared right in the middle of their group! With a wave of its long arm, it sent Harper stumbling backward. Then it swung at the others. Jodi and Morgan were both hit.

"OH NO, YOU DON'T!" said Po, and he readied his weapon. If it weren't such a serious moment,

Harper would have laughed at the sight of a butterfly armed with a sword. Funny or not, Po's attack was useless. The enderman teleported away again, and Po's sword swept through empty air.

"IT'S FAST," said Po.

"Unusually fast," said Morgan. Then the enderman appeared right behind him, striking him again before blinking away.

"Ow!" said Morgan. He looked around the clearing, frantic. "I don't think I can take many more hits like that one."

"Everyone, clump up!" said Harper. "Put your backs together so it can't sneak behind us."

"No, we should go on the offensive!" said Theo. **"I'VE FOUGHT PLENTY OF ENDERMEN BEFORE."**

Po and Morgan joined Harper. They drew their weapons and stood back to back. **Fighting mobs was not Jodi's preferred way of experiencing Minecraft,** but she knew a good idea when she heard it. She quickly joined them in the defensive circle.

Theo, however, stood alone.

"Don't be careless," said Po.

"Theo," Jodi hissed to get his attention.

"Get over here," said Harper.

Thunder rumbled overhead. Suddenly, the enderman reappeared right in front of Harper.

She slashed with her sword, and its eyes flashed—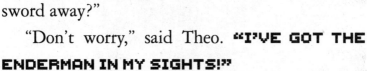

And her sword disappeared.

"What was that?" she said, shocked. "Did it just teleport my sword away?"

"Don't worry," said Theo. **"I'VE GOT THE ENDERMAN IN MY SIGHTS!"**

Theo lobbed his splash potion at the mob, which quickly blinked away—and the splash potion splattered all over Harper and her friends.

"Watch it, Theo!" said Morgan.

Morgan was in bad shape. Harper worried that he must be very low on health. "I think we need to retreat so Morgan has a chance to heal."

"YOU GUYS GO," said Theo. "I'll cover you."

"Don't be ridiculous," said Harper. **"IT'S TOO DANGEROUS."**

Just then, thunder rumbled once more, and it began to rain. From somewhere nearby, the enderman shrieked as if in pain. Harper whirled around in a circle, but the hostile mob was nowhere to be found.

"They hate the rain," said Morgan. He grimaced. "I don't think it's coming back. We got lucky, and just in time. My hearts are low."

"Drink this," Harper said, and she handed Morgan a healing potion.

"THAT WAS A DISASTER," said Po. "That thing almost handed us our blocky butts."

"We had it under control," said Theo. "It was just an enderman!"

Harper wasn't so sure about either of Theo's points. It hadn't felt like they'd had things under control. **In fact, with Ash gone and Theo here, it felt like their teamwork just wasn't clicking like it had before.**

As for it being "just an enderman" . . . Harper couldn't shake the feeling that there was something different about the mob they'd just fought. It was a little too fast. A little too strong.

And its eyes had glowed red with rage and hate . . . and intelligence. Those eyes would haunt her dreams that night.

Chapter 6

FRAZZLED TEACHERS, MAD SCIENTISTS, UNWANTED APPAREL . . . AND THAT'S ALL BEFORE THE END OF LUNCH!

Those red eyes haunted Morgan, too.

Morgan was known throughout Woodsword Middle School as a walking encyclopedia of Minecraft—especially Survival Mode. He knew which mobs could be tamed. He knew the exact elevations to find specific gems. He knew strategies for fighting every hostile mob . . . **and he knew that the enderman they had fought was not normal.**

On their walk to school the next day, he told Jodi all about it. "Endermen are supposed to have purple eyes," he said. "That thing's eyes were red. And I've never heard of any mob being able to

disarm a player like it did Harper. We never did find her sword. . . ."

Jodi nodded along as he spoke. She looked lost in thought.

Morgan continued, **"It wasn't like any enderman I've seen.** It was like some kind of . . . Endermonster."

"I'm more worried about the Evoker King," said Jodi. "Did the Endermonster destroy him? And what were those icky mobs we saw in the smoke? There was definitely more than one, right?"

"I'll bet it's Theo's fault," Morgan grumbled.

"Morgan!" said Jodi. "Be nice."

"What? You heard him," said Morgan, waving his arms in the air. **"He's been installing mods behind our backs.** And he was a total mess during the Endermonster fight. It's like he's

never even *heard* of teamwork before!"

Jodi frowned at him. **"Maybe he'd be better at teamwork if you treated him like part of the team."**

"You think it's *my* fault?" Morgan asked. "You can't blame me for his mistakes."

Jodi shook her head. "I'm not blaming you. I'm just pointing out that you aren't always very welcoming to new people. Remember when Ash moved here? You didn't want to include her in anything. But when you started being nice, she became one of your best friends."

"Well, that's the whole problem," said Morgan. **"Theo is no Ash."**

"Just promise me you'll make an effort," said Jodi. "Be a little more welcoming. Please?"

Morgan crossed his arms. "Yeah. Okay. Fine," he said. "I'll make an effort."

Morgan knew he wouldn't have a chance to talk to Theo until lunch. He hoped for an easy, quiet morning in the meantime.

But homeroom got off to a weird start. **"Pop quiz time,"** said Ms. Minerva. "Everyone ready?"

The students shared a confused look. Finally, Morgan raised his hand. "Um, Ms. Minerva?" he said. "This is homeroom. We don't actually have quizzes or grades in homeroom, right?"

Ms. Minerva straightened her glasses. **They were smudged, and her hair was in disarray.** "Oh, yes," she said. "What was I thinking? You're right, Mulligan."

Mulligan? Now Morgan was really worried. "Uh, my name is—"

Morgan was interrupted by the squeal of the loudspeaker coming to life. "Today's morning announcement is as follows," said a voice. **It wasn't the usual robotic voice of the school's announcement AI.** This voice sounded human—but weird. Like someone was

trying to disguise their voice. "The faculty lounge's *exquisite* combo coffee maker and weather prediction device is out of order. Do not expect repairs until *somebody* apologizes for insulting it."

Morgan turned to Jodi. **"Is that . . . Doc?"** he whispered.

"This concludes the morning announcements," said the voice. "Good luck out there!"

Morgan turned back to get a better look at Ms. Minerva. She looked rough. Was this what happened she missed her morning coffee?

"I'm fine!" Ms. Minerva said. She rummaged through the lost-and-found box beneath her desk and pulled out a juice box. She squinted at the ingredients. **"Water . . . kiwi and pineapple extract (Pineapple? That's weird) . . . monodextrosomething concentrate . . . Why don't they make these things with coffee?"**

"Those two need to make up," Jodi whispered into Morgan's ear.

Morgan agreed. He spent the rest of homeroom

hoping Ms. Minerva would hurry to apologize to Doc between classes.

Apparently, there was no apology.

Doc stopped by their table at lunch. **"Greetings, my little Minecrafters!"** she said. "I come to you seeking aid."

Harper perked up, as she always did at the chance to learn from Doc. "What do you need?" she asked. "Is it . . . a science side quest?"

Doc chuckled. "You know me too well. Yes, in fact. I need a few students to take some measurements in the butterfly sanctuary after school."

Po's face drooped. "Aw, I can't," he said glumly. "I have drama club."

"That means we won't be playing Minecraft," said Morgan.

"How come?" said Theo. "We could still play without Po there, right?"

Po gasped theatrically. "Don't you

dare!" he said, outraged by the thought.

"It's an unspoken rule," Jodi explained to Theo. **"If one of us can't make it, we usually don't meet up."**

"You guys have a lot of unspoken rules," Theo said. "Maybe you should write them down."

He chuckled as he said it, so Morgan knew he was trying to make a joke. But it rubbed Morgan the wrong way—like Theo was calling them bossy.

"Anyway," Harper said, glaring at her friends before turning back to Doc, **"I'll help with the measurements."**

"Yeah," Jodi said. "Morgan and I will, too."

"Much appreciated," said Doc. "I would do it myself, you know . . . but Ms. Minerva has decided not to give me a ride to my evening badminton match. Which means I have to take my bike. Which means it will be a mad dash to get there in time."

"Gosh," Jodi said. **"That sounds stressful."**

"Oh, I wouldn't want to get a ride in Minerva's car today anyway," said Doc. "Not after I fill it with beetles . . ."

The kids looked shocked.

"Eh-hem . . . I'm just kidding, of course," Doc said as she nervously cleared her throat. "Well, see you in class."

Then she quickly walked away.

"I feel like we're kidding when we call her a mad scientist," said Po. **"But . . . maybe she's actually a mad scientist?"**

"Someone has got to get those two back on the same page," said Jodi. Morgan could see the wheels turning in her head. His sister couldn't stand to see people (or animals) in conflict.

Theo rapped his knuckles on the table to get their attention. "I have a surprise for you all," he said. "I was going to hand these out at the library tonight. But if we're not meeting, I'll give them to you now."

"A surprise?" Morgan echoed. **"I hope it's not a splash potion."** Jodi elbowed him in the ribs.

"I felt bad about how things went yesterday," Theo continued. "So I stayed up late to make these."

Theo pulled a T-shirt from a beat-up old

cardboard box. It was bright green, and quite large, and in big, blocky letters it said **BLOCK HEADZ.**

"There's one for everybody!" he said, and he passed out the T-shirts.

"Interesting color," said Po. **"Sort of a . . . booger green."**

"I don't understand the 'Z' at all," said Harper.

"What's a blockhead?" asked Jodi.

"We are!" said Theo. **"I figured we should have a team name. So . . . Block Headz."**

"That's so nice, Theo," said Jodi, and she elbowed Morgan again. "Don't you think so, big brother?"

Morgan held up his T-shirt. It was all wrong. He understood that Theo was trying to be nice, but . . . he just hated the shirt. *Hated it!*

"It's a nice gesture, man," said Po.

"I'll be sure to wear it soon," said Harper.

"Maybe I'll get matching . . . um . . . nail polish!" said Jodi.

Morgan realized he had been silent for a long time. Everyone was looking at him.

"It's . . . cool," he said. **"Thanks, Theo."**

But he didn't sound very convincing. He could

tell by the disappointed look on Theo's face.

Just then, the bell rang. Lunch was over, and everyone started packing up their things.

"Saved by the bell," Morgan muttered under his breath.

Jodi gave him a dirty look. But what could he do? **Morgan didn't want to be mean, but from his perspective, Theo made it hard to be nice.**

Chapter 7

"METAMORPHOSIS" IS A BIG WORD THAT MEANS "CHANGE." LET'S JUST HOPE IT'S FOR THE BETTER. . . .

After school, Jodi made her way to the butterfly sanctuary, previously known as the computer lab.

When she opened the door, she was pleasantly surprised to see a familiar face.

"Baron Sweetcheeks!" she said. "What are you doing here?"

The class hamster squeaked as if to say hello. He had been put into a plastic hamster ball, and he rolled right up to Jodi. She picked him up, ball and all.

Harper poked her head out from behind an elephant-ear plant. "I brought him along," she said. "I'm on hamster duty this week, and I thought he could use some exercise. He seems to like it here. It's almost like being outside."

"Yeah, what happened to the air-conditioning?" Morgan pulled at his sweaty shirt. "It's sweltering in here. **like it's an actual jungle!**"

"That's on purpose," said Harper. "Doc was keeping all the caterpillars in a terrarium so she could control the temperature and humidity levels for them. But now . . . since they escaped . . ."

"This whole room is the terrarium," said Morgan. "Got it."

"We just have to take some measurements," said Harper. "We'll report back to Doc, and she'll figure out if she needs to bring in more plants or adjust the thermostat or anything like that."

"I hope these little guys appreciate all this," said Morgan, squinting to get a good look at a cocoon.

"I'm sure they do!" said Jodi. "When they hatch, they'll know we took good care of them. Like the baron here." She placed the hamster

ball back on the ground, and Baron Sweetcheeks resumed rolling around the room.

"It's weird, though," said Morgan. **"These things were caterpillars less than a week ago.** And they're going to be butterflies?"

"That's right," said Harper. "They're going through *metamorphosis*—which is a fancy word for 'change.'"

Morgan frowned. "I feel like we're all going through metamorphosis. Nothing is the same as it was before."

Jodi patted her brother on the back. "Nothing is ever the same as before," she said. **"Change is constant."** She looked over her shoulder. "I just wish we would sprout wings. That's a change I could really enjoy!"

Just then, **Harper's backpack chimed.**

"Ooh!" Harper said. "That's my phone." She rummaged around in a pocket. Then she pulled out the phone she had once upgraded with some of Doc's old equipment—to strange results. "It's a video call," Harper said with a grin. "From our old friend—"

"Ash!" cried Jodi. She squeezed in close to Harper so that she could get a better look. "How are you? I like your hair! What's the weather like over there?"

"Hi, Jodi," said Ash. "Everything's good here, but I miss you guys."

"We miss you, too," said Morgan. He squeezed in on Harper's other side.

Baron Sweetcheeks squeaked at the sound of Ash's voice, and Harper laughed. "Baron Sweetcheeks says hi. Either that or he's asking for dinner."

"Baron Sweetcheeks is the best," said Ash. **"My new class pet is a snake,** you guys. A snake! It gives me the creeps."

Baron Sweetcheeks squeaked in agreement.

"Aw, snakes are all right," said Jodi. She wouldn't mind having a snake, if only she could find one that didn't eat cute little rodents. Were there vegetarian snakes? She made a note to look that up next time they were in the library.

"Are we playing Minecraft tonight?" asked Ash. "I'm finally free!"

"Bad timing," Harper said glumly. "We're helping Doc with a project. And Po's got a club meeting."

"Aw, too bad," said Ash. "I keep missing you guys. But we'll find time soon, I'm sure."

"I hope so," Morgan said. "It's not the same without you. Theo is *super* annoying."

"**Yikes,**" said Ash. "That's pretty harsh, Morgan."

"It's the truth!" he said. "I don't understand his jokes. He's a terrible team player—he just always acts like he's in charge, and then he gets in the way. **He likes to tell us he's some sort of coding genius, but I'm beginning to think he couldn't hack his way out of a paper bag.**"

"Ouch," said a voice. Jodi's heart sank immediately. She knew whose voice that was.

They turned to see Theo standing in the doorway. He was holding a pizza box and wearing his Blockheadz shirt. And he looked utterly, completely heartbroken. "I was just . . . I thought you guys might want some pineapple pizza, but . . ."

He couldn't finish the sentence. He spun around and bolted into the hallway.

"Theo, wait!" said Jodi. She hurried after him, but she had to step around plants and a hyperactive hamster in a ball. By the time she got to the door, **Theo was gone.**

Morgan face-palmed. "That wasn't great," he said.

"No, it wasn't," Jodi said crossly. "I was already worried about Doc and Ms. Minerva fighting. Now I have to worry about you two. What did I tell you about being nice?"

"I didn't know he was there. I'll make it up to him," said Morgan. "Somehow." His face was red. *At least he has the good sense to be embarrassed,* Jodi thought. *That's a start.*

"It sounds like there's a lot happening over there," Ash said through the phone. "Do you guys want to fill me in?"

Morgan, Jodi, and Harper all sighed at the same time.

"It's a long story," said Harper.

"I've got time," said Ash. "Tell me all about it."

Jodi smiled and picked up Baron Sweetcheeks in his hamster ball. Ash always made her feel better. **And Ash always made their problems feel solvable.**

It was nice to know that the distance between them didn't change that.

Chapter 8

LET'S BE HONEST: PINEAPPLE ON PIZZA IS JUST WEIRD, EVEN IF IT PROVIDES A BALANCE BETWEEN SWEET AND SAVORY.

Theo felt a terrible mix of emotions in his belly. He was angry at Morgan for the things he'd said. He was worried that all his friends might feel the same way Morgan did. Worst of all, he felt guilty.

Because what if Morgan was right? What if Theo's mods had broken the game somehow? **What if the Evoker King had been destroyed ... and it was all his fault?**

After Theo stormed out of the butterfly sanctuary, he didn't stop moving until he'd made it across the street to Stonesword. He didn't even realize he was still holding the pizza box until

Mr. Malory pointed it out to him.

"Sorry, Theo," he said. "No food allowed."

"Oh," Theo said, looking at the box in his hands. "Do you want it, sir? I'm not really hungry anymore. **It's pineapple. . . .**"

Mr. Malory grimaced as he took the pizza box. "Not my favorite. But I'll put it in the break room. The volunteers from the high school will eat anything." He looked toward the door, as if expecting other students to file in behind Theo. **"Where's the rest of the group?** I thought you all traveled together."

"Sometimes," Theo said, looking a little embarrassed. "But other times, they treat me like

I'm not really part of the group. I don't get it. I try so hard to fit in. . . ."

Mr. Malory nodded. "I've been there. We've *all* been there," he said. "But sometimes, trying to fit in is the wrong thing to do. **Because if you try too hard, you're not being yourself. And your friends should like you for who you are.**"

For a moment, Theo was silent, his jaw working like he was chewing a piece of sticky caramel.

"Thanks, Mr. Malory," he said, a smile slowly returning to his face. "You've given me something to think about. **Are the computers free?**"

"They are today," he said. "But eventually, other kids are going to find them. I might have to limit screen time. . . ."

Theo's smile dropped again. "Really?" he said.

Mr. Malory chuckled. "You go right ahead and enjoy yourself. Forget about your problems for a while."

"Okay," said Theo. But he didn't intend to forget about his problems. **He intended to fix them.**

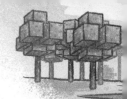

Because Mr. Malory had told him to be himself. **And who he was . . . was a problem-solver.**

Even when that meant breaking the rules.

Theo had played Minecraft by himself plenty of times. But he still wasn't used to being alone in the strange VR goggle version of Minecraft. The silence made him feel nervous.

Of course, he probably *should* be nervous, he thought. **The Endermonster was out there somewhere.**

And Theo meant to find it.

Theo raided one of the Shack's many storage chests. He selected a set of diamond armor, a diamond sword, and some healing potions. He felt a lot safer now . . . **but he would have to be sure to put everything back,** or Morgan would be even more annoyed with him.

He crept carefully through the forest, retracing their path from the day before. In the clearing

where they'd battled, **the footprints made a big, messy jumble of squares.** But Theo picked up the Endermonster's tracks just outside the clearing.

The mob's trail led him out of the forest, across a sunflower plain, and right to the foot of a low mountain. The footprints disappeared occasionally, and Theo was forced to wander around until he found where they picked up again. There was only one explanation for the gaps in the trail: **the mob was teleporting as it traveled.** It never teleported very far, but still, Theo was losing precious time. The sun had set, and darkness had fallen on the Overworld. Using a torch to see more clearly, Theo picked up the Endermonster's trail once more.

Even in his diamond armor, Theo felt a shiver of fear.

It was when the night felt its darkest that he found the Endermonster. **He saw its eyes first.** Those frightening red eyes seemed to glow in the dark.

Then Theo realized his mistake. If he could see those eyes . . .

. . . those eyes could see him, too!

The Endermonster emitted a terrible scream. The sound chilled Theo to the core. He lifted his sword to defend himself—

But it was teleported right out of his hands!

Okay, thought Theo. *That's fine. I didn't want to hurt him anyway. I just wanted to get a good look at him.*

That goal would be easier to achieve now—since the Endermonster had teleported right into Theo's face!

Theo took a quick step backward, barely avoiding the hostile mob's swinging fist. He forced himself to stay calm. He had a theory about what the mob *really* was . . . but he needed proof. He needed some sign that this wasn't an enderman at all, that it was actually—

POW! The Endermonster's second swing connected. Theo almost fell over.

This mob hit *hard.* But at least Theo had powerful armor to protect him.

The Endermonster emitted a low howl. **Its eyes flashed bright red.** And Theo's diamond chest plate . . . disappeared.

The Endermonster had teleported his armor right off him!

Now Theo worried he was really in trouble. Maybe he shouldn't have tried to do this by

himself. Maybe everything Morgan had said about him was true.

Theo backed up against a tree. The Endermonster stepped closer. It loomed above him. Theo searched its face for any sign of intelligence or compassion. **"PLEASE,"** he said.

Something strange happened then. The Endermonster opened its mouth, as if ready to howl again.

This time, it spoke words.

"DON'T LOOK AT ME!"

Theo gasped. The Endermonster had spoken . . . with the Evoker King's voice.

Theo realized that his theory was correct. The

Evoker King's code hadn't been destroyed. It had been changed.

Changed . . . into *this*.

He tried to take comfort in that knowledge as the Endermonster raised its arms to strike him down.

Suddenly, a flask flew through the air. It struck the Endermonster square in the back. The mob's eyes went wide with surprise—**and then it teleported away in the blink of an eye.**

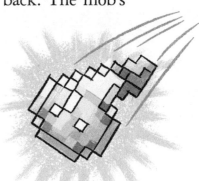

With the Endermonster no longer right in front of

him, Theo saw that someone else had followed its trail. Someone very unexpected—but a welcome surprise.

"ASH?!" said Theo.

"Are you all right, Theo?" she asked.

"I am now." He rubbed his aching head. "Your timing was perfect. What did you hit that mob with?"

"Just water," she answered. "Morgan and Harper filled me in. **I KNOW THAT THING ISN'T A NORMAL MOB . . .** but it seems to hate water just as much as any other enderman."

"I should have thought of that," Theo said, scolding himself. "MY WEAPON SURE DIDN'T HELP. AND NOW I'VE LOST OUR ONLY DIAMOND SWORD."

"You mean this diamond sword?" Ash held it up for Theo to see. "I found it under a tree nearby. I WAS WONDERING WHERE IT CAME FROM."

Theo smiled slightly. "That's a relief. Now Morgan will just yell at me a little, instead of yelling at me a lot."

Ash chuckled. "I might know a thing or two about that," she said. "Remember, it wasn't so long ago that I was the new kid." She handed him the

sword. **"LET'S GET OUT OF HERE BEFORE THAT THING COMES BACK.** Then you can tell me what you're doing here alone . . . and maybe I can give you some advice for dealing with Morgan."

Theo smiled a real smile this time. "That would be great."

As they walked back to the Shack, they kept their eyes open. They didn't see the missing diamond armor. But they didn't see any red eyes beneath the trees, either. So Theo considered himself lucky.

"Here's the thing about Morgan," said Ash. "He is the kindest, most loyal friend a person can have. **BUT HE'S VERY PICKY ABOUT WHO HE CONSIDERS A FRIEND."**

"I definitely got that impression," said Theo. "I know he thinks I'm bad at teamwork."

"TEAMWORK IS SKILL. It's like . . . playing the piano," said Ash. "Anyone can do it. But it takes constant practice to do it well. Even Morgan has to practice it. He likes being in charge. But sometimes he needs to be reminded that he's not the boss of Minecraft." Ash chuckled. "I got very good at reminding him of that."

"So where do I start?" asked Theo. "I don't think I can go into school tomorrow and say, 'HEY, MORGAN, PLEASE STOP BEING BOSSY.'"

"No, that won't help," said Ash. "You need to show him that you care about the team. You need to show him he can *trust* you. That means being honest . . . including telling the truth about what you're up to in here."

Theo thought about that. **He still hadn't been honest about all his modding.**

"What if the truth just makes him angrier?"

Ash thought about that for a moment. "It might. But you can't let fear get in the way of being honest. Not if you want a *real* friendship with Morgan and the others."

Theo sighed. It sounded so simple when Ash said it. But he knew she was right.

As they approached the Shack, Theo caught a glimpse of something out of the corner of his eye. **A glimmer of light shone in the sky.**

At first he thought the Endermonster had found them. But it was something else. . . .

"Hey, Ash," said Theo. "Do you see that?"

Ash squinted. "That's definitely weird," she agreed. "Let's climb that hill and get a better look."

They got closer to the anomaly, but it was hard to see. It was like a patch of deeper black in the darkness. But its edges glimmered like an oil slick.

It was a hole. **A tear in the sky.**

Theo had never seen anything like it. Neither had Ash.

"SOMETHING ELSE TO WORRY ABOUT," said Theo.

"One thing at a time," said Ash. "You've got a big conversation with Morgan and the others tomorrow. Focus on that for now."

"Right," Theo said. **That conversation—his confession—felt more terrifying than some random glitch in the Minecraft sky.**

And he wasn't looking forward to it. Not at all.

Chapter 9

A REVELATION!
A EUREKA MOMENT!
A CHANGE OF HEART!
ALL LIKE BUTTERFLIES
TAKING FLIGHT!

Po was eating a peanut butter sandwich for lunch when Jodi and Harper presented their plan for saving their teachers' friendship. Morgan nodded along as he took a bite of banana. Theo sat listening in silence.

"We have to do *something*," said Jodi. **"We can't just sit by while their friendship ends over some cocoons and a cybernetic coffeepot."**

"But what can we do?" Po asked.

"We've already started," Jodi answered. "After we finished in the butterfly sanctuary yesterday, I removed the beetles from Ms. Minerva's car. Doc was *not* joking."

"And I got permission to go to the faculty lounge this morning," said Harper. **"I was able to get the coffee machine up and running."**

"I thought Ms. Minerva seemed better this morning," said Morgan. "She got my name right during attendance, anyway."

"You're a genius, Harper," Po said. "How did you fix the high-tech coffee machine so quickly?"

Harper grinned. "It wasn't broken. Doc had just unplugged it, and nobody had thought to check the power cord."

"Mad science," said Po. "I'm telling you! Right, Theo?"

Theo didn't say anything. In fact, he had hardly said anything all morning. **His mind was clearly elsewhere.**

"Here's what we do next," said Jodi. "We're going to ask the yearbook club for photos—lots of photos. *Years* of photos. Everything they have of Doc and Ms. Minerva."

"We'll make a photo album," said Harper. "And then we'll scan it. I'll upload a digital version of the album to Doc's tablet while the rest of you sneak the physical album into the library. You can shelve it next to the young adult vampire novels, where Ms. Minerva will definitely find it eventually."

"She does love those vampire novels," Po said.

"And there you have it!" Jodi said. "Violins swell, they realize their friendship is precious, and we have saved the day."

"It's brilliant," said Po. And he took a big bite of his sandwich.

Theo chose that moment to finally speak. **"I have to tell you all something,"** he said. **"I made a mistake."**

Po tried to ask, "What do you mean?" But with his mouth full of peanut butter and bread, it sounded more like, "Waddle a meme?" Everyone gave him a weird look. But Theo answered his question anyway.

"I've been modding," he said. "You all saw the footprint mod. But that's just the tip of the iceberg. I've been making all kinds of stuff. And . . ." He took a deep breath. "I've even been messing with some of Doc's mods."

"I knew it!" Morgan growled, and the others all shushed him.

"Go on, Theo," said Harper.

"I didn't mean to cause problems," Theo continued. "But the best way to learn coding is by playing with somebody else's code. I thought if I figured out what Doc had done to the game . . . if I could wrap my head

around all her modding . . . then I could figure out what went wrong with the Evoker King. I thought it would help me fix him."

Jodi pressed her palms to her cheeks. "Theo," she said. **"Did . . . did your modding . . . did it destroy the Evoker King?"**

"No. Maybe." Theo said. "I don't know. But the Evoker King isn't gone. He's just . . . different."

"What do you mean?" asked Harper. "Different how?"

"The Evoker King didn't explode. He transformed," Theo said. **"He transformed . . . into the Endermonster."**

Po gasped. He was lucky he didn't choke on his sandwich.

"That creepy thing is . . . was . . . our friend?" Jodi asked.

"Poor Bob," said Po.

"Is it permanent?" Harper asked. **"Can we fix it?"**

"I . . . I don't know," said Theo. "I think so. I'll do whatever it takes to try."

Po noticed Morgan wasn't saying anything.

Theo was afraid to even look in his direction.

Before anybody could say anything else, **the cafetorium doors burst open.** Doc hurried over to their table. "Sanctuary volunteers!" she cried. **"The cocoons are hatching! Come quick!"**

Doc didn't wait for them to respond. She was running out the door before Po had even processed what she had said.

"Let's go!" said Jodi.

"We're not done discussing this," Morgan said.

Harper was already out of her seat. "We can talk in the sanctuary. Come on," she said, tugging on Theo. "I am *not* missing this!"

Po trembled with anticipation. **A few of the butterflies had already emerged,** but most of the cocoons were just beginning to hatch. He marveled at the sight. Each new butterfly stepped lightly out of its shell, as if uncertain or shy. But then it slowly spread its wings and gave them a test flap or two. Some instinct told it how to use those wings, and it quickly took flight.

He had thought they would all look the same. But each butterfly was a different color. Blue, orange, pink, green. **It was like being inside a living prism.**

A butterfly with light-blue wings landed on Po's nose. It tickled, and when he laughed, the startled insect flew away.

"It's kind of amazing," he said. "They grew wings while inside their cocoons. They just grew a whole new body part!"

"And not just the wings," said Harper. "They also develop longer legs and antennae and more complex eyes. Metamorphosis is complicated— they need those cocoons to keep them safe while they're going through all those changes." She frowned. "It's weird. **I actually thought I saw a butterfly in the game recently.** Right after the Evoker King split open."

"Me too!" said Po. "I saw a bunch of them through the smoke."

Theo went pale. "That's strange," he said.

"A butterfly was one of the mods I made. I was inspired to do it because I knew we'd be learning about them in Doc's class."

"So you made digital butterflies," Morgan said, "and now they're loose in the game?"

Theo shook his head. "That's not possible. After I made sure that mod worked, I uninstalled it. **The code for butterflies exists now, but it isn't active.**"

Po saw Jodi's eyes light up. "It's almost like . . . like someone is trying to tell us something."

Harper gave Jodi a long look. "What do you mean?"

"Think about it," Jodi said. "According to Theo, the Evoker King just went through a major transformation. **A metamorphosis!** And then, as soon as that happened, butterflies appeared in the game."

"So you think the Evoker King was trying to tell us what had happened?" Po said. "By using Theo's butterfly code?"

Jodi nodded enthusiastically. "Yeah! I mean, we kept saying he was 'solid stone.' *Petrified.* But what if the stone was more like a protective shell? A *cocoon,* keeping him safe while he changed?"

"It sort of makes sense," Harper said. "He wasn't programmed to be our friend. He *decided* to do that. And he was learning emotions and how to deal with them. His program was changing, and rapidly. **What if he spun a cocoon to protect himself while his code rewrote itself into a new and improved Evoker King?"**

"But that would mean . . ." Theo grinned. "That would mean it isn't my fault that he changed! He was changing anyway."

Harper frowned. "We don't know anything for sure. But I don't think he would have become the Endermonster. I think his programming was in flux . . . it was *vulnerable*. . . ."

"And when I messed with Doc's code, **I created a monster.**" Theo hung his head.

The door to the sanctuary opened. Po wasn't surprised to see Doc enter. But he was surprised to see Ms. Minerva following right behind her, holding Baron Sweetcheeks in her hands.

"You see, Minerva?" said Doc. "It's just like I said!"

"What a marvel," said Ms. Minerva. **"I never imagined I'd witness something like this."**

The two teachers—and the hamster—shared a smile.

Po whispered to Jodi, "I guess they aren't fighting anymore?"

Jodi whispered, **"I'm still making that photo album just in case."**

Morgan looked at the teachers oohing and aahing at each new butterfly. Then he looked at Theo, who seemed miserable with guilt.

Morgan must have been inspired by the sight of the teachers putting their grudge aside. **He put a hand on Theo's shoulder** and said, **"It's not your fault."**

Po hadn't expected that.

"You were trying to help," Morgan continued. "We all understand. And now that you've been honest with us . . . **we can fix it somehow.**"

"You mean it?" asked Theo.

"That's what teams are for," said Harper, and she put a hand on Theo's other shoulder. "We share

the problem. We solve it together."

"Where do we start?" asked Jodi.

"Well, first, we should probably make sure the Endermonster doesn't wander off," said Theo. "If it does, we might never find it again."

"So we need to capture it?" said Po. "That sounds hard, considering we can't even look at it."

"Well, I do know one trick we can use," said Morgan. **"It's a way to look at an enderman**

without angering it. It should work on the Endermonster, too."

"Okay, so with Morgan's trick, we can look directly at the scary mob," said Po. "Next problem: How do you capture something that can just teleport away?"

"I had an idea about that, actually," said Harper. "What if we use its power against it? **What if it teleports . . . right into a trap?**"

"I like that," Po said, and he felt a little thrill at the idea.

Time to show the Endermonster that it had messed with the wrong team.

Chapter 10

PUMPKINS! THEY'RE WHAT ALL THE MONSTER HUNTERS ARE WEARING THIS SEASON.

Harper had changed her skin to an outfit better suited for capturing a hostile mob. She figured if Po could change his skin for every new adventure and whim, she could change hers for more practical reasons. But at the moment, she felt ridiculous.

"Morgan, **TELL ME AGAIN WHY I HAVE TO WEAR THIS PUMPKIN ON MY HEAD,**" she demanded.

"It's safer this way. I promise!" Morgan told her. "The Endermonster has powers that an enderman doesn't have. But it still acts like an enderman." **He put a pumpkin**

on his own head. "And an enderman attacks anyone who looks at it . . . unless that person is wearing a pumpkin."

"Personally, I am a big fan of this plan," said Po. "I could really *lose my head* over how cool it is!" In addition to the pumpkin head, **he was wearing all black clothes, with a dark cape hanging from his shoulders.** He looked like the Headless Horseman in "The Legend of Sleepy Hollow."

Harper sighed. She couldn't shake the feeling that Morgan was playing a prank on them. But she knew he wouldn't be so silly when they were on such an important mission.

They had to capture this mob or whatever it was if they had any hope of saving their digital friend.

"Let's review the plan," Harper said. "We need to dig a pit and then line the pit with soul sand, which I picked up last time we were in the Nether."

"Because according to Morgan, endermen can't teleport when they're standing on soul sand," said Jodi.

"That trick only works during the day," said Morgan. **"So we have to time this just right."**

"So we'll get the Endermonster to teleport into the pit," said Po. "It won't be able to teleport out of the pit, and it will be too deep to climb out."

"That just leaves the question of bait," said Theo. "What do we use to lure the Endermonster into the pit?"

"Not what," said Morgan. *"Who."* He turned his pumpkin-head gaze to Theo. "How serious were you when you said you'd do anything to fix this?"

Harper knew that it wasn't really possible, but she thought Theo's avatar looked a little queasy.

The Endermonster was easy to find. It still hadn't traveled very far from the site of their first battle. **The mob shuffled from tree to tree,** moving blocks around seemingly at random.

Harper passed out flasks of an electric-blue liquid. "Everybody drink up," she said.

"It looks like a sports drink," said Po.

Harper grinned. "You're sort of right. These are potions of swiftness. **WE NEED TO BE QUICK AGAINST AN ENEMY WHO CAN TELEPORT.**"

Theo drank his potion down. "I feel faster already," said Theo. "Wish me luck."

"We've got your back," Jodi promised.

Theo removed the pumpkin from his head. He looked right at the Endermonster.

"PEEK-A-BOO!" he cried. "I see you, Endermonster!"

The Endermonster whirled at the sound of Theo's voice. It emitted a bloodcurdling shriek.

"Now, Theo," said Harper. "Go. Run!"

Theo turned and ran, hoping he would be fast enough. At the same moment, the Endermonster teleported to where Theo had just been standing, slamming its fists down on empty grass.

The mob shrieked in frustration. It scanned the forest with its sinister red eyes. When it spotted Theo, it teleported again. Once again, it just missed him.

"THEO'S STAYING AHEAD OF IT, THANKS TO THE SWIFTNESS POTION!" said Harper.

"And we need to keep up with them so we can help if his luck—or his speed—runs out," said Morgan. "Come on, everybody!"

They all ran, weaving around the trees of the forest. **Theo was in the lead, screaming his head off.** The Endermonster was right at his heels. And Harper and her friends followed in the Endermonster's wake, their pumpkins protecting them from its anger.

Finally, they reached the end of the forest and the edge of the pit. Theo didn't even slow down. He leapt right into the hole. **He would probably take some fall damage.** Still, that would hurt less than a direct punch from the creature pursuing him.

But would it follow? Harper held her breath.

Then she let out a whoop of triumph. **The Endermonster took the bait**—it teleported itself right into the pit.

Theo dodged one more swing of its arms. Then he leapt for a ladder on the pit's far side. He quickly climbed out of reach of the creature's long limbs, and as soon as he was back on the grass, Morgan was there, smashing the ladder to bits with a pickaxe.

They'd done it. Their plan had worked. **They'd captured the Endermonster!**

But now that they had it . . . what would they do with it?

Ash found her friends near the Shack. They stood at the edge of a great pit, and they looked very serious.

But their eyes lit up with joy when they saw her.

"ASH!" cried Jodi, and **she flung herself into Ash's blocky arms.**

"Hey, Jodi," said Ash. "Good to see you, too. But, um . . . why is Po wearing a pumpkin on his head?"

"Fashion!" said Po. He threw his arms around both Jodi and Ash, and then Harper and Morgan joined in, **making for an epic group hug.** Theo kept his distance, though. Shyly, he waved hello from the edge of the pit.

"We caught it, Ash," said Theo. "We have the Endermonster trapped."

"For now," said Morgan. He looked at the sun, already lowering in the sky. "When the sun sets, the mob will be able to teleport again. And we might not get a second chance."

"So what do we do now?" asked Harper. **"WE NEED MORE TIME TO FIGURE OUT HOW TO FIX THE EVOKER KING."**

"Could we make a cage?" Po asked. "Some kind of box the Endermonster can't teleport out of?"

"Maybe we need to strike it down," said Morgan. "If we got its health down, it might respawn in its original form." He pulled out a bow. "From up here, it would be like shooting fish in a barrel."

"That is *risky,* big brother," said Jodi. "And kind of mean."

"Letting him run free is risky, too," said Morgan.

Ash looked down at the mob. It paced on the soul sand. It seemed anxious, even scared. It looked up at her, and its red eyes met hers.

It shrieked. It shook. It tried to teleport . . . But it was stuck.

"Don't look at me!" it cried. "Don't look at me! **STOP LOOKING AT ME!"**

Ash took a step back. It was too strange, hearing

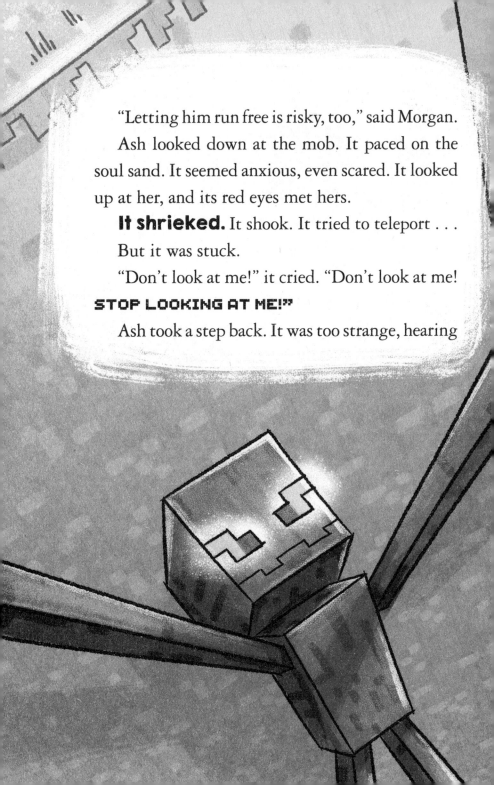

the Evoker King's voice coming from the monster.

"It sounds angry," said Po.

"Not angry," Ash said. "Terrified." She turned to Morgan. **"PUT THE WEAPON AWAY,** Morgan. Attacking it doesn't seem right."

Morgan put the bow back in his inventory. But he still had a hard look in his eyes. "What else can we do?" he asked.

Ash put her fists on her hips. **"HAS ANYONE TRIED TALKING TO IT?"**

"Talking?" said Po. "To Creepy McGlowyEyes down there?"

"It can speak with the Evoker King's voice," Ash replied. "Does that mean it can listen with the Evoker King's ears?"

Everyone was silent for a moment.

"I'll try it," said Theo.

Then he thought about what he'd just said. "But only if the group agrees," he added. "From now on, **I WON'T MAKE DECISIONS THAT AFFECT ALL OF US** unless I discuss things with the team first."

"What exactly are you offering to do?" asked Morgan, raising a rectangular eyebrow..

"I want to go back down into the pit," Theo answered. "I want to talk to the Endermonster. **JUST ME. ALL ALONE.**"

Chapter 11

THE ENDERMONSTER IS WHAT? YOU'RE PULLING MY STONE LEG!

Theo didn't put the pumpkin back on his head. He wanted the Endermonster to really *see* him. **Maybe the part of it that was once the Evoker King would recognize Theo as a friend.**

He would just have to avoid making eye contact. He wanted to be very careful not to anger it again, now that the mob had finally calmed down.

He could feel his friends' eyes on him as he descended the ladder into the pit. They were nervous. Morgan, especially. **Because Morgan didn't like it when things were out of his control.**

And this time, it all came down to Theo.

Once he was off the ladder, Theo kept his eyes on the ground. The soul sand was eerie. As if this situation weren't frightening enough!

"I, uh, I come in peace," he said. **"I JUST WANT TO TALK."**

The Endermonster didn't say anything. But it didn't attack, either.

"Do you remember me? I'm Theo. We were both going to be 'the new kid' at the same time."

He took a shuffling step forward. **"YOU CALLED YOURSELF THE EVOKER KING."**

The mob made that horrible shrieking sound. Theo flinched, and he held his hands up in front of him. But he kept his eyes on the ground.

The shriek faded. **And the Endermonster spoke.**

"Not Evoker King," it said. "Evoker King's . . . **FEAR."**

"Fear?" Theo felt it himself. "I don't understand."

"Evoker King . . . **WAS ONE.** Evoker King . . . **IS SIX.**"

It took Theo a moment to make sense of what the Endermonster was saying. He gasped as the truth sank in.

Did he understand correctly? **Was such a bizarre metamorphosis possible?**

The Evoker King hadn't just become this new mob. He had become *six* new mobs.

Theo remembered the moment when Jodi had convinced the Evoker King to be their friend. The

Evoker King had been scared. **He was terrified of change.**

Was the Endermonster that piece of him? The part of him that was afraid?

"Listen to me," Theo said. "I know what it's like . . . to be afraid. I know what it's like to not want people to see you. Because what if they don't like what they see?" He took a deep, shaky breath. "It feels safer to be invisible. **SAFER . . . BUT IT'S SO LONELY.** Aren't you lonely?"

The Endermonster didn't say anything. But Theo could hear it making the strange, otherworldly

sounds of an enderman. It was close.

He took another small step forward.

"I'm going to look at you now," he said. "I know it's scary. But I want you to be brave. Because I'm your *friend*. And you have to let your friends see the real you."

Theo raised his square chin. He gazed into the Endermonster's face. **He looked right into its bloodred eyes.**

"Not afraid," it said.

"Good," said Theo. "That's good."

The mob's eyes glowed red. Its whole body glowed. It leaned forward and whispered something in Theo's ear.

Theo didn't have a chance to respond. The Endermonster was engulfed in a burst of light— **light in the shape of blocky, pixelated butterflies.** There was a swarm of them, and they washed over Theo, filling his vision with color. He had to shield his eyes and look away.

When the butterflies had all faded or flown away, **Theo saw that the Endermonster was gone.** Where it had stood just a moment before, there was now a long, rectangular block.

"What *is* that?" asked Jodi.

"It's a leg," said Theo. **"IT'S THE FIRST PIECE OF THE EVOKER KING."**

"The first piece?" said Ash.

"You mean . . . that was just the beginning?" Morgan asked.

"I'll explain everything," said Theo. **He poked the leg.** "But first, we need to figure out who's putting that leg in their inventory."

Chapter 12

ASIDE FROM THE STRANDS OF TWISTED CODE AND AN OMINOUS WARNING OF IMPENDING DOOM, THIS IS A TOTALLY HAPPY ENDING!

With Doc's permission, **THEO RETURNED TO STONESWORD LIBRARY DURING HIS LUNCH PERIOD** the next day. He had promised to uninstall his mods—at least until the team had a chance to vote on which ones would be helpful.

That part was easy. But when Theo saw Doc's code, he gasped.

Lines of code were missing. **Files had been deleted.** The mod code that made their Minecraft game so special . . . was no longer complete.

Theo didn't know enough about programming to know exactly what this meant. But he knew enough to realize that it would be trouble.

Clearly, it wasn't just the Evoker King who had changed. **THE GAME ITSELF HAD CHANGED.**

On his way out of the library, Theo saw Ms. Minerva, Doc, and Mr. Malory taking a lunch break together. **They were sitting by the Stonesword statue.** They were all smiling and laughing.

Mr. Malory spotted him first. "Hey, Theo," he said. "Did you solve that problem you were having with your friends?"

"I think so," Theo said. "I took your advice to be myself, and I took my friend Ash's advice to be honest, and I sort of mashed both pieces of advice together." He shrugged. **"I want my friends to see and accept the real me.** I think it's going to be fine."

Ms. Minerva nodded. "Wise words, Theo," she said. "Just remember—friendship takes work. And that work is never really done."

"*Some* friendships take more work than others," Doc said, and she cackled when Ms. Minerva gave her a look.

"I don't get it," Theo said. "I mean . . . I don't want to be rude . . . but two days ago, **I thought you two hated each other.**"

Doc clucked her tongue. "We could never hate each other. We've been friends too long for that."

"Sometimes friends disagree," added Ms. Minerva. "Sometimes they disagree *strongly.* And that's okay. As long as you respect each other and can agree on the big things."

"The big things?" Theo echoed.

"Sure," said the teacher. "For instance, Doc and

I both believe in the importance of education. **We agree that there's real joy to be found as a teacher.** And we think you kids deserve the very best."

"And we agree that the butterfly sanctuary is a wonderful addition to the school," Doc added. "Especially if it gives me the chance to update some of our systems. **Woodsword is going to be truly cutting-edge before I'm done!**"

Ms. Minerva threw up her hands in surrender. "Sometimes a little chaos is all right, I suppose."

"Oh!" said Mr. Malory. "That reminds me." **He plucked the VR headset from Theo's hands.** "We can't have these things floating around. We need to get them checked into the system."

"But . . . ," said Theo. "But we've been taking those home at night. To keep them safe."

"They're perfectly safe here, Theo," said Mr. Malory. "What could go wrong in a media center?"

Mr. Malory smiled, but that didn't make Theo feel any better. **And it was clear that**

Theo would have to leave the goggles behind . . . where just about *anybody* could use them.

Maybe moving the computer lab to Stonesword wasn't going to be such a good thing after all.

Another problem for later, Theo thought. Those seemed to be stacking up lately. **Like a tower of blocks that was bound to come crashing down.**

Theo crossed the crosswalk, stepping back onto school grounds . . . and right into a very welcome surprise.

A very welcome, very green surprise.

"We're still not calling ourselves the Blockheadz," said Morgan. **"But I admit the shirts are kind of fun."** Morgan, Harper, Po, and Jodi were all in a row, wearing their T-shirts with pride. And Harper was holding a pizza box.

"We figured we owed you a pizza," she said.

"We even got pineapple."

"On *half* of it," said Po. **"It's a weird topping, man."**

"Call it a compromise!" Jodi said. She held up Harper's phone. "Right, Ash?"

"That's right," Ash said through the phone. "Welcome to the team, Theo! For real this time."

"And . . . ?" said Jodi, and she gave her brother a look.

"I am sorry for making you feel unwelcome—you're not as annoying as I said you were," Morgan mumbled. Then he grinned. "As Ash and Jodi have reminded me, I can be a little intense."

Theo smiled. "It's all right. I can be intense, too, in my own way." He rubbed the back of his head. "I made a lot of decisions without checking with you guys first. **I kept secrets. I did it because I was afraid to make you mad."** He shrugged. "I've never had a close group of friends like this.

It's taking me some time to get used to it."

"We'll work it out," said Morgan. "We're good at solving problems. **Although I still don't understand how my diamond armor ended up in a tree. . . .**"

Theo kept his lips sealed about that. And on the phone Ash smirked, keeping mum as well.

"Then it's settled," Ash said happily, changing

the subject. "Now, if only I could figure out how to eat pizza through the phone, this would be a totally happy ending!"

Everybody laughed at that. Theo felt his worries float away on the sound of their happiness.

Most of his worries. He couldn't forget what he had seen in the mod code, and he couldn't forget the Endermonster's final whispered words of warning.

"Beware," it had said. **"THE FAULT . . . WILL DESTROY THE OVERWORLD."**

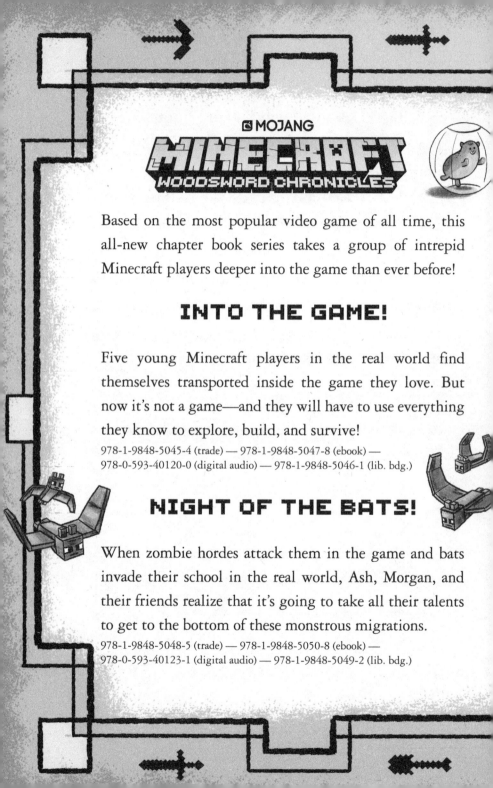

MOJANG

MINECRAFT

WOODSWORD CHRONICLES

Based on the most popular video game of all time, this all-new chapter book series takes a group of intrepid Minecraft players deeper into the game than ever before!

INTO THE GAME!

Five young Minecraft players in the real world find themselves transported inside the game they love. But now it's not a game—and they will have to use everything they know to explore, build, and survive!

978-1-9848-5045-4 (trade) — 978-1-9848-5047-8 (ebook) — 978-0-593-40120-0 (digital audio) — 978-1-9848-5046-1 (lib. bdg.)

NIGHT OF THE BATS!

When zombie hordes attack them in the game and bats invade their school in the real world, Ash, Morgan, and their friends realize that it's going to take all their talents to get to the bottom of these monstrous migrations.

978-1-9848-5048-5 (trade) — 978-1-9848-5050-8 (ebook) — 978-0-593-40123-1 (digital audio) — 978-1-9848-5049-2 (lib. bdg.)

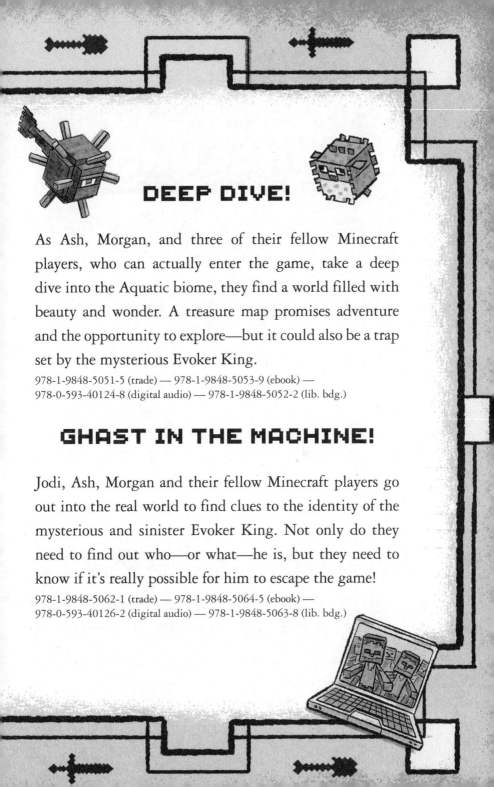

DEEP DIVE!

As Ash, Morgan, and three of their fellow Minecraft players, who can actually enter the game, take a deep dive into the Aquatic biome, they find a world filled with beauty and wonder. A treasure map promises adventure and the opportunity to explore—but it could also be a trap set by the mysterious Evoker King.

978-1-9848-5051-5 (trade) — 978-1-9848-5053-9 (ebook) — 978-0-593-40124-8 (digital audio) — 978-1-9848-5052-2 (lib. bdg.)

GHAST IN THE MACHINE!

Jodi, Ash, Morgan and their fellow Minecraft players go out into the real world to find clues to the identity of the mysterious and sinister Evoker King. Not only do they need to find out who—or what—he is, but they need to know if it's really possible for him to escape the game!

978-1-9848-5062-1 (trade) — 978-1-9848-5064-5 (ebook) — 978-0-593-40126-2 (digital audio) — 978-1-9848-5063-8 (lib. bdg.)

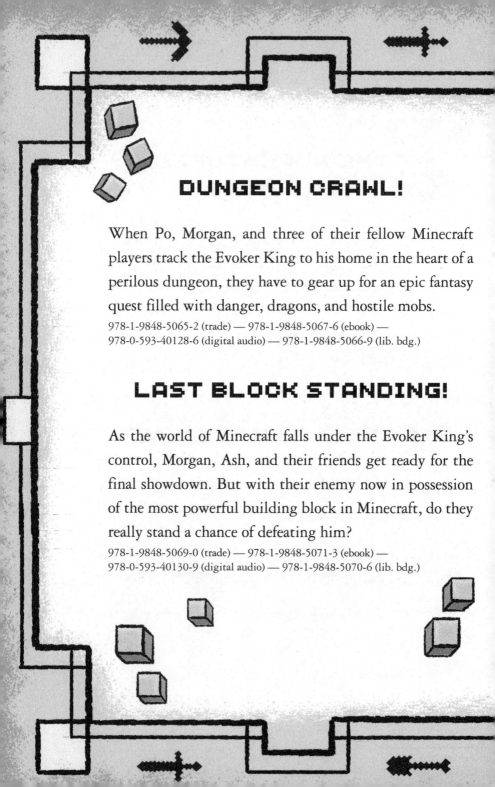

DUNGEON CRAWL!

When Po, Morgan, and three of their fellow Minecraft
players track the Evoker King to his home in the heart of a
perilous dungeon, they have to gear up for an epic fantasy
quest filled with danger, dragons, and hostile mobs.

978-1-9848-5065-2 (trade) — 978-1-9848-5067-6 (ebook) —
978-0-593-40128-6 (digital audio) — 978-1-9848-5066-9 (lib. bdg.)

LAST BLOCK STANDING!

As the world of Minecraft falls under the Evoker King's
control, Morgan, Ash, and their friends get ready for the
final showdown. But with their enemy now in possession
of the most powerful building block in Minecraft, do they
really stand a chance of defeating him?

978-1-9848-5069-0 (trade) — 978-1-9848-5071-3 (ebook) —
978-0-593-40130-9 (digital audio) — 978-1-9848-5070-6 (lib. bdg.)

THE ADVENTURES CONTINUE IN

MINECRAFT
STONESWORD SAGA

CRACK IN THE CODE!

Someone—or something—has turned the Evoker King to stone. And now a new player, Theo, has joined the team on their quest to return their former enemy to normal. Theo has modding skills that could come in handy, but does he have what it takes to be part of the team, or will his meddling put a crack in the game code that none of them will survive?

978-0-593-37298-2 (trade) — 978-0-593-37300-2 (ebook) — 978-0-593-40132-3 (digital audio) — 978-0-593-37299-9 (lib. bdg.)

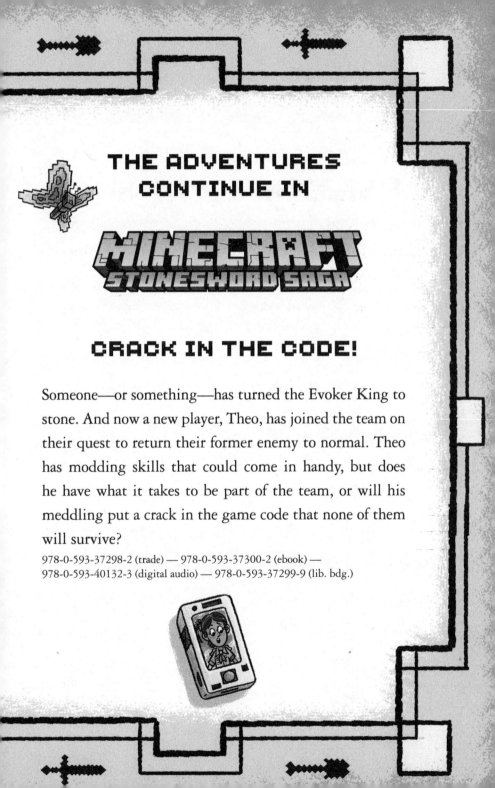

MINECRAFT is a game about placing blocks and going on adventures. Build, play, and explore across infinitely generated worlds of mountains, caverns, oceans, jungles, and deserts. Defeat hordes of zombies, bake the cake of your dreams, venture to new dimensions, or build a skyscraper. What you do in Minecraft is up to you.

Nick Eliopulos is a writer who lives in Brooklyn (as many writers do). He likes to spend half his free time reading and the other half gaming. He cowrote the Adventurers Guild series with his best friend and works as a narrative designer for a small video game studio. After all these years, endermen still give him the creeps.

Alan Batson is a British cartoonist and illustrator. His works include *Everything I Need to Know I Learned from a Star Wars Little Golden Book, Everything That Glitters is Guy!,* and *Spider-Ham.* Being extremely fond of cubes and travel to exotic places, he has recently begun to lend his talents to several different books on adventures in the world of Minecraft.

Chris Hill is an illustrator living in Birmingham, England, with his wife and two daughters and has been loving it for twenty-five years! When he's not working, he spends time with his family and trying to tire out his dog on long walks. If there's any time left after that, he loves to go riding on his motorcycle, feeling the wind on his face while contemplating his next illustration adventure.

JOURNEY INTO THE WORLD OF

MINECRAFT™

—BOOKS FOR EVERY READING LEVEL—

OFFICIAL NOVELS:

FOR YOUNGER READERS:

OFFICIAL GUIDES:

DISCOVER MORE AT READMINECRAFT.COM

THE END OF THE OVERWORLD!

© 2024 Mojang AB. All Rights Reserved. Minecraft, the Minecraft logo, the Mojang Studios logo and the Creeper logo are trademarks of the Microsoft group of companies.

Published in the United States by Random House Children's Books, a division of Penguin Random House LLC, 1745 Broadway, New York, NY 10019, and in Canada by Penguin Random House Canada Limited, Toronto. Random House and the colophon are registered trademarks of Penguin Random House LLC.

rhcbooks.com
minecraft.net

Library of Congress Cataloging-in-Publication Data is available upon request.
ISBN 978-0-593-56294-9 (trade)—ISBN 978-0-593-56295-6 (lib. bdg.)—
ISBN 978-0-593-56296-3 (ebook)

Cover design by Diane Choi

Printed in the United States of America
2nd Printing

THE END OF THE OVERWORLD!

By Nick Eliopulos
Illustrated by Alan Batson and Chris Hill

Random House 🏠 New York

MORGAN

ASH

HARPER

LAYERS!

PO

JODI

THEO

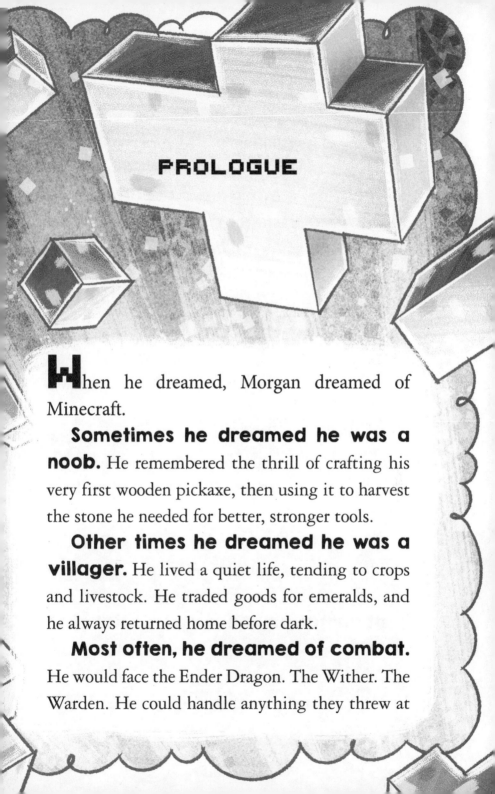

PROLOGUE

Hen he dreamed, Morgan dreamed of Minecraft.

Sometimes he dreamed he was a noob. He remembered the thrill of crafting his very first wooden pickaxe, then using it to harvest the stone he needed for better, stronger tools.

Other times he dreamed he was a villager. He lived a quiet life, tending to crops and livestock. He traded goods for emeralds, and he always returned home before dark.

Most often, he dreamed of combat. He would face the Ender Dragon. The Wither. The Warden. He could handle anything they threw at him. (Even the time he dreamed that the Ender Dragon had given him a pop quiz in chemistry. It had spoken in Doc's voice. That was weird!)

Tonight, Morgan dreamed a nightmare vision of a Minecraft that had been broken into pieces. The sky was a starless void. The horizon was a lifeless sea of bedrock. Morgan was standing on a tiny patchwork island: a bit of grass, some rocky rubble, a jungle tree, and a few mushrooms. That was all that was left of the game Morgan had loved with all his heart.

It seemed as if Minecraft was dying—breaking down into a digital abyss. **And unless he wanted to go down with it, Morgan had to escape.**

Luckily, he had planned for this. He had obsidian in his inventory. With the speed of a master builder, he constructed a portal on the grass. **That portal, he knew, was his ticket to safety.**

But he didn't have any way to turn it on.

Morgan cursed himself for forgetting to craft

the flint and steel he needed to light the portal and make his escape. He would have to mine for the materials. It was his only hope.

Morgan brought his pickaxe down hard.

Too hard.

The force was too great for the little island. **It shattered like glass.** The final fragment of the Overworld had been destroyed by Morgan's own carelessness.

And there was no more solid ground for him to stand on.

Morgan fell into the void, screaming.

He was still screaming when he awoke in his bed.

He was safe. But was Minecraft?

Chapter 1

IT WAS A DARK AND STORMY AFTERNOON! SO OBVIOUSLY AN OMINOUS WARNING OF THINGS TO COME!

A storm was raging outside Woodsword Middle School, but Morgan Mercado barely noticed.

Because a storm of a different kind was raging inside his heart.

Morgan loved Minecraft. If he wasn't playing the game, he was often thinking about it and discussing it with his friends. Every birthday, he had a cake in the shape of a different Minecraft mob. His school folders and notebook were covered with Minecraft stickers and sketches. He had dressed as an Enderman for Halloween two years in a row!

And now the game he loved was in trouble. **How could Morgan let anything distract him from that?**

The bell rang, signaling that school was over for the day. **But Morgan's work was just beginning.** He leapt out of his chair, threw his backpack over his shoulder, and hurried past rows of desks and a brightly decorated bulletin board. He was the first student out the door.

His sister, Jodi, was waiting for him at his locker. She had a smudge of paint on her nose and more paint stains on her fingertips. It looked like she'd just come from art class.

"I thought math was your last class of the day," said Morgan.

"It is," Jodi replied. "I thought it would be a great idea to use watercolor paints on my math test." She wiggled her paint-stained fingers. **"I was right!"**

Morgan shoved his textbooks into his locker and zipped his backpack. "Do you need to wash up?"

"There's no time," Jodi said. **"We have to get to the library as soon as we can.** We have to get *into Minecraft* as soon as we can."

Morgan grinned. He couldn't agree more.

The siblings hurried down the hallway. Students were gathering for after-school activities. They saw a group of kids in neckerchiefs and badge-bedecked sashes. **Those were the Wildling Scouts.** Their friend Ash Kapoor had been in this scouting troop before she moved away. Morgan and Jodi recognized a few of them and smiled hello as they passed.

The next cluster of kids were members of Woodsword's student government. **Morgan's best friend, Po Chen, was one of them.**

Po saw them and waved. Then he turned to Shelly Silver, the class president. "Sorry, Shelly," he said. "I've got to head to the library with Morgan and Jodi."

"No problem," said Shelly. "I'll let you know what you miss. Maybe I'll drop in and join you guys for Minecraft sometime!"

"You play Minecraft?" Morgan asked.

13

"Doesn't everybody?" said Shelly, and she turned to enter a nearby classroom.

Po rolled his wheelchair alongside Morgan and Jodi. "Perfect timing," he told them.

"Are you sure you can miss the meeting?" asked Jodi.

"I'm in a lot of clubs," Po reminded her. "Student government, basketball, and theater. But with what's going on in Minecraft, we need to tackle that first. You know that!"

Morgan grinned. His friends were the best.

And two more of those friends were just ahead.

"Today's the day," said Theo Grayson. **"We have to fix the Fault before it's too late."**

"And more important, we have to save the Evoker King," said Harper. "The EK is made up of game code. If the game falls apart, he falls apart with it."

They weren't saying anything that Morgan didn't agree with.

The Evoker King was an artificial intelligence—a digital being—who existed inside their current Minecraft campaign. But the Evoker King had split up into six separate mobs at the same time that a "Fault" of broken pixels had appeared in the Minecraft sky. **That Fault had grown to swallow nearly the entire Overworld.** But Morgan and his friends hoped that putting the Evoker King back together would fix the game, too.

It was the best idea they had. And they were close. They'd already gathered five of the six "Evoker Spawn." Only one of the strange mobs remained.

They could do this. They could restore the Evoker King and reverse the damage caused by the Fault. **They could win the day!**

But first they had to cross the street. The computer that hosted their Minecraft game was in the Excalibur County Library and Media Center, aka **Stonesword Library**, immediately across from their school. And so were the special VR goggles that allowed them to actually project themselves into the game.

Morgan pushed open the front doors of the

school. To his surprise, a strong wind grabbed the door and slammed it open with a loud *KLANG!* He could see the library just ahead, through heavy sheets of rain. **Thunder rumbled overhead.**

"I forgot my umbrella," said Harper.

"I have one," said Theo. "But it's not big enough for all of us."

"We're getting wet, then," said Po.

"Oh, good," said Jodi. "I could use the wash!"

"On three, everybody," said Morgan. "One. Two. Three!"

Morgan charged ahead into the storm. The crossing guard helped them cross the street, holding up a small stop sign to stop road traffic. Morgan found himself wishing the sign would work on the rain and wind. Water was seeping down the back of his shirt and into his shoes. It was everywhere!

Morgan was surprised to see Mr. Mallory, the library's media specialist, standing outside the front entrance. He was wearing a poncho and standing beneath an awning, but neither was doing a very good job of keeping him dry. He cradled the library's hamster, Duchess Dimples, to his chest. **It looked like he'd been crying.** But that was probably just the rain wetting his cheeks, right?

"Mr. Mallory?" said Harper. **"Is everything okay?"**

Mr. Mallory blinked, then finally seemed to realize they were there.

"I'm sorry, kids," he said. "The library is closed."

"But why?" said Theo. "It's only three o'clock!"

"You don't understand," said Mr. Mallory. "I mean the library is closed *indefinitely*. The roof collapsed. The building is flooding. It's a disaster in there!"

Morgan's eyes went wide. "The tech equipment!" he said. "Is it okay?"

Mr. Mallory frowned. **He pulled an object from beneath his poncho.** It was dripping with water.

"Th-that's one of the VR headsets we use for Minecraft," Morgan said.

"Not anymore," said Mr. Mallory. "I'm sorry, kids, but all five headsets were caught in the flood. It looks like they got the worst of it. **They're drenched!**"

Chapter 2

WATER: BANE OF BOOKS! ENEMY OF ELECTRONICS! HONESTLY, WHY DO WE EVEN KEEP WATER AROUND?

Harper tossed and turned all night long. She couldn't stop thinking about the damaged library. As she usually did when she learned about a big problem, she wished desperately that she could fix it.

Harper was an amateur scientist. And she believed that science, *good* science, was all about solving problems.

But it was too late to prevent the damage to the library. Was it also too late to save their Minecraft campaign?

As she lay awake, she reminded herself that Minecraft itself wasn't

going away. She and her friends would always be able to play their favorite game. They could generate a new world from scratch and work together to gather the materials they'd lost. **They could craft all their favorite gear, weapons, items, potions, and so on.** It was fun to occasionally start over from the beginning.

But the version of the game she'd shared with Morgan, Jodi, and the others was special. And not just because of the experimental VR goggles that had transported them into the game. **What had really made their game unique was the Evoker King.** As an evolving, self-aware artificial intelligence, the Evoker King was truly one of a kind. She thought of him as a friend. And because he was made of programming, he was stuck in that world. He was *part* of that world.

If that world was destroyed, **her friend would be destroyed with it.**

How was Harper supposed to get any sleep with thoughts like that on her mind?

The next day, Harper could tell she wasn't the only one who'd had trouble sleeping. Jodi had bags under her eyes, and **Theo yawned** as he greeted her in front of the school.

But Morgan looked as awake and intense as Harper had ever seen him.

"There must be something we can do," he said. "Harper, Theo, do you two have any ideas?"

They were all gathered in Woodsword's gym before the first bell. Usually, they would meet on the front lawn, beneath their favorite tree. **But the storm was still raging.** The wind rattled the doors, as if trying to find its way inside.

"Hey!" said Po. "Why are you asking Harper and Theo for ideas? We're all equally smart on this team."

"You're right, Po," said Morgan. "I'm sorry. Did you have an idea?"

Po grinned. He waggled his fingers as if casting a magic spell. **"Time travel,"** he said.

Morgan sighed, and Jodi patted Po on the head. "We'll work on it," she promised.

"There's not much we can do without the VR goggles," Theo said, and he yawned again. "The specific instance of Minecraft that we've been playing . . . or visiting . . . is keyed to those devices. **The world itself is hosted on a library computer, but without the goggles, we have no way of accessing it."**

Harper nodded in agreement with Theo. She saw the desperate hope in Morgan's eyes. He wasn't ready to give up on the Evoker King. She admired that about him. But she couldn't think of a single encouraging thing to say. And she saw the hope in Morgan's eyes start to fade away.

"I can see you're all upset about the

library," said a voice. "I am, too."

Harper turned, and at first, she thought she was seeing a ghost. A tall figure loomed before them, dressed all in black, its face obscured by a shadowy veil. But there was no disguising the frizzy red curls that belonged to their homeroom teacher.

"Ms. Minerva!" said Harper. "Are you going to a funeral?"

"In a manner of speaking," said the teacher. "I'm mourning the destruction of the library. It's a terrible loss for our community, isn't it? **All those poor, defenseless books, lost to the ravages of nature.** It's almost Shakespearean!"

"Oh, Minerva, must you be so dramatic?" said another voice—one that Harper recognized instantly. **Her favorite teacher, Doc Culpepper, approached them with a skip in her step.** "You know what I always say: every setback is an opportunity for invention. And I think we can all agree that what the library needed all along was a state-of-the-art force field!"

Harper couldn't see Ms. Minerva's expression with the veil in place, but she could sense her rolling her eyes. "Even a force field lets light through," Ms. Minerva said. **"And light can damage books, too, given enough time."**

"Challenge accepted!" said Doc. "If you can get me funding, I will invent a barrier that will block both rain *and* light."

"But . . . that's just a roof, isn't it?" said Theo.

Doc narrowed her eyes. **"Then I will make a**

state-of-the-art roof. With science!"

"Why are the teachers hanging out with us?" Po whispered. "It's weird, right?"

Harper elbowed him. It was her way of saying *Shush!*

"**look there,**" said Doc. "Is that Mr. Mallory?"

Harper saw immediately that Doc was right. The media specialist was coming in from the rain. Doc and Ms. Minerva waved him over.

"Are you here to check on Duchess Dimples?" asked Ms. Minerva. "She's settling in just fine."

"**Or are you here to request a force field?**" asked Doc. "Because I'm still puzzling out an appropriate power source."

Mr. Mallory raised his eyebrow. "Nothing like that," he answered. "I'm here to greet some student volunteers. A troop of Wildling Scouts has volunteered to help us

with all the cleanup."

"It will be heartbreaking," said Ms. Minerva. "Sifting through the ruin of the library."

Mr. Mallory shook his head. "The flooding made a mess, and it destroyed some of our physical collection. **But a library is more than just a building.** I can continue to serve the community while the roof is being repaired and books are being replaced." He smiled. "And since many of our materials are available online, you'll still be able to access our collection. I just turned the computers on this morning."

"And the Wildling Scouts are going to help you?" asked Theo. "Won't they miss class?"

"Aw, no fair," said Po. "That's, like, the *one* club I'm not in."

"The Wildling volunteers are coming from a neighboring town, actually," said Mr. Mallory. "Their school calendar is different from Woodsword's. They're on break this week. Ah! Here they are now."

They all peered out the window. Through the rain, Harper saw a school bus pull up to the curb. Its door opened, and a stream of Wildling Scouts stepped out, holding their umbrellas high.

One of them was familiar.

"Everybody, look! It's Ash!" cried Harper. **"Ash is here!"**

Chapter 3

WELCOME BACK, ASH! I HOPE YOU LIKE WHAT WE'VE DONE WITH THE PLACE.

Ash Kapoor had been away too long. Although she had kept up with her friends since moving away, she hadn't seen Woodsword Middle School in a while.

There were a lot of little changes, which she noticed right away. The gardening club had been hard at work, and flowers were in bloom in little gardens all over the school grounds. The school's ancient, rusty weathervane had been replaced with a shiny new model in the shape of an atom. **(That had to be Doc's doing.)** While riding in on the bus, she had even spotted a beehive!

But the important things hadn't changed at all.

30

For example, her friends still gave the best group hugs.

"**Okay, enough hugging!**" said Morgan, pulling free from their group embrace. "We've got to update Ash on everything that's happened."

"Brace yourself," warned Jodi.

"So it isn't good news," said Ash. "**Has the Fault gotten worse?**"

"That's an understatement," said Theo. "The last time we played, the Overworld was ninety percent Fault."

"But that's not the worst of it," said Harper. "Our VR goggles were destroyed in the flood."

"Oh no!" said Ash. "So there's only one left?"

"No," said Morgan. "**All five were wrecked.**"

"But Doc made six of them," said Ash. "Remember?" She dug around in her backpack. "I took one with me, when I moved." **Grinning, she pulled something from the pack and held it out for them all to see.** "And I brought it with me."

Everyone's eyes went wide. They all started talking at once.

"I can't believe we forgot. . . ."

"Ash to the rescue . . . again"

". . . have a real chance now."

". . . corn dogs for lunch."

Morgan, however, was quiet. His lower lip trembled with emotion. Then he leapt forward, his arms held out wide. "One more hug, everybody!" he cried. "Come on! Everybody get in on this!"

Ash smiled. It was good to be back. **For a moment, it felt like she'd never left.**

But then there was a tremendous crash. It echoed through the gymnasium, so loud and sudden that Ash nearly dropped the headset right out of her hands.

"Careful!" said Morgan.

"I've got it," said Ash. "But what was that sound?"

"It wasn't thunder," said Harper. **"It sounded like a train hit the school."**

"Or a ravager," said Po. "Which I actually had a dream about last night." He gasped. **"Does this mean I'm psychic?!"**

"No," said Theo.

Po gasped again. "I knew you'd say that!"

Ash noticed that Doc and Ms. Minerva were hurrying out into the hallway. "We should follow them," she suggested. "If we want to see for ourselves what just happened."

Jodi led the way. She put on a pair of sunglasses,

popped up her collar, and stepped lightly on her feet. **Ash recognized Jodi's "spy mode" immediately.** But there was no need to be sneaky. Plenty of other students had wandered into the hallway, curious about the noise.

Doc and Ms. Minerva were both running ahead. **"So much for no running in the halls,"** Po said.

The teachers came to a stop before a closed classroom door. Ash wondered how they knew this was the source of the sound they'd heard.

Then she saw water seeping out from beneath the door. It pooled in the center of the hallway.

"My lab!" cried Doc.

Ms. Minerva pushed the door open just as Ash and the others caught up. Ash peered around the teacher. Her jaw dropped at what she saw.

A tree had fallen outside and crashed right through a window in Doc's laboratory classroom. **Rain poured into the opening, and sodden leaves and fragmented branches littered the tabletops.** At least one microscope lay broken on the ground.

Ash had never seen such destruction in a classroom. It was as if Woodsword was under siege. **And the storm wasn't finished yet.**

Chapter 4

ASH STANDS ALONE! SHE ALSO RUNS, JUMPS, AND FIGHTS ALONE. BUT I'M SURE SHE'S GOT THIS. SHE'S VERY CAPABLE!

The damaged lab was quickly blocked off and the hallway mopped, and **school resumed as normal, although students and teachers all watched the classroom windows with concern.** While Morgan and the others tried to focus on their school lessons, Ash and the rest of the visiting Wildling Scouts spent the day across the street at Stonesword Library.

Hours later, after a full day of carrying ruined books and furniture out to a dumpster, Ash's muscles ached. She wanted a shower and a nap.

But her friends needed her. **The Evoker King needed her.** Ash decided that going into Minecraft might actually reinvigorate her.

The decision wasn't that difficult when she saw the look of pure exhilaration on Harper's face.

They were meeting in the cafetorium, with Ms. Minerva's permission. She'd even given them some snacks: fresh fruit and little cartons of milk.

"I've got an idea," Harper said. "Mr. Mallory mentioned that the library's computers are still on, and that should include the networked PC we use for Minecraft. If I can connect your headset to that computer remotely by piggybacking off the school's Wi-Fi, **then one of us should be able to get into the game from here."**

"That all makes sense, kind of," said Ash. "But why is Po covered in aluminum foil?"

"Because I'm helping!" said Po. He held a spoon high up in the air. **"It's possible that by taking on the aspect of a giant antenna,**

I'll boost the signal and help Harper's plan work."

"It is technically possible," said Theo. He rubbed his chin doubtfully. "Likely? No. Possible? Sure."

"**Good enough for me!**" said Po, pulling out a second spoon and holding it in the air.

Harper turned back to Ash. "Doc's already

boosted the school Wi-Fi to a ridiculous extreme. That's what makes this plan possible. Well, that and your headset."

"Which is why you should be the one to go into the game," said Morgan.

"Me?" said Ash. "I was sure *you* would want to."

"I do," said Morgan, smiling. **"But I've gotten better at sharing.** And it's your headset, so fair is fair." His smile dropped. "But be *careful*. It felt like the entire Overworld was falling apart. Who knows what you'll find when you connect?"

"Only one way to answer that," said Ash, and she donned her goggles. **"I'm ready when you are, Harper."**

With Morgan's warning ringing in her ears, Ash expected the worse as she pulled the goggles into place and logged in.

To her surprise, her avatar appeared just where she'd left it, on a tranquil, grassy plain, near a smattering of flowers. The sun was just peeking over a snow-capped mountain range, and Ash's bed, chest, and inventory were all just as she remembered.

So far, so good.

A low groan alerted her to new danger. She turned to see a zombie approaching her from the edge of a heavily shaded forest. As it stepped into the sunlight, the zombie's

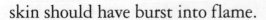

skin should have burst into flame.

But the zombie didn't burst into flame. It didn't seem bothered by the sun at all.

And Ash was standing there, unarmed.

"Sword," she mumbled. **"WHERE'S MY SWORD?"**

She quickly rifled through her inventory, selecting her best weapon: a diamond sword, enchanted with Sharpness. It would make exceptionally short work of a lowly zombie. Even if that zombie seemed strangely unbothered by sunlight.

Ash thrust with her sword.

But the sword never connected with the mob.

She watched in amazement as her weapon broke apart into pixels before her very eyes. One moment it was a gleaming sword. The next it was gone. A few stray pixels floated away, as if carried off by the wind.

But there was no wind in Minecraft, of course.

Or was there? Ash suddenly had to rethink everything she thought she knew about the game.

The zombie swiped at her, growling. Ash was strangely relieved that the zombie, at least, was acting like a zombie.

She swiped back, hitting it with her bare, blocky fist. The zombie was knocked backward—

And the block beneath it broke apart as if it had been hit with a powerful pickaxe. Grass and dirt shattered apart. The zombie fell through the new hole **. . . and kept falling.**

Ash crept carefully to the edge and peered inside. It was too dark to see very far, but she had the impression that the hole went a very long way indeed. Perhaps all the way down to bedrock.

Then she wondered: *Does bedrock even exist anymore?*

As Ash watched, the blue sky glitched out, replaced by black. The sun still hung in the sky, but it gave off little light. And the one-block-wide hole at Ash's feet began to grow larger, one block at a time.

The Overworld wasn't just broken and in

trouble. **It had become dangerous and unpredictable.**

And there was no sign of the one thing she so desperately hoped to see.

"Where are you, butterflies?" she asked. **"WHERE IS THE FINAL PIECE OF THE EVOKER KING?"**

The pixelated sky only grew darker and gave no answer.

Chapter 5

THE WISDOM OF BUTTERFLIES: EMBRACE CHANGE. SEEK SHELTER FROM THE STORM. AND EAT YOUR GREENS!

Morgan listened anxiously as Ash spoke. She told them all about her zombie encounter, the disappearing sword, and the bottomless pit. When the sky had glitched out, she'd quickly disconnected, and Morgan didn't blame her.

It sounded totally chaotic. And dangerous. Far too dangerous for any one of them to go in alone.

"We need more goggles," he said. "It's the only way."

"I tried," Harper said. "Mr. Mallory let me take a pair home. All the electronics inside were totally fried."

"So we can't fix them," said Po. "Can we make new ones?"

"We can't," said Theo. "But we know someone who might be able to."

Jodi opened the cafetorium door and peered through the rain. **"Her car's still in the parking lot. She hasn't left yet!"**

"Okay." Morgan smiled despite all the grim details Ash had shared. This was starting to sound like an actual plan. "Doc made the original goggles.

So we'll ask her to do it again." He clapped his hands together. **"Let's find her! Come on!"**

Doc wasn't in her laboratory classroom, sorting through the wreckage. She wasn't in the teachers' lounge. Just as Morgan began to worry they wouldn't find her, Po squeaked.

"I saw her through that window," he said. **"She's in the butterfly sanctuary!"**

Morgan chuckled. He'd honestly forgotten that the school had a room just for butterflies. It had once been Woodsword's computer lab, before the insects had taken over.

"Oh!" said Ash. "I've never seen it in person."

"Then you're in for a treat," said Harper.

"Unless you dislike insects," added Theo. "If you dislike insects, you really won't enjoy this at all."

Judging by the excitement on her face, Ash did not dislike insects. She opened the door, and **she motioned for the others to hurry inside, before any butterflies could escape.**

Doc was holding a terrarium in her hands.

47

It was like an aquarium, but full of leafy plants instead of water. Morgan counted at least four cocoons attached to those plants. He leaned in for a closer look . . . and then a butterfly landed on the tip of his nose.

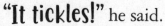

"It tickles!" he said.

"It's a good look for you," Ash said in a teasing voice. "The wings really bring out the color of your eyes."

"How about the color of his cheeks?" said Jodi. "He's blushing!"

"I am not," said Morgan, and he blew the butterfly off his nose.

"Hello, Ash," said Doc. "It's good to have you back, even if it's just for a little while."

"Thanks, Doc," said Ash. **"Are you gathering cocoons?"**

"I am," said the teacher. "This used to be our computer lab. But I'm sure you remember that. You spent a lot of time here!"

"Those were the best weeks of her life," said Po, pretending to sniffle with emotion.

"**Anyway, after the incident at the laboratory, we need all the space we can get,**" Doc explained. "I'm going to set the adult butterflies free. And I'll find a safe place where the cocooned ones can finish their metamorphosis."

"Are you injecting them with super chemicals?" asked Jodi. "**Mutating the butterflies into giant beasts you can ride into battle with the school board?**"

"I like the way you think," said Doc. "But Minerva made me promise not to do any genetic tampering on school grounds, alas. Care to help me gather the remaining cocoons?"

"**I'll help,**" said Harper, perking up at the chance to assist her favorite teacher.

Theo cleared his throat. "Actually, we're here to ask *you* for help, Doc."

"These VR goggles you made." Ash held up the last remaining pair. "They're very special to us. But we lost five of them when the library flooded. Do you think you could make new ones?"

"And quickly?" added Theo.

Harper shushed him. "**Theo, be polite!**"

"I'd rather be honest," said Theo. "We need more headsets in order to help the artificial—"

"*Our friend,*" Morgan interrupted. "**We need more headsets so we can help our friend.**"

"It sounds very serious indeed," said Doc. "But I don't have all the parts I would need. It could be weeks before I can rebuild even a single set." On seeing their reactions, Doc laughed. "Don't look so glum!" she said. "There's a quick, temporary solution to your problem. Look here."

Doc took Ash's headset in her hands. She lifted a small panel to reveal input and output jacks. "These goggles were meant to be networked. In fact, with a few ethernet cables, a memory card or two, and dollar-store sunglasses, **you could rig up a whole circuit of VR goggles by piggybacking off the software of this single pair.**" She handed the goggles back to Ash. "I'm sure Harper can handle it, but I'm available if you have trouble."

"**I can do that!**" said Harper excitedly. Morgan hadn't totally understood, but Harper seemed to grasp exactly what Doc was suggesting. "I've got everything we need except sunglasses."

"I've got you covered," said Jodi. She turned her backpack upside down, and several pairs of sunglasses in different styles fell out.

"Why?" asked Po. "Just . . . why?"

Jodi shrugged. "They're for my spy kit. **You can never have too many disguises.**"

"I accept this explanation," said Po, and he chose a glittery pink pair from the pile.

"There's one more thing I have to do," said Doc. "The rain has stopped for a moment, so now's my chance. Everybody ready?"

Morgan wasn't sure what he needed to be ready for. So he was caught by surprise when Doc threw open the nearest window.

Wind swirled around the room. **The adult butterflies immediately took notice,** and one by one flew out of the classroom and into the late-afternoon sky.

"Will they be okay?" asked Morgan.

"They'll be marvelous," said Doc. **"After all, they were born to fly.** And we could all learn a thing or two from butterflies."

"Like what?" asked Po.

"Embrace change," answered Doc. She was smiling as she watched all the colorful insects fly into the distance.

Chapter 6

WEARING SUNGLASSES INDOORS? TOTALLY ACCEPTABLE IF THEY'RE HOT-WIRED WITH IMPROVISED VR TECH!

Fo had to admit it: he was impressed. Where yesterday there had been one set of VR glasses, now there were six. **The styles ranged from classic aviators to sci-fi new-wave shades**—all with wires and computer-chip gizmos attached.

"Harper, you're amazing! You did all this last night?" he asked.

Harper smiled at the compliment. "It was easy once Doc explained how it worked," she said. "I'm just glad Jodi had so many sets of sunglasses."

"I feel a little silly," said Theo. He was

trying on a set of goggles that clearly belonged at a swimming pool.

"You look awesome," Po promised. "Honestly, it's about time this group started experimenting with new styles."

"I don't care how we look," Morgan said. **His glasses were oversized and clunky,** as if they belonged in an old-school video game. "I'd wear a burlap sack and mismatched socks if it got us back into Minecraft."

"I'm with Morgan on that," said Ash. "We only have a little bit of time before you have to be in class and I have to be at the library." She slipped her goggles on. **"Let's make the most of our time."**

Po gasped as his digital form took shape. Evidence of the Fault was all around him. He saw it in the black sky. He saw it in a strangely glitching tree, which seemed to blink in and out of existence.

But that wasn't why Po was gasping.

He was gasping . . . **because his avatar was half bee and half axolotl.**

And that was awesome.

"Look at me!" he cried. "Look at me!"

"Oh no!" said Jodi. "Your skins got all mixed up."

But Po was laughing. "I'm a whole new creature! CALL ME A BUMBLOTL!"

"I won't call him that," Theo said to the group.

"BE CAREFUL, PO," Morgan warned. "I can tell you're excited, but we should all stay close together."

"MY SWORD IS BACK IN MY INVENTORY," Ash said, and she drew a diamond blade. "But . . . I think it's got a different enchantment than before."

"THERE DOESN'T SEEM TO BE ANY RHYME OR REASON TO ANY OF THIS," said Harper. She was standing in a patch of snow.

"You can say that again," said Jodi, who stood next to Harper. Yet Jodi appeared to be in a miniature desert biome, complete with sand and a cactus.

Morgan bonked his fists against his square forehead. "I feel like I'm losing my mind!" he said. "Minecraft is supposed to have rules. And I have all those rules memorized. But this . . . ? It's just absolute chaos!"

"WE'LL FIX IT," Ash promised. "We'll find the last piece of the Evoker King. Fixing him will fix the game. Right?"

Theo shrugged his blocky shoulders. "That's our theory. AND IT'S JUST A THEORY. But it's the best idea we've got."

"Then we need to find the butterflies," said Jodi. "They've led us to all the other pieces."

"IT'S GOING TO BE LIKE FINDING A NEEDLE IN A HAYSTACK," said Po. "If the haystack was moving. And occasionally transformed into a bear."

"Well, here's some good news," said Theo, and he swung his pickaxe into the dirt. "We can still mine."

"AND WE CAN STILL CRAFT!" added Harper. She lifted a freshly crafted sword from a crafting table. "As long as we can do those things, we can survive here."

Jodi picked up the dirt block that Theo had knocked loose. "LET'S BUILD A TOWER," she suggested. "Maybe from up high, we'll be able to see what we're looking for."

Po joined in. "I've got a lot of cobblestone. **WE CAN USE IT TO BUILD.**"

But as Po began laying the foundations for a tower, he noticed something strange. The blocks he set down were a variety of colors, each different from the last. "Do you all see this?" he asked.

"THAT'S NOT COBBLESTONE," said Theo.

"It was cobblestone when it was in my inventory!" insisted Po.

Everyone gathered around, and those with extra building materials pitched in. It was the same for everybody. They would try to place cobblestone, but the block they set seemed to be chosen at random. Sometimes Po could barely tell the difference. He couldn't always distinguish one type of stone block from another. But as blocks of obsidian, glass, slime, and dyed wool appeared, nobody could deny what was happening.

"THIS IS TOO WEIRD," said Harper.

"But sort of beautiful," said Jodi.

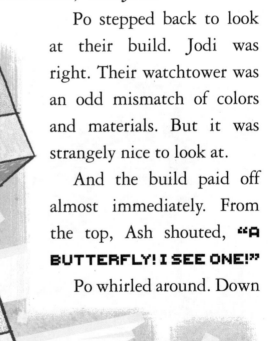

Po stepped back to look at their build. Jodi was right. Their watchtower was an odd mismatch of colors and materials. But it was strangely nice to look at.

And the build paid off almost immediately. From the top, Ash shouted, **"A BUTTERFLY! I SEE ONE!"**

Po whirled around. Down

on the ground, he was nearest to it. He took off in pursuit, while the others followed close behind.

They didn't make it far before they came to the edge of the plains biome. **Normally, that wouldn't have been a problem.** Normally, one Minecraft biome blended into another, and another.

But there was nothing normal about this situation. The biome ended in a sheer drop into an inky void. From the edge, Po could see a swamp biome floating nearby, and a jungle biome beyond that. A great mass of ocean floated in the distance. It didn't appear to be connected to anything. It was like a great blue bubble suspended in space.

It looked like the game was being pulled apart into separate pieces. **The Overworld was a collection of disconnected islands.**

"WE NEED TO BUILD A BRIDGE," said Morgan.

Jodi put a steadying hand on his shoulder. "It's too late. The butterfly's gone."

"And we just used up most of our building materials on the watchtower," Po said.

Morgan grimaced. "WE ALMOST HAD IT!"

"This is a good thing," said Theo. "Now we know we're close."

"AND WE HAVE A DIRECTION TO TRAVEL," added Harper.

"If we work together, we can do this!" said Ash.

"That's right," said Po. He clapped Morgan on the back. "Cobblestone let you down? Don't worry, bud." He grinned. "WE'LL BE YOUR ROCK."

Chapter 7
THE DUCHESS ON HOLIDAY! (ALSO, THERE ARE SOME IMPORTANT PLOT DEVELOPMENTS, BUT IT WILL BE A WHILE BEFORE THEIR RELEVANCE BECOMES APPARENT.)

Even after spending time in Minecraft that morning, Morgan and the others still arrived early to homeroom. Ms. Minerva sat at her desk grading papers. Nearby, a wastebasket was set out to catch water droplets from the leaky ceiling.

The storm seemed to be passing, but not quickly enough for Morgan. He didn't know how much more rain and wind the school could take!

Jodi ignored the wastebasket and ran over to the hamster cages. **"I need to see how Duchess Dimples is adjusting to her vacation home!"** she said.

"Vacation?" echoed Ms. Minerva. "I'm afraid it might be a permanent relocation."

Thunder rumbled outside, making the teacher's statement sound ominous.

"Permanent? What do you mean?" asked Morgan.

Ms. Minerva realized she'd spoken louder than she'd intended. "Oh! Of course Dimples is welcome to stay as long as she likes. She's not the problem. **I'm simply worried that the library will never be entirely fixed.**"

"But . . . why not?" asked Po. "Ash and her troop are over there now. They're helping Mr. Mallory clean up the mess."

"That's true," said Ms. Minerva. "But the scouts can't replace the roof. And I'm afraid that the people of this town don't care enough about the library to save it."

"No way!" said Po. "The library is awesome. We used it to learn about bees."

"And code-breaking," Harper added.

"I've got a backpack full of programming books that I checked out," said Theo. "It's weighs a ton. I can barely lift it!"

Ms. Minerva smiled. "That's a pleasant surprise. I thought you were only going to the library to use the computers."

"Well, that, too," Theo confessed. "But that's what makes the library—or media center, or whatever you want to call it—so special. There are books and computers and electronic media like DVDs. There are even board games you can check out."

"And classes!" Jodi said, turning away momentarily from

the hamster cages. "Our mom attended a basket-weaving class there."

Ms. Minerva's smile deepened. "Well, good!" she said. "Perhaps I was worried for nothing. Perhaps this town *does* care about its library."

"As much as Baron Sweetcheeks cares about Duchess Dimples, I bet," said Jodi. **"look at these little fur balls!** They're having so much fun."

Morgan looked over at the cages, and he saw that they had been connected by a piece of PVC pipe. That way, each hamster had their own space, but they could also visit each other. **At the moment, Duchess Dimples was using Baron Sweetcheeks's exercise wheel** while the baron watched her. **It almost looked**

like he was cheering her on!

And Morgan remembered when Ms. Minerva had cheered them on. She had watched over them during their conflict with the Evoker King, using one of the headsets to appear in the game as a mysterious figure they knew only as the Librarian. **It was easy to forget, sometimes, that his teacher loved Minecraft, too.**

"We should tell you what's going on in our game," said Morgan. "Things have gotten . . . a little out of hand."

And to the surprise of his friends, Morgan told her everything. About how they'd befriended the Evoker King. **About how the Evoker King had split apart into six different mobs.** About the Fault that appeared in the sky at around the same time. About how that Fault had grown and seemed ready to swallow the entire game.

"That all sounds very stressful," said Ms. Minerva. **"Have you considered starting a new game?** You don't need Doc's strange technology to enjoy it. I've been logging a lot of hours at home. I've just built my forty-third bookshelf!"

Morgan shook his head. "We can't just leave our game behind. **Not until we know if the Evoker King can be saved.**"

"I respect that," said Ms. Minerva as their other classmates began filing in for homeroom. "And I'm glad you told me about it. Doesn't it feel good to share?"

"It does," Morgan confessed. And it was true. **He felt a little less worried** now that he'd spoken his worries out loud.

"There's a lesson in there somewhere," said

Ms. Minerva. "Secrets and exclusive clubs are fun. But they can make us feel all alone with our problems. **The bigger your community, the smaller your problems can become.**"

"We'll keep it in mind," said Morgan. But he was eager to change the subject. His classmates were listening in now, and they seemed curious to know what Ms. Minerva was talking about. And despite Ms. Minerva's advice, **Morgan wasn't ready for everyone to know his business.**

Chapter 8

IT'S TOTALLY VEXING, BUT LET'S GO OVER A FEW THINGS FOR THOSE WHO HAVEN'T BEEN PAYING ATTENTION. WE'RE LOOKING AT YOU, PO.

After school, they gathered once again in Minecraft. Jodi was on high alert for anything strange. **"LET'S NOT WASTE BUILDING MATERIALS THIS TIME,** if we can avoid it," she suggested.

Before Doc had invented the VR goggles, Jodi had played Creative Mode. She still missed flying sometimes. Flying would have come in handy when they were hunting the strange Minecraft butterflies!

"I WANT TO TRY SOMETHING," she said. "A sort of art project."

"I'm not sure now's the time," said Theo.

"It'll only take a minute," Jodi said. "Do you still have one of the Evoker King's legs? **GIVE IT HERE!**"

Her time in Survival Mode had taught Jodi a lot about combat and resource management. But what she would always love most about Minecraft was that it allowed her to make art.

The others had set down their Evoker King pieces. **Jodi began putting the pieces together like a jigsaw puzzle.** She started with the legs.

"I see what she's doing," said Harper. "Do you think this will work, Theo?"

Theo shrugged. **"IT'S WORTH A TRY,"** he said. "But without the final piece, there's still a hole in the code."

"Explain that to me," said Ash. "I've never fully understood the connection between the Evoker King and the Fault."

"OH, GOOD! I THOUGHT IT WAS JUST ME," said Po. "Sometimes I zone out a little bit. Especially when Theo and Harper talk about coding and math."

As Theo watched Jodi connect the Evoker King's torso, he said, "The Evoker King was never supposed to be a part of the game. He was an invasive artificial intelligence who accessed the game through Doc's high-tech virtual reality equipment."

"Like an invasive species," Harper suggested. **"IN THE REAL WORLD, SOMETIMES ANIMALS THAT DON'T BELONG IN A PARTICULAR ECOSYSTEM FIND THEIR WAY INTO THAT ECOSYSTEM.** Because they have different ways of surviving than the normal species in that environment, everything can get thrown out of balance."

"... so science stuff?" Po said.

"Right," said Theo. "But in this case, the game and the invader found a new balance. The Evoker King, who is made up of programming code, and this game of Minecraft, which is also made up of programming code, grew intertwined. When the Evoker King transformed, he left a hole right in the heart of the game's code. And the hole has been expanding. It's like a sweater slowly unstitching because somebody pulled on a thread."

"But a sweater can be knit back together . . . ," Ash said.

"Exactly," said Theo. "And we hope the code

will fix itself once the Evoker King is put back together and the hole gets plugged."

Jodi had finished assembling the various Evoker King fragments. There was a torso, two arms, and two legs. But they were still missing one crucial piece.

"He looks like a Christmas tree without a star on top," said Ash.

"OR A HEADLESS SCARECROW," said Morgan.

"Ooh! That gives me an idea," said Po. He approached the headless form and plopped a carved pumpkin on top.

They all waited expectantly.

"I guess that didn't do anything," said Harper.

"Sure it did," said Po. "It made me feel better."

Jodi cocked her head to give the pumpkin-headed creation a good look. It was obvious to her that they needed to find the Evoker King's true head. She stepped forward to remove the pumpkin.

And she saw something blue out of the corner of her eye.

She thought it was a butterfly. She turned around quickly, already pointing.

To her surprise, it wasn't a butterfly at all. It was blue, but a much paler shade than the butterflies she'd seen. Like a butterfly, it flew, but on tattered, wispy wings. **It was small, shaped like a human, and held a dark sword in one of its hands.**

So: definitely not a butterfly.

"IT'S A VEX!" said her brother.

"But . . . that doesn't make sense," said Theo. "What would a vex be doing out here?"

Seeing the confusion on Jodi's face, Ash explained, **"NORMALLY, A VEX ONLY APPEARS WHEN SUMMONED BY AN EVOKER."**

Everyone's eyes went wide at the same time.

They looked from the partially completed Evoker King to the vex, and they knew: **this was the final mob they needed.**

"Grab it!" cried Morgan, and he lunged forward.

The vex easily dodged him, flying just beyond his reach.

Jodi dashed forward. The vex was now flying

in her direction. "I'll box it in," she said, and she began laying blocks in a wall formation.

To her surprise, the wall didn't stop the vex. It passed right through the blocks, like a ghost.

"Hey, that isn't fair," complained Jodi.

Po waved a sword at the vex as it approached him.

"DON'T HURT IT," warned Harper.

"I'm not!" said Po. "I'm trying to get it to fly in the other direction."

"Oh, good idea, Po," said Ash. "If we can get it to land on the Evoker King's empty shoulders, then all his pieces will be in the right place!"

"TALK TO IT!" said Theo. "That worked with the other Evoker Spawn."

"Mr. Vex," said Po. "Please stop being so vexing!"

"It's not going to listen," Jodi said. She could see in the mob's erratic flight pattern that it was upset. **"WE'VE SCARED IT, AND NOW IT JUST WANTS TO GET AWAY."**

"Please don't go!" said Morgan, but as they

watched, the vex passed through the ground.

Morgan ran forward, lifting his pickaxe high. He began digging frantically near the spot where the vex had disappeared.

But it didn't do any good. **The mob was nowhere to be found.**

Chapter 9

I SCREAM! YOU SCREAM! THEN WE GET IN TROUBLE FOR YELLING, SO WE USE OUR INSIDE VOICES TO ASK POLITELY FOR ICE CREAM.

Dark clouds blanketed the sky, and thunder rumbled in the distance. **But the rain, at last, had stopped falling, and the wind had calmed to a gentle breeze.** Ash was happy for the break in the weather. She was only in town for a few more days, after all, and she still had several favorite locations she wanted to visit.

There was the bat house that she had helped build, on the edge of school property. A bookstore that had a huge selection of graphic novels and manga. **And the best ice cream shop around, with dozens of flavors and uncountable toppings.**

She asked Morgan to join her for ice cream. She thought it was about time the two of them had a very important talk. **And she was worried that he wouldn't like what she had to say.**

But in Ash's experience, ice cream made everything a little bit better.

That was especially true about ice cream with a friend. And not just human friends. Morgan had gotten permission to bring the hamsters home for the evening. **Baron Sweetcheeks and Duchess Dimples were each in their own plastic ball,** rolling around at Ash's feet.

"It's so hard to choose," Ash said as they waited

in line. **"There are so many options!"**

"Yeah," Morgan agreed. But when it was his turn to order at the shop window, he asked for a cup of simple vanilla ice cream.

They sat on a nearby swing set, and Morgan's eyes bounced between his plain white scoop and the multicolored confection Ash had chosen: **three flavors of ice cream, topped with bright sprinkles, gummies, walnuts, and a drizzle of butterscotch.**

Ash laughed as Morgan goggled. "You can't get this specific combination anywhere near my house," she explained.

"It looks so chaotic," he said. "Is it *good*?"

"Of course it's good," Ash answered, and she licked her lips. "It's all sugar, after all."

"I guess I could be a bit more daring," Morgan said. "But I get worried about what could happen. I know for a fact that I like vanilla ice cream. **So why risk getting something I won't like as much?"**

Ash laughed again. "Because you might find something you like even more. **You can't know unless you try!"**

"I guess," Morgan replied, looking skeptical.

Ash watched him poke at his ice cream with his spoon. She took a breath. It was now or never.

"That's actually what I wanted to talk to you about," said Ash.

Morgan looked confused. "My ice cream selection?"

"No," said Ash. **"Your reluctance to try new things."**

"Oh." Morgan watched the hamsters rolling around beneath his feet. "This sounds serious."

"It's not a big deal," Ash promised. "It's just that I have an idea. **And I want to make sure you really listen to it.** And I hope that you'll consider it before you try to shoot it down."

"I don't shoot ideas down," Morgan said a little defensively. Then he added, "Do I?"

"Not always," said Ash. "But when we

needed help deciphering a code, I thought we should ask my Wildling troop for help. **And you weren't happy about that.**"

"Well, that's certainly true . . . ," said Morgan. He took a scoop of ice cream without taking a bite.

"Or what about our decision to let Theo join the club? You didn't like that." She grinned. "And you were the same way when I joined, remember?"

"That was a long time ago!" Morgan said, leaning back in his swing. **"I've changed.** I'm way more relaxed and open."

"Good," said Ash. "In that case, I've got an idea." She pulled a sheet of graphing paper from her pocket with her free hand before unfolding it and handing it to Morgan. **The paper contained her design for something she was calling a slime engine.** "Really, it was Po's idea. He inspired me when he tried to force the vex to move toward the Evoker King fragments. This device should help us do that."

Morgan took a moment to wrap his head around Ash's design. She had labeled everything clearly, but there were a lot of different elements. **The slime engine made use of sticky pistons, redstone blocks, and slime blocks.** But at heart, the idea was simple. The slime engine would crawl forward on its own, using a wall of slime to push anything in its path.

"Because slime blocks can push vexes!" Morgan said. He wanted to slap his forehead with the realization, but his hands were full of ice cream and blueprints. "Ash, this is brilliant." He furrowed his brow. "Only, to cover a large space, we'd need a lot of these engines, all coming from different directions."

"Right. My thinking exactly," said Ash. "And that brings us to the part I'm nervous to say out loud, but here goes: Morgan, I think we should invite more kids to join us in Minecraft."

"No way!" Morgan said automatically. "Our team is special. And it's hard enough getting Po and Jodi to take it seriously sometimes. And the Evoker King is depending on us, and, and—

I'm doing the thing where I shoot down an idea, aren't I?"

Ash took a prim bite of her ice cream and gave him an innocent shrug that said *What do you think?*

Morgan sighed loudly. **"I'm sorry. I'll hear you out."**

"Thank you," said Ash. She anchored her feet and twisted her swing around so that she was facing him. "Here's the thing. Keeping our club or whatever you want to call it secret made sense when we only had a few headsets. **But if we can make five of them, we can make ten. Maybe more!** And with that many of us working together, we can build these slime engines, find the vex, and restore the Evoker King. At least, we'll have a better chance of doing all that before time runs out."

Morgan stared into his ice cream as if it held the secrets of the universe.

"Well?" Ash said finally. "Say something."

Morgan frowned. "What if we do this . . . and nothing is ever the same again?"

"That's what change is. You can fight it or you

can embrace it. But it comes eventually, either way." Ash lifted her feet, and her swing spun around as its chains untwisted. "And wouldn't you rather embrace it, if it gives us a better chance to help the Evoker King?"

Morgan's eyes glittered in the shop's neon lights. He reached down and gently picked up Baron Sweetcheeks's hamster ball. **"What do you think, Baron?"**

Baron Sweetcheeks scratched his chin vigorously and then ran around in a small circle three times.

"You're right. We're just going to keep running in circles if we keep doing things my way," Morgan said. "And you're right, too, Ash. **To save the Evoker King … we have to try something new."**

He stood up, sliding out of the swing.

"Where are you going?" Ash asked, surprised at his intensity. "We can't really do anything until tomorrow."

"You're wrong. There's something I can do right now," said Morgan. **"I can ask them to put sprinkles on my ice cream!"**

Ash gasped. "Are you sure?"

"I'm tired of being afraid to try new things," he said. "And to be honest, they look delicious."

"They are!" Ash said, and as the sun broke through the clouds for the first time in days, she put a spoonful of dessert into her mouth. **Nothing had ever tasted sweeter.**

Chapter 10

A BRIGHT AND SUNNY AFTERNOON! A HOPEFUL SIGN OF THINGS TO COME! NOTHING TO GO WRONG JUST YET.

The sun was finally shining outside Woodsword Middle School, but Morgan barely noticed.

Because a light of a different kind was shining inside Morgan's heart.

The bell rang, and Morgan leapt out of his chair. He was the first one out the door, and Jodi was waiting for him just outside. Her hands were stained with multicolored paints.

"I got all the posters finished and hung up," she said. "Things got a little messy."

Morgan gave her a high five. He didn't mind getting a little color on him.

The siblings hurried down the hallway. They passed the classroom where student government meetings were held. Po was there, taping a red sign to the door. It read MEETING CANCELED.

"Dude!" Po said to Morgan. He wheeled alongside Morgan and Jodi as they continued down the hallway. **"Shelly canceled today's meeting. I think she saw one of Jodi's posters."** He turned to Jodi. "Which are beautiful and excellent," he added.

Jodi beamed. "Aw, shucks. I bet you say that to everybody who uses elements of French Expressionism in their school flyers."

Po shrugged. "I like color."

They ran into Harper and Theo soon after.

"Today's the day," said Theo. "Are you sure this is a good idea?"

"I just hope I made enough headsets," said Harper.

"We're about to find out," said Morgan. He pushed open the doors to the cafetorium.

Just as he'd hoped, **a group of eager students was waiting on the other side.**

"Are we in the right place?" asked Shelly Silver. She held up one of Jodi's flyers, still wet with paint. **"Is this the Minecraft club?"**

Morgan realized that she had directed the question at him. Everyone's eyes looked his way, and he felt queasy. He tried not to let them see how nervous he was. He forced himself to grin. He hoped it looked like the confident smile of a leader.

"You're in the right place," he said. "Thanks for coming, everybody."

Morgan looked over the crowd. There were about a dozen kids there, and he recognized all of them. He saw several of Po's basketball teammates, a couple of drama kids, some cheerleaders, and more. Ash waved at a few Wildling Scouts. Even Po's older cousin Hope was there.

"I'm here as the chaperone," Hope explained, and **she handed Morgan a small corn dog on a stick.** "And to promote my new food truck."

Ned Brant, a reporter for the school's podcast, held a microphone in Morgan's direction. "Can you tell us why the Blockheadz are so eager for new members?"

"We're not calling ourselves that," Morgan grumbled.

Theo crossed his arms, bashfully hiding the BLOCKHEADZ logo on his T-shirt.

"We asked you here to help us with an experiment," Harper explained, and she began passing out the jury-rigged sunglasses. "We've got some pretty fun technology built into these glasses. **It's a whole new way to play Minecraft!**"

"But there's bad news, too," said Morgan. "The Minecraft you're about to experience is broken. We need your help to accomplish a specific task. If you get into trouble, don't worry. Hope will be able to unplug your glasses, and you'll be safely back here."

"Back here?" echoed Shelly. "I don't understand. Where are we going?"

Morgan grinned. **"Into the game."**

Chapter 11

TWO IS COMPANY. THREE IS A CROWD. BUT WITH ODDS LIKE THESE? THE MORE THE MERRIER!

Ash had never seen Minecraft so crowded.

And it had never been so loud, either.

"WOO-HOO!" cried Ned as he punched a tree into free-floating blocks of wood.

"This is so cool!" Shelly shouted. She ran her hands over a sheep. "It feels so real."

"A-W-E-S-O-M-E!" Tony the cheerleader spelled out.

"Po, is that you?" asked Raul, one of Po's basketball teammates. "Why do you look like a cat?"

"Maybe the question is why don't *you* look like a cat?" asked Po, who was wearing a cat suit.

Raul seemed to think this was very deep. "Huh," he said, nodding slowly.

"BUT WHAT'S WRONG WITH THE SKY?" asked Ricky, another teammate of Po's. "And why aren't the biomes connected? It all seems . . . disconnected." Ricky tapped the headless Evoker King, but nothing happened.

"Inquiring minds want to know," said Ned.

"Why is there a phantom out during the daytime?"

"PHANTOM?" echoed Harper. "Where?"

But the answer was soon obvious. The flying undead mob swept down from the sky, cutting a path through the players. Shelly was nearly knocked off her feet. Raul took a swing with a brand-new wooden sword, but the phantom had already flown beyond his reach.

"It's circling back around," said Ned.

"Raul, Raul, you can do it," cheered Tony.

"Come on now, there's nothing to it!" added Po.

The phantom flew low again, aiming for Raul, who readied his sword.

"Wait, be careful," Ash warned. "We don't know if—"

Before Ash could finish her sentence, the

phantom began to flash red. It reminded Ash of how a creeper flashed . . . right before exploding.

"RAUL, GET CLEAR!" she cried.

Raul barely jumped out of the way in time. The phantom exploded, taking a big chunk of the plains biome with it. Now there was a gaping hole at the base of their mismatched watchtower. Ash hurried over to plug it up and to check on Raul.

"I'm okay," he said. "But why did that thing explode? AND WHY WAS IT OUT IN THE DAYLIGHT TO BEGIN WITH?"

"That's what I meant when I said this version of the game is breaking down," said Morgan. "The code has gotten all wrong. We're never sure what's going to happen next."

"Which means we need to make the slime engines immediately," said Ash. "Before things get worse."

"SLIME ENGINES? What are those?" asked Shelly.

"It's what we're here to build," answered Morgan. "Ash, Po, Jodi, Harper, and I all have the design memorized. But we need materials:

redstone, wood planks, and slime. A lot of slime! Can you all help with that?"

"It's going to mean doing our best to hold this place together a little bit longer," said Harper. **"WE'LL NEED BRIDGES OR STAIRCASES TO CONNECT THE BIOMES.** We'll need to plug holes in the ground and fight off mobs that might be extra dangerous and unpredictable."

Po eyed the nearby sheep with suspicion. "Don't try anything funny," he warned them.

"THEY WOULD NEVER!" Jodi insisted.

"Tony, as a cheerleader, you're good at being heard from a distance," said Ash. "Can you climb the watchtower? **IF YOU SEE A VEX, LET US KNOW IMMEDIATELY."**

"Aye aye, captain," said Tony.

"Wildling Scouts, you're on slime ball duty."

"Where will we find slime balls?" asked a scout.

"THERE'S A SWAMP NEARBY," Morgan explained. "Make yourselves some weapons and go hunting for slimes."

Jodi added, "Or if you're not interested in combat, find some pandas! If you're lucky, a sneezing baby panda will leave a slime ball behind."

"WE'VE GOT THIS," said Shelly.

"Go team!" said Tony.

As Ash watched them, she saw the kids take

naturally to teamwork. **Ned mined,** providing the material Shelly needed to build a piston from scratch. The drama kids crafted an entire bridge, linking the plains biome to a swamp in a matter of minutes, and Wildling Scouts rushed across on their hunt for slimes.

"This could work," Morgan said beside Ash.

"I just hope we're ready before the vex appears," said Ash. "We need to be ready to seize our chance."

Morgan agreed. "Yeah," he said. **"BECAUSE IT MIGHT BE THE LAST CHANCE WE GET."**

Chapter 12

MEANWHILE: THEO'S SIDE QUEST! WHAT CHALLENGES AWAIT HIM? WILL HE REAP AN EPIC REWARD OR FACE HIS FINAL DOOM?

Theo hadn't entered the game with the rest of them. He planned to join them soon. **First he had to make sure their hardware could handle the strain.**

"And that's how you get the perfect golden-brown color," Hope was saying. **"There's nothing less appetizing than a yellow corn dog."**

"I believe you," said Theo. He was only half listening. He and Harper had set up a fairly complicated

computer network in the cafetorium. At the heart of the network was a single PC that Theo had brought in from home. **He had built the computer himself!** (Well, his dad had helped.) But he hadn't realized it would be pushed so hard so soon.

More than a dozen VR goggles were all using the software installed in Ash's set, which were plugged into Theo's PC, which was remotely networked to the server in the library. It was a web of connections. **And like a web, it was beautiful but delicate.** One broken thread could cause the entire thing to collapse. They just hadn't had time to make it better.

Theo was relieved to see that everything seemed to be working. It wouldn't work for long, but it didn't have to. **Just long enough for them to find that vex, herd it in the right direction, and restore the Evoker King.**

Hope finally stopped talking about corn dogs—a very strange food, in Theo's opinion. In the sudden silence, he overheard new voices. Theo realized they were coming from a little side office connected to the cafetorium. **The adult voices were hushed and urgent, and curiosity got the best of him.**

He crept closer, recognizing Ms. Minerva's voice. "I'm telling you, it's an inspiration. They're all in the game right now, working together. The rules changed on them, and they adapted."

"They're wonderful kids." That was Doc's voice. "Although the technology they're using is also pretty wonderful."

"When it works!" said Ms. Minerva.

"So we know they can adapt," said Mr. Mallory. **"That will be important if we select them for this program."**

"It sounds like we're in agreement," said Ms. Minerva. **"It will be a big change. . . ."**

"But change can be a good thing," said Doc. "I have the paperwork right here. We can make it official."

Theo heard the rustling of papers. He peeked around the corner. All three adults were huddled over stacks of paper and manila file folders. He saw his school photo clipped to one of the folders. **Was that his permanent file?**

"This school won't be the same without them," said Ms. Minerva.

"Or without us," said Doc.

"But it's the best solution for everyone," said Mr. Mallory. "Now how about we take a break? I was promised snacks."

"Po's cousin has her food truck parked outside," said Doc. "I'll treat."

"Oh, good," said Ms. Minerva. "Who doesn't love a corn dog?"

Chapter 13

VEXES ARE VEXING! NO SURPRISE THERE. BUT THIS ONE IS SOMETHING SPECIAL....

Morgan felt a rush of relief when he saw Theo's avatar appear beside him.

"IS EVERYTHING LOOKING GOOD IRL?" he asked.

"I'm not sure," said Theo. "The adults are up to something."

"I MEAN WITH YOUR COMPUTER," said Morgan. "Everything else can wait. As long as the network is working."

"It is, for now," said Theo. "But my PC could break down at any second. **THIS MIGHT BE OUR LAST CHANCE."**

"Then we'll make the most of it," said Harper.

"JODI IS IN POSITION," said Morgan.

"And we've already built a bunch of slime engines," said Ash. "The scouts did a great job of finding slime balls."

"THERE REALLY SHOULD BE A MERIT BADGE FOR THAT," said Po.

At that moment, they heard Tony cry out, "Vex! There's a vex on the move, north by northeast!"

"IT'S TIME," said Morgan. "Come on, team. This is it!"

They hurried to the northeast edge of the plains biome. **There was a new bridge there, built by their classmates.** Its colorfully mismatched blocks made it look a little like the rainbow bridge from Norse mythology.

The bridge led to a mushroom field. Morgan saw the vex floating low among the mushrooms. **He couldn't believe their luck!** Mushroom fields were mostly flat, so the vex didn't have many places to hide.

"I'll get it over the bridge," said Morgan. "Then it will be up to the rest of you."

"I'll make sure everyone is ready," promised

Ash. "Good luck, Morgan!"

Morgan ran across the rainbow bridge, but he slowed down as he entered the first patch of mushrooms. **He didn't want to spook the vex.** It might attack him, or worse, fly away. But he had to slip past it so that he could move it in the right direction.

He constructed one more slime engine. By now, he could do it quickly. He attached a few slime blocks to a sticky piston, added some cobblestones for stability, then placed redstone blocks where they would keep the piston powered. With the push of a button, **the piston surged forward**—and because it was a sticky piston, it pulled the whole build forward.

The engine lurched ahead, a fully automated battering ram. Although something about its movement and green-and-red coloring made Morgan think of a caterpillar. An attack caterpillar! Po would get a kick out of that image.

Morgan had positioned the engine perfectly. It crept up on the vex, and when it reached the mob, the pistons slammed the slime blocks into the unsuspecting mob. **The vex was shoved forward,** onto the rainbow bridge. And as the slime engine moved forward, it continued shoving the vex all the way across the bridge and onto the plains island.

So far, so good. But would the others do their part?

"THE VEX IS BELOW!" cried Tony. "Heading southeast!"

The vex, tired of being bumped, had flown ahead of Morgan's engine. It flew past the tower, past the Evoker

King fragments, and toward the edge of the plains biome. **If it flew off into the void, it would be lost to them.**

But Shelly Silver was on the southeast edge of the island. At Tony's warning, she set her slime engine in motion. It knocked the vex back, away from the edge and toward the center of the biome.

And so it went. Po's engine in the west, Harper's engine in the northwest and Raul's to the northeast, and more. Each of them was activated in turn so that blocks of slime lurched across the biome, **closing in on the vex like a cage,** preventing it from flying off.

But it could still fly *up.*

"THE VEX IS TAKING TO THE SKIES,"
Ash warned.

"We'll see about that," came a voice from atop the tower. It wasn't Tony this time, but Jodi. **She leapt off the tower and into the sky!**

For a terrifying instant, Morgan watched his sister fall. But she spread the elytra that she'd kept after winning the challenge of the golem. **She drifted down,** aiming right for the vex.

Tony cheered her on from above. "Be aggressive, Jodi! *B-E* aggressive!"

"I LOVE FLYING!" she cried, and she batted

the vex downward, doing only light damage. Her aim was perfect; the vex landed atop the shoulders of the incomplete Evoker King.

Morgan held his breath. **This was it!**

As Jodi alighted on the ground, the vex still crouched atop the Evoker King's headless avatar with gleaming eyes. **It flapped its wings and made a strange giggling sound.** It appeared ready to fly away again.

"WE NEED TO TALK TO IT," said Theo. "That might calm it down."

"What should we talk about?" asked Po.

"Because I don't think I have much in common with a vex."

"Maybe not," said Ash. "On the other hand, this place—Minecraft—is the vex's home. **AND MINECRAFT HAS BEEN LIKE A SECOND HOME FOR ALL OF US.**"

"Yeah!" said Po. "It's a great place you've got here, Vexter. **WHEN I'M PLAYING MINECRAFT, I FORGET ALL MY REAL-LIFE WORRIES.** And I can stop putting so much pressure on myself to succeed. Here, I get to be whoever I want to be. **LOOK HOWEVER I WANT TO LOOK.**" Po grinned. "When I'm playing Minecraft, I feel totally free."

"I spend so much of my time worried," said Harper. "I worry about big stuff like climate change and small stuff like my grades. But in Minecraft, I don't worry so much. **HERE, EVERY PROBLEM HAS A SOLUTION.** Usually a lot of solutions, if you apply a bit of creativity!"

"It's the creativity I love most," said Jodi. "The Overworld is beautiful on its own. But it's also a canvas. **IT'S A BLANK SHEET OF PAPER**

WHERE I CAN CREATE ANYTHING I CAN DREAM UP!"

"And then you can share your creations with friends," said Ash. "I think that's my favorite part. MINECRAFT IS SOCIAL. IT BRINGS PEOPLE TOGETHER." She swept her arms out toward her friends. "It brought all of you into my life. And it kept us together when I moved away."

"I'm also grateful for the friendships," said Theo. "I CAN HAVE TROUBLE MAKING FRIENDS. LIFE IS SCARY AND CONFUSING. BUT EVERYTHING MAKES SENSE HERE. There are rules. Logic." He frowned up at the black sky. "Usually."

Suddenly, they were all looking at Morgan. "What about you?" asked Jodi.

"Yeah," said Ash. "WHAT DO YOU LOVE ABOUT MINECRAFT?"

"Everything." Morgan knew that avatars didn't cry. But he could almost swear his vision was blurring with tears. "Minecraft is all the things you said. It's art and it's science. It feels like it's my space, where I can do anything I want. But it's also something we all share." He reached out to hold hands with Ash and Po, who were closest to him. Following his lead, the others joined hands to form a circle. "Learning to share was a difficult lesson for me. **BUT MY LIFE IS SO MUCH BETTER BECAUSE I'VE BEEN ABLE TO SHARE THIS ADVENTURE WITH ALL OF YOU."**

While they had spoken, their schoolmates had

quietly gathered around them, and **the vex had stopped trying to escape.** It had fixed its eyes on them as they spoke, each in turn. Now, with Morgan's speech ended, the mob giggled. It began to glow.

"What did you guys do?" asked Ned.

"We're . . . not *really* certain," said Theo.

"IS THE GLOWING GOOD OR BAD?" asked Po warily.

"Let's hope for the best," said Ash.

Morgan watched intently as the vex's glow spread to the Evoker King's body, radiating down into the torso before spreading to the arms and legs. And they heard a voice:

"THANK YOU, MY FRIENDS," the familiar voice of the Evoker King boomed all around them. "Before, I transformed because of my fear and uncertainty. I needed more data to understand this world and my place in it. But now, I am whole again. And I will be in control of my next metamorphosis."

"YOU'RE CHANGING AGAIN?" asked Ash. **"WHY?"**

"I wish to experience Minecraft from . . . a new perspective."

"Wh-what do you mean?" asked Morgan.

But there was no answer.

Only a great flash of light that shone from the Evoker King . . . and grew to consume the entire Overworld.

Chapter 14

A HINT OF THINGS TO COME! BECAUSE IN MINECRAFT, WE NEVER STOP BUILDING.

Ash **blinked furiously.** The light had blinded her, but only for a moment. As her vision returned to her, she realized she was no longer in Minecraft. **She was back in the Woodsword cafetorium,** surrounded by students and scouts, all of them removing their headsets and rubbing their eyes.

"Oh," said Ash, and she realized her own headset was blinking red. She didn't know much about electronics, but blinking red lights were usually not good.

And Theo's computer was smoking and shooting out sparks.

"I'm on it, kids!" said Hope. **"Nobody panic!"**
As Ash watched, Po's cousin doused the computer
with a fire extinguisher. That took care of the fire
hazard. But Ash figured the computer was ruined
for good.

Theo didn't seem worried. "Did we do it?" he
asked. **"Did we succeed?"**

"I don't know what just happened," said Shelly.

"But it was awesome."

"Right?" said Po. **"Nice job, prez!"**

Morgan turned to Harper. "Why did we get booted from the game?" he asked.

Harper held a magnifying glass to the circuit board she'd welded to her sunglasses. "The whole network was overloaded. It burned out." **She put the glasses back on her face.** "These are nothing more than shades now."

"I think my headset is broken, too," said Ash. "That might have been our last hurrah."

"But did we fix the game in time?" Jodi asked. "Did we save the Evoker King? **Did we fix Minecraft?"**

"It looked like it," said Theo. "But we can't know for sure until we get access to the library's computer."

"That might take a few days," said Ash. "We still have a lot of work to do at the library."

"Then we'll have to wait," said Morgan. **He watched as the kids around them all discussed their adventure excitedly.**

They didn't seem to mind that it had been cut short. **"And we just have to trust that we did everything we could,"** he added.

The very next morning, Morgan was right back in the cafetorium. The school staff had pulled

out the bleacher seats, and several teachers and administrators were on the stage. Mr. Mallory was there, too.

"Does this have something to do with the library?" Morgan asked his friends.

Theo shrugged. Po yawned. And Harper said, "*Shhh!* The assembly is starting."

Ms. Minerva welcomed them all, **and she reminded everyone about the flood at the library and the smashed school lab.** (As if anyone could forget.)

Morgan's mind began to wander. And then he thought he heard his teacher say "iron sword."

"What was that?" he said, a little too loudly. Jodi chuckled.

Ms. Minerva clucked her tongue. "As I was saying, the storm system has passed. But the damage done to the school and library was more extensive than we hoped. **It will take some time to make repairs, and we have no choice but to close an entire wing of the school."**

"School's canceled?!" asked Po.

Ms. Minerva crossed her arms. **"Absolutely not."**

Doc leaned over and took the microphone from Ms. Minerva. "What my verbose colleague is trying to say is this: To avoid overcrowding our classrooms, some Woodsword students will be attending another local school for the rest of the

school year. And they'll be joined by a few familiar teachers."

"And media specialists," added Mr. Mallory.

Morgan felt his stomach sink. He looked around at his friends. "How will you choose?" he asked. "Who stays . . . and who goes?"

"Not to worry, Morgan," said Doc. "We've taken care not to split up any tightly knit groups of friends."

"That's right," said Ms. Minerva, and she looked from Morgan to Jodi, from Po to Harper and Theo. **"Get ready for a new adventure, Minecrafters. We'll see you at the Ironsword Academy!"**

Chapter 15

EVERY ENDING IS A NEW BEGINNING. THANKS FOR ALL THE BLOCKS!

After relying on Doc's experimental VR tech for so long, Morgan felt relieved to load into their game of Minecraft the good old-fashioned way. He was using his own game controller, which was decorated with Minecraft stickers; it felt so comfortable and familiar in his hands that he almost believed it had been custom built just for him. He wore headphones to immerse himself in the sounds of the game . . . and to make it easy to chat with his friends.

For a moment, he worried that the game would be gone. What if the Fault had

spread over the Internet like a virus? What if every instance of Minecraft across the world had been consumed or warped by the crack in the code?

But his worries lifted as soon as the game loaded. **Here was Minecraft, just as he remembered it.** The Overworld had reset. The sun was high in a blue sky. The ground was solid beneath his feet.

And his friends were there at his side. Even Ash, who was back home now but able to connect from afar.

"This is what I expected, from looking at the code," said Theo. "We plugged the hole in the game's programming when we put the Evoker King back together, but it caused a full reset. **OUR ENTIRE GAME HAS BEEN REBOOTED.**"

"Aw, but all our stuff!" said Po. "Our diamond pants! Our enchanted fishing rods! **MY HUGE LIBRARY OF SKINS!**"

"Sorry, Po," said Jodi, and she patted his head gently. "But look at it as an opportunity. Out with the old and in with the new."

Po perked up. "Hey! You're an artist," he said. "You want to help me design some new looks? That half bee and half axolotl skin gave me some ideas."

"I would be delighted," said Jodi, bowing.

"I'm going to ask what everyone's thinking," said Ash. **"IS THE EVOKER KING HERE SOMEWHERE?** Does he even exist anymore?"

"He said he wanted to experience the game in a new way," said Theo. "He must be here somewhere."

"Sounds like we have our first mission," said Harper. **"BUT WHERE DO WE START?"**

"We start like we always do," said Morgan. **He**

struck a tree until it produced wood.

"We gather resources. And we make tools."

"AND PETS!" said Jodi. **"WE'RE GOING TO NEED PETS!"**

"Somebody grab that pig!" said Po, and he and Jodi chased a poor confused pig in circles.

Morgan felt totally at peace. As he crafted planks and sticks from blocks of wood, he took a moment to appreciate the pleasure of starting a game from the beginning. **Everything felt so**

simple all of a sudden.

"**DON'T FREAK OUT,**" whispered Harper. "But someone's watching us from the trees."

Po and Jodi settled down, and Morgan looked up from his work. Harper was right. A figure

stepped forward from behind a tree trunk.

Morgan braced himself for a fight. But the figure wasn't any kind of mob, hostile or otherwise. **It was a kid.**

"Hi," said the boy. "I really thought I was all alone here."

"Who are you?" asked Morgan. "Are you a Woodsword student? **DO YOU GO TO IRONSWORD?**"

"I'm not sure," said the boy. "I don't think so. **I'M ... NEW.**"

"New in what way?" asked Ash.

The boy shrugged. "Just . . . new."

"DOES HE LOOK FAMILIAR?" asked Theo.

"Yes," said Harper. "He definitely *evokes* a memory of someone we used to know."

Morgan smiled. "Let me guess. **YOU WANT TO EXPERIENCE EVERYTHING THIS WORLD HAS TO OFFER.**"

"That's right," said the boy, returning Morgan's smile. "But monsters come out at night. I could use some allies. Maybe . . . maybe some friends."

He took a hesitant step forward. "I don't know why. But I feel like I can trust you all."

"You *can* trust us," promised Ash.

"That's right," said Morgan. "You want to learn all about Minecraft? Well . . ." Morgan extended his blocky fist in greeting. **"WE'VE GOT A LOT TO SHOW YOU."**

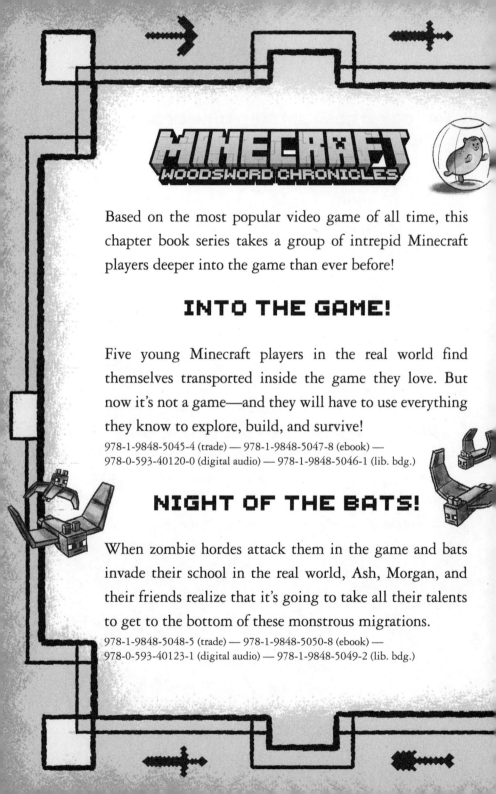

MINECRAFT
WOODSWORD CHRONICLES

Based on the most popular video game of all time, this chapter book series takes a group of intrepid Minecraft players deeper into the game than ever before!

INTO THE GAME!

Five young Minecraft players in the real world find themselves transported inside the game they love. But now it's not a game—and they will have to use everything they know to explore, build, and survive!

978-1-9848-5045-4 (trade) — 978-1-9848-5047-8 (ebook) — 978-0-593-40120-0 (digital audio) — 978-1-9848-5046-1 (lib. bdg.)

NIGHT OF THE BATS!

When zombie hordes attack them in the game and bats invade their school in the real world, Ash, Morgan, and their friends realize that it's going to take all their talents to get to the bottom of these monstrous migrations.

978-1-9848-5048-5 (trade) — 978-1-9848-5050-8 (ebook) — 978-0-593-40123-1 (digital audio) — 978-1-9848-5049-2 (lib. bdg.)

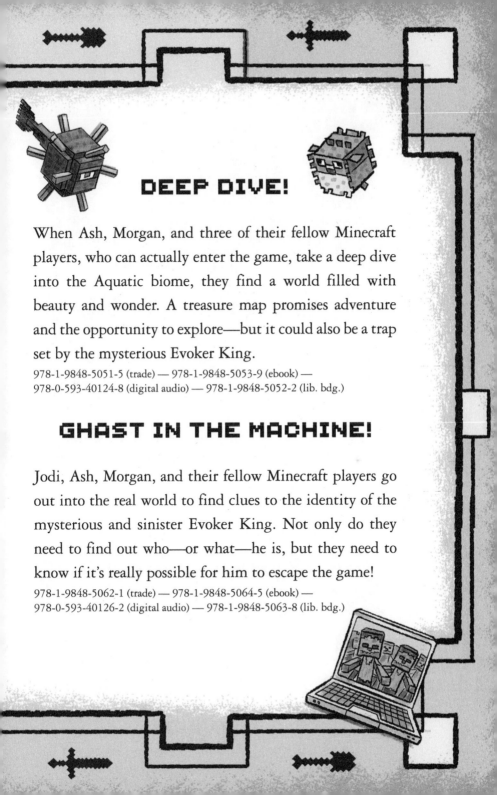

DEEP DIVE!

When Ash, Morgan, and three of their fellow Minecraft players, who can actually enter the game, take a deep dive into the Aquatic biome, they find a world filled with beauty and wonder. A treasure map promises adventure and the opportunity to explore—but it could also be a trap set by the mysterious Evoker King.

978-1-9848-5051-5 (trade) — 978-1-9848-5053-9 (ebook) —
978-0-593-40124-8 (digital audio) — 978-1-9848-5052-2 (lib. bdg.)

GHAST IN THE MACHINE!

Jodi, Ash, Morgan, and their fellow Minecraft players go out into the real world to find clues to the identity of the mysterious and sinister Evoker King. Not only do they need to find out who—or what—he is, but they need to know if it's really possible for him to escape the game!

978-1-9848-5062-1 (trade) — 978-1-9848-5064-5 (ebook) —
978-0-593-40126-2 (digital audio) — 978-1-9848-5063-8 (lib. bdg.)

DUNGEON CRAWL!

When Po, Morgan, and three of their fellow Minecraft players track the Evoker King to his home in the heart of a perilous dungeon, they have to gear up for an epic fantasy quest filled with danger, dragons, and hostile mobs.

978-1-9848-5065-2 (trade) — 978-1-9848-5067-6 (ebook) — 978-0-593-40128-6 (digital audio) — 978-1-9848-5066-9 (lib. bdg.)

LAST BLOCK STANDING!

As the world of Minecraft falls under the Evoker King's control, Morgan, Ash, and their friends get ready for the final showdown. But with their enemy now in possession of the most powerful building block in Minecraft, do they really stand a chance of defeating him?

978-1-9848-5069-0 (trade) — 978-1-9848-5071-3 (ebook) — 978-0-593-40130-9 (digital audio) — 978-1-9848-5070-6 (lib. bdg.)

THE ADVENTURES CONTINUE IN

MINECRAFT STONESWORD SAGA

CRACK IN THE CODE!

Someone—or something—has turned the Evoker King to stone. And now a new player, Theo, has joined the team on their quest to return their former enemy to normal. Theo has modding skills that could come in handy, but does he have what it takes to be part of the team, or will his meddling put a crack in the game code that none of them will survive?

978-0-593-37298-2 (trade) — 978-0-593-37300-2 (ebook) — 978-0-593-40132-3 (digital audio) — 978-0-593-37299-9 (lib. bdg.)

MOBS RULE!

Po, Harper, and their friends must travel underground and into a web of danger. But that's the easy part, because in the real world, Po decides to run for class president, and before he knows it, the ground feels like it's opening under his feet!

978-1-9848-5075-1 (trade) — 978-1-9848-5077-5 (ebook) — 978-0-593-50552-6 (digital audio) — 978-1-9848-5076-8 (lib. bdg.)

NEW PETS ON THE BLOCK!

When the third piece of the Evoker King takes the form of a Minecraft witch and sends Jodi, Morgan, and their friends on a quest to bring back an extremely rare animal mob, Jodi is determined to make sure that the mob stays safe no matter what!

978-1-9848-5094-2 (trade) — 978-1-9848-5096-6 (ebook) —
978-0-593-55978-9 (digital audio) — 978-1-9848-5095-9 (lib. bdg.)

TOO BEE, OR NOT TO BEE!

The bees around the school and the Stonesword Library are disappearing—and a splinter of the Evoker King has taken on the form of a bee colony with a hive mind! Could there be a connection? And to make matters worse, the rip in the Minecraft sky is growing bigger and darker.

978-0-593-56288-8 (trade) — 978-0-593-56290-1 (ebook) —
978-0-593-66817-7 (digital audio) — 978-0-593-56289-5 (lib. bdg.)

THE GOLEM'S GAME!

The next splinter of the Evoker King takes the form of a golem and challenges each member of the team to run a dangerous obstacle course. Forced to face the challenge alone, the team is not sure they are going to survive the golem's unwinnable game.

978-0-593-56291-8 (trade) — 978-0-593-56293-2 (ebook) —
978-0-593-68053-7 (digital audio) — 978-0-593-56292-5 (lib. bdg.)

MINECRAFT is a game about placing blocks and going on adventures. Build, play, and explore across infinitely generated worlds of mountains, caverns, oceans, jungles, and deserts. Defeat hordes of zombies, bake the cake of your dreams, venture to new dimensions, or build a skyscraper. What you do in Minecraft is up to you.

Nick Eliopulos is a writer who lives in Brooklyn (as many writers do). He likes to spend half his free time reading and the other half gaming. He cowrote the Adventurers Guild series with his best friend and works as a narrative designer for a small video game studio. After all these years, endermen still give him the creeps.

Alan Batson is a British cartoonist and illustrator. His works include *Everything I Need to Know I Learned from a Star Wars Little Golden Book, Everything That Glitters Is Guy!,* and *Spider-Ham.* Being extremely fond of cubes and travel to exotic places, he has recently begun to lend his talents to several different books on adventures in the world of Minecraft.

Chris Hill is an illustrator living in Birmingham, England, with his wife and two daughters and has been loving it for twenty-five years! When he's not working, he spends time with his family and trying to tire out his dog on long walks. If there's any time left after that, he loves to go riding on his motorcycle, feeling the wind on his face while contemplating his next illustration adventure.

JOURNEY INTO THE WORLD OF MINECRAFT

THE GOLEM'S GAME!

© 2023 Mojang AB. All Rights Reserved. Minecraft, the Minecraft logo, the Mojang Studios logo and the Creeper logo are trademarks of the Microsoft group of companies.

Published in the United States by Random House Children's Books, a division of Penguin Random House LLC, 1745 Broadway, New York, NY 10019, and in Canada by Penguin Random House Canada Limited, Toronto. Random House and the colophon are registered trademarks of Penguin Random House LLC.

rhcbooks.com
minecraft.net

Library of Congress Cataloging-in-Publication Data is available upon request.
ISBN 978-0-593-56291-8 (trade) — ISBN 978-0-593-56292-5 (lib. bdg.) —
ISBN 978-0-593-56293-2 (ebook)

Cover design by Diane Choi

Printed in the United States of America
4th Printing

THE GOLEM'S GAME!

By Nick Eliopulos
Illustrated by Alan Batson and Chris Hill

Random House 🏠 New York

MORGAN

ASH

HARPER

LAYERS!

PO

JODI

THEO

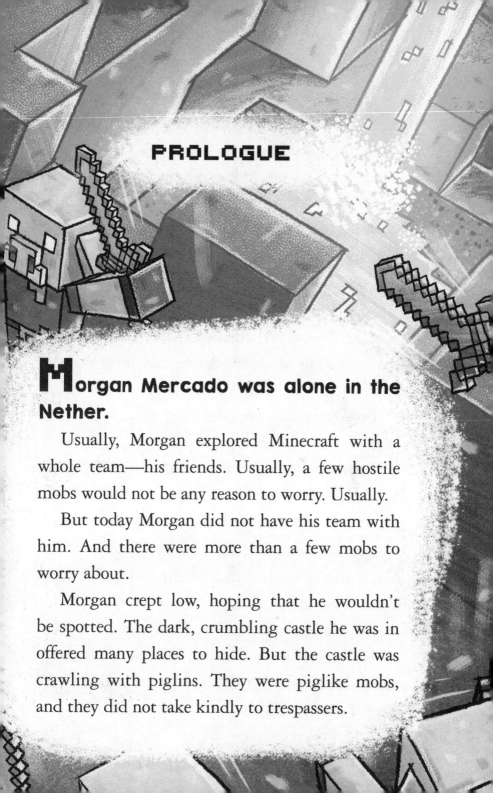

PROLOGUE

Morgan Mercado was alone in the Nether.

Usually, Morgan explored Minecraft with a whole team—his friends. Usually, a few hostile mobs would not be any reason to worry. Usually.

But today Morgan did not have his team with him. And there were more than a few mobs to worry about.

Morgan crept low, hoping that he wouldn't be spotted. The dark, crumbling castle he was in offered many places to hide. But the castle was crawling with piglins. They were piglike mobs, and they did not take kindly to trespassers.

Morgan couldn't turn back, though. There was something of immense value in this fortress. And going back to his friends empty-handed simply wasn't an option.

A bloodcurdling squeal rang through the air. Morgan knew he'd been spotted.

Sneaking was no longer an option, either. Fortunately, he had the best sword and armor in the game. He was more than a match for a piglin or two. Or three. Maybe four . . .

But the piglins kept coming! There were more of them than he could count.

Morgan leapt into battle. With his sword in front of him, he carved a path through an endless wave of enemies.

One after another, the piglins fell to Morgan's blade. But it seemed like for every one that went down, two took its place. And even through his armor, Morgan could feel their attacks.

He knew it was only a matter of time before . . . **well, best not to think about it and just keep swinging.**

Chapter 1

MORGAN MERCADO: STAR OF TRACK AND FIELD! OR MAYBE HE'S MORE LIKE A METEOR, CRASHING AND BURNING SPECTACULARLY!

Hoodsword Middle School had been **transformed overnight.** Colorful pennants hung from the low ceilings, and the hallways were decorated with posters that offered words of encouragement to the students.

One poster showed a cartoon brain with arms, legs, and sunglasses lifting weights. A banner above it said: WINNER!

Another poster said: WINNERS NEVER QUIT! It featured a group of smiling kids all holding up gleaming medals.

And a third: TEAMWORK MAKES THE DREAM WORK! It showed a squirrel, a chipmunk, and a

9

WINNER!

hamster standing atop one another's shoulders in order to reach a steaming pie on a high window ledge.

Jodi Mercado smiled. She loved color and art, and above all else, she loved animals. **However, she was pretty sure that hamsters didn't eat pie.** (She decided to test that theory as soon as possible with the class hamster, Baron Sweetcheeks, and the library's official mascot, Duchess Dimples.)

"Hey, Jodi!" a familiar voice called out. She turned to see her friend **Po Chen.** He sounded full of energy, as usual. "Do you like what we've done with the place?"

"I love it," said Jodi, nodding enthusiastically. "But why are you decorating?"

"This Friday is Field Day," said Shelly Silver. She was in student government with Po. Once they had been challengers for class president, but now they worked side by side. "We're going to be celebrating all week."

"Field Day!" said Jodi, slapping her own forehead. "I almost forgot. My brother isn't going to be happy about this."

"Why not?" said Po. "He's on a team with Harper and Theo, isn't he?"

"There might be a small complication," said Jodi. "I had better find **Harper** and **Theo.**

Keep up the good work!"

Jodi gave Po and Shelly each a thumbs-up (two thumbs total), then she ducked beneath the hanging pennants and began her search.

She looked for Harper and Theo in the science lab, where they sometimes helped out before school. They weren't there, but Jodi did find their science teacher, Doc Culpepper. The teacher was jumping in place and waving her arms as if trying to get someone's attention. Glass beakers and test tubes rattled with every jump.

"Doc Culpepper?" said Jodi. "What are you doing?"

"Jumping jacks!" answered the teacher. "I'm the coach of Team Red for Field Day, and I've got to be ready!"

Jodi was pretty sure the Field Day coaches only needed to take attendance and hand out ribbons. It was unclear to her what jumping jacks had to do with that. But since Doc seemed laser-focused on her exercise, Jodi just shrugged, gave Doc a little wave, and backed out of the room.

Next, she looked for Harper and Theo in the school's butterfly sanctuary. (It *used* to be a computer lab, but . . . long story.) Her friends weren't there, either, but Ms. Minerva was. Their homeroom teacher sat cross-legged on the floor. Her eyes were closed, and butterflies were resting in her frizzy hair and on her arms and shoulders. One was even perched on her ever-present coffee cup.

"**Ms. Minerva?**" said Jodi. "Are you okay?"

Ms. Minerva jumped with surprise, and the startled butterflies took to the air. "Oh! Jodi, you scared me," said the teacher. "I was meditating. I'm the coach of Team Blue, you see, and I've got to get *in the zone,* as they say."

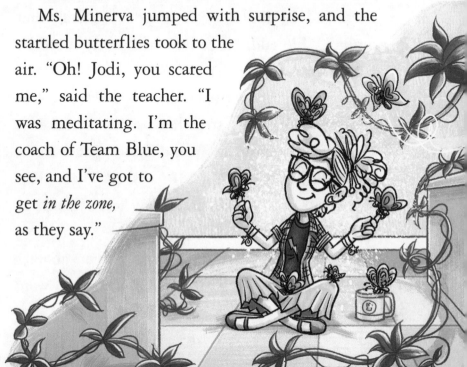

Jodi wasn't sure anybody actually said "in the zone," and she didn't know what meditating had to do with Field Day. But she smiled politely and nodded, and she was careful to close the door gently on her way out.

She finally found her friends outside. They were beneath the large tree in front of the school.

Harper Houston gave Jodi a welcoming hug. "Good morning!" she said. "Theo was just showing me his new shoes."

Theo Grayson lifted one foot. His shoe was clean and bright. "It's designed specifically for running," he said. "It could increase my speed by as much as twelve percent!"

"I'm using my normal shoes," said Harper. "But I learned some new stretches over the weekend. They'll help me run faster, and I won't get as sore."

"What about Morgan?" asked Theo. "Did he practice this weekend? A relay team is only as fast as its slowest member."

"That's what I wanted to talk to you about," said Jodi. She knew that Harper and Theo were

counting on her brother, **Morgan.** The three of them had signed up to be in a relay race for Team Blue. That meant they all had to take turns running as fast as they could.

But there was one problem with that plan.

"Hi, guys," said a voice. "Sorry I'm late."

Jodi recognized her brother's voice immediately. She also recognized the looks on her friends' faces.

Harper immediately looked surprised.

Theo instantly looked worried.

And Morgan already looked frustrated as he limped up to them. He was unsteady on a pair of crutches. His foot was in a brace.

"Morgan, your foot!" said Harper.

"What happened?" asked Theo.

"I had a small accident," said Morgan. "Don't worry, though. **It's just a sprain.** It's not as bad as it looks."

But Jodi did worry. As she watched her brother struggle to balance on his crutches, she worried he would fall over.

"Our pediatrician told you to take it easy," said Jodi. "I thought you'd stay home this week."

"And miss Field Day?" said Morgan. **"No way."**

"Hold on," said Theo. "You still want to be in the race?"

"Morgan, I'm not sure that's a great idea," said Harper.

"It'll be fine," said Morgan. "You'll see."

Then he almost fell, and Jodi caught him.

It was going to be a long week. She could tell.

Chapter 2

BLUE FIRE! GREAT FOR SETTING A SPOOKY SCENE. NOT SO GREAT FOR MAKING S'MORES!

Morgan set one blocky foot in front of the other. **In Minecraft, his injury didn't bother him at all.** It was a relief that he didn't have to worry about it while he was here, inside a hyper-realistic, VR-augmented version of his favorite game.

Of course, there were other things to worry about here.

Morgan and his friends were on a quest to save the Evoker King, a former enemy turned friend. The Evoker King was an artificial intelligence—a digital life-form—who had been split into pieces. So far, they had retrieved four of the pieces. Each time, a digital butterfly had led them where they needed to go. **The butterflies had been an obvious clue,** because they didn't exist in a normal game of Minecraft. And Morgan would know. He prided himself on being an expert on all things Minecraft.

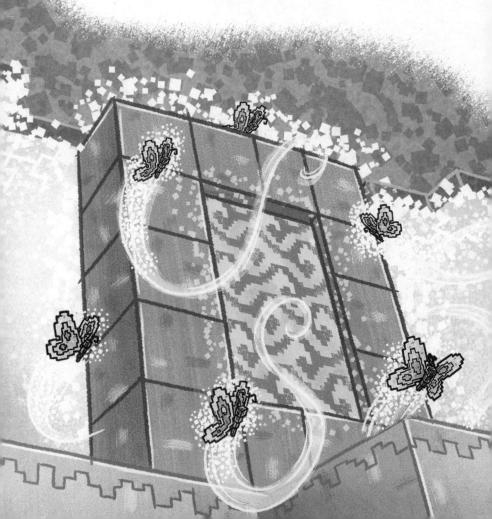

Now, a few butterflies flittered around a rectangular four-by-five-block structure of darkest obsidian. It was a portal to another Minecraft dimension. It glowed purple, daring them to step inside. Morgan's friends were ready to accept that dare. But Morgan wasn't so sure.

"CHECK YOUR INVENTORIES," he said. "Let's make sure we have everything we'll need."

"That sounds impossible," said Harper. "How can we know what we'll need before we need it?"

"We can handle anything the Nether throws at us," said Po. His avatar was wearing a toga, with a laurel circling his head. "We got this far, right?"

"And time is running out," Theo added. "THE FAULT HAS EATEN THE ENTIRE SKY." He pointed to where the Overworld sky had been replaced with a mass of dark, swirling pixels. Every few moments, lightning flashed.

"Morgan, what's wrong?" asked Jodi. "Usually you're the first one to leap into danger."

"In the Overworld, maybe," said Morgan. "BUT THE NETHER IS DIFFERENT."

"We've been there before," said his sister. "Back

when we thought the Evoker King was our enemy, remember?"

Morgan shook his head. "There was an update. The Nether has *changed* since then. **IT'S MORE DANGEROUS THAN EVER.**"

"Well, lucky us!" said Jodi, and she put her blocky hand on Morgan's shoulder. "We have a Minecraft *expert* leading the way."

Morgan grinned, but his heart sank a little. **He had read all about the Nether, of course.** And he had visited on several occasions.

But between the recent school election, and the bee crisis, and Jodi's pet-walking misadventure, he'd been awfully busy. He hadn't traveled to the Nether in quite some time.

And despite how he liked to think of himself as an expert, he had never really mastered all the challenges in the Nether. He realized that might be a problem, but at the moment he didn't think making that particular confession was going to help them. He cleared his throat.

"Let's just keep our eyes open," Morgan said. "I have a feeling . . . **THIS QUEST IS ABOUT TO GET A LOT MORE DANGEROUS.**"

"We can handle it," promised Po.

"Together," added Harper.

"Probably," said Theo.

Morgan nodded, but he was wrestling with his own thoughts. The Fault above them crackled with lightning, and a strange wind seemed to pick up, causing the pixelated grass and leaves to sway. *There is no wind in Minecraft,* he thought. The Fault—**the hole in the game's code that appeared when the Evoker King had**

been broken—was wreaking havoc, causing Minecraft to change in unexpected ways.

Morgan always loved Minecraft. When Doc Culpepper had created a set of VR goggles—goggles that allowed them to travel into the game—his love had only grown. This version of Minecraft was just for them, and it had been a little strange from the start. Morgan didn't know what he would do if they lost it all to the Fault.

"ALL RIGHT," he said. **"BUT WE STICK TOGETHER IN THERE.** And we don't leave anybody behind, no matter what."

Morgan held his breath as he stepped through the portal. He was ready for a fight. But everything was peaceful on the other side of the portal. They were in a clearing within a strange blue-green forest, with tall trees and a thick covering of vines. Someone had set up a campsite, with a series of treasure chests ringing a campfire. The fire burned an eerie shade of blue, and an iron golem stood motionless nearby.

"It looks like a camp," said Jodi. **"IS THAT GOLEM HERE TO GUARD IT?"**

"Let's not loot any treasure chests until we know for sure," said Harper.

"Aw," said Po, who had started reaching for the nearest chest.

"I've never seen a golem that color before," said Theo.

Morgan took a closer look. At first, it was hard to tell. **The Nether was dark, and the blue fire made everything seem a little strange.** Morgan realized that Theo was right about the golem. Morgan had thought it was an iron golem, but they were light gray in color, like iron armor. This one was darker.

"Is that . . . netherite?" he asked.

To his surprise, he got an answer!

"Yes," said the golem, and it turned to gaze at them. **"IT'S ABOUT TIME YOU GOT HERE.** I've been waiting for you. **AND TIME IS OF THE ESSENCE."**

Chapter 3

THE GOLEM SPEAKS! WILL HE TALK ABOUT THE WEATHER, OR ISSUE A DIRE CHALLENGE THAT WILL TEST THE VERY LIMITS OF FRIENDSHIP AND SKILL?

When the golem spoke, Morgan reacted without thinking.

He already had his sword in his hand. And he was on edge, expecting trouble as soon as they'd entered the Nether. The golem seemed like trouble. So when it surprised him by speaking, he lashed out with his sword.

It was a diamond sword. One of the most powerful weapons in Minecraft.

It didn't seem to hurt the golem at all.

"NOW. NOW. THERE'S NO REASON TO BE IMPOLITE," said the golem.

"Uh . . . sorry?" said Morgan. He eyed his sword,

a little awed and irritated that it had had no effect.

"Put that sword away, Morgan!" said Jodi. "You're lucky you didn't cut that poor golem in half!"

"NETHERITE IS MUCH STRONGER THAN DIAMOND," Harper explained. "It's also extremely rare. I've never seen a golem made of it before."

"That's because it isn't possible," said Theo. "Not in a normal game of Minecraft, at least."

Po turned to the golem, his eyes wide with awe.

"YOU'RE WHO WE'RE LOOKING FOR. YOU'RE

ONE OF THE EVOKER SPAWN."

Morgan thought Po must be correct. When the Evoker King had shattered, he had taken the form of six different mobs. So far, all of the mobs were familiar Minecraft creatures, but with strange powers and personalities. This golem certainly seemed to fit the pattern.

"THAT'S CORRECT," the golem said, its voice rumbling in its massive chest. "When the Evoker King fell, my siblings and I rose in his

place. And you are—"

"We're hoping to put him back together," said Theo, interupting enthusiastically.

"By bringing you and your 'siblings' together," Harper added.

"LIKE A FAMILY REUNION!" Jodi suggested enthusiastically.

"I know what you're doing," said the golem. "Or should I say: I know what you're *trying* to do. But will you succeed? I am not so certain."

"Then help us," said Jodi.

"Yeah!" said Po. **"THAT WOULD BE A NICE CHANGE OF PACE, ACTUALLY."**

The golem swept its bright red eyes over them. It seemed to gaze at

Morgan an especially long time.

"I WILL GIVE YOU WHAT YOU SEEK," said the golem. "I will rejoin with my siblings."

"All right!" said Po.

"But *first . . . ,*" continued the golem. "You must pass my test."

Po shrieked in horror, and the golem tilted its head in confusion. "What is wrong with that one?"

"Ignore him," said Jodi. **"HE'S JUST BEING DRAMATIC."**

"He does hate tests," said Harper.

"I'M NOT AFRAID OF ANY TEST," said Morgan. He squared his shoulders and lifted his chin. The golem still towered above them, but Morgan was determined to show no fear. "You want to test us? Well, so did that witch. And the swarming hive mind."

"Don't forget the creepy cave spider," said Jodi, shuddering.

"And the Endermonster!" said Theo.

"Wow, it really has been a weird few weeks," said Po, scratching his square chin with his block hand.

"My point is, we're undefeated," Morgan told the golem. **"WE'VE PASSED EVERY TEST. WE'VE MASTERED EVERY CHALLENGE.** And we'll survive anything *you* decide to throw at us."

The golem had no mouth. That made it especially strange when it tilted its head back . . . and laughed.

Morgan frowned. "What's so funny?" he demanded.

"You are correct," said the golem. **"SO FAR, YOU HAVE PASSED EVERY TEST . . . AS A TEAM."** Its eyes glittered in the blue campfire. "You have learned to work together. But this time, you will be tested . . . as individuals."

With that, the golem raised its massive slate-gray arm.

"Tomorrow, I will expect one of you to run my

GAUNTLET. ALONE."

It waved its blocklike fist before them, and Morgan's vision filled with purple. He closed his eyes. And when he opened them . . .

He was back in the real world. Back in the Stonesword Library's computer area, with Doc's special VR goggles on his face.

He looked around. His friends were taking off their own goggles. They all looked as surprised as he felt.

"What just happened?" he asked.

Harper shook her head. "It shouldn't be possible. But somehow—"

Theo finished her thought. **"Somehow the Netherite Golem kicked us out of the Minecraft!"**

Chapter 4

P.E.: IT STANDS FOR PIGLIN EDUCATION! HONEST, GO LOOK IT UP. I'LL WAIT.

Morgan needed answers, and Theo was his best chance to get them.

"What just happened, Theo?" he asked. **"And how do we stop it from happening again?"**

"I—I don't know," Theo stammered.

"But you're the team programmer," said Morgan. "You understand computers better than any of us."

"I still have a lot to learn," said Theo. He waved his headset around. "These are the highest of high tech. Even Doc doesn't understand how they work, and she created them!"

"It's all right that you don't have answers,

Theo," said Harper. She placed a steadying hand on his shoulder. "But if you have any *theories,* now is the time to share them."

Theo ran his fingers through his hair. "Well, as you all know, I've been keeping an eye on the game's code. **Ever since the Evoker King transformed, there's been a hole in that code.**"

"Right," said Po. "That's why we're trying to put the guy back together again. **We're hoping that will fix the hole.**"

"In the meantime, the hole is getting worse," said Theo. "It's getting bigger, and it's starting to warp other lines of code. It's like the whole game is mutating." He shrugged. "So my theory is that the Netherite Golem is somehow able to use that to its advantage. The game is changing, and the golem has some power over *how* it's changing. The golem is like a modder who's able to alter the code in real time . . . from the inside."

"Then let's hope the golem doesn't cheat when it's testing us," said Harper.

Po groaned. "Why does it have to be a test?" he asked.

"Hey, if it's a test . . . then we can study for it," said Morgan. He grinned. "Which means I've got some research to do."

The next day, during gym class, everyone was given free time to practice for their upcoming Field Day event. Harper and Theo ran the track, Po shot hoops, and Jodi worked on her throwing skills.

Morgan was stuck on the bleachers. But that suited him fine. **He had a lot of Minecraft reading to catch up on.**

The previous night, Morgan had loaded up his tablet with information about the Nether. **He was determined to prepare for the golem's test.** And he wasn't sure that he would be ready in time.

Morgan had only been to the Nether a handful of times since it had been updated with new biomes. Once, while playing alone at home, he'd gotten hopelessly lost. Another time, he'd been surprised by a blaze and knocked off a high perch, and he fell to his doom. **Of course, when you ran out of health in a normal game of Minecraft,** you respawned. But that time, Morgan had lost all of his best equipment in the Nether. He hadn't gone back since.

And now he had no choice. **And he had**

no idea what would happen if he ran out of health in the strange version of Minecraft that the Evoker Spawn called home.

"Skipping gym? I don't blame you," said a voice. Morgan looked up and saw Mr. Mallory, the media specialist. "Most days, I would rather read than play sports."

Morgan lifted his injured foot. "It isn't up to me," he said. "I'm supposed to stay off my foot. I hurt it when I was climbing a tree over the weekend." He thought about that for a second. "Actually, the climbing part didn't hurt. It was falling *out* of the tree that caused the problem."

Mr. Mallory winced. "And that's exactly why

I prefer books." He peeked at the screen of Morgan's tablet. "Although *that* book might give me nightmares. Is that a pig-man?"

"A piglin," Morgan answered. "They're from Minecraft."

"I thought so," said Mr. Mallory. "You take that game very seriously, don't you?"

Morgan shrugged. "I'm part of a team," he said. "My teammates count on me to know everything about the game."

"It sounds like they put a lot of pressure on you," said Mr. Mallory. "Unless you're putting the pressure on yourself?"

Morgan wasn't sure what the librarian meant by that. He was about to ask him, when Ms. Minerva's voice rang out: "There you are, Mr. Mallory! Did you bring my books?"

Mr. Mallory smiled as the teacher approached them. "That's why I'm here," he said.

"Disappointing!" said Doc as she hurried over from another direction. "I had hoped you were here to deliver the hamster!"

"I'm here for both reasons," said Mr. Mallory.

"I'm not choosing sides, remember?"

Now that Morgan saw the three adults in a row, he noticed something about their clothing. Ms. Minerva wore blue for her team, and Doc wore red for hers. Mr. Mallory was wearing *purple*. Morgan knew that purple was a combination of red and blue.

"You're still determined to stay neutral?" prodded Ms. Minerva.

"A pity!" said Doc. "Only supporters of Team Red will be allowed to use my high-tech massage chairs on Field Day."

Ms. Minerva clucked her tongue. "Those chairs will vibrate the fillings right out of your teeth."

Mr. Mallory didn't say anything. He put his backpack down on the bleachers, then zipped it open. He pulled out a small stack of books for Ms. Minerva. They were all about exercise and healthy eating.

"Knowledge shall win the day!" she said, and hurried off.

Next Mr. Mallory pulled out a small cage. Inside was Duchess Dimples, the library's hamster.

"Now both teams have a hamster," said Doc. "It's only fair!" She picked up the hamster's enclosure and scampered toward the school building.

Mr. Mallory shook his head. "See?" he said. "Sports do strange things to people. You're lucky you get to skip Field Day."

Morgan flushed red. **"I'm not skipping Field Day,"** he said. "I'll be better by then."

Mr. Mallory glanced at Morgan's injured foot. "I hope you're right," he said. "Good luck, Morgan, and feel better." With that, he headed back to the library, just as Harper and Theo approached.

Morgan quickly hid his tablet. He didn't want his friends to know that he was unprepared for the Nether. He especially didn't want Theo to realize it. **Theo's knowledge of Minecraft was almost equal to Morgan's,** and that sometimes made Morgan feel self-conscious. It felt a little bit like he and Theo were in competition, even though they were on the same team.

"Was that Duchess Dimples?" asked Harper. "What's she doing here?"

"Rooting for Team Red, apparently," answered

Morgan offhandedly.

"Speaking of Field Day," said Theo. "We have some concerns."

Morgan crossed his arms. "Like what?"

"We talked to Jodi," Theo said. "She said you'll be on crutches for at least another week."

"That isn't true!" Morgan insisted. "The doctor said it's impossible to know for sure. She said that everyone heals at their own speed!"

Harper raised her hand in a calming gesture. "We understand. And that's exactly why we're worried. We want you to heal, however long it takes. If you push yourself too hard, you could make your injury worse."

"We talked to Ms. Minerva," said Theo. "She said you can switch events. We just have to find a replacement."

"You want to *replace* me?" Morgan's jaw dropped. "No way! I'm telling you, I'll be fine. I feel a lot better already!" He turned to look directly at Harper. **"Don't give up on me, please."**

"Well, okay," Harper said hesitantly. "If you're sure."

"I'm sure," Morgan insisted. *"Really."*

Morgan made certain that his voice was steady and his eyes were calm. **But his leg hurt a little even as he said it.**

Chapter 5

IN A VAST VIDEO GAME FANTASY WORLD, THERE'S NOTHING QUITE LIKE NETHERITE, AMIRITE?

That afternoon, they returned to the Nether. The soul campfire was still burning. The Netherite Golem stood just where they had left it.

"We're ready," said Morgan. **"WE ACCEPT YOUR CHALLENGE."**

The golem's dark eyes twinkled. "Very good," said the mob. "Which one of you will be tested?"

Morgan tried to appear calm and confident as he stepped forward. It wasn't easy. The golem was much larger than him, with massive arms, broad shoulders, and dark eyes. Red vines twisted along its netherite body.

"Me. I'll go," said Morgan. "We took a vote."

The vote had been nearly unanimous, except Theo had voted for himself. And Po had voted for the class hamster, but Jodi had pointed out that the VR goggles wouldn't fit Baron Sweetcheeks.

The golem said, **"SO BE IT. LISTEN CAREFULLY, AND I WILL TELL YOU WHAT YOU MUST DO."**

Morgan nodded.

"North of here, there is a fortress. In the heart of that fortress is a chest. Within that chest is an item that I hold dear. Retrieve it, and I shall surrender to you."

"That's it?" Morgan said. **"I JUST HAVE TO FETCH YOUR PROPERTY?"**

"That's it," said the golem. Its square eyes gleamed with amusement. "But do not take the task lightly. The Nether is a dangerous place. Very dangerous. And you must each face it alone."

"WHAT IF HE FAILS?" asked Theo.

"Theo!" said Harper. "Have a little faith in Morgan."

"I'm not saying that I don't," said Theo. "But this is important information."

"If he fails, then another must try," answered the golem. "And then another. Until the item is retrieved . . . **OR UNTIL ALL FIVE HAVE FAILED."**

"So we have five chances," said Theo.

"We don't need five chances," said Morgan. "You guys, I've got this."

"We know you do," said Po.

"We believe in you!" said Jodi.

"The chests are full of useful items," said the golem. **"TAKE WHATEVER YOU LIKE."**

Morgan felt a thrill at those words. It never failed: opening a Minecraft chest to see what it held was even more exciting than unwrapping a birthday present.

And the golem's chests held quite a lot.

"Is this . . . netherite armor?" he asked. "And a sword! It would take forever to find enough netherite to make all of this!"

"WHAT'S NETHERITE?" asked Jodi.

"It's the strongest, most durable material in the whole game," Morgan answered, a huge smile on his avatar's face.

"I thought that was diamond," said his sister.

"It used to be," said Theo. "Netherite was added in an update."

Jodi threw up her blocky hands. "I can't keep up!" she said.

Morgan was still smiling. "All you need to know is that this stuff will make me unbeatable!" He began swapping out his old armor for the brand-new dark-gray upgrade.

"Hold on," said Theo. "Are you sure you should take the whole set?"

"Sure, I'm sure," said Morgan confidently. "Why wouldn't I?"

"Well . . . ," said Theo. **Morgan saw him trade a look with Harper.**

"I . . . think I see where Theo is coming from," said Harper. "Suppose you . . . don't succeed. Then one of *us* will have to go. And we'll have to do it without any netherite armor."

"What if you just took one piece?" suggested Theo. "Then there's some left for the rest of us."

"THAT'S A TERRIBLE SUGGESTION," said Morgan. "If I leave good gear behind, then

I'm making it less likely that I'll succeed. **IT'S SMARTER TO MAXIMIZE MY CHANCES."** He turned to Po and Jodi. "You two agree with me, right?"

Jodi nodded. "I want my brother to come back safe and sound. We can share the armor *after* you're back."

"Po?" prodded Morgan.

"Don't look at me," Po said. **"I VOTED FOR**

BARON SWEETCHEEKS!"

As far as Morgan was concerned, that settled it. If Theo or Harper was upset with him, he could apologize later, after he returned with the golem's trophy . . . or whatever it was.

"What am I looking for, by the way?" he asked the golem. "These chests are full of valuable loot. So what's the item that you're missing?"

"AN ITEM OF LITTLE VALUE . . . BUT GREAT WORTH," said the golem. "Bring it to me, Morgan Mercado." Its eyes glimmered in the light of the campfire. "Fail . . . and the consequences will be more severe than you can imagine."

Chapter 6

MORGAN MERCADO: ALONE IN THE NETHER! HE'S GOING TO NEED THAT ARMOR. AND A LOT OF LUCK!

Morgan's solo adventure in the Nether started off well.

He felt confident in his full set of netherite armor. And that's not all he'd taken from the golem's stash. He had a bow and arrows, cooked food, a shield to protect him from fireballs, and potions to provide a variety of benefits. In short, he felt prepared for whatever the Nether had to throw at him.

His first task was to travel through the warped forest. **It was full of Endermen,** but that was okay. Morgan had taken a pumpkin from the golem's chests. He wore it now, which allowed him

to pass among the Endermen untroubled.

If this whole challenge was a test, then so far, Morgan was on track for a perfect score.

The forest ended at a steep cliff wall. Morgan climbed it by carving out a staircase. He used a diamond pickaxe, which made it easy.

At the top of the cliff, Morgan gasped. He could see far off in the distance. The Nether was every bit as strange as he remembered. Great creatures floated in the air; they didn't see him yet. A ceiling blocked any view of sky, sun, or stars. **A vast ocean of lava stretched out before him,** leading to a soul sand shore. And past that, hazy in the distance, was a structure.

It was a bastion remnant. That had to be the "fortress" the golem had mentioned. **That's where he'd find its treasure.** He was sure of it.

He spared a brief glance backward. The warped forest spread out behind him. His friends were down there, depending on him. He couldn't see them through the trees, but he knew that they were there. He wouldn't let them down.

Morgan descended the cliff. **The sea of lava was below him.** It stretched out for a hundred blocks or more. He would have to find some way to cross it.

Unless . . . what if he went underneath?

It was a risky choice. But all his choices were risky, and digging a tunnel would at least keep him from drawing the attention of the flying mobs.

So he dug. He started by making a hole. When he was twenty blocks below ground level, he cut his way forward. Soon he was beneath the lava, traveling through an underground hallway of his own creation. **He placed torches as he went,** and he counted his steps.

Morgan knew that even a diamond pickaxe would wear down eventually. He took a quick look at the tool's durability bar, and he saw that it wouldn't last much longer. He had hoped to dig all the way to the fortress, but that would be impossible. So after counting one hundred steps, he started digging upward at an angle.

He struck lava almost immediately!

Clearly, one hundred steps had not been far enough. Morgan was still under the lava lake. And now the lava was surging forward, filling his tunnel. It reached for him like a hot, glowing hand, and as it touched him, he burned.

Morgan quickly placed a pair of netherrack blocks. The blocks were a dam, holding the lava back. But Morgan was still on fire!

He had thought something like this might happen. There were a lot of fire-related hazards in the Nether. **He pulled a Potion of Fire Resistance from his inventory,** and he drank it quickly. It kept him relatively safe while

he waited for the fire to go out.

In this version of Minecraft, Morgan could feel when he took damage. The lava and flames had been uncomfortable, and the potion's effect was cool and soothing on his digital skin.

"LET'S NOT DO THAT AGAIN," he said, and then he realized he was talking to himself. He missed his friends even more than he had thought he would.

Morgan cut his tunnel sideways, going around the spot where lava had filled it. He didn't try to dig upward again until he'd counted another hundred steps. This time, he drank a Potion of Fire Resistance first, but there was no lava. Only sky— or whatever passed for sky in the Nether.

Morgan hopped up aboveground. He knew he would need to identify what biome he was in quickly. **Every biome in the Nether carried new threats.**

He was immediately struck by arrows. He felt them, even through his powerful armor. He turned to run, but he was so *slow.* The sand at his feet was like wet cement.

He was in a soul sand valley.
Skeletons surrounded him, launching arrows in an endless attack.

Morgan drew his sword.
This was going to be a long day.

When he finally made it to the bastion remnant, Morgan was exhausted. He'd had to fight the whole way, and his armor and weapons were worn down nearly to breaking. He was out of potions, out of *food,* and his health was dangerously low.

Now he realized that he didn't have the one thing he needed most: **gold.**

The bastion remnant was crawling with piglins.

They were intimidating and strange. Morgan had encountered piglins in the past, of course. But not nearly as often as he'd seen the various mobs of the Overworld.

To Morgan, the most interesting fact about piglins was that they loved gold. **A hostile piglin would even become friendly for a time, if a player gave them gold.**

Wearing gold armor also worked. And there had been a gold helmet in the Netherite Golem's war chest. But Morgan had passed it up for a netherite helmet instead.

And his netherite armor had taken a lot of damage.

Morgan decided that a stealthy approach would be smart. He had a Potion of Invisibility . . . but he would have to remove his armor in order to become fully invisible. And that felt like too much of a risk, **even with his armor damaged.**

So Morgan took it slow. He hid behind a wall, then crouched as he worked his way to another wall. There were a lot of dark corners he could hide in. But that meant there were a lot of places

for piglins to hide, too. **Could he possibly avoid them all?**

The answer was no. One of the piglins spotted him. It made a horrible piglike sound.

Morgan leapt forward, swinging his netherite sword. He knocked back the piglin—too late. Its noises had already drawn the attention of its snouted siblings. With their swords and axes raised, they rushed to attack Morgan.

He swung his own sword in a wide arc. **He couldn't fight so many mobs.** But he hoped he could keep them back as he ran through the fortress.

Through a gap in the horde, he saw a lone treasure chest sitting out in the open. He was so close.

But also too far. One piglin attacked from behind, and as he turned to knock it away, two more got hits in.

They were swarming him now. There were too many. He felt like he was drowning.

Morgan buckled. He dropped to his knees.

"NO!" he said defiantly. **"NO, I WON'T LOSE. I CAN'T!"**

But Morgan did lose.

He lost consciousness and fell to the ground in utter defeat.

Chapter 7

BATTERED AND BEATEN. THE BITTER TASTE OF DEFEAT. WORSE THAN EATING YOUR VEGETABLES!

Jodi was startled. One second, she was with her friends in Minecraft, gazing into the eerie blue fire and waiting for her brother to return.

The next second, she was back in the computer lab at Stonesword Library.

Theo tore off his VR goggles. "We're back! It happened again."

Jodi quickly looked to make sure that Morgan was with them. He was, although he didn't look very happy about it. As he took off his goggles, he looked angry, and more than a little embarrassed.

"I . . . I failed," he said, gripping his goggles tightly.

They all gasped. Even Jodi; she couldn't help herself.

Her brother was the master of Minecraft. He never failed!

"I came close," he said. **"Really close!** I could *see* the chest."

"I'm sure you did your best, Morgan," said Harper.

"I'll bet it was epic," said Po. **"Did you go down swinging?"**

"Yeah." Morgan smiled a little. "Yeah, I didn't give up without a fight."

"Well, there's some good news here," said Theo. "We've never been defeated in this version of Minecraft before. I was afraid there would be real-world consequences." He looked Morgan up and down. "But you seem to be okay. Do you feel all right?"

"I feel fine," said Morgan. He stretched. "I feel normal. But being defeated . . . it hurt. I could feel every blow, even through the netherite armor."

"And that's the bad news," said Theo. "You took all the best armor. And if this is working like Minecraft normally works, all your gear is now just lying there where you fell. It's not going to do us any good."

For a second, **Jodi thought that Morgan would say he was sorry.**

She thought that her brother might tell them what he'd seen, so that they could all learn from his defeat.

But Morgan obviously didn't like the way Theo was talking to him. It sounded like Theo was blaming Morgan for wasting the golem's loot.

So Morgan didn't apologize. He yelled instead. **"The netherite armor wouldn't help you!** If I couldn't win this challenge, none of you stand a chance. Armor isn't going to change that."

Jodi looked back at her brother, stunned. "Morgan!" she said. **"You don't mean that."**

"Good luck in the Nether, whoever goes next," said Morgan. "I'm not sticking around to watch you all fail one by one."

Then Morgan stormed out of Stonesword Library as fast as his crutches could take him.

For the next few hours, Jodi tried to make peace with her brother. But Morgan didn't make it easy for her.

He sulked on the ride home, gazing out the window the whole way.

He hid in his room before dinner, playing music loud enough to drown out her knocking.

She knew better than to bring up their **top-secret, high-tech, AI-infested, VR-infused Minecraft game** at dinner, where their parents would have all sorts of questions. Not

to mention the wild and dangerous adventures they sometimes faced.

But after dinner, she found him outside.

"What are you doing?" she asked him.

"**Practicing,**" he said.

It looked a little reckless to Jodi. She watched as he hurried down the walkway, practically flinging himself across the stones. It was the fastest she'd ever seen someone move on crutches.

"Morgan, slow down!" she said. "**You're going to fall.**"

"No, I'm not," he said through gritted teeth. But even as he said it, he stumbled badly. Luckily, he fell toward Jodi. She was able to catch him.

"Do I get to say I told you so?" she said.

Morgan scowled, and he pulled out of her grip. "You don't understand. I've got to get faster before Field Day. I don't want to slow Theo and Harper down. And I don't . . . **I don't want them to replace me.**"

Jodi crossed her arms. "I don't know whether to try to make you feel better . . . or to tell you that you're being selfish."

Morgan sighed. He sat on the low garden wall. **"I vote for the first one,"** he said.

Jodi sat next to him. "Would it really be the end of the world if they did the relay race without you?"

"It's not just the relay race," said Morgan. "It's all this stuff with Minecraft and the Nether. I'm supposed to be the team expert! But Doc's VR goggles changed the game in weird ways, and then the Evoker King changed all sorts of things. And

today I couldn't even handle the Nether on my own. If I'd worn just a single piece of gold armor, I could have won."

"**You can still win**," said Jodi. "By helping *us* win. Harper is taking the challenge tomorrow. Tell her everything you know. Everything you saw! Were there giant piglins? Or Endermen with pitchforks?"

"It doesn't matter." Morgan shook his head. "Like Theo said, I wasted all the good items. I'm sorry, Jodi, but Harper doesn't stand a chance tomorrow." He got up and limped away. "And I won't be there to watch her be defeated. **She'll have to do it without me.**"

Chapter 8

HARPER, HARPER, YOU CAN DO IT! RIGHT? BECAUSE, REALLY, THE WHOLE TEAM IS COUNTING ON YOU.

When the golem asked for the next volunteer, Harper stepped forward. She didn't hesitate. And though she felt a sliver of fear run through her, she didn't show it. **Whatever happened, her friends were there, cheering her on.**

Well . . . *most* of her friends were there. Morgan hadn't shown up at the library that day.

"Choose your tools," said the golem.

"IF THERE'S ANYTHING GOOD LEFT," Theo muttered, just loud enough for her to hear.

But Harper wasn't too worried about that. Morgan had taken a lot of useful items, but he hadn't bothered taking the useful *ingredients.*

Harper figured she would make her *own* items.

As luck would have it, the first chest she checked held an abundance of nether wart.

"This is perfect!" she said. **"MORGAN TOOK ALL THE POTIONS. BUT WITH THIS, I CAN BREW MY OWN."**

"What will you use potions for?" asked Jodi.

"There's a lot of lava in the Nether," said Harper. "Lava is very dangerous . . . **UNLESS YOU DRINK A POTION OF FIRE RESISTANCE.** Then it can't hurt you."

Po's mouth dropped open. "So you're planning

to *swim* in lava? Harper, you're my hero!"

Harper grinned. "Pretty cool, right? Just don't try this at Field Day, kids."

Harper traveled through the warped forest, over the cliff, and down to the shore of the great lava lake. It stretched out nearly as far as she could see. She would have to be quick.

She drank down her freshly brewed, orange-hued potion in a single gulp. Then she prepared to dive—but she hesitated. She had faith in her potion; she was sure she'd done it right. Still, the thought of entering the lava made her nervous.

But there was no turning back now. **She dove headfirst into the lava.** She didn't feel a thing!w

Harper began swimming. She knew she had only a few minutes before the potion would wear off, so she had to move quickly..

When she had made it halfway across the lake,

she realized she would not make it the rest of the way in time. But that was okay. **Harper had planned for this.**

She set some stone blocks in front of her, creating a small, two-by-two stone island in the middle of the lake. She hopped onto the island and set down her brewing stand. Then she made another potion, and she drank it immediately.

She decided to leave the brewing stand where it was. It would be useful on the way back. She even left some key ingredients behind, so that she'd be able to brew again in a hurry.

As Harper swam, **a shadow passed over**

her. It startled her. There were no clouds in the Nether. What could it be?

She looked up, and a great, fearsome ghast was just above her. Its tentacles hung low, and it made a strange mewing sound.

Harper dove beneath the surface. Had the ghast seen her? She waited for several seconds. Soon, she could wait no longer. **She had to come up for a breath!**

Harper swam up. To her relief, the ghast had drifted away.

But then Harper realized she had lost precious seconds. How long had she been beneath the lava?

She hesitated with indecision. Should she hurry toward the far shore? Should she turn around and return to her island of stone and brew another potion?

The hesitation cost her. **Her time was up.**

Harper could suddenly feel the heat of the lava. It gripped her like a fiery fist. She could see the flames all along her arms!

Harper yelled for help, **but no one was close enough to hear her.**

"Harper! Are you okay?"

Harper blinked. She realized she was safe in the library. Theo and the others looked at her with concern. **Had she been yelling in real life?**

Mr. Mallory came hurrying around the corner. "What's going on?" he asked.

"I'm sorry, Mr. Mallory," she said. "I was playing a video game, and my avatar was trapped in lava. It . . . it seemed so real."

Theo frowned as he realized what

this meant. Harper had failed the golem's challenge.

But Mr. Mallory smiled. "Thank goodness. I thought something was really wrong."

"Everything's fine, honest," Harper said. She was embarrassed by all the attention. **Her cheeks grew hot.**

It felt a little bit like she was still in that unforgiving lake of lava.

Chapter 9

THEO, THEO, HE'S OUR MAN! IF HE CAN'T DO IT, NO ONE CAN! BUT NO PRESSURE. NOPE, NONE AT ALL.

Theo was determined to succeed where his friends had failed. He didn't even wait for the golem to ask. He strode right up to the mob and announced: "I'm next."

"CHOOSE YOUR TOOLS," said the golem. Theo thought there was a hint of amusement in the golem's tone.

Theo rummaged through the chests in search of anything that might be useful. There wasn't much left. But to his surprise, there was a particularly useful—**and especially rare**—item in the last chest he checked.

"ELYTRA!" he said, his voice full of awe. He

turned to his friends, smiling.

"I don't need to swim across the lava.
Not when I have wings!"

"Wow!" said Jodi. **"DO THOSE THINGS LET YOU FLY?"**

"It's more like gliding than flying," Theo said. He tried on the elytra, which were similar to some sort of geometric beetle wings that attached to his shoulders. "I'll have to start from up high so I can drift across the lava."

Minutes later, as Theo looked out upon the great orange sea, he realized that the cliff separating the warped forest from the lava lake was not nearly high enough.

So Theo built. Jumping in place, he dropped blocks of dirt beneath his feet. Soon, he stood atop a narrow column of dirt. He could see the bastion remnant!

But he still wouldn't be able to glide that far. He would have to aim for the soul sand valley on the other side of the lava. It was the closest point.

Theo wished he had fingers to cross. Instead, he pressed his blocky fists together. "I got this," he said.

And then he jumped into the air.

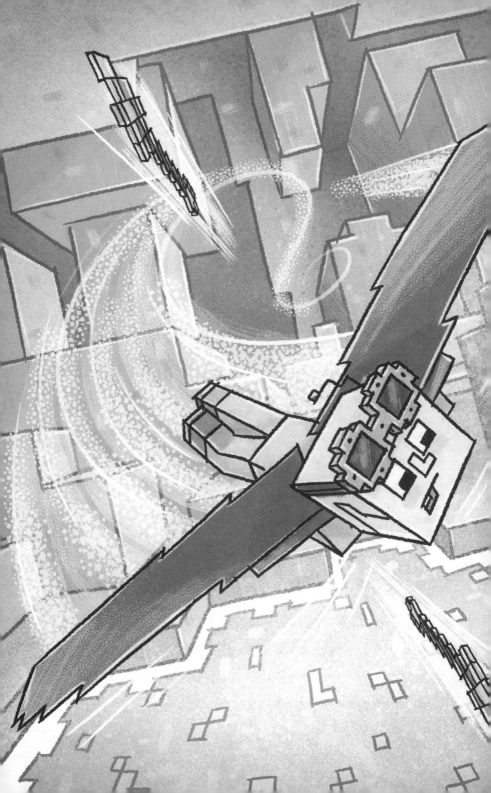

The experience was thrilling. Theo had always enjoyed flying in Minecraft, back when he had played in Creative mode. But this was a different experience. Doc's VR technology made him feel as if he were really, truly gliding through the air!

Theo's excitement slowly faded, and fear grew in its place. He was losing height every second, getting closer and closer to the lava below—even starting to feel the heat. He was pretty sure he would make it to the other side. But it was going to be close.

And then an arrow whizzed by him.

Theo veered wildly in the air. Where did that come from?

He found the answer below and ahead of him. On the shore of the soul sand valley, a cluster of skeletons had gathered. **Each one held a bow, and each one was looking his way.**

Up in the air, there was nowhere to hide, and no way to fight back. Theo would just have to hope he could reach land before he took too many hits.

As more arrows flew in his direction, Theo went

on the defensive. **He rolled, he banked, he dove.** He did anything and everything he could to avoid the projectiles.

And he did a great job. He didn't get hit even once!

Unfortunately, Theo realized too late that there was a problem. All of his fancy moves had cost him precious time in the air. He wasn't much closer to land.

But he was much, much closer to the lava. Too close!

Theo splashed down into the glowing orange liquid. His avatar caught fire, wings and all.

Back in the computer lab, Theo angrily removed his goggles.

"**That wasn't fair!**" he said. "I was a sitting duck for those skeletons."

"It's okay, Theo," said Harper. "At least you're safe."

"Sure," said Theo. "And I learned an important lesson, too. **Flying is for the birds!**"

Chapter 10

WE MEANT PO. IF HE CAN'T DO IT, NO ONE CAN! AND WE HOPE HE CAN DO IT, BECAUSE WE ARE REALLY STARTING TO RUN OUT OF OPTIONS!

Po had never thought of himself as much of a builder.

Some Minecraft players liked to mine. Others liked to craft. **Po enjoyed the exploration and adventure aspect of the game the most.** He liked imagining himself as a heroic character, finding new biomes, and striking down gruesome undead enemies.

But as he prepped by the golem's fire with his friends, he realized something. After accepting the golem's challenge and looking through the mostly empty chests, he realized: he would have to build . . . something.

"IT'S MOSTLY DIRT AND STONE AND NETHERRACK LEFT," he said. "Although there is another pair of elytra, and a gold helmet."

Theo shook his head. "The elytra won't do you any good. Maybe if we had a rocket, but we don't. And there's no gunpowder to make one."

"AND YOUR DIAMOND HELMET IS WAY BETTER THAN A GOLD ONE," said Harper.

"It looks nicer, too," Jodi added.

"I know!" said Po. "It sparkles."

"Focus, Po!" said Theo. "Do you have a plan for crossing the lava?"

"I've got a lot of building material," said Po. "SO IT LOOKS LIKE I'LL BE BUILDING A BRIDGE."

Po's inventory was almost entirely full of blocks. He was glad they didn't weigh anything. He wouldn't want to carry around stacks of stone cubes in real life.

Building a bridge wasn't the most exciting

experience. He was a little jealous of his friends. Theo had flown through the air! Harper had done the butterfly stroke in hot lava!

But as Po peered over the side of his makeshift bridge and into the lava below, he shuddered. He was actually quite happy to be on solid ground and away from the molten red-hot rock he could feel even at this distance.

And then, mere minutes after he had started, **Po realized he was running out of blocks.**

"Huh," said Po. He stood at the unfinished edge of his bridge. The far shore was still quite far.

He saw the problem now. **He'd been**

making his bridge too wide. He didn't exactly want to walk a balance beam across the lava. But a narrower bridge would reach farther.

Po quickly dismantled the structure, removing the blocks and starting again. It just might work if his building materials held out. **He wished his block hands had fingers so he could cross them for good luck.**

As Po turned around to retrieve more blocks from behind him, he looked back at his starting point. He could see the warped forest, and there was movement between the trees. **It was a tall figure with glowing eyes.** Was the golem watching him? The figure looked at Po, and Po looked right back.

And then Po realized his mistake. That wasn't the Netherite Golem. That was an Enderman!

Po looked away quickly. He knew Endermen didn't like to be looked at. Had he turned away in time?

A low moan sounded from nearby. Po looked up and saw that he was no longer alone on his partial

bridge. The Enderman had teleported right next to him!

Po shrieked. Unarmed, he slapped at the Enderman, hoping it would teleport away.

But the Enderman slapped right back. Po leapt backward to avoid the blow—right over the edge of his structure . . .

And into the waiting lava below.

"Oh, man," said Po. He had opened his eyes to find himself back at Stonesword Library. **"That's it. From now on, I'm wearing a pumpkin everywhere I go."**

"A pumpkin?" said Jodi.

"Let me guess," said Harper. "You must have run into an Enderman problem."

"You're not supposed to look directly at them," said Theo.

"I know, Theo!" said Po. "I didn't do it on purpose." He shook his head. **"They say curiosity killed the cat.** But they *should* say that curiosity got Po knocked off the edge of his bridge and into the lava."

"It's kind of a mouthful," said Jodi.

"It's true, though," said Po. **"And it means we've only got one more chance to win."**

Chapter 11

A TWIST OF FATE! A TWIST OF ANKLE! THIS CHAPTER'S GOT MORE TWISTS THAN THE LATEST DANCE CRAZE.

Morgan felt a little guilty, hearing how his friends had fared without him.

They were gathered on the Woodsword playground, and Po was telling the story of his half-built bridge. "I'm telling you, I've got a fear of heights after that experience," he said. **"And also a fear of teleporting monsters, and lava, and sad clowns wearing little hats."**

"Wait, there were clowns there, too?" asked Jodi in surprise.

"No," said Po. "I've just always been creeped out by them. The sad ones, especially." He shuddered.

Harper patted Po's arm. "I really thought that

plan would work," she said. **"The Nether is too dangerous."**

"That means it's up to you, Jodi," said Theo. "You're our last hope."

Jodi chuckled nervously. "Wow! No pressure, though, right?"

Theo frowned. "It's quite a lot of pressure, actually."

Jodi rolled her eyes and said, "Does Woodsword have any classes on understanding sarcasm? Because you might learn a thing or two." Then she groaned and dropped her head into her hands.

Morgan cleared his throat. "I have an idea," he said.

Po shook his head. "If your idea is to tell the golem all about Baron Sweetcheeks, you're too

late! I chatted the golem's ear off the whole time Theo was running the challenge."

"It's true," Harper confirmed. "You know, the golem doesn't close its eyes, but I could almost swear it dozed off once or twice."

"I'm pretty sure it was just drinking it all in," Po replied with a huff.

Theo frowned. "Or maybe Morgan's idea is to go back in time and help us before we all suffered a series of defeats?"

"Not helpful, Theo," Harper said in a singsong voice.

"I guess he *does* understand sarcasm after all," Jodi said. Then, without lifting her face from her hands, she asked her brother, "What's your idea, Morgan?"

"Let me try again, said Morgan. **"Jodi can give me her spot, and I'll use what I learned last time to succeed."**

Jodi lifted her head. *"That's not fair!"*

"It might be smart, though," Theo said. "I mean, he has a point."

"Were you even excited for your turn, Jodi?" Po

asked. "It seemed like you were worried."

"That's not the point," Jodi said.

"I'm not sure the golem will allow it," Harper said. "It told us we had five chances. But it strongly implied we'd only get one chance each."

"The golem's a computer program," said Theo. "If our argument is logical, we can convince it."

"First you've got to convince me!" said Jodi.

Morgan excused himself, leaving his friends to debate his proposal.

Field Day was only a day away. And he had to fit in one last practice.

Morgan was getting faster. He was sure of it. His underarms were rubbed raw, and his good foot was getting a blister, but that was the price he had to pay for speed.

He set a stopwatch. He wanted to time how long it took him to make one circuit around the school track.

Everyone else was at lunch. That's why Morgan chose to practice now. He wanted some privacy.

But there was one problem with that.

It meant that when he fell . . . nobody was there to catch him.

Chapter 12

NURSE YOUR WOUNDS, NOT YOUR GRUDGES! WOUNDS HEAL, BUT GRUDGES JUST GET WORSE.

Morgan spent a good part of the afternoon in the nurse's office. He had twisted his ankle. The pain had been excruciating—even worse than the first injury—but there was good news.

"**Nothing's broken,**" said Doc. "And you didn't do any permanent damage. But you have *got* to rest, Morgan. You'll never heal if you keep landing on it funny."

Morgan nodded. "I've learned my lesson. **Pain is a great teacher.**"

"As long as *this* great teacher isn't a pain!" said Doc. She chortled at her own joke, but Morgan could only moan.

"It sounds like he's in pain!" cried Jodi as she pushed her way into the cramped office. Harper, Theo, and Po were right behind her.

"I'm afraid we can't save his sense of humor," said Doc. "But his foot will be fine . . . in a couple of weeks."

"Doc?" said Harper. "I didn't know you were our school nurse."

"Just filling in while Glenda is on vacation," Doc said. "As long as nobody needs a kidney transplant, I can handle it." She seemed to sense

some tension between Morgan and his visitors. "I'll let you all talk, but I'll be right outside if you need me."

Po waited until Doc had left, and then he turned to Morgan. "Dude, we were so worried!" he said. "When you weren't in class, we didn't know what happened."

"We even called Ash," said Harper. She held up her phone. **Morgan could see the face of their long-distance friend, Ash, on the screen.**

"Hi, Morgan," said Ash. "I'm glad to see you're

okay. Jodi thought you'd run away to join the circus."

"Or to play Minecraft without us," said Theo. "We actually checked the library first."

Morgan shook his head. "I guess I haven't been much of a team player lately, have I? But I wouldn't have gone behind your backs like that."

"Can you tell us why you've been so upset?" Ash asked.

"Well . . ." Morgan felt his cheeks get hot. "I

guess it's because I like being a part of this team so much. And I worry sometimes that you don't need me. Or even that I'm holding you back."

"Holding us back?" said Po. "That's the opposite of what you do."

"But I'm supposed to be the Minecraft expert," said Morgan. "And I've been so busy that I haven't been able to keep up like I used to. I wasn't prepared to face the Nether alone, and sometimes Theo knows more than I do."

"Two heads are a lot better than one," said Theo. "When it comes to knowledge, everybody contributes."

"Theo's right," said Harper. "I mean, I've always been better at remembering crafting formulas."

Jodi chuckled. "That's true! Just like I'm good at taming cute animal mobs."

"And if we have to replace you on a relay race, that *wouldn't* mean we're replacing you as a friend, you know," Harper continued. "We don't even care that much about winning the race. We just didn't want you to get hurt again."

"Mission *not* accomplished," Po said, pointing at Morgan's freshly rebraced foot.

"I guess I took it too personally," said Morgan. "I was looking forward to being on a team with you two for Field Day. I didn't want to miss out. But I have to face facts. And that means staying off my foot for a while." He looked from Harper to Theo. "What will you do now?"

"We'll think of something," said Theo. "In the relay race *and* in Minecraft."

"I'm sorry I tried to take your spot,

Jodi," said Morgan.

She sighed. "That's okay. Honestly, I'm worried. I wish we could all do the golem's challenge together."

"Maybe, in a way . . . you can," Ash said through the phone.

Morgan grinned. "It sounds like you have an idea."

Ash nodded. "The golem is making you work as individuals. But maybe you can treat its game less like a competition." She smiled. "And more like a relay race."

Chapter 13

JODI AND THE PIGLINS. SOUNDS LIKE A BAND! AND SPEAKING OF MUSIC, ARE YOU READY TO NETHERRACK AND ROLL?!

The golem didn't ask for a volunteer. It looked at the five avatars gathered around the campfire and said, "Jodi. Choose your items."

Jodi was ready. She had given it a lot of thought and consulted her friends. The elytra would help, and so would an empty flask and the gleaming golden helmet.

But the real tool Jodi had was knowledge. Her friends had told her everything she would need to know **in order to survive the Nether and return with the golem's prize.**

At least, she hoped so.

She kept her head down as she navigated the

warped forest. There were Endermen all around her, and her gold helmet wouldn't offer much protection from them. But as long as she minded her own business, they would leave her alone.

She climbed the cliff and saw Po's bridge right away. It extended out over the sea of lava like an Olympic diving platform. She saw the hole to Morgan's tunnel, too. But she knew the tunnel would lead her right into the heart of a soul sand valley—and lots of skeletons to get past. The bridge was the safer choice. **She walked to its very edge.** She could see the soul sand valley in the distance.

Jodi donned her elytra. With a running start, she leapt off the edge of Po's platform.

It was exhilarating to fly again after so long. **Jodi used to fly all the time in Creative mode.** She couldn't help laughing as the Nether stretched out before her.

But she knew better than to glide all the way to the soul sand. The skeletons there would only shoot her out of the sky, as they did to Theo.

Instead, she aimed for a small stone island in the middle of the lava. It was easy to spot from the air, and she reached it with no problems.

Harper had left the brewing stand behind, **with just enough material for one more Potion of Fire Resistance.** Jodi had never made one before, but she remembered Harper's instructions. Within seconds, her empty flask was filled with a liquid that looked a little like orange soda.

Jodi drank the potion. Then she looked at the lava with a bit of dread. But Harper had told her there was nothing to worry about . . . as long as she was quick. **So, without wasting another second, she dove into the lava.** She stayed beneath the surface, where she would be safe from any ghasts flying overhead.

Her brother had had to fight his way through the soul sand valley, where the sand was hazardous and the monsters were numerous. Jodi went around the other way so that she could travel through a crimson forest instead. There were dangers here, but they were easier to avoid. She took it slow, darting from tree to tree. Soon, she had arrived at the bastion remnant.

The structure was crawling with piglins. They saw her approach, and she held her breath. **There was no way she could fight them all!**

But the piglins didn't attack. They didn't seem the least bit bothered by her. A baby piglin even walked right up to her. It was cute!

Morgan's advice had worked. **As long as she wore a gold helmet,** she would be safe

among the piglins.

Still, she didn't want them to see her stealing from them. She waited until she was alone before she approached the treasure chest at the center of

the bastion. Would she find glittering jewels, precious materials, or framed works of art?

Instead, the chest held a random assortment of items. **There was a**

black disc, a saddle, and a fishing rod with a strange-looking mushroom on its hook.

There was also an illustration. It showed Jodi what to do with the fishing rod and saddle.

"NO. WAY," she said, smiling excitedly in the moment.

She still had to get back to the others, which meant crossing the lava once more.

But this time, she would be traveling in style.

Jodi's friends were waiting for her on the far shore. She could see the looks of surprise and delight on their faces as they realized she was riding a strider.

The strider was a strange creature,

unlike anything Jodi had seen in the Overworld. It was boxy and red, with stringy white hair, wide-set eyes, and a downturned mouth that looked like a frown. Even though it looked grumpy, the strider was very gentle.

And it loved mushrooms! **Jodi used the fishing rod to dangle the warped fungus in front of the strider.** This allowed her to steer it wherever she wanted to go.

And Jodi wanted to go right over the surface of the lava and back to her friends.

They all cheered her as she set foot

safely on shore. She cheered them right back. After all, thanks to Ash's idea, this had been a team effort. Jodi was only able to win because her friends had paved the way for her. Even better, they had shared what they had learned, and Jodi was able to avoid making the same mistakes.

She patted the strider and placed the weird fungus on the ground in front of it. "Thanks for the lift, Stri-Guy," she said.

"YOU HAVE THE ITEM?" asked the golem.

"I think so," said Jodi, and she held out the black disc. "But I thought it would be a treasure. What makes this thing so valuable?"

"The item itself is not precious," said the golem. **"BUT THE JOY IT BRINGS IS PRICELESS."**

With that, the golem directed Jodi to place the disc into a slotted brown box. It was a jukebox, and once the disc was in place, music poured forth.

"Is that . . . ?" asked Morgan.

"'Pigstep'!" said Theo.

"Pig does what now?" asked Po.

Harper laughed and said, **"'PIGSTEP.' IT'S THE NAME OF THE SONG."**

"It's catchy!" said Jodi, and she began dancing to the beat. The other kids joined in . . . and to Jodi's surprise, so did the golem.

The mob had been so stony and unemotional. But at the sound of the music, **the golem seemed to truly come alive.** It swayed its hips. It waved its arms. And its eyes glinted with delight.

This was the Evoker King's joy, Jodi knew. The golem was the part of their friend that delighted in all the wonders of Minecraft.

As they danced, the golem began to glow. **Then its body transformed into a swirling mass of butterflies.** The butterflies fluttered and swayed in their own dance before rushing past Jodi on their way back toward the portal.

They left behind a piece of the Evoker King. Morgan called it the torso.

Jodi smiled, knowing it was really the Evoker King's heart.

Chapter 14

FIELD DAY! IN WHICH BARON SWEETCHEEKS SHOWS HIS TRUE COLORS AND EVERYONE HAS A GREAT TIME!

Field Day had come at last to Woodsword Middle School. Morgan wouldn't have missed it for the world—even though he was still on crutches, and on strict orders to stay off his foot.

"Good to see you, Team Blue!" Ms. Minerva said when Morgan entered the school. He was wearing his team color and a bib with his participant number: 43. She checked him off a list.

"Wait a minute," said the teacher. She looked at his crutches. **"Number forty-three, I have you down for the relay race. That can't be right."**

"**Sure it is,**" said Morgan. "I missed the deadline to change my event. So participant number forty-three will definitely do the relay race."

Po came forward on his wheelchair to greet Morgan with a high five. (It made Morgan wobble, but he didn't fall.) Po was also wearing blue, and his bib number was 13. **He was already set to deck his wheelchair out like an ancient Greek chariot!**

"You ready to make the trade?" Po asked him.

Morgan grinned. "Let's do it."

As Ms. Minerva watched, the boys removed their numbered bibs—and traded them. Morgan affixed **number 13** to his shirt, while Po took **number 43** for his own.

Ms. Minerva smiled. "A brilliant display of problem-solving," she said. "Participants forty-three and thirteen, enjoy your events. **And do Team Blue proud out there!**"

Later that morning, wearing Morgan's bib, Po

took his place on the track. Theo and Harper were there, too, along with the relay runners for the red, gold, and green teams.

Morgan and Jodi watched from the bleachers, along with a couple of very special guests—**Baron Sweetcheeks and Duchess Dimples!**

"Let's go, Team Blue! Let's go, Red!" cried Jodi. "Duchess Dimples is rooting for both of you!"

Theo called from the sidelines, "Actually, hamsters are almost entirely color-blind!"

Jodi called back, "She is no longer rooting for you! She's just squeaking enthusiastically in your general direction!"

A bell sounded, signaling the start of the race. Harper took an early lead, sprinting ahead of her competition. But she used too much energy too soon, and the other teams caught up just as she handed the baton to Theo.

Theo stumbled a little as he started, and the other racers pulled ahead. But as Morgan watched, Theo churned his arms and legs. He kept his eyes ahead of him, and he quickly reached Po sooner than they thought he could.

Po shot forward in his wheelchair, as fast as Morgan had ever seen him move. Po's time on the basketball court had obviously made him quite adept at bursts of speed.

Po started in last place. He overtook Team Gold, and then Team Green . . . but Team Red finished just ahead of him.

"Second place!" said Jodi. **"That's great!"**

"It is," said Morgan, clapping furiously … while being careful not to knock Baron Sweetcheeks and Duchess Dimples over.

The hamster seemed unimpressed with the race. **The whole time, he only had eyes for the Duchess.**

Jodi's event was discus throwing. **She got first place in the competition despite a wild first throw that almost gave Ms. Minerva a surprise haircut.**

And then it was Morgan's turn. At first, he felt pressure to do as well as his sister had. Winning first place would feel really good!

But then he remembered: he was supposed to be having *fun,* not stressing himself out. At Ms. Minerva's suggestion, **he even tried meditating.** It calmed him down a little. He especially liked focusing on his breathing.

The free-throw basketball event would not have been Morgan's first choice. He wasn't a natural at

shooting hoops. But because Woodsword had a title-winning wheelchair basketball team, no one had any problem with Morgan making his shots from a seated position. That way, he was able to stay off his feet, and he didn't have to worry about losing his balance.

He only made two baskets, though. That left him in last place.

It didn't matter. **He laughed when he missed a basket, and he hooted with joy when he made one.**

And his friends were there on the sidelines, cheering him on the whole time.

Chapter 15

EVERYBODY LOVES A HAPPY ENDING! WHICH MEANS YOU'RE PROBABLY GOING TO REALLY HATE THIS PART.

A few days passed before Morgan and his friends were able to return to Minecraft. It was their first time donning their goggles since they had won the golem's game.

There was just one more piece of the Evoker King to retrieve. Just one!

They spawned at the blue soul fire camp, where they checked the golem's chests for good measure. The chests were empty. They had already gone through every bit of the golem's loot.

"WE'RE RUNNING REALLY LOW ON . . . EVERYTHING," said Harper.

"That's all right," said Theo. "We'll be able to

resupply in the Overworld."

"I am so ready to get out of this place," said Po.

"I'll sort of miss the piglins, to be honest," said Jodi.

Morgan shuddered thinking about the piglike mobs. "Not me. **COME ON, LET'S GO.**"

At the portal, Morgan wondered briefly what they'd see on the other side. It had been more than a week since they'd been in the Overworld. The last time they'd seen it, **the Fault had swallowed the entire sky.** He hoped it hadn't gotten any worse.

That hope was in vain.

Morgan's virtual jaw dropped open as he stepped out into the Overworld. It was unrecognizable. The Fault was everywhere. **A pixelated, lightning-lanced abyss of darkness stretched out above, before, and below them.** The landscape was still there—he had land beneath his feet—but it was cracked and segmented. It looked more like the floating islands of the End than the Overworld he knew and loved.

His friends came through the portal behind

him. One by one, they all gasped.

"What happened here?" asked Jodi.

"We're too late," Morgan told her. **"THE FAULT . . . IT'S SWALLOWED THE WHOLE OVERWORLD!"**

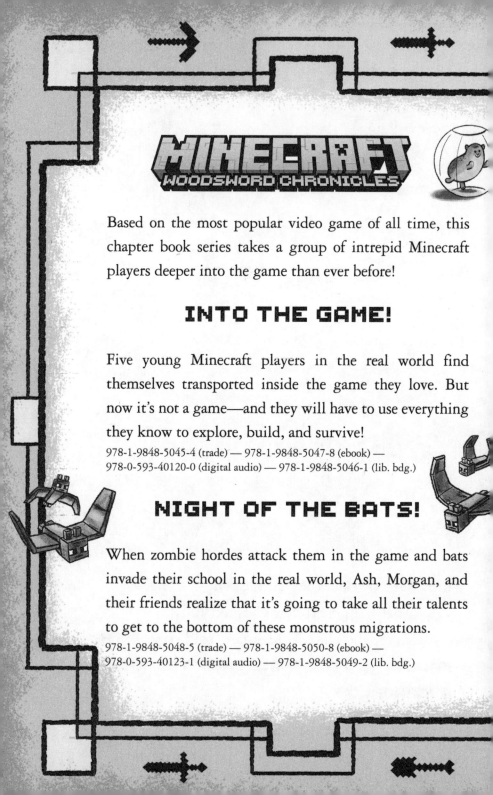

MINECRAFT
WOODSWORD CHRONICLES

Based on the most popular video game of all time, this chapter book series takes a group of intrepid Minecraft players deeper into the game than ever before!

INTO THE GAME!

Five young Minecraft players in the real world find themselves transported inside the game they love. But now it's not a game—and they will have to use everything they know to explore, build, and survive!

978-1-9848-5045-4 (trade) — 978-1-9848-5047-8 (ebook) — 978-0-593-40120-0 (digital audio) — 978-1-9848-5046-1 (lib. bdg.)

NIGHT OF THE BATS!

When zombie hordes attack them in the game and bats invade their school in the real world, Ash, Morgan, and their friends realize that it's going to take all their talents to get to the bottom of these monstrous migrations.

978-1-9848-5048-5 (trade) — 978-1-9848-5050-8 (ebook) — 978-0-593-40123-1 (digital audio) — 978-1-9848-5049-2 (lib. bdg.)

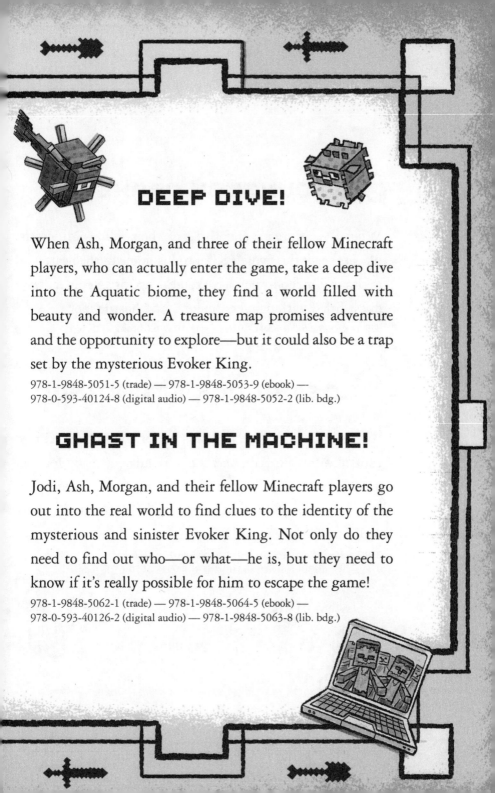

DEEP DIVE!

When Ash, Morgan, and three of their fellow Minecraft players, who can actually enter the game, take a deep dive into the Aquatic biome, they find a world filled with beauty and wonder. A treasure map promises adventure and the opportunity to explore—but it could also be a trap set by the mysterious Evoker King.

978-1-9848-5051-5 (trade) — 978-1-9848-5053-9 (ebook) —
978-0-593-40124-8 (digital audio) — 978-1-9848-5052-2 (lib. bdg.)

GHAST IN THE MACHINE!

Jodi, Ash, Morgan, and their fellow Minecraft players go out into the real world to find clues to the identity of the mysterious and sinister Evoker King. Not only do they need to find out who—or what—he is, but they need to know if it's really possible for him to escape the game!

978-1-9848-5062-1 (trade) — 978-1-9848-5064-5 (ebook) —
978-0-593-40126-2 (digital audio) — 978-1-9848-5063-8 (lib. bdg.)

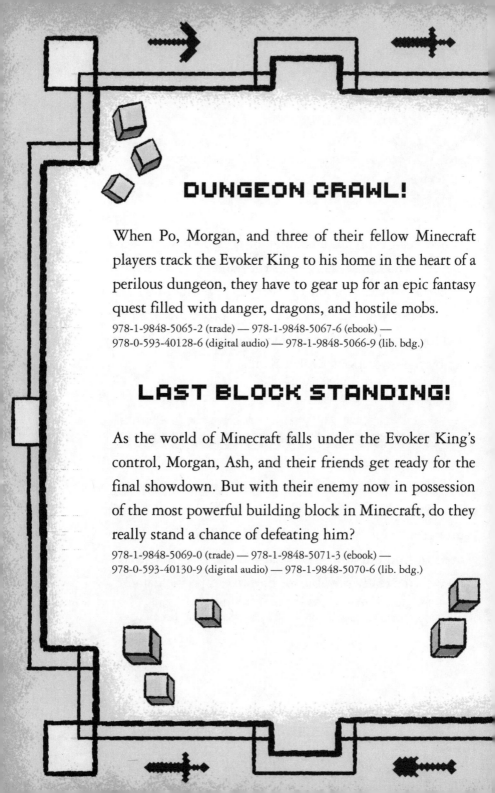

DUNGEON CRAWL!

When Po, Morgan, and three of their fellow Minecraft players track the Evoker King to his home in the heart of a perilous dungeon, they have to gear up for an epic fantasy quest filled with danger, dragons, and hostile mobs.

978-1-9848-5065-2 (trade) — 978-1-9848-5067-6 (ebook) —
978-0-593-40128-6 (digital audio) — 978-1-9848-5066-9 (lib. bdg.)

LAST BLOCK STANDING!

As the world of Minecraft falls under the Evoker King's control, Morgan, Ash, and their friends get ready for the final showdown. But with their enemy now in possession of the most powerful building block in Minecraft, do they really stand a chance of defeating him?

978-1-9848-5069-0 (trade) — 978-1-9848-5071-3 (ebook) —
978-0-593-40130-9 (digital audio) — 978-1-9848-5070-6 (lib. bdg.)

THE ADVENTURES CONTINUE IN

MINECRAFT
STONESWORD SAGA

CRACK IN THE CODE!

Someone—or something—has turned the Evoker King to stone. And now a new player, Theo, has joined the team on their quest to return their former enemy to normal. Theo has modding skills that could come in handy, but does he have what it takes to be part of the team, or will his meddling put a crack in the game code that none of them will survive?

978-0-593-37298-2 (trade) — 978-0-593-37300-2 (ebook) —
978-0-593-40132-3 (digital audio) — 978-0-593-37299-9 (lib. bdg.)

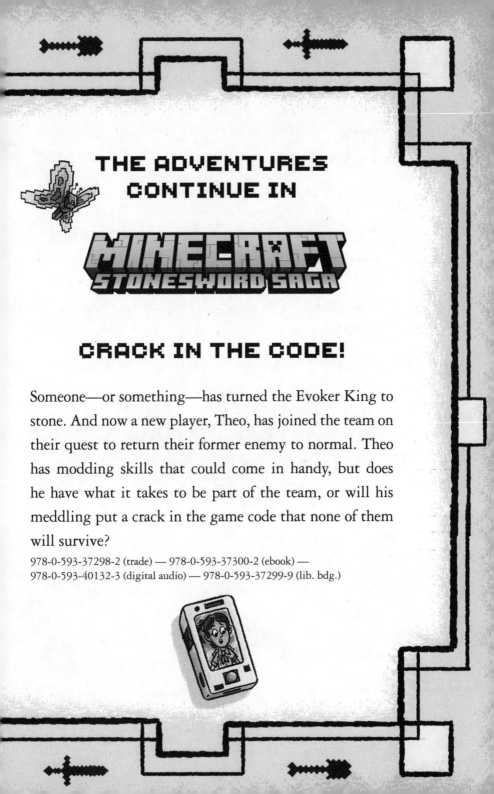

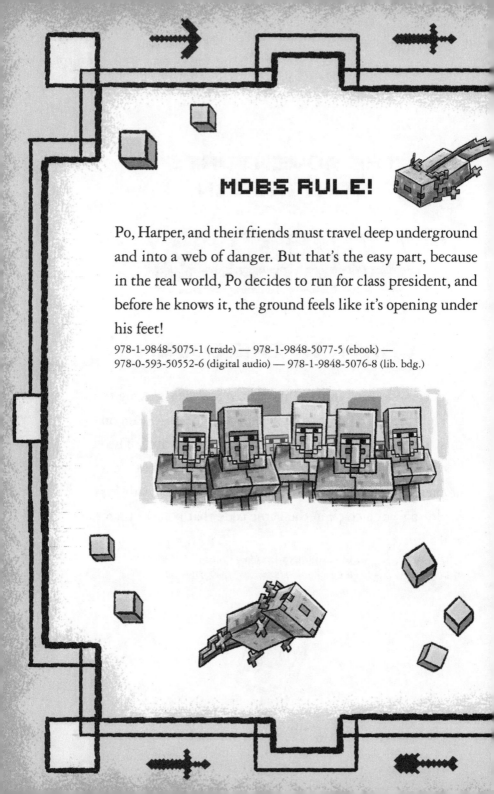

MOBS RULE!

Po, Harper, and their friends must travel deep underground and into a web of danger. But that's the easy part, because in the real world, Po decides to run for class president, and before he knows it, the ground feels like it's opening under his feet!

978-1-9848-5075-1 (trade) — 978-1-9848-5077-5 (ebook) —
978-0-593-50552-6 (digital audio) — 978-1-9848-5076-8 (lib. bdg.)

NEW PETS ON THE BLOCK!

When the third piece of the Evoker King takes the form of a Minecraft witch and sends Jodi, Morgan, and their friends on a quest to bring back an extremely rare animal mob, Jodi is determined to make sure that the mob stays safe no matter what!

978-1-9848-5094-2 (trade) — 978-1-9848-5096-6 (ebook) —
978-0-593-55978-9 (digital audio) — 978-1-9848-5095-9 (lib. bdg.)

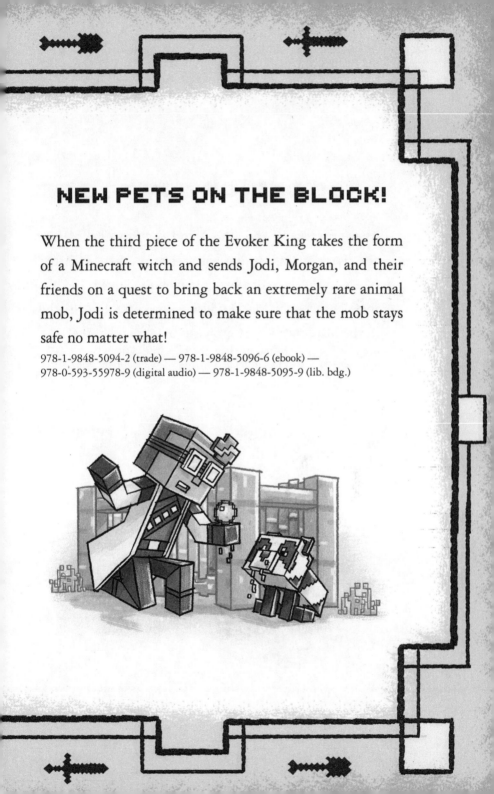

TOO BEE, OR NOT TO BEE!

The bees around the school and the Stonesword Library are disappearing—and a splinter of the Evoker King has taken on the form of a bee colony with a hive mind! Could there be a connection? And to make matters worse, the rip in the Minecraft sky is growing bigger and darker.

978-0-593-56288-8 (trade) — 978-0-593-56290-1 (ebook) — 978-0-593-66817-7 (digital audio) — 978-0-593-56289-5 (lib. bdg.)

GET READY FOR THE EPIC CONCLUSION TO THE STONESWORD SAGA IN BOOK 6—COMING SOON!

MINECRAFT is a game about placing blocks and going on adventures. Build, play, and explore across infinitely generated worlds of mountains, caverns, oceans, jungles, and deserts. Defeat hordes of zombies, bake the cake of your dreams, venture to new dimensions, or build a skyscraper. What you do in Minecraft is up to you.

Nick Eliopulos is a writer who lives in Brooklyn (as many writers do). He likes to spend half his free time reading and the other half gaming. He cowrote the Adventurers Guild series with his best friend and works as a narrative designer for a small video game studio. After all these years, endermen still give him the creeps.

Alan Batson is a British cartoonist and illustrator. His works include *Everything I Need to Know I Learned from a Star Wars Little Golden Book, Everything That Glitters Is Guy!,* and *Spider-Ham.* Being extremely fond of cubes and travel to exotic places, he has recently begun to lend his talents to several different books on adventures in the world of Minecraft.

Chris Hill is an illustrator living in Birmingham, England, with his wife and two daughters and has been loving it for twenty-five years! When he's not working, he spends time with his family and trying to tire out his dog on long walks. If there's any time left after that, he loves to go riding on his motorcycle, feeling the wind on his face while contemplating his next illustration adventure.

JOURNEY INTO THE WORLD OF MINECRAFT

1481d  rhcbooks.com

TO BEE, OR NOT TO BEE!

© 2023 Mojang AB. All Rights Reserved. Minecraft, the Minecraft logo, the Mojang Studios logo and the Creeper logo are trademarks of the Microsoft group of companies.

Published in the United States by Random House Children's Books, a division of Penguin Random House LLC, 1745 Broadway, New York, NY 10019, and in Canada by Penguin Random House Canada Limited, Toronto. Random House and the colophon are registered trademarks of Penguin Random House LLC.

rhcbooks.com
minecraft.net

Library of Congress Cataloging-in-Publication Data is available upon request.
ISBN 978-0-593-56288-8 (trade)—ISBN 978-0-593-56289-5 (library binding)—ISBN 978-0-593-56290-1 (ebook)

Cover design by Diane Choi

Printed in the United States of America

3rd Printing

TO BEE, OR NOT TO BEE!

By Nick Eliopulos
Illustrated by Alan Batson and Chris Hill

Random House New York

MORGAN

ASH

HARPER

LAYERS!

PO

JODI

THEO

Prologue

Harper didn't want to hurt the bees.

They weren't making it easy for her, though.

They were buzzing all around her. One of them broke loose from the swarm, diving at her. It aimed its stinger right at her face.

She lifted her shield just in time, batting it away. But she knew it would try again.

A hissing sounded at her back. **She spun around as a spider lunged at her.**

"Bad spider!" she said, swatting at it with her empty hand. That knocked it back, giving her some room. Maybe she could escape. . . .

But more buzzing forced her to whirl around

again. Another bee struck her shield.

And then another.

And another.

The spider hissed behind her. **She could sense its approach.**

She turned . . .

And again . . .

And again . . .

She couldn't keep this up for long.

It was a battle of the bugs. And both sides wanted to destroy her.

And the worst part was this: if she fought back, she and her friends—and maybe the entire Overworld—were **doomed.**

Chapter 1

TO BEE, OR NOT TO BEE MARKED ABSENT IS NOT A GOOD QUESTION TO ASK THIS EARLY IN THE MORNING.

Woodsword Middle School was abuzz with excitement.

Harper Houston had never really understood that expression before today. But as she stood on the front lawn of the school, surrounded by her classmates, she could hear it. **It was the sound of dozens of students whispering at once.** Their voices were too low—and too numerous—for Harper to make out any individual words. But those voices, overlapping and reverberating across the lawn?

Together, they sounded distinctly like a *buzz*.

Harper's entire grade had been instructed to

meet their homeroom group on the lawn. Now her homeroom teacher, Ms. Minerva, was attempting to take attendance while a hundred kids chattered and squirmed with excitement. She seemed a little flustered. **Her hair was extra frizzy, and her eyes were a little intense.** She took a long sip of her coffee, followed by a deep breath.

"Theo?" she said, raising her voice to be heard over the racket. **"Is Theo Grayson here?"**

"Present!" said Theo, and he cut through the crowd, waving his hand in the air. "I wasn't late, honest! I just got a little lost."

Ms. Minerva checked off his name on her clipboard. "Harper Houston?" she said.

"Here," said Harper, then turned to greet Theo.

"What's going on?" Theo asked her. **"This is highly unusual . . . even for Woodsword."**

"Nobody knows for sure," said Harper. "But I'm pretty sure I heard Ms. Minerva muttering under her breath about how this is all Doc's fault."

"Oh no," said Morgan Mercado. He cradled the class hamster, **Baron Sweetcheeks**, against his chest. "If Doc's involved, it could be almost anything. She didn't try to replace the lunch ladies with robots again, did she? It took weeks to clean all the Sloppy Joes off the ceiling. . . ."

Po Chen chuckled. "That's nothing," he said. "Remember when the computer lab became a butterfly sanctuary? **Maybe the whole school has become an iguana habitat!**"

Jodi Mercado, Morgan's little sister, pressed her hands together

with delight. "That actually sounds adorable," she said. She loved animals of all kinds.

"I know, right?" Po laughed again. "Iguanas need an education, too!"

Harper grinned. **She was fairly certain that the school hadn't been taken over by reptiles or robots.** But her friends were right about one thing. Doc—their nickname for Dr. Culpepper, their science teacher—could be unpredictable. Harper didn't mind. In fact, she looked up to Doc.

A loud horn sounded, interrupting Harper's thoughts and nearly jolting her out of her skin. She looked up—along with every other person on the lawn—and saw a pick-up truck rounding the corner. It pulled to a stop at the curb, blocking their view of the library across the street. And driving the truck . . . was **Doc Culpepper** herself.

The science teacher honked twice more, and the kids broke into cheers. There was something strange and delightful about seeing their teacher at the wheel of the big vehicle.

Doc hopped out of the cab, joined by a man who

had been sitting beside her in the passenger seat. **The man had white hair and wrinkles around his eyes, and he wore cowboy boots.** Harper guessed that he was the owner of the truck.

But what was the truck hauling? The back was covered with a massive tarp, making its contents a mystery.

"What do you think is in there?" Harper asked.

"Iguanas...or puppies," said Jodi hopefully.

"Robot custodians," suggested Morgan.

"Alien spaceships!" Po guessed.

"It could be anything," said Theo. Then he thought about it. "Probably not spaceships."

"Bonjour, mes étudiants!" Doc said, speaking through a high-tech bullhorn. She laughed, pressing a button. "Oops. I had it on the wrong setting. Let's try that again. Good morning, students!"

The buzzing of the crowd stopped as voices rang out in unison: "Good morning!"

"I'd like to introduce a friend of mine," said Doc. She gestured to the man standing beside her. "This is Mr. Shane. He has a very interesting job—one that takes him all over the country. For the next few weeks, he'll be right here in our hometown. And he's brought a few thousand of his closest friends." Doc winked at the man. "Whenever you're ready, Mr. Shane."

Mr. Shane gripped a corner of the tarp, and he pulled. The tarp fell away, revealing stacks of crates, **all of them swarming with insects.** They flew into the air, buzzing around the truck, immediately taking the opportunity to explore the area.

"**Bees!**" said Harper. She'd never seen so many bees in all her life.

"Mr. Shane is a bee wrangler—or an apiarist, if you want to use the scientific term," Doc said into her bullhorn. "His truck is loaded with beehives, and he brings the hives—and the honeybees who live in them—wherever they're needed."

"Wherever they're *needed*?" Morgan said to his friends. "Aren't they pests?"

"I don't know," said Jodi. "**I love animals. But stinging insects aren't exactly cuddly.**"

"And they follow an outdated form of government," Po said, motioning dramatically toward the truck. "Down with the monarchy! We're a democratic republic in *this* country, honeybees."

Theo shushed them. "I'm trying to listen!" he said.

Harper nodded at him, grateful. She wanted to hear what Doc had to say, too.

"I can tell you all have questions," said Doc. "And that's a good thing! **We'll be talking more about bees all week in science class.**" She handed the bullhorn to Mr. Shane.

"Bees are fascinating creatures," he said. "And they're important to the ecosystem. I've spent my life learning about them. And I *still* learn something new, most days."

"Mr. Shane has to drive his truck over to the town orchard this morning," said Doc. "But he's agreed to leave one hive behind for a few days. We'll keep it on library property, right across from the school, where we can keep an eye on it—and maybe learn a thing or two ourselves." She placed a hand on the man's shoulder. "Let's all make a

promise to Mr. Shane. Let's promise we'll take care of the insects he's entrusting to us. Promise?"

"**Promise!**" Harper called, along with many of the other students.

But after she'd said it, she felt a little anxious. How did a person take care of insects, exactly? How could she keep them safe from harm?

Harper had a sinking feeling it might be harder than it sounded.

Chapter 2

THE SECRET TO SUCCESSFUL ANIMAL FRIENDSHIPS? LOTS OF SNACKS!

I think we need to talk about the giant hole in the sky," said Harper.

They were in Minecraft—not just playing the game, but inside it. Together, Harper and her friends were experiencing a hyper-real simulation that they could only access with special Doc-enhanced VR goggles. It never ceased to amaze Harper that they were in the world of Minecraft. Thanks to Doc's mad science, their favorite game had come to life!

But now, she feared that something was very wrong with that world.

"Do we have to focus on the negatives?"

complained Po. "I'm moooo-dy enough as it is."

Po liked to wear different skins to express himself. Today, he was in a mooshroom skin, in honor of their recent temporary teammate, a mushroom-covered cow named Michael G. "I really miss that guy," Po said.

"He was an excellent addition to the team," Jodi agreed. "But he's safer not following us around. WE TEND TO GET INTO A LOT OF FIGHTS."

"And talking about the Fault isn't 'focusing on the negatives,'" Morgan argued. "If we're going to find a solution, we have to acknowledge the problem."

"What we really need to do is find the Evoker King," said Theo. "OR THE 'EVOKER SPAWN,' I GUESS. AT LEAST, THAT'S WHAT I'M CALLING THE PIECES HE BROKE INTO." He gazed worriedly at the rift overhead. "Finding them is our best hope of bringing this place back from the brink of disaster."

Harper figured Theo knew what he was talking about. As the group's only programmer, he'd spent some time studying the computer code at the heart of the game. It was Theo who had figured out what happened to their former enemy turned friend, the Evoker King, an artificial intelligence who had lived inside this version of Minecraft. **The Evoker King's very essence had been split into six distinct pieces.** Those pieces had taken the form of unusual mobs. So far, Harper and her friends had confronted three of those mobs. They had been successful in retrieving half of the Evoker King's code.

They needed three more pieces to save the Evoker King . . . to put him back together again and stop the rest of the program from breaking down entirely.

The sixth member of their team, Ash Kapoor, had joined them for the day's scouting mission. Ash lived in a different town, **but distance didn't matter in this virtual world.** Harper felt as if she were truly standing right beside Ash. She reached out and put her arm around Ash's shoulder. Even though she was only touching an avatar, it felt solid to the touch.

"I'm glad you're here," Harper told her. "An extra set of eyes could come in handy."

"It can't hurt, right?" said Ash. "Especially when we're looking for something as small as a butterfly."

Butterflies weren't a normally occurring Minecraft mob, and they only showed up whenever one of the Evoker Spawn was near. They were like digital ghosts, virtual echoes of the Evoker King's metamorphosis.

They were *clues.* And Harper knew they desperately needed clues.

Suddenly, she saw a flash of movement out of the corner of her eye. Not a butterfly—it was a rabbit, darting across the grass.

Po screamed. **"LOOK OUT!"** he said.

Harper gave him a funny look. "It's just a rabbit," she said.

"Am I the only one who remembers that time we were attacked by rabbits?" he asked. "I still see their beady little eyes in the dark when I'm trying to get to sleep."

"Those rabbits were being mind-controlled by a giant cave spider with self-esteem issues," Theo reminded him.

"That doesn't make it any less weird," said Po. "Or more forgettable . . ."

"Oh, cute!" said Jodi. "Look. The bunny has a friend."

Harper looked where Jodi was pointing. **A fox hurried past them, heading the**

same way the rabbit had gone.

"HE WENT THAT WAY!" Jodi told the fox. "If you hurry, you should be able to catch him." She sighed, then turned to her friends. "I love animal friendships. I have a whole notebook full of cute animal photos I found online."

"Uh, Jodi," said Morgan. "You realize—"

Ash cleared her throat, cutting Morgan off. She shook her head at him, signaling that he shouldn't say what he was about to say.

"What?" said Jodi. "What is it?"

"NEVER MIND," Morgan said. "Don't worry about it."

Harper knew what Morgan was thinking. She knew he was a good big brother—too kind and protective to upset Jodi unnecessarily.

Harper *also* also knew that Theo was not as careful with other people's feelings.

"They aren't friends," said Theo. "The fox is going to catch and eat the rabbit."

Harper was reasonably sure that avatars couldn't blush or blanch. **Yet Jodi's blocky face appeared suddenly pale.** Her mouth

dropped open. "What?" said Jodi. "That's awful!"

"No, it isn't," said Theo. **"IT'S JUST NATURE."**

"Nature or not," said Po, "I'm rooting for the rabbit. Run, little guy! All is forgiven!"

"Can't we do something to help?" asked Jodi.

"That's a kind thought," said Harper.

"But it's pointless," said Theo. "You shouldn't try to disrupt the food web. Even if you *could,* it would be a disaster."

Harper sighed, turning to Jodi. "Theo is a little blunt," she said. "But he isn't wrong. We learned all about this in science class, remember? **HERBIVORES, LIKE RABBITS, EAT GRASS. CARNIVORES, LIKE FOXES, EAT OTHER**

ANIMALS. If you saved all the rabbits, the foxes would starve. And there wouldn't be enough grass to feed the rabbits."

"It's all part of the circle of life," Ash said, agreeing with Harper. "The Minecraft fox is programmed to act like a real-world fox. **IT ISN'T EVIL OR MEAN . . . IT'S JUST DOING WHAT IT NEEDS TO DO TO SURVIVE."**

Morgan put his arm around Jodi's shoulders. "Don't worry," he said. "The rabbit might get away! And if it doesn't, there are a lot more rabbits out there. We'll see another one soon, I bet."

"MAYBE THAT BUTTERFLY WILL LEAD US TO ONE," said Po.

"Sure," said Morgan. "That's something I love about this game. You never know what you're going to— Wait." His head snapped up. "What butterfly?"

Po grinned, pointing. **A luminous, pixelated insect fluttered nearby.**

"FOLLOW IT," said Theo and Morgan simultaneously.

"It's surely what Michael G. would have wanted," Po added.

Chapter 3

CALLING LIGHTNING DOWN FROM A MYSTERIOUS RIP IN THE SKY ... AND OTHER QUESTIONABLE IDEAS

Jodi tried not to think about the rabbit. Had it gotten away? **Or had the fox caught it in the end?**

She would never know. But she *could* learn where the butterflies were leading them.

"Focus on the butterflies," she said to herself.

There had been only one of them at first. But as it led them across the taiga biome, **OTHER BUTTERFLIES HAD JOINED IT.** Now there were four of them, flittering around each other. Fortunately, they were all moving in the same direction.

"I bet if a parrot swooped down and started

eating those butterflies, you'd try to stop it," she said to her brother.

"I don't know," said Morgan. "It might be interesting to see what would happen. Any theories?"

Theo tapped his chin. "If the butterflies are stray bits of the Evoker King's code . . . maybe the parrot would be transformed by eating them?"

"THE EVOKER PARROT!" said Ash. "Sounds cute."

"I agree," said Po. "Maybe if I wore my pirate skin, he'd hang out on my shoulder."

The kids laughed. Then lightning crackled

from the Fault overhead and the sound of thunder made them jump! All at once, they remembered what was at stake.

Jodi knew they were entering a new biome when the trees changed. There had been nothing but spruce trees in the taiga biome. Now they were walking among a cluster of oak and birch trees.

Jodi wasn't a plant person, really. But she knew her Minecraft trees. They all provided wood of different colors, and that was important to know when planning a colorful build.

For the same reason, she was trying to learn all the flowers of Minecraft. But there were so many different types! Some of them could be used to make dyes, but not all of them. And usually, they were spread across an assortment of different biomes.

But as Jodi stepped past the trees, she saw a huge array of flowers growing on the gentle slopes ahead. It was like a rainbow had come down to nestle in the grass.

"WHAT IS THIS PLACE?" she asked in awe.

"IT LOOKS LIKE A FLOWER FOREST BIOME," said Theo. "Almost every kind of flower grows here."

"Could the butterflies be attracted to the flowers?" asked Harper.

"I don't know," said Ash, pointing with her blocky hand. "They seem more interested in *that*."

Jodi saw what Ash meant. The butterflies had all gathered around a block that was hanging from a nearby oak tree. The block was yellow with bands of brown. Small openings in its sides made it look almost like a miniature house.

"IT'S A BEES' NEST!" said Morgan.

"Why are the butterflies gathered around it?" Harper asked.

"Do you think the next Evoker Spawn could be **A GIANT BEE?"** asked Ash.

But Jodi wasn't paying attention. She'd spotted a sheep grazing among the flowers. Pressing herself again a nearby birch, she scanned the area for wolves and other predators. For now, the sheep appeared safe. But how long would that last?

"Psst," Jodi whispered. "Hey, Po."

While the others were gathered around the bees' nest, Jodi pulled Po aside. "Do you still have that trident?" she asked him.

Po gave her a suspicious look. "Yeeeah," he said, and **he glanced up at the lightning that flashed around the edges of the Fault.** "What do you need it for?"

"I had an idea," Jodi said. "Your trident has a special enchantment on it, right? It causes lightning to strike."

"When it's raining, sure," said Po. He looked

up again at the Fault. "You think it'll work on the lightning that's flashing around the Fault?"

"I THINK IT MIGHT WORK," Jodi said.

"Okay," said Po. "But why do you *want* to call lightning down?"

Jodi looked around to make sure her brother couldn't hear her, and then she fixed Po with her most serious expression. She asked him, "Do you remember what happened when a pig got struck by lightning?"

Po nodded. **"UH, YEAH! THE PIG WAS TRANSFORMED INTO A MONSTROUS, UNDEAD MOB PIG-HUMAN HYBRID THINGY."**

He shuddered. "It's not the sort of thing a person forgets."

"Do you think it

would work on other animals, too?" asked Jodi. "Like that sheep over there?"

"Jodi," said Po, and he put his blocky hands on her shoulders. **"YOU KNOW I LOVE A GOOD BAD IDEA.** But why would you want to transform another animal into a monstrous, undead hybrid? Are you worried that Piggy Sue is out there somewhere, terribly lonely?"

"I'll bet Piggy Sue doesn't have to worry about being eaten by predators," said Jodi. **"IF WE CAN TRANSFORM THAT SHEEP, THEN IT'LL BE SAFE, TOO."**

Po thought about it for a minute. "Yeah," he said at last. "I support this idea one hundred percent. It's unusual. Which I *always* mean as a compliment." He handed her the trident. "Want to do the honors? You'll have to throw it at the sheep."

Jodi hesitated. "You don't think anything bad will happen? **THE LIGHTNING FROM THE FAULT IS PROBABLY JUST LIKE NORMAL LIGHTNING, RIGHT?"**

Po rubbed his square jaw for a moment, and

then said, "It will be fine. **WHAT'S THE WORST THAT COULD HAPPEN?"**

Jodi smiled, gave Po a fist bump, then turned and crept toward the sheep. **The animal looked up from its grazing,** and Jodi waved. Then it went back to what it was doing, obviously deciding that she wasn't a threat.

"Good choice," said Jodi. "I'm here to help, after all."

Just as she took aim with the trident, Po said, "Um—but I just remembered that this will kill the sheep."

"WHAT?!" Jodi yelled as she let go of the trident. Luckily her shock caused her to throw the trident into the air and way off course.

Lightning from the Fault leapt out at the trident, causing a massive flash. Hot sparks showered down from the sky. **NEARBY TREES AND BRUSH BEGAN TO SMOLDER AS THE SPARKS HIT. THE SHEEP RAN AWAY.**

Po and Jodi looked at each other. Po said, "I think the sheep has the right idea. Let's go."

The two friends took off through the trees hoping to find their friends—and hoping nothing too bad would come from the sparks caused by their failed experiment. Jodi soon heard a strange sound. **She looked up and saw that the tree contained another bees' nest.** And it was buzzing with activity.

"Something's happening!" said Morgan. "Jodi? Po?"

"We're over here!" said Jodi, and she grabbed Po and pulled him toward the others.

THERE WAS A BUZZING COMING FROM BEHIND THEM. AND TO THE SIDE. AND UP AHEAD . . .

They were surrounded by the sound of buzzing insects.

"What's happening?" Po asked as their friends came into view.

"MORGAN DISTURBED THE BEES," said Theo.

"I did not!" said Morgan. **"I ONLY POKED**

THE NEST A LITTLE BIT."

"It's so loud!" said Harper, covering her ears.

"I hate to say this," said Ash, "but we should be ready for a fight. Just in case . . ."

As Ash drew her sword, the first bee appeared. It floated out from the first nest they'd found, wings beating furiously.

Jodi wasn't always fond of insects. But this insect was decidedly cute, with big eyes and itty-bitty antennae sticking out from its head. "Oh!" she said. "I don't want to fight it."

"It's okay," said Morgan, and he put his hand on Ash's sword. "It isn't hostile right now."

"How can you tell?" she asked.

Morgan frowned. "BELIEVE ME. IF IT WERE HOSTILE, YOU'D KNOW."

Two more bees appeared from the first nest. They flew into the air, joining their hive mate. And they weren't alone. More bees approached, flying in from all over the forest. There must have been a dozen nests nearby, and now all those bees were coming together in a great, billowing swarm.

The buzzing grew in intensity as dozens of wings vibrated at the same time.

"Fascinating," said Harper. "It almost looks like they're dancing in the air."

As Jodi watched, the insects spun and swirled in a great mass. They sped up, moving so fast that their wings and bodies blurred, and the buzzing grew louder than ever. And then, to Jodi's astonishment . . . the bees made a shape.

It was the shape of a *human*. Some of the bees lined up like limbs. Others clumped together to form a torso. And the head . . .

The head appeared to be looking right at them.

"That's . . . new," said Morgan.

"Shh!" said Ash. "Do you hear that?"

Jodi strained to catch the sounds. But all she heard was **the buzzing.**

And then she realized that the buzzing almost sounded like a word, repeated over and over: *Lzzn. Lzzn.*

Listen.

As Jodi watched, the bees' wings began to move in perfect unison. The pitch of the buzzing changed as their wings went faster or slower. **The bees were trying to tell them something.**

"*Lizzzzen,*" they said. "*Youuu . . . muzzzzt . . .*"

It was then that a great bolt of lightning struck a nearby tree.

Jodi gasped in surprise.

The bees broke apart, each one flying away in a different direction.

And nearby . . . **a fire began to rapidly spread through the forest.**

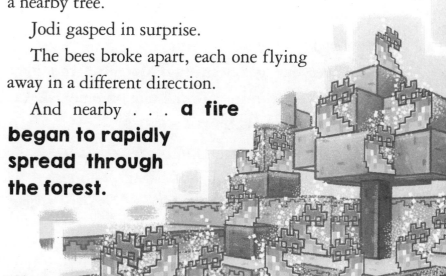

Chapter 4

EXCUSE ME, FELLOW MINECRAFT PLAYERS, WE DON'T WANT TO ALARM YOU, BUT FIRE!!!

As he watched the flames spread through the forest biome, **Theo froze with inaction.**

Fire was dangerous and destructive. No one would blame Theo for being afraid.

But Theo *wasn't* afraid. He was too busy feeling annoyed.

"Everyone, get clear," said Morgan. "And don't panic! We can retreat to the taiga biome. **WE'LL COME BACK WHEN IT'S SAFE.**"

"No!" said Theo. "It might be too late by then."

"Too late?" said Ash. "What do you mean?"

"THOSE BEES," said Theo. **"THEY WERE**

TRYING TO COMMUNICATE WITH US. They were trying to tell us something. And now . . . Oh no!"

Theo's heart sank as he saw it happen. Fire had spread to a nearby oak tree . . . destroying one of the bees' nests in a matter of seconds.

"We have to do something," said Theo. **"WE HAVE TO GIVE THE BEES ANOTHER CHANCE TO DELIVER THEIR MESSAGE."**

"I see what Theo means," said Harper. "If the bees are destroyed, we might lose our chance to fix the Evoker King."

"It would also be bad for the bees," said Jodi. "I'm sure they would love to not be destroyed today."

"Okay," said Ash. "New plan. **STOP THE**

FIRE! SAVE THE BEES!"

They scattered, each doing their best to stop flames from spreading.

Morgan and Ash ran to a nearby stream and filled their buckets with water. **"DO YOU THINK THIS WILL MAKE A DIFFERENCE?"** asked Ash.

"It will if we use this water to set up a whole new water source," said Morgan. "We could actually create a river in the heart of the forest."

"Sounds like a plan," said Ash.

"I'LL DIG SOME CANALS," offered Harper, and she pulled out her shovel. "Even if we don't fill them with water, the gaps should stop the fire from spreading across the grass."

As Harper started carving lines through the landscape, Theo finally sprang into action. He followed close behind Harper, grabbing the dirt blocks that she left in her wake. "I can use these to make walls of dirt. **THEY'LL BE LIKE**

BARRIERS AGAINST THE FLAMES."

"DON'T TRAP THE ANIMALS!" said Jodi. She ran ahead of Harper and Theo, moving toward the heart of the forest with a sheaf of wheat in her hand. "If they get stuck behind your canals or your walls of dirt, they'll be in a lot of danger!"

"I'd better get the trident we left behind," said Po. "The last thing we need is a second lightning strike."

Theo stopped. "TRIDENT?" he echoed. "Po, did you cause this fire?"

"Busy now," said Po as he rushed past them. "Talk later!"

Jodi emerged from between the trees, leading a sheep to safety. "IT'S MY FAULT," she said. "I put the trident down and then forgot about it. I'm really sorry."

"Tell that to the bees," Theo said. As he watched, another nest fell into the flames.

"**WE HAVE TO GET THOSE NESTS OUT OF HERE,**" said Theo. "We're losing too many of them."

"There's a nest right over there." Harper pointed at a nearby tree with her shovel. "Should I cut it out of the tree?" she asked.

"Wait!" said Morgan. "If you use that, you'll just destroy it."

"We need a pickaxe with a Silk Touch enchantment," said Ash, and she ran to Harper's side. "**I HAVE SOME LAPIS.** Do you have an enchanting table?"

Harper nodded, placing the workstation down beside the tree. On either side of the enchanting table, she set down bookcases. "I'm going to need a minute," she said. "Someone keep an eye on the fire, please."

"I've got your back," said Theo, and he placed a dirt barrier all around the tree—and around Harper, who was now free to work without fear of the flames reaching her.

The pickaxe she was working on glowed purple with magic, but Harper shook her head. "That didn't work right," she said. "It's a Fortune enchantment."

"KEEP TRYING," said Theo, and he handed her a spare pickaxe. "You'll get the right enchantment eventually." He just hoped it happened before they ran out of materials in their inventory.

"THAT DID IT!" Harper said after the third try. She lifted the glowing tool from the enchanting table and tossed it to Ash, who was closest to the nest.

Ash smiled, and her new pickaxe seemed to glow more brightly as it swung through the air, cutting the bees' nest loose from the tree.

Harper caught the nest and carried it to safety.

Theo hoped that would be enough. He hoped the bee being wasn't lost to them forever.

But as he looked over the smoldering ruins of the forest . . . beneath the growing wound in the sky . . .

He found it hard to be very hopeful at all.

Chapter 5

FLIGHT OF THE HONEYBEE. FRIGHT OF THE STUDENTS. A CHANCE TO JOIN THE DANCE!

The next day in science class, Po was still feeling guilty. He had known the trident wasn't a toy. And he really, really should have realized that leaving it in the middle of a forest was a bad idea.

"You didn't do it on purpose," Morgan said. "Don't be so hard on yourself."

"And that goes double for me," said Jodi. "Right?"

"*You* should have known better," said Morgan. "I mean, a mutant sheep beast? Even if that was possible, why would you want to see it?"

"A sheep beast would have been able to protect itself from wolves. It might have protected other sheep, too," said Jodi. Morgan raised an eyebrow. "Well, it *seemed* like a good idea at the time!"

"It really did," said Po. **"Your sister can be very convincing."**

Class hadn't started yet, and Po was just pulling out his textbook when Harper slumped into a nearby seat.

"Everything okay?" asked Morgan.

"I was up late reading about bees," answered Harper. "I wanted to get a head start on today's lesson."

Po nodded sagely. "Yeah, doing extra homework would bum me out, too."

"No, you don't understand," said Harper. "I ended up reading about something called *colony collapse disorder*. It's when an entire colony of bees just . . . dies. Scientists don't totally understand why, but it's happening a lot." **She dropped her head on the desk.** "You know how I get when I start worrying about the environment."

"Man," said Morgan. **"Everyone has a lot of feelings today, huh?"**

"Bees," Doc said so suddenly and so forcefully that Po jolted to attention. "They are marvels of nature. Without them, we would have no fruits! No flowers! And . . . no honey!"

Po gasped. **"But . . . but my mom puts honey in her peanut butter and honey sandwiches.** It's a key ingredient!"

"You have the humble honeybee to thank for your sandwiches, Po," said Doc. She thought about it for moment. "You should also thank your mother. Honestly, you're probably old enough to be making your own sandwiches."

Po gasped again.

Their classmate, Shelly Silver, raised her hand. "But *why* do bees make honey?" she asked. "They aren't just doing it to be nice, are they?"

"No indeed," said Doc. "Bees make honey so that they'll have something to eat during the winter, when there are no flowers in bloom. Typically, a bee's diet consists of nectar. That's why you'll see them buzzing around flowers so often."

Theo entered the classroom late, which was unusual for him. "I'm so sorry, Doc," he said. "I was with Ms. Minerva. She . . . uh, she wanted me to read this note to you."

"Go ahead," said Doc.

Theo cleared his throat, then read aloud from

a sheet of paper. "Dear Doc, Please excuse Theo's tardiness to science class. **He is a member of our school's newest extracurricular club, the Woodsword Gardening and Landscaping Club.** We have our work cut out for us ever since *someone* thought it would be a good idea to have a hundred students all trample the front yard. Sincerely, Ms. Minerva." Theo grinned bashfully. "And she drew a little smiley face. But it sort of looks like it's scowling. . . ."

"Thank you for your service to our school, Theo," said Doc. "Please have a seat, and I'll compose a reply for you to take back to Minerva. Honestly, if she'd just used my combination lawn mower, woodchipper, and hedge trimmer, the yard would be in fine shape by now. 'Too many blades,' she said."

Theo slipped into his seat, obviously less than enthusiastic about running notes back and forth between the teachers.

Po gave him a little pat on the back and a sympathetic smile.

"The problem here is that Minerva is a bit of a queen bee . . . and so am I," said Doc. "A bee colony has only one queen—no more and no less."

"What other sorts of bees are there?" asked Morgan. **"King bees? Royal vizier bees?"** **"Court jester bees?"** asked Po.

Doc shook her head. "Aside from the queen, every adult bee in the colony is either a drone or a worker. The drones are male bees. They have no stinger, and they stay behind to tend to the queen. But the workers, ah! The workers are female bees, and they go out and explore the world."

As if Doc had somehow summoned it, a bee flew in through the open window. The teacher smiled, obviously happy to have a visitor.

"It's a bee!" cried Morgan.

"Look out, here it comes!" yelled Po.

Someone screamed, and then half the kids in class were on their feet, ducking and dodging to stay out of the bee's path.

"Students, students!" said Doc. She held up her hands to signal for calm. **"There's no reason to panic."**

"Sure there is," said Po, and he kept his eyes on the bee as he spoke. "Bees use their stingers to inject venom. The venom can cause pain, irritation, and even an allergic reaction."

"Aw," said Harper. "You *did* do the homework."

"A bee uses its stinger to defend its hive and its queen," said Doc. "They aren't aggressive, and they won't attack unless you give them a reason to."

"So we should all just stay calm," said Harper. **She walked toward the bee and, with a sheet of paper, guided the insect back out the window.**

"Well!" said Doc. "That was one

worker bee who had a little adventure. She didn't find any nectar in here, so she'll keep looking."

"**What will the worker bee do when she finds nectar?**" asked Jodi. "Imagine she finds a garden that's full of flowers—full of food! She can't bring it all back by herself, can she?"

"No, she cannot. She'll need help," said Doc. "Where do you think she'll find it? What would *you* do?"

"**I would go back to my hive,**" said Po. "I'd want to tell all the other worker bees about the garden. Then they could help me bring back all the nectar."

"But how are you going to do that, Po?" said Doc. "**You're a bee! You can't talk.**"

"Oh," said Po. "Uh . . . could I point?"

"You're not far off," said Doc. "When a honeybee wants to communicate with the hive . . . they communicate with movement. Through a complicated series of gestures, they can relay information about where to find a food source, as well as the quality and quantity of the food there."

Jodi couldn't help imagining—**because**

her imagination was always a little wild—Doc dancing with a human-sized bee at a fancy party. They looked so elegant as they danced around and around.

"I'm sorry," said Po. "But are you saying . . . that bees *dance* to communicate?"

"That's what I'm saying," confirmed Doc.

Po's jaw dropped. He could feel his eyes go wide.

"I want to be more like a bee," he said. "Less talk! More rhythmic movement." Po performed a bold interpretive dance with his arms, making full use of his wrists and fingers. It looked like he was weaving spells in the air. Jodi joined in, waving her hands above her head.

"This dance is communicating . . . that

Harper should cheer up!" said Jodi.

Harper laughed. "Well, it's working!"

"I think Jodi and Po have the right idea," said Doc. "Come on, class. Let's all be a little more . . . bee."

The class cheered. Some of them stood. Some stayed seated. **But they all danced to their own imagined beat.**

And Po couldn't help feeling like he had the very best colony a kid could ask for.

Chapter 6

IN A WORLD OF EMAILS, TEXTS, AND POP-UP ADS, THE MESSAGE HAS BEEN RECEIVED . . . SORT OF.

Harper laughed when she saw Po's new Minecraft skin.

"Do you like *thizzz*?" he said.

"Very much," said Harper. "In fact, I'd say that outfit is very *bee*-coming."

Po, naturally, had found a bee skin. It was yellow with brown stripes, with short antennae sticking out from the head and a couple of wings in the back.

"Do the wings work?" asked Jodi.

"I wish," said Po. "But no. They're just for show."

"IT'S TOO BAD WE DON'T HAVE ANY ELYTRA WINGS," said Morgan. "Then you'd be able to fly. Or glide, at least."

"You know, I might be able to do something about that," said Theo. "I could import some elytra into this version of the game from my home computer."

"Maybe not until we've solved that," said Morgan, and he pointed up at the Fault. **"I DON'T THINK WE SHOULD BE MESSING WITH THE CODE RIGHT NOW. WE COULD MAKE THINGS WORSE."**

"We sort of did make things worse," said Jodi, and she gazed miserably out at the ruined forest. Most of the trees and flowers had burned away entirely. **"I FEEL ROTTEN ABOUT CAUSING SO MUCH DAMAGE."**

"Me too," said Po. "I think we should stay here for a little while. Maybe we can repair the forest."

"No way!" said Theo. "The butterflies—the

mission! That's all that matters."

"Aren't you in the landscaping club?" said Po. **"I'D SAY THIS AREA NEEDS SOME LANDSCAPING."**

"That's in real life," said Theo. "The flower forest isn't a real place with real plants, remember? It's just programmed to appear that way. It doesn't really matter if it looks nice or not."

"I'm with Theo," said Morgan. "The fire was a huge distraction. We need to get back to our mission."

"MAYBE THIS IS THE MISSION," said Jodi. "Maybe we need to fix our mistake."

"*That* is what we need to fix," said Morgan, pointing to the Fault again. "We're clearly running out of time."

"Ash would agree with Po and me, I bet," said Jodi.

"Ash isn't here today," said Morgan. **"SHE HAD A SCOUT MEETING AT HER NEW SCHOOL."** He turned to Harper. "So it's up to Harper to cast the deciding vote."

Harper squirmed a little. She didn't enjoy being

the decision maker for the entire group. And she could see both points of view so clearly!

But it felt wrong to leave such damage and destruction in their wake. "What's a flower forest biome without flowers and trees?" she said. **"We can fix this place up a little and keep an eye out for bees and butterflies at the same time.** As a matter of fact . . ." From her inventory, Harper pulled out the nest they'd saved.

"I'd forgotten that!" said Theo.

"I've been studying it," said Harper. "I think there are bees inside, but they won't come out while I'm holding it. SO THE FIRST STEP OF OUR FOREST RESTORATION PROJECT CAN BE FINDING A NEW TREE FOR THIS NEST."

"That feels like a good compromise," said Morgan.

"I actually have some flowers in my inventory," said Jodi. "I was going to use them to make dyes, but I could replant them here instead."

"And I've got a couple saplings," said Theo, holding up a small tree. "I picked them up when

I was gathering wood recently. I bet we could get some more in a nearby biome."

"*Buzz buzz,*" said Po. "I like *thizz* plan!"

They got to work. And Harper found herself having fun. When they'd reacted to the fire, they had all tried different tactics. The energy had been frantic, and they'd all panicked a little. But now they were working together as a team.

They discussed where to put each flower. **"THESE DANDELIONS LOOK SO HAPPY IN THIS PATCH OF SUNLIGHT,"** said Jodi.

They worked out the best place to plant saplings. "If we put four of them together like this, they'll grow into a single big tree," said Morgan.

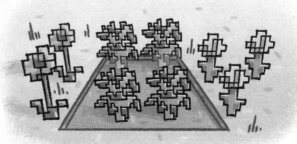

They all looked for the perfect spot to leave the bees' nest. "That oak tree looks *juzzt* right," said Po, pointing.

Harper did the honors. She climbed a staircase of dirt and placed the nest high in the tree. Almost as soon as she did so, it buzzed with activity.

"It's working," said Harper, hopping back down the staircase. "Here they come!"

Three bees emerged from the nest.

They spread out in the air around the tree.

"I think they approve of their new home," said Jodi with delight.

"But will they swarm together again?" asked Morgan. "Will they form a shape and finish what they were saying before?"

Harper shook her head. "Three bees aren't enough. I don't hear any more buzzing out there." She frowned. **"I THINK**

THESE ARE THE ONLY BEES TO SURVIVE
THE FIRE."

"And they look . . . glitched," said Theo. He
couldn't keep the disappointment from his voice.
"Look. They're just making the same movements
over and over again."

Theo was right. Each bee was making a different
motion, seemingly caught in a type of loop. "That
one's just moving in circles," said Harper.

"Movement," said Po. Then his eyes lit up
beneath his antennae. "What if the movements
mean something?" he said. "Just like in real life.
THEY COULD BE TRYING TO COMMUNICATE
WITH MOTION!"

The bees suddenly buzzed in unison, as if in
agreement.

"Is the circle supposed to be a zero?" asked
Theo.

"Or the letter *O*!" said Jodi. "Because this one
looks like it's making a capital *P*."

"Aw, you guys," said Po. "THEY'RE
SPELLING MY NAME!"

Harper laughed. "I think it's a coincidence.

Because the third bee is making the letter *R*."

"'Pro'?" said Morgan. "Short for professional? Does that mean anything to anyone?"

"It could be an abbreviation," said Theo. "Like FBI stands for Federal Bureau of Investigations."

Harper tried to puzzle it out. "PRO could stand for all sorts of things. Or it could be POR, OPR . . ."

Morgan groaned. **"THIS IS IMPOSSIBLE."**

"Not impossible," said Harper. "But we need to do some studying." She smiled. **"WHO'S UP FOR A LITTLE RESEARCH IN THE LIBRARY TOMORROW?"**

Chapter 7

TIME TO HIT THE BOOKS!
BUT NOT LITERALLY,
BECAUSE THAT WOULD
BE RUDE.

The next day after school, **Morgan and his friends gathered at the Stonesword Library, as they often did.**

But this time, they didn't head right for the computers and VR goggles. Morgan went to the information desk instead.

"Hi, Mr. Mallory," he said, greeting the media specialist. "What sorts of books do you have on codes and ciphers?"

Instead of answering him, Mr. Mallory tapped on the desk.

"Uh," said Morgan. "Mr. Mallory, did you hear me?"

The media specialist broke into a grin. "I guess you don't know Morse code," he said. "I just tapped out an answer to your question: we have *many* books on that topic. Come on, follow me!"

Within a few minutes, Morgan had joined Harper, Po, and Jodi in a small conference room **to work through the stack of books Mr. Mallory had pulled for them.** Harper was using her smartphone to search for online resources, too.

"This is a lot to wrap our heads around," said Po, rubbing his temple.

"I'll admit, I wish Theo were here," said Morgan. "He's good with brainteasers."

"I hope he's good at gardening, too," said Jodi. "I saw him with Ms. Minerva's landscaping club when I was walking here."

"Oh!" said Harper as her phone chimed. "Ash is calling me back. Hang on. . . ."

Harper set her phone up against a stack of books. Ash's face appeared on the screen, and she waved in greeting

"Hi, team!" she said. "Harper filled me in earlier. I'm here to help any way I can."

Morgan could feel himself growing calmer. Ash usually had that effect. Morgan liked to think of himself as the team's leader, but that wasn't always an easy thing to be. He had long ago realized that Ash was a natural problem solver. She also had a calm, confident energy that made challenges seem less overwhelming.

Jodi held the library's hamster up to the screen. "Say hello to Duchess Dimples, Ash!"

Ash bowed. "It's an honor to see you again, my duchess."

The hamster squeaked with pleasure.

"Okay, Ash," said Harper. "We've started in on all the books at Stonesword. Do you want focus on abbreviations?"

"I still think the answer could be 'Please reheat oatmeal,'" said Po.

Morgan sighed. "I put it on the list, but I have a lot of doubt about it."

"I'm on it," said Ash. "And actually . . . what do you guys think if I ask some of my fellow scouts to help?"

Morgan's cheeks prickled. "I don't know about that," he said, without even really stopping to think about it first.

Harper peered at him over his open book. **"Why not?"** she asked. "If we're looking for an abbreviation, we're talking about thousands of possibilities. The more people sharing ideas, the faster it will go."

"Yeah," Morgan said. "I know. It's just . . ."

"Morgan doesn't like to share his toys," said Jodi. "He's always been that way."

Morgan scowled. "Only because my little sister used to *break* every toy she *borrowed.*"

"I understand where you're coming from, Morgan," Harper said. "After all, we haven't told anyone about Doc's VR goggles. People think we're just playing regular Minecraft every day, not transporting to a virtual world where we're trying to rescue a broken artificial intelligence."

Po laughed. "I'm not sure people would believe us if *did* tell them."

"Harper's right," said Morgan. **"I like keeping the secret of the goggles to ourselves.** And I like having a club that feels special and is just ours. Remember, I wasn't very welcoming to Ash or to Theo."

"And look how that turned out," Jodi said. "It feels like they've *always* been part of the team."

Morgan thought about it for a long moment.

"Okay," he said at last. **"We need more people working on this puzzle.** Just . . . don't tell them more than they need to know, okay?"

"Got it," said Ash. "Thanks, Morgan. I'll hang up now and get to work."

After that, they returned to their books, poring over the pages for any hint at how to translate the bees' message. Twenty minutes passed in silence before Mr. Mallory appeared in the doorway.

"I found another book," he said. "Although I feel bad interrupting. **look at this hive mind at work!**"

"Hive mind?" said Po. "What does that mean?"

"I was just pointing out how well you were all working together," said Mr. Mallory. "A hive mind

is a phenomenon you see in social insects, like the bees we're keeping here on the library grounds. It refers to the idea that every individual insect is doing its own thing . . . but they're all contributing to the good of the colony. **Almost like the bees were little parts of a single organism— like how your bodies are made up of lots and lots of little cells."**

Morgan had a thought. "Mr. Mallory?" he said. "What would happen if most of the colony wasn't there anymore?"

Mr. Mallory thought about it. "Well, if there weren't enough bees to perform all the tasks, then the colony would suffer. Perhaps it would be wiped out entirely." He shrugged. "But if there was still a queen bee to lay eggs, then the lost bees would be replaced. The new bees could take over for any bees that were lost, growing up to be either a drone or a worker."

A huge grin spread over Morgan's face. "Thanks, Mr. Mallory. That was a big help."

"It was?" said the media specialist. "Well, okay. **I'm not sure what hive minds have to do**

with codebreaking." He smiled. "But I do like it when kids are enthusiastic about learning. Maybe I should have been a teacher. . . ."

As Mr. Mallory departed, Morgan turned to his friends. "I think that's the answer," said Morgan. "I don't think there are enough bees left after the fire to give us the whole message." He snapped his fingers. **"They're probably spelling out what they were going to say before the lightning struck!"**

"We don't need to crack a code," Harper said with a sudden revelation. "We need to breed more Minecraft bees!"

"That's right," said Morgan. "Once the bee colony is large enough, every bee will contribute to the message." He looked at the clock. "I don't know if we have enough time to play today, but if we meet up tomorrow—"

Just then, Theo

73

came barging into the room looking for Harper. His nose was pink from the sun, and he wore thick gardening gloves. "You're still here," he said. "Thank goodness!"

"You're just in time, Theo," said Harper. "We've had a breakthrough."

"That'll have to wait," said Theo. "I was heading here from the school . . . **and I walked past the beehive that Mr. Shane left behind, and—**"

"What is it?" asked Harper.

"There's something wrong with the bees," said Theo. "They're sick. **I think the bees are dying.**"

Chapter 8

ALAS, POOR BUZBY!
WE HARDLY KNEW YE.
(SNIFF.)

Harper knelt in the grass beside the beehive. Some of the bees seemed fine. They flew to and from the hive on their errands, buzzing as they went.

Other bees were obviously not well. They were having trouble flying. Harper saw one drop right out of the sky, and she went to pick up the little creature.

"Careful," warned Morgan. "You don't want to get stung."

"These gardening gloves are thick," said Theo. **"Here, Harper, use this extra pair."**

With one glove each, Harper and Theo worked

their way through the grass, lifting honeybees off the ground and placing them back atop the hive. "At least they won't be stepped on," said Harper. "But we still don't know what's causing the problem."

"Oh no!" said Jodi. **"It's too late for this one."** She cradled a bee in her palm. It was completely still, curled up in a little ball.

"Poor guy," said Po. **"We should give him a proper burial."**

"You all should set that up," said Harper. "I'm off to see a doctor."

Harper needed answers. And she knew only one place to go in order to get them.

"Doc!" she said, storming into the school lab. "Something's wrong with the bees."

At last, a bit of luck: Doc was still there, even though school had ended nearly an hour ago. **She looked up from an experiment in progress,** flipping her safety goggles up to her forehead. "Harper? What is it?"

Harper held out a gloved hand. She had a bee in her palm. The bee was alive but very still. It didn't try to fly away. It didn't try to do anything at all.

"This one dropped right out of the sky," she said. **"The same thing happened to several of them. One of them died."**

"Bring it here," said Doc. "Let's take a closer look."

Doc rummaged through her drawers until she found a device Harper had never seen before. **It looked almost like a microscope, but instead of sitting on a table, it fit over Doc's face.** She watched as Doc fiddled with the settings. "Place the bee on my desk," she said, and Harper did as she was told.

Doc leaned over the bee. The device whirred and clicked. **"This is a magnification device of my own making,"** she said. "Handy when examining anything smaller than a salamander but too big for a microscope."

"What are you looking for?" asked Harper.

"Parasites," answered Doc. "It's a common problem for bees. Little red mites will affix themselves to the bee's body and suck it dry." She shook her head. "I don't see any sign of them on this one, however."

She looked at Harper.

Her eye looked huge through the magnification lenses.

"There must be some other problem," Doc said. "I'll take a look at the hive and see what I can find."

"I'm coming with you," said Harper.

While Doc examined the beehive, Jodi approached Harper with a matchbox. "Buzby is in here," said Jodi. "Theo is digging a little hole for him, and Morgan is going to give the eulogy."

Morgan's eyes went wide. **"I am? But I didn't**

even know him!"

"Morgan!" Po said in a scolding tone. "Don't speak ill of the dead."

Morgan tugged at his collar. "I guess I could come up with something nice to say."

Theo was on his knees, using his garden trowel to dig up dirt at the base of a tree.

"This is a nice spot, Theo," said Harper. "Good choice."

Theo nodded, then wiped the sweat from his brow. "That should be deep enough," he said.

Jodi carefully lowered the box into the hole. "Go ahead, Morgan," she said.

"Uh, we gather here today to pay our respects to a fallen honeybee," said Morgan. **"I used to be afraid of bees, but now I know they aren't so scary.** And since he was a drone, Buzby didn't even have a stinger. So . . . I guess he was all right, in my book."

"He just wanted to hang out at home and eat honey," said Po. "I totally get that."

They all stood in silence, looking down at the little box in the hole. Theo lifted his trowel. "Anything else?" he asked. "Or should I fill the hole now?"

"I have something to say," said Harper. She put her hands over her heart and closed her eyes. "I'm sorry this happened to you, Buzby. I'm sorry that the world wasn't a safer place for you."

"We're all sorry, Buzby," said Jodi.

"But we're going to do something about it," promised Harper. "We're going to figure out what happened to you. And we're going to save the rest of your colony. No matter what it takes."

Chapter 9

LET'S GIVE NATURE A HAND. . . . AFTER ALL, NATURE GAVE US HANDS TO START WITH!

There was nothing more they could do for the Stonesword bees. Doc needed time to run tests, but she promised to tell Harper as soon as she'd learned anything.

In the meantime, **the kids had a flower forest biome to rebuild.** Their saplings had already grown into adult trees, but the Minecraft bees wouldn't multiply on their own.

"Okay, Morgan," said Harper. "You're the expert. How do we breed bees?"

"It's easy," Morgan answered. **"TO START, WE JUST NEED FLOWERS."**

"Oh!" said Po, who was dressed as a giant

flower. "It's so nice to be needed."

Theo rolled his eyes. "You won't be so happy when the bees mistake you for lunch," he said.

"IT'S WORKING!" said Jodi, and she ran past them, laughing. She held a purple allium flower in her hand, and a bee was following her wherever she went.

"We don't know how many bees we'll need in order to receive their message," said Morgan. "But let's assume it's a big number. We'll want a lot of flowers."

"WE CAN EXPLORE THE NEARBY BIOMES," said Harper. "We'll gather whatever flowers we find and bring them back here."

"Even better if we find some bone meal," said Theo. "That will encourage new flowers to grow."

"PICKING FIGHTS WITH SKELETONS?" said Po. "Who knew that raising bees would be so adventurous?"

The work went quickly once everyone had their assignments. Jodi in particular enjoyed the task of finding various flowers, and Theo liked replanting them in the flower forest. Morgan proved adept at flushing skeletons out of caves and leading them into an ambush. Po especially liked defeating the undead mobs while dressed as a flower.

Harper took on the task of breeding more bees. She would wait until Jodi and Theo had an extra flower to spare, then she would feed the flower to the nearest bee. Soon, several little baby bees fluttered through the forest.

"They need a place to live," Harper said of the baby bees. "There's no room for them in the nest."

"I've got an idea for that," said Morgan. **"BUT WE NEED HONEYCOMB FIRST."**

Morgan showed Harper how the Minecraft bees acted much like their real-world counterparts. "Watch," he said. "The bees will fly to a flower to collect nectar. Then they'll return to their nest to make honey with it."

Harper noticed that little flecks of yellow stuck to the bees' bodies when they interacted with a flower. **"IS THAT POLLEN?"** she asked.

"Yeah," said Morgan. "Again, it's just like real life. The bees get pollen on them, and the pollen spreads all over the forest. It can make some plants grow faster. Crops and berry bushes, for instance."

"We should plant some berry bushes," Harper suggested. "I think they'd look nice in our forest."

Sometime later, after the sun had gone down, Harper saw what Morgan had been waiting for. "Look," she said. **"THEIR NEST IS DRIPPING WITH HONEY."**

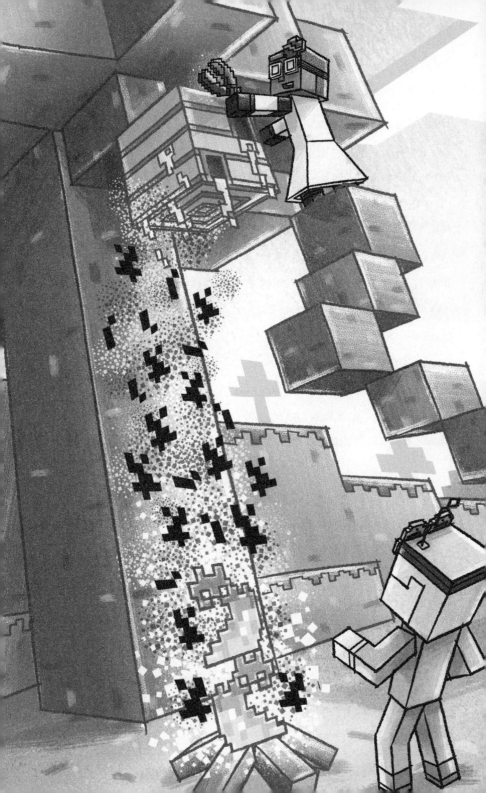

"We'll have to be careful with this next part," he said. "Since it's night, the bees are inside their nest, and we don't want to upset them. Get your shears ready. But don't use them until I say."

Harper watched as Morgan lit a campfire beneath the honey-heavy nest. **"SMOKE FROM THE FIRE WILL KEEP THE BEES CALM,"** he said. "Now you can use the shears on the nest to cut away some honeycomb."

Harper did just as he said. With a quick snip, several pieces of honeycomb fell into her inventory.

"Perfect," said Morgan. "With honeycomb and wood, we can make beehives, which means the new bees will have a place to live, and— Look out!"

Harper whirled around just in time to see a zombie lurching toward her. She ducked out of the path of its attack.

MISSING HER, THE ZOMBIE STRUCK A NEARBY BEE INSTEAD.

"Hey, watch it!" said Harper, and she drew her sword to defend the insect.

But to her surprise, the bee could take care of itself. It dove at the zombie, flipping around and striking the undead mob with its stinger. **The zombie flared red as it took damage.**

"Ooh, that looked like it hurt," said Harper.

"Only a little bit," said Morgan. "Normally, a bee will poison whatever it stings. But poison doesn't work on zombies."

"Then I'd better help it out," Harper said. With the zombie focused on the bee, **Harper easily finished off the undead mob with her sword.**

"Did you see that, Morgan?" Harper said. "That bee and I make a good team!"

But when she turned around, she saw Morgan

gazing at the bee. **"IT LOST ITS STINGER WHEN IT ATTACKED THE ZOMBIE,"** he said. **"IT CAN'T SURVIVE FOR LONG WITHOUT IT."**

And true to Morgan's word, the bee dropped moments later, disappearing in a cloud of dust.

"No!" said Harper. "Not when we were finally making progress!"

"I guess it's an important lesson," Morgan said. **"THESE BEES NEED TO BE PROTECTED, JUST LIKE THEIR REAL-WORLD COUSINS."**

Morgan held out a plank of wood and asked, "Do you have that honeycomb? We should get these bees a new home before there's any more trouble."

Chapter 10

HONEYBEES DON'T GET WEEKENDS OFF, BUT THEY DON'T GET POP QUIZZES, EITHER!

In the real world, it was the weekend, and Harper and her friends had decided to go on a fact-finding mission.

Harper's parents were more than a little confused by her request. "Are you sure you want to go to the orchard *today*?" they asked. "Apple-picking season is weeks away."

"That's *why* I want to go today," said Harper. "I'm not interested in the apples. I'm interested in the bees that are *pollinating* the apple blossoms."

In the end, they'd agreed, and they dropped Harper off at the orchard while they ran errands nearby.

Her friends were there waiting, and they'd already found Mr. Shane. **The man had traded his cowboy attire for a beekeeper suit.** He had taken the beehives off his truck and set them all over the orchard grounds. When Harper arrived, he had just removed a tray from one of the hives, and he was scraping fresh honey off of the tray and into a glass bottle. **Bees were crawling all over him, but he didn't seem to mind.**

Po frowned at the sight, though. "I'd go up and say hi," he said, "but even if bees aren't aggressive, I don't want to be outnumbered a hundred to one."

"I'll do it," said Harper, and she strode forward, waving her arms. "Hi!" she said. "Sorry! Mr. Shane? It's important!"

Theo grinned. "I guess she means business."

"She made a promise on Buzby's grave," Jodi reminded him. **"Nothing's more serious than that."**

Mr. Shane held up a hand to keep Harper from coming too close. He put the hive back together, grabbed the bottle of honey, and came toward them. "Can I help you?"

"We're hoping that *we* can help *you,* actually," Harper said. **"Your bees are in trouble. The ones you left by the school, I mean. And we're trying to find out why."**

Mr. Shane came closer, removing his helmet. The skin around his eyes crinkled as he smiled at them. "You must be Doc Culpepper's students," he said. "She called me about the problem. I'll tell you what I told her: it's sadly pretty common, these days." He sighed. "I lose a lot of bees."

"Why?" asked Harper. **"Why do honeybees need so much help to survive?"**

Mr. Shane tipped his head at her. "I'm happy to tell you more," he said. "But let's walk while we talk."

Harper had been to the orchard before, but never when the trees were in full bloom. It was a beautiful sight. "I didn't realize apple blossoms were so pretty," she said.

"They're pretty . . . and they're an important part of the natural balance," he said. "I'm sure Doc's told you all about how this works. Bees seek out flowers for nectar to eat. That's where honey comes from. But while the bees are getting what they need from the flowers . . . the flowers are getting what *they* need from the bees. The insects spread pollen from the flowers all around. Then the flowers become fruit, and the seeds from the fruit ensure that more trees grow." He patted a nearby tree trunk. **"It's a pretty good system. Worked well for millions of years.** Then people came along, and things got complicated."

Po crunched loudly into an apple.

"Oh," said Po. "Sorry! I didn't think that was going to be so noisy."

"Where did you even get that?" asked Theo. "There aren't any apples here yet!"

"It's from the grocery store," said Po.

"Aha!" said Mr. Shane. "See, that's interesting. We know it isn't apple season around here. The bees are only now doing the work of pollinating. But it's apple season somewhere—in another climate, maybe another hemisphere. And people have gotten used to having year-round access to every kind of fruit and vegetable you can imagine."

"Thafsa good fing," Po said around a mouthful of apple.

"It's not a bad thing—not always," agreed Mr.

Shane. "Believe me, I'm happy to have year-round access to avocados. But sometimes we put our own needs and our convenience ahead of the needs of the planet." **He shook his head.** "Truth is, this orchard shouldn't need an old cowboy coming through with a truck full of bees. The bees should be in this area year-round; they should find the orchard without my help. But we've got the environment all mixed up. You see this patch of wild growth over here?"

Mr. Shane had led them to the edge of the orchard, where tall grasses, weeds, and wildflowers grew in a tangle.

"What a mess!" said Theo, and he pulled out his garden trowel. "You want me to clean this up? **I'm getting good at landscaping."**

"You're proving my point for me, son," said Mr. Shane. "You think this looks chaotic. You think it needs to be fixed. **But this is nature!** And this is what bees need to survive." He clucked his tongue. "This town's perfect lawns might look nice in a picture, but bees starve without the tangled growth and bountiful flowers. And all the

herbicides, fungicides, and pesticides are murder on the poor fellows. Literally."

"**P-pesticides?**" said Theo. "Pesticides hurt the bees?"

"Naturally," said Mr. Shane. "Gardeners will spray poison to keep pests away. But poison hurts all sorts of creatures, not just the pests."

Harper watched as Theo went pale before her very eyes.

"**What's wrong, Theo?**" she asked.

"Woodsword's landscaping club," he said. "We

use that stuff. Herbicides, fungicides, pesticides . . . we were trying to fix up Woodsword's lawn, to make it look *better.*"

"Dude," said Po. "Stonesword is right across the street from the school. **All it would take is a breeze, and those chemicals would spread to the library.**"

"And I'm sure the bees can't resist crossing the street to visit the school's plants," Harper added.

"I've seen them," said Jodi. "They were buzzing right outside the window during homeroom yesterday."

"It's my fault, isn't it?" said Theo. **My new club is killing the bees!**"

Chapter 11

CLASH OF THE TEACHERS— OR JUST ANOTHER EPIC SCHOOL DAY AT WOODSWORD?!

"Let me talk to Ms. Minerva," said Theo. "I think she'll listen to me."

But he wasn't as confident as he tried to sound.

It was early Monday morning, and Harper and Theo had arrived early at school. Their mission was simple: **they had to convince Ms. Minerva to stop using harsh chemicals on Woodsword's lawn.**

It did not go as well as they had hoped.

"Can't you just move the bees?" asked Ms. Minerva.

"Well . . . ," said Theo, "I suppose . . ."

"We could move this particular hive," said

Harper. "But this is part of a bigger problem. **We want bees to thrive in this area.** It's better for the ecosystem if they do."

"*Not* if it means letting the schoolyard become overrun with weeds," said Ms. Minerva. "Nobody wants that. Your parents would be the first to write angry letters. A school needs to look presentable."

"But at what cost?" asked Harper. "Here, Ms. Minerva. I got this for you."

She handed the teacher an apple blossom.

"A flower? I don't understand."

"There's a tradition where students give teachers a bright, shiny apple. But an apple at this time of year would have to be shipped in from another country on a carbon-emitting plane or boat. And for the apple to be perfectly bright and shiny, that probably means the farmers used chemicals, and threw away anything with a blemish." **Harper shrugged.** "Maybe we should be happy with what we have."

"Hear, hear," said a voice from the doorway. Harper turned to see Doc. "I couldn't agree more,

Harper. And I'm eager to see what changes will be made to the landscaping club."

"Hold on," said Ms. Minerva. **"I haven't agreed to anything yet."**

"After such an impassioned speech?" said Doc. "If you'd been there for Buzby's funeral, you wouldn't be so heartless."

"Who in the world is Buzby?" asked Ms. Minerva.

"A fallen friend," said Doc. **"He was poisoned**

by the landscaping club."

Minerva rolled her eyes, clearly thinking, *Now what?!* "My club isn't poisoning anybody."

"Well, not on *purpose,*" said Theo.

"We've got a problem on our hands, Minerva," said Doc. "Fortunately, I've come up with some solutions."

"Oh, I can just imagine your solutions," said Ms. Minerva, and she squeezed the bridge of her nose. "A lot of sharp objects on wheels, roaming the school grounds?"

"I would phrase it as 'automated landscaping,'" argued Doc.

"I'd really prefer that you not replace my students with robots," said Ms. Minerva.

"It's your chemicals I want to replace," said Doc. "Listen, how sensitive is your nose? Because I've got a new fertilizer formula, but the result is *very* pungent. . . ."

Harper tried a few times to get a word in. But the teachers were firmly locked in their debate, with Doc pushing for the landscaping club to change the way it worked to something greener **. . . and possibly more technologically robust.** But she pushed too hard, relying on science that Ms. Minerva simply didn't trust.

When Harper and Theo finally slipped out of the classroom, the teachers didn't even seem to notice they were leaving.

Chapter 12

A SPELLING BEE TO REMEMBER! IF ANYONE (INCLUDING THE BEES) GETS OUT ALIVE . . .

Harper took comfort in the fact that things were going better in Minecraft than they'd been going at school.

"THIS IS IT!" said Jodi. She held up a bright blue cornflower. "This is the last flower we needed for our forest restoration project. Now we've got at least one of everything."

"Except blue orchids," said Theo. "They only grow in swamps, so they would be out of place here."

"SAME WITH SUNFLOWERS," said Morgan.

"Oh, and we didn't include Wither roses," added Theo. "For obvious reasons."

Jodi squinted her virtual eyes. "You guys are so *technical*. The point is, we're done gathering flowers. AND THEO AND I CAME UP WITH A DESIGN TO MAKE SURE OUR FLOWER FOREST IS AS BEAUTIFUL AS POSSIBLE."

Theo grinned. "We were inspired by the orchard, actually. All those perfect rows of planted trees. We wanted our forest to feel organized." He turned to Harper. "I think you'll like what we've done so far."

But when Harper saw the state of the forest, **she didn't like it one bit.**

"It's . . . nice," she said.

But she couldn't fool Theo.

"What?" he said. "WHAT'S WRONG?!"

Harper gazed out at the field of flowers, all organized by color and arranged in artful rows. It actually *did* look nice. But it didn't look like a flower forest biome. It looked like a garden rather than a natural space.

"I think we're worried too much about how it looks," suggested Harper. "WE SHOULD BE THINKING ABOUT WHAT THE BEES NEED."

"SHE'S GOT A POINT," said Morgan. "The bees will only leave their hives if there are flowers nearby. We should move some of these flowers, to make sure that happens."

Theo slapped his forehead. "I'm doing it again, aren't I? It's the same mistake I made in the real world!" He shook his head. "I just like symmetry. And order. I like things to be neat and to make sense."

"I know," said Harper. "And that's a really good thing when you're programming or doing a research project. Or cleaning your room!" She put her arm around him. **"BUT NATURE DOESN'T MIND A LITTLE CLUTTER. AND WE SHOULD LEARN TO BE OKAY WITH THAT."**

Theo sighed. "Technically, this isn't nature. It's a randomized digitally generated re-creation." Harper started to react, but he smirked good-naturedly and quickly added, "Still, I know what you mean."

"I don't know what *anybody* is talking about," said Jodi. "Just keep the yellow flowers close to the purple flowers, okay? They're complementary!"

With the final flowers in place, the forest was alive again. **Harper saw chickens, a rabbit . . . and bees.**

They'd successfully bred and created homes for a great number of bees.

"There they go," she said. "That one is making a P again. And an R . . . O . . . T . . ."

"Eep, hold on!" said Jodi. "There's a spider over there! Two of them, in fact."

Harper turned to look. Jodi was right. Two spiders skittered beneath nearby trees.

"It should be fine," said Theo. **"IT'S LIGHT OUT, SO THEY WON'T BE HOSTILE."**

"But that will change when the sun goes down," said Morgan. "And if they get into a fight with the bees, we might have to start all over again."

"Jodi and I can take care of the spiders," said Po. "Easy. And to be honest, I'd rather do that than play Spelling Bee."

"Okay," Morgan said reluctantly. "But holler if you need help."

"You know me," said Po, and he drew his sword. "I scream really good when I'm in trouble."

"And sometimes when he isn't!" said Jodi, running after him.

Harper kept one eye on her friends and one eye on the bees. There was an *E* . . . and a *C* . . .

"They're telling us to protect someone," said Harper. "Or something."

"Check this out!" said Po, and **he pelted a spider with arrows.**

"Uh, we might need some help, actually," said Jodi. "There are . . . sort of a lot of . . ."

"I got this," Morgan said. "Spiders are so easy." He leapt into battle, swinging his sword.

"Should we help?" asked Theo.

"You go ahead," said Harper. **"I'LL SEE WHAT THE BEES HAVE TO SAY."**

"PROTECT THE . . . SOMETHING," said Theo. "Let me know!" And he joined the fray.

Harper spared a quick glance. There really were a lot of spiders all of a sudden. Where were they all coming from?

Fortunately, her friends were equal to the task. **The spiders didn't get anywhere close to the bees.** And the bees, one after another, performed their dance for Harper.

In the end, the wording of their message was clear, even if the meaning was not.

"PROTECT THE BALANCE," Harper said after the last bee had completed its movement. "Protect *what* balance?"

Before Harper could puzzle out the meaning, an alarming change came over the assembled bees.

Their eyes turned red.

Their buzzing grew more intense.

Some of them turned their stingers in her direction.

"Hey, everyone!" she yelled. "We have a problem here."

"Sort of busy!" Po shouted back.

And Harper realized she was trapped between hostile spiders on one side . . .

. . . and angry bees on the other **. . . and both were closing in on her fast!**

Chapter 13

ANGRY BEES TO THE LEFT OF ME! SPIDERS TO THE RIGHT! (BUT AT LEAST THERE'S GOOD SYMMETRY!)

Harper ran to rejoin her friends as quickly as she could.

It wasn't fast enough to avoid being stung in the back.

"OW!" she cried, and she felt the bee's poison weakening her. Worse, she knew that the bee that had stung her would die.

She didn't want that to happen. She didn't want to fight the bees. **She'd just spent days bringing them back from the brink of disaster!**

"What did you do?" asked Morgan.

"Nothing!" said Harper. She held up her shield,

blocking a dive-bombing bee. "They delivered their message, and then they got really mad."

Morgan swatted the nearest bee away with his hand, clearly afraid that a sword would do too much damage. "What was the message?" he asked.

"Protect the balance," Harper said. **"ARE THEY MAD BECAUSE WE AREN'T DOING THAT?"**

"Uh," said Po, also swatting a bee. "Jodi and I did sort of cause a forest fire."

"We're very sorry about it!" said Jodi as she ran in circles, pursued by angry bees.

"But we fixed that damage," said Theo. "We restored the balance. They should have forgiven us for that." As he focused on dodging a bee, a spider struck him from behind. "Yowch! Okay, this is ridiculous. *Where* are the spiders coming from?"

"I THINK THEY'RE COMING OUT OF THAT HOLE!" said Jodi, motioning over her shoulder as she ran past. "Over that way!"

Theo and Harper fought their way through the spiders, working in the direction Jodi had indicated. They found the hole, and inside it . . .

"A dungeon," said Theo. **"WE MUST HAVE**

MADE THIS HOLE BY ACCIDENT WHEN WE WERE LANDSCAPING."

"And there's a spawner inside," said Harper. She could see the glow of its fire, flickering in the dark. The spawner would keep making spiders as long as they could defeat them.

"I'VE GOT TO DESTROY IT," Theo said. "That'll take care of the spiders, at least." He traded his sword for a pickaxe and carved a bigger hole, giving him easy access to the spawner.

He raised his pickaxe, ready to destroy it.

And Harper yelled, **"STOP!"**

Theo did stop, but his confusion was obvious. "Why am I stopping?" he asked, holding his pickaxe just above the spider spawner.

"The bees' message," Harper said. "The balance. **WE'RE DISRUPTING THE BALANCE!** We had no right to attack the spiders like we did. We started the fight. Just like we started the fire."

"So what can we do about it now?" asked Theo.

"We can leave," said Harper. "We put this biome back together. Now we should . . . just leave it be."

Theo trusted Harper, but Morgan wasn't happy with

the plan. "It feels like we're retreating," he said. "Like we're giving up."

Then another stingerless bee fell at his feet, and he reconsidered. "But it's obvious that we're causing harm to the bees all over again." He sighed. "Okay. Let's get out of here."

Harper and her friends fled the forest as quickly as they could. The spiders soon gave up the chase, dropping their hostility and returning to their business. The bees, however, pursued the group to the very edge of the forest.

"MAYBE THEY WON'T FOLLOW US INTO THE TAIGA," said Po.

But as they watched, the bees flew above the trees of the flower forest in a great black swarm.

They roiled and rippled like a dark cloud before descending. The swarm was aiming directly for the kids.

Harper hefted her shield, ready for another fight. . . .

But the swarm didn't attack. The bees moved in an intricate dance, once more positioning themselves into a shape that looked humanoid. The buzzing noise of their wings grew louder, and then harmonized.

The buzzing once more sounded like a voice.

"Zzank youz . . . ," it said. *"For rezztoring zee balance. Rezzpecting. Protect-zing."*

Harper stepped forward. She tried to look the

being in its eyes, but it didn't have any. Or rather, it had too many. **The eyes of dozens of bees all looked back at her.**

"You're . . . you're welcome," she said. "We'll be more careful in the future. We care about this place."

"WE WANT TO FIX THE FAULT!" Theo added, stepping forward. "Please. **CAN YOU HELP US?"**

"Findz. Findz . . . golem," said the bees. *"Findzzz*

golem . . . or elzzzzze."

Their message delivered, the buzzing bees fused together in a flash of light . . . to form the missing arm of the Evoker King.

A kaleidoscope of butterflies lowered the piece of her friend gently into Harper's outstretched hands. They dispersed as soon as she gripped it.

Chapter 14

ALL'S WELL THAT ENDS WELL...EXCEPT FOR THAT BIG HOLE IN THE SKY.

A few days later, Harper wore her new T-shirt to an afterschool ceremony. As the newest member of the **Woodsword Gardening and Landscaping Club,** she wanted to show off her club pride.

"Thank you all for coming," said Shelly Silver. She stood before Woodsword's new garden. Harper hoped it would be the first of many.

Shelly continued, "As class president, it's my honor to preside over the grand opening of the school's first wild garden. Free of chemicals, the plants and flowers within this garden will be allowed to grow naturally—**and will still give**

our gardening club an opportunity to work their green thumbs. It's only the start of a plan for expanding greener practices to all of Woodsword."

"We've chosen plants that are native to the area," added Ms. Minerva. "And the gardening and landscaping club is committing to pulling harmful weeds by hand—*without* resorting to chemicals . . . or robots." She smiled. "But Doc Culpepper did provide some wonderful ideas for improving the nutrients in our soil. So I guess it's fair to say she and I have buried the hatchet . . . just as we've buried some flower bulbs that will bloom next spring!"

The crowd cheered as Ms. Minerva used a pair of garden shears to cut the ribbon around the garden. The teacher smiled, and Harper understood why. Even though the garden was wild, it was well maintained. Instead of using harsh chemicals to make the garden look "nice," Theo and the rest of the club had promised to use elbow grease. **Pulling weeds the old-fashioned way would take the work of many hands.**

That was why Harper had agreed to sign up. **And it was why she gave Theo a big hug, right there in front of the garden.**

"Thank you for convincing Ms. Minerva to try this," she said. "I know she won't regret it."

Theo blushed. "*I definitely don't regret it.*"

"However," said Harper, and she took the gardening shears from Ms. Minerva. **"I do have some ideas about how to make our equipment more efficient.** I bet Doc has some digital technology that could really make these shears work wonders."

Ms. Minerva ran her hands through her hair. "Let's not go overboard, now, Harper."

Doc herself was just across the street, helping Mr. Shane retrieve the Stonesword hive. She called Harper over to say goodbye.

"I'll be back again, same time next year," said Mr. Shane. "In the meantime, enjoy some local apples and think of my bees, all right?"

"We will," promised Harper. **"I'm just sad the bees can't stay behind."**

"Well, speaking of that," said Mr. Shane. "You and your friends did such a good job taking care of them that I thought I'd leave you with a present. I can't leave a whole hive behind, of course . . ." **Mr. Shane handed Doc a tray from the hive.** It had several bees crawling on it. "But I can leave you with a few bees, including a brand-new queen. It's enough to start a colony of your very own."

Harper gasped with delight. **"We'll take good care of them,"** she promised.

"The whole landscaping club can work together to keep them happy and safe," said Theo. "They'll have all the flowers they could want."

"That's what I like to hear," said

Mr. Shane, and once he was done loading up his truck, he stepped into the cab. The tarp had been tied firmly in place, and **Harper knew the bees beneath it were off to their next adventure.**

But she had plenty of adventure to look forward to right here at home. And she was glad that the bees—some of them, at least— were here to stay.

In Minecraft, however, Harper's happy ending was soon forgotten in the face of a very large hole in the sky.

"THE FAULT'S GOTTEN EVEN BIGGER," she said. "I didn't think it was possible."

"I worry about what will happen when it fills the sky," Theo said, looking across the Overworld. "Will it spread to the ground beneath our feet?"

"It won't come to that," said Morgan. **"WE'LL FIND A WAY."**

"I believe you, Morgan," said Po, and he pointed. "Because I just saw a butterfly heading that way."

"Already?" said Jodi. "We're in luck!"

They all moved together as a group, pursuing the butterfly through a cluster of trees.

On the other side, a mass of the insects fluttered their colorful wings. **They were all flying around a familiar object.**

"So much for luck," said Harper. **"THAT'S A PORTAL TO THE NETHER."**

"I guess we know where we'll find **THE GOLEM,**" said Morgan. **"READY . . . OR NOT."**

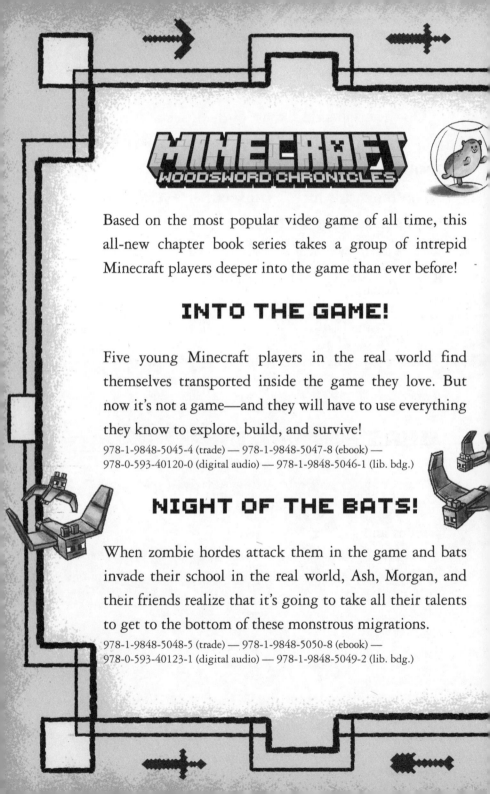

MINECRAFT
WOODSWORD CHRONICLES

Based on the most popular video game of all time, this all-new chapter book series takes a group of intrepid Minecraft players deeper into the game than ever before!

INTO THE GAME!

Five young Minecraft players in the real world find themselves transported inside the game they love. But now it's not a game—and they will have to use everything they know to explore, build, and survive!

978-1-9848-5045-4 (trade) — 978-1-9848-5047-8 (ebook) —
978-0-593-40120-0 (digital audio) — 978-1-9848-5046-1 (lib. bdg.)

NIGHT OF THE BATS!

When zombie hordes attack them in the game and bats invade their school in the real world, Ash, Morgan, and their friends realize that it's going to take all their talents to get to the bottom of these monstrous migrations.

978-1-9848-5048-5 (trade) — 978-1-9848-5050-8 (ebook) —
978-0-593-40123-1 (digital audio) — 978-1-9848-5049-2 (lib. bdg.)

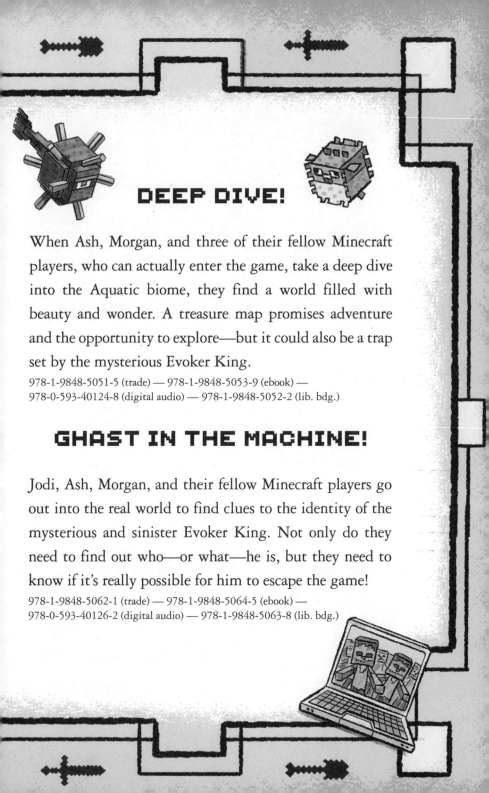

DEEP DIVE!

When Ash, Morgan, and three of their fellow Minecraft players, who can actually enter the game, take a deep dive into the Aquatic biome, they find a world filled with beauty and wonder. A treasure map promises adventure and the opportunity to explore—but it could also be a trap set by the mysterious Evoker King.

978-1-9848-5051-5 (trade) — 978-1-9848-5053-9 (ebook) — 978-0-593-40124-8 (digital audio) — 978-1-9848-5052-2 (lib. bdg.)

GHAST IN THE MACHINE!

Jodi, Ash, Morgan, and their fellow Minecraft players go out into the real world to find clues to the identity of the mysterious and sinister Evoker King. Not only do they need to find out who—or what—he is, but they need to know if it's really possible for him to escape the game!

978-1-9848-5062-1 (trade) — 978-1-9848-5064-5 (ebook) — 978-0-593-40126-2 (digital audio) — 978-1-9848-5063-8 (lib. bdg.)

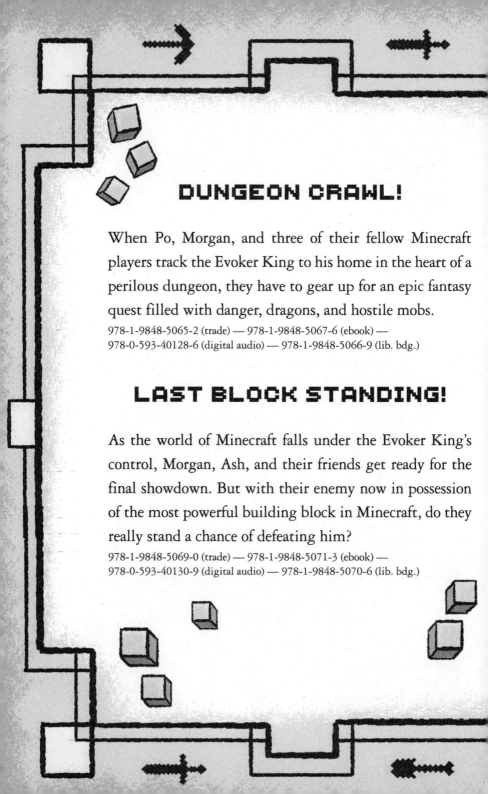

DUNGEON CRAWL!

When Po, Morgan, and three of their fellow Minecraft players track the Evoker King to his home in the heart of a perilous dungeon, they have to gear up for an epic fantasy quest filled with danger, dragons, and hostile mobs.

978-1-9848-5065-2 (trade) — 978-1-9848-5067-6 (ebook) —
978-0-593-40128-6 (digital audio) — 978-1-9848-5066-9 (lib. bdg.)

LAST BLOCK STANDING!

As the world of Minecraft falls under the Evoker King's control, Morgan, Ash, and their friends get ready for the final showdown. But with their enemy now in possession of the most powerful building block in Minecraft, do they really stand a chance of defeating him?

978-1-9848-5069-0 (trade) — 978-1-9848-5071-3 (ebook) —
978-0-593-40130-9 (digital audio) — 978-1-9848-5070-6 (lib. bdg.)

THE ADVENTURES CONTINUE IN

MINECRAFT STONESWORD SAGA

CRACK IN THE CODE!

Someone—or something—has turned the Evoker King to stone. And now a new player, Theo, has joined the team on their quest to return their former enemy to normal. Theo has modding skills that could come in handy, but does he have what it takes to be part of the team, or will his meddling put a crack in the game code that none of them will survive?

978-0-593-37298-2 (trade) — 978-0-593-37300-2 (ebook) —
978-0-593-40132-3 (digital audio) — 978-0-593-37299-9 (lib. bdg.)

MOBS RULE!

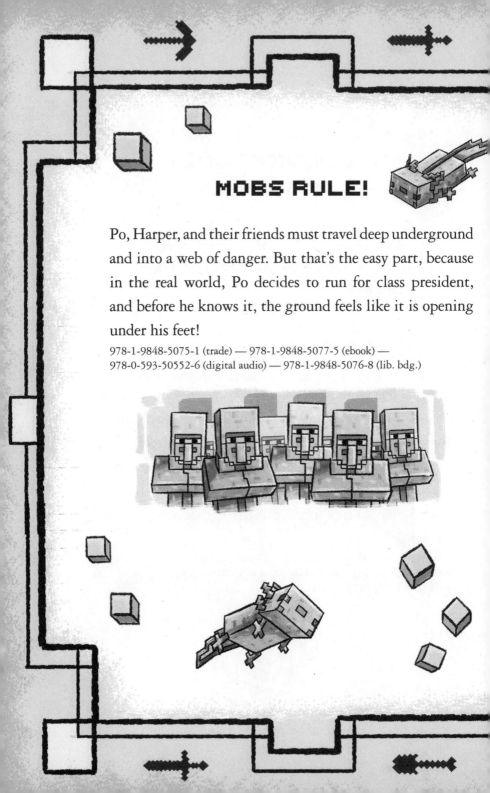

Po, Harper, and their friends must travel deep underground and into a web of danger. But that's the easy part, because in the real world, Po decides to run for class president, and before he knows it, the ground feels like it is opening under his feet!

978-1-9848-5075-1 (trade) — 978-1-9848-5077-5 (ebook) — 978-0-593-50552-6 (digital audio) — 978-1-9848-5076-8 (lib. bdg.)

NEW PETS ON THE BLOCK!

When the third piece of the Evoker King takes the form of a Minecraft witch and sends Jodi, Morgan, and their friends on a quest to bring back an extremely rare animal mob, Jodi is determined to make sure that the mob stays safe no matter what!

978-1-9848-5094-2 (trade) — 978-1-9848-5096-6 (ebook) —
978-0-593-55978-9 (digital audio) — 978-1-9848-5095-9 (lib. bdg.)

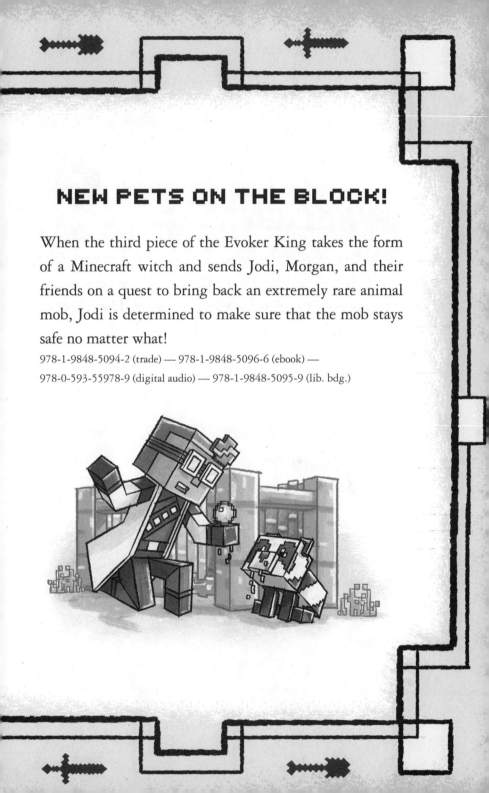

MINECRAFT is a game about placing blocks and going on adventures. Build, play, and explore across infinitely generated worlds of mountains, caverns, oceans, jungles, and deserts. Defeat hordes of zombies, bake the cake of your dreams, venture to new dimensions, or build a skyscraper. What you do in Minecraft is up to you.

Nick Eliopulos is a writer who lives in Brooklyn (as many writers do). He likes to spend half his free time reading and the other half gaming. He cowrote the Adventurers Guild series with his best friend and works as a narrative designer for a small video game studio. After all these years, Endermen still give him the creeps.

Alan Batson is a British cartoonist and illustrator. His works include *Everything I Need to Know I Learned from a Star Wars Little Golden Book, Everything That Glitters is Guy!,* and *Spider-Ham.* Being extremely fond of cubes and travel to exotic places, he has recently begun to lend his talents to several different books on adventures in the world of Minecraft.

Chris Hill is an illustrator living in Birmingham, England, with his wife and two daughters and has been loving it for twenty-five years! When he's not working, he spends time with his family and trying to tire out his dog on long walks. If there's any time left after that, he loves to go riding on his motorcycle, feeling the wind on his face while contemplating his next illustration adventure.

JOURNEY INTO THE WORLD OF
MINECRAFT

—BOOKS FOR EVERY READING LEVEL—

OFFICIAL NOVELS:

FOR YOUNGER READERS:

OFFICIAL GUIDES:

DISCOVER MORE AT READMINECRAFT.COM

NEW PETS ON THE BLOCK

© 2022 Mojang AB. All Rights Reserved. Minecraft, the Minecraft logo and the Mojang Studios logo are trademarks of the Microsoft group of companies.

Published in the United States by Random House Children's Books, a division of Penguin Random House LLC, 1745 Broadway, New York, NY 10019, and in Canada by Penguin Random House Canada Limited, Toronto. Random House and the colophon are registered trademarks of Penguin Random House LLC.

rhcbooks.com
minecraft.net

Library of Congress Cataloging-in-Publication Data is available upon request.
ISBN 978-1-9848-5094-2 (trade)
ISBN 978-1-9848-5095-9 (library binding) — ISBN 978-1-9848-5096-6 (ebook)

Cover design by Diane Choi

Printed in the United States of America

10 9 8 7 6

NEW PETS ON THE BLOCK

By Nick Eliopulos
Illustrated by Alan Batson and Chris Hill

Random House 🏠 New York

MORGAN

ASH

HARPER

AYERS!

PO

JODI

THEO

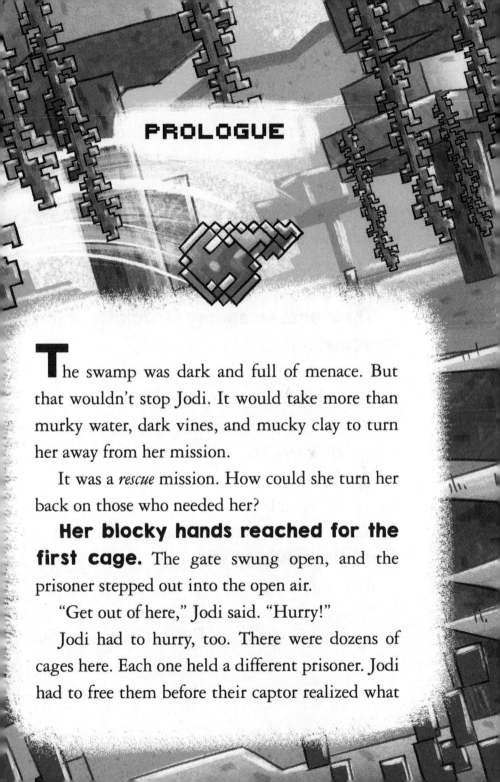

PROLOGUE

The swamp was dark and full of menace. But that wouldn't stop Jodi. It would take more than murky water, dark vines, and mucky clay to turn her away from her mission.

It was a *rescue* mission. How could she turn her back on those who needed her?

Her blocky hands reached for the first cage. The gate swung open, and the prisoner stepped out into the open air.

"Get out of here," Jodi said. "Hurry!"

Jodi had to hurry, too. There were dozens of cages here. Each one held a different prisoner. Jodi had to free them before their captor realized what she was doing. Unless Morgan stopped her first.

"JODI, STOP!" he cried. "We need to talk about this."

But as far as Jodi was concerned, there was nothing to talk about. She opened another cage, and another.

That was as far as she got . . . before they were attacked.

Their unseen enemy struck from the shadows, quick and merciless.

Po was the first to fall.

Theo and Harper were next.

When Morgan was defeated, Jodi was all alone against their attacker.

She knew she had to be brave. She knew everyone was counting on her. She wouldn't back down!

But in the end, it didn't matter. **This was a fight she couldn't win.**

And as Jodi fell to her knees, cursed by some foul magic . . . their enemy laughed.

Jodi wondered if it would be the last sound she ever heard.

Chapter 1

PLEASE HOLD YOUR QUESTIONS UNTIL THE END OF THE PRESENTATION! (BUT YOU CAN OOH AND AHH AS MUCH AS YOU LIKE.)

Jodi Mercado knew how important it was to dress for battle.

When fighting a boss mob, diamond armor was hard to beat.

When dodging fireballs, a shield was quite useful.

When confronting an Enderman, a pumpkin helmet was a smart accessory.

But when it came to a war of words in the real world . . . Jodi chose to wear her very best dress.

"As you can see, animals are adorable," she said. She aimed a red laser pointer at the screen behind her, drawing everyone's attention to the image of a cute, floppy-eared puppy. **She clicked a button on the pointer**—*click!*—and the image changed from the puppy to a kitten with a tiny pink nose. "I would like to hug every animal," she said. "Except for spiders." *Click! Click! Click!* The image changed from kitten to hedgehog to gerbil to gecko.

"Just look at those faces!" Jodi squealed enthusiastically. For a moment, she forgot all about her presentation.

Someone in the audience cleared their throat.

It was a gentle reminder to Jodi that she should stay on topic. She looked down at her notecards, where she had her entire speech written down.

"I love every kind of animal," she read from the final card. "And isn't love the greatest gift of all? Therefore, I think you will agree that I am ready for a pet of my own. Amen. The end. Thank you for listening!"

The small audience broke into eager applause. Jodi grinned from ear to ear as she looked out at them.

Her best friends were all there, gathered in a

meeting room in Excalibur County Public Library. **(They called it Stonesword Library, which was less of a mouthful.)**

Harper Houston cheered from her seat. A whiz with math and science, Harper had helped Jodi with the technological parts of her presentation. She had even created Jodi's one-of-a-kind laser pointer. **It looked like something right out of Minecraft!**

Po Chen whooped and hollered. He could be a goofball, but he was always supportive of his friends. During Jodi's presentation, he had laughed the loudest at her jokes.

Theo Grayson clapped politely. Theo was good with computers, but Jodi wasn't sure he liked animals very much. Even so, he had helped Jodi download all the pictures for her slideshow.

Ash Kapoor waved her hands in silent applause. Although Ash lived in a different city and couldn't be there in person, she had used video software to watch the presentation through Theo's laptop. Her smile lit up the screen.

Even the class hamster, Baron Sweetcheeks,

had his eyes on Jodi. He couldn't cheer for her, but Jodi felt that he was providing excellent emotional support.

Morgan Mercado was another story. Although he clapped, too, he seemed uncertain. Hesitant. Jodi knew her big brother well, and she could tell he was less excited than everybody else.

What was that about? After all, any pet Jodi brought into their home was a pet Morgan could hug, too.

He was probably thinking about Minecraft, Jodi decided. He usually was!

"So?" said Jodi. "What did everybody think? Is this enough to convince my parents that I'm ready to take care of a pet?"

"Absolutely," Ash said from the laptop's speakers. "You made a very smart argument."

Harper added, "The part about using eco-friendly poop bags was a nice touch."

"Gross, Harper!" said Po, wrinkling his nose. "Don't say *poop* and *touch* in the same sentence." He and Harper both laughed.

Theo raised his hand. "I wonder if you should say *vertebrates* instead of *animals*," he suggested. "All the images you used were of animals with a backbone. And I assume you don't want a pet cricket or earthworm." Harper elbowed him. "Oh, but other than that—good job," he added quickly.

Jodi could feel her heart swell with cheerfulness . . . **and hope.** She had wanted a pet for years, and her parents had never agreed to it. They always said no. They said it wasn't the right time for a pet. They told her to wait until she was older.

Well, Jodi had made up her mind: now, at last, was the right time. She was old enough. She was responsible enough! And when her parents heard her presentation after dinner tonight, she was sure they would agree with her.

She was pretty sure, at least.

But when she snuck a glance at Morgan, she saw that he was frowning. **And a dark cloud of worry passed over Jodi's heart.**

Chapter 2

ANIMALS OF THE OVERWORLD! I'LL NEVER GET OVER HOW CUTE THEY ARE.

The next day, Morgan, Jodi, and their friends returned to the library. This time, they weren't there for a meeting room. Instead, they collected a set of special VR headsets from the front desk. The goggles felt electric in Morgan's hands. He gripped his set tightly as he led Jodi, Po, Harper, and Theo to a row of networked computers in the back.

The computers would allow them to play Minecraft together.

And the VR goggles would allow them to live Minecraft together.

Morgan had given up on ever understanding

how the goggles were able to transport them into **the world of their favorite game.** Their science teacher, Doc Culpepper, had done . . . *something* to the goggles, supercharging them somehow. Her experiments were known mostly for going wrong in spectacular ways, but in this case, she had gotten something very right. In the end, he didn't really care *how* they worked. So long as they worked.

He took a seat, booted up the game, and slipped the goggles over his eyes.

The next thing Morgan knew, he was standing in a simple rectangular house. It was just big enough for five beds, a crafting table, a furnace, and a chest of supplies. **There was a single iron door, operated by a button, and there were two torches set into one of the house's stone walls.**

This build didn't have any of the comforts of home. But that was because they wouldn't

be staying here for long. They were constantly exploring, going deeper into Minecraft. And right now, they had a mission.

"All right, let's get started," said Morgan. He clicked the button on the wall. The door swung open, and he stepped outside. It was a clear, sunny day in the Overworld. Morgan smiled . . . and then he looked up, and he frowned. **The Fault was plainly visible high above him.** It looked like someone had taken the bright blue sky and just . . . *ripped* it.

"We really need to figure out what that Fault is," said Harper as she stepped outside the house. **"I'M SURE IT'S GETTING BIGGER."**

Theo was giving the rip a long look. He turned and nodded to Harper in agreement with her assessment. "It *is* getting bigger."

"One problem at a time," said Morgan. "First we need to find the next piece of—"

Suddenly, Jodi came bursting out of the house, running at top speed and shouting at the top of her lungs. "Look at that bunny!" she yelled.

"I WANT TO PET THE BUNNY!"

The bunny, it seemed, did not want to be petted. It bounded away, disappearing over a hill.

Jodi didn't follow. She was immediately distracted by a cow. Then a sheep. Then a pig. She ran back and forth across the plain, petting them all. She was definitely not "on mission" at the moment.

"Maybe I'll get a piglet in real life," she said.

Po laughed. His avatar was especially detailed today. Even though he was as blocky as the rest of them, the carefully placed pixels of his outfit made him look almost *fluffy*. Morgan thought he must be a cloud. Or a sheep? She wasn't sure. Po never stuck with one look for long. **He had a huge collection of skins, and he was constantly changing them.**

"Or maybe I should get a pet chicken!" said Jodi. She patted a hen, which flapped and clucked at the attention.

"I guess the presentation went well," Po said.

Jodi flashed a grin. Even in avatar form, it was easy to see how happy she was. "It went so well!" she cried.

"So your parents said yes?" asked Theo.

"They said 'we'll see,'" answered Jodi as she ran circles around a nearby horse. "Which is basically the same thing as yes."

Morgan kept his expression neutral,

and he tried to keep his voice neutral, too. "I don't think you should get your hopes up yet," he told his sister.

"TOO LATE!" She cackled, then started poking around at the edge of a lake. Morgan thought she was probably hoping for a glimpse of an axolotl— even though she should know by now that those mobs are only found way underground. Morgan rolled his eyes.

"Morgan!" Po whispered. "What gives? **YOU'RE BEING SO NEGATIVE."**

"Po's right," Harper said gently. "You could be a little more supportive."

Before answering, Morgan made sure his sister wasn't listening. "You don't understand," he said. "You didn't see my parents' faces during that presentation. They did *not* think getting a pet was a good idea." He shook his head. "Besides, when has 'we'll see' *ever* meant 'yes'?"

"He's got a point," said Theo. **"IN MY EXPERIENCE, PARENTS SAY 'WE'LL SEE' WHEN THEY REALLY MEAN 'NOT IN A MILLION YEARS.'"**

"Exactly," Morgan said.

"But she's so happy," said Po. **"ISN'T THERE SOMETHING YOU CAN DO?"**

"Me?" said Morgan.

"Maybe you could change your parents' minds," said Harper. "If she can't convince them . . . maybe *you* could convince them that she's ready for a pet."

"MAYBE . . . ," said Morgan.

Theo rubbed his blocky chin and gave Morgan a long look. "Morgan . . . you *do* think she's ready for a pet, don't you?"

Morgan hesitated. He wasn't sure how to answer that question.

"You guys!" said Jodi, and Morgan was happy for the interruption. "Does anybody have a bone?

THERE'S A WOLF BY THE TREES, AND I WANT TO GIVE HIM A TREAT."

"What a coincidence," said Po. He did a little twirl. "My avatar skin is a wolf today."

Theo frowned. "Are you sure? I thought you were a sheep."

"Aha! That's what I was going for," said Po. "See, I'm actually a wolf in sheep's clothing."

"SO YOU'RE PO... DRESSED AS A WOLF... DRESSED AS A SHEEP," SAID THEO.

Po laughed. "Baaah-sically, yeah."

"Let me check my inventory for a bone," Harper said. "I'm pretty sure I have one."

Morgan looked over Jodi's shoulder, and he saw the wolf in the distance. It was standing at the edge of a nearby forest. His sister obviously hoped to tame the wolf by giving it a bone.

"Are you sure you want to do this?" Morgan asked her. "Even digital wolves are a lot of responsibility. **YOU'LL HAVE TO FEED IT AND KEEP IT AWAY FROM LAVA.**"

Jodi waved around the bone that Harper had given her. "Sure I'm sure," she said. "Keeping away from lava is one of my favorite things!"

Morgan and the others followed as Jodi ran up to the wolf. She offered the bone to the animal, and the wolf took it, but no little red hearts appeared around its head. That meant it hadn't been tamed.

"SOMETIMES ONE BONE ISN'T ENOUGH," said Theo. "But you could try again."

Harper shook her head. "I don't have any more bones," she said. "Sorry, Jodi."

"Aw. It's okay," said Jodi. "Lobo Joe here just

wants to be free!"

Lobo Joe that was the wolf's name now, Morgan figured turned to go. It walked across the plain and disappeared from view.

It disappeared from view *very suddenly,* in fact.

"Where did it go?" asked Harper, startled.

"LOBO JOE?" said Jodi. "What happened to you?"

The kids all ran in the direction the wolf had gone.

They didn't see the pit until it was almost too late.

Morgan called, "Stop!" And he threw his arms out to the side. The others skidded to a stop just behind him, at the edge of a large hole.

The hole was full of animals. Not just Lobo Joe, but ocelots and chickens and more. **Several of the animals looked at the wolf with worry in their eyes. But maybe because of the strange situation they found themselves in, the animals mobs were staying calm . . . at least for the moment.**

"They fell into a hole, the poor things," Jodi said. "We should help them."

"We can dig some steps out of the dirt," offered Harper. "Then they can climb back up."

"This reminds me of that time we trapped a bunch of angry bunnies in a pit," Po said, pulling a pickaxe from his inventory. "Good times!"

Morgan nodded slowly. Po was right—perhaps more so than he realized.

The pit had a purpose.

Someone had *dug* this hole in the Minecraft dirt. Someone had trapped these animals on purpose!

Chapter 3

OUT OF THE PIT. INTO THE SWAMP! (I'LL TAKE ANY OTHER OPTION YOU'VE GOT, PLEASE.)

Jodi didn't get mad very often. But when Morgan told her what he suspected, she was furious.

"You think someone set this trap on purpose?" she said. She sputtered and shook. **"BUT . . . BUT WHY WOULD ANYONE WANT TO CAPTURE ALL THESE POOR ANIMALS?"**

A newly freed chicken clucked as it hurried past. To Jodi, the clucking sounded a little like "thank you."

"I don't know who would do this, or why," said Morgan. "I just know that hole didn't look natural. There were loose blocks of dirt around the edges."

"Maybe a creeper exploded," Theo suggested. "There *could* be a simple explanation."

"Maybe," said Morgan. But he didn't seem convinced. His gut was clearly telling him that something strange was happening here.

And then they saw the butterfly.

Butterflies were not a natural occurrence in the world of Minecraft. But when Jodi and her friends accessed the game with their headsets, the version of Minecraft they experienced was sometimes . . . a little different, or even downright bizarre.

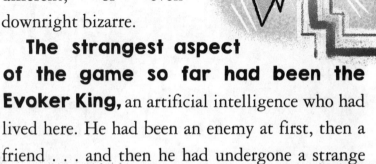

The strangest aspect of the game so far had been the Evoker King, an artificial intelligence who had lived here. He had been an enemy at first, then a friend . . . and then he had undergone a strange transformation. **The Evoker King had split into six different mobs,** each containing a piece of his programming and personality.

And when those mobs were nearby, the kids often saw digital butterflies—mobs that were definitely not a feature in the Vanilla game.

"Did you see that?" said Morgan. "A butterfly just flew by! We need to follow it."

"What? No!" said Jodi. "We have to find out who trapped these animals."

"Jodi," Morgan said, using his most serious "big brother" voice. "That butterfly could lead us to the next piece of the Evoker King. **THAT'S OUR MISSION, REMEMBER?"**

"It's more than just a mission," said Harper. "The Evoker King is our friend, and it's up to us to put him back together again."

"I WANT TO HELP HIM," said Jodi. "You know I do! But I want to help these animals, too."

"Maybe we can do both somehow," Po suggested.

"We can't do two things at once," Morgan said, huffing. "Jodi, you just gave us all a big speech about how responsible you are. Don't you see how irresponsible it is to get distracted from our quest?"

Jodi suddenly wished that Minecraft avatars had laser vision. **She knew one big brother who deserved a face full of laser right now.** She settled for scowling at him.

"Uh, guys?" said Theo. "I do not want to be in the middle of this. Not even a little bit. But—"

"—the butterfly is almost out of sight." Harper finished. "Are we going after it or not?"

Jodi sighed. "Fine. But somebody mark this spot on our map. **WE'RE NOT DONE WITH THIS ANIMAL MYSTERY."**

She tried to keep the frustration out of her voice. But she didn't try very hard.

Morgan almost lost sight of the butterfly more than once. It fluttered between the trees of the forest. The sun was high in the sky, so the leaves cast dark shadows. But with all five of them on the lookout, they were able to stay on the insect's trail.

Morgan hoped that following the butterfly was the right decision. He knew his sister was worried about the animals they had found. He admired her kindness and compassion. But he wanted to put the Evoker King back together more than anything.

Following the butterfly led them out of the forest and into a biome of dark, shallow water.

"IT'S A SWAMP," said Po. He made a face as he pulled his foot out of a puddle.

"It's kind of creepy," said Jodi, and Morgan agreed. Dark vines hung from oak trees, and the water was a murky green instead of blue.

"It's just like any other biome," said Theo. "It's programmed to look gloomy, that's all."

"And there are some unique resources here,"

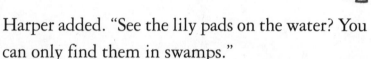

Harper added. "See the lily pads on the water? You can only find them in swamps."

Po turned up his wolfish nose. "I am *not* going into that water," he said.

Theo plucked a light blue flower, and he handed it to Harper. **"BLUE ORCHIDS ARE UNIQUE TO SWAMPS, TOO,"** he said. Harper accepted the flower with a shy smile.

Po also made a face at that.

"Hey, look!" Jodi said. "Somebody built a house out here."

Morgan saw it. It was a boxy wooden structure, and it was built right above the water. Four wooden pillars like stilts kept the house above the muck.

"It's not a house," he whispered. **"IT'S A SWAMP HUT."**

"Okay, sure," Po whispered back. "But why are we whispering?"

"Because swamp huts have another name," Morgan answered. "They're also called *witch huts.*"

As soon as he said those words, **Morgan saw a shape moving behind the hut's windows.** "And there's someone inside," he said.

"What's the big deal?" said Po. "We can handle a witch, right?"

"An ordinary witch? Sure," agreed Morgan. "But look."

Morgan pointed to the roof of the hut. **The butterfly had landed right on top of it.**

Harper gasped. "Do you think the mob in that hut is one of the Evoker Spawn we're looking for?" she asked.

Morgan nodded. "Probably. And if it's anything

like the last two, it will be a lot more dangerous than your average mob. **WE'LL NEED TO BE QUIET . . . AND CAREFUL, AND . . .** Wait." He looked around. "Where's Jodi?"

"UH-OH," said Po, and he pointed.

Jodi was running at top speed, splashing through the shallow water. She wasn't trying to hide. She wasn't trying to be quiet.

And she was heading right for the witch's hut.

Chapter 4

WELCOME TO THE ZOO!
COME FOR THE PANDAS.
STAY FOREVER. . . .

Jodi knew she was taking a big risk. **The creepy house on stilts was obviously not the kind of place she wanted to be.** But as she splashed through the shallow water, she wasn't thinking about the hut. She was thinking about what she had seen *behind* the hut.

"JODI!" her brother hissed. He was quickly catching up to her, and the others were close behind him. "What are you doing?"

"I'm helping," she said. "I'm helping *them*."

Jodi stepped onto dry land, just a short distance from the swamp hut. There were fences there. *Cages.* They were built from the same spruce and oak as the hut. **And they held just about every animal Jodi had ever seen in Minecraft.**

"Whoa," said Po. "Check out all the animals." He peered between the bars of the nearest cage. "Is that a panda? I forgot Minecraft even *had* pandas."

"THEY ONLY SPAWN IN JUNGLES," Morgan said. He leaned in closer. "It sort of looks like a jungle biome inside the cage, doesn't it? There's bamboo growing in there." He frowned. "That shouldn't happen in a swamp."

"And there," said Harper, pointing at another cage. "The turtle's cage is full of sand and water. It looks like a small beach."

"Someone is recreating the home biome of each animal," Theo said. "There's even an aquarium over there. **IT'S FULL OF DIFFERENT KINDS OF FISH."**

"That panda is just a baby," Jodi said. "It looks so sad!"

"That's just your imagination," said Theo. "It can't be sad. It isn't a real panda."

Before Jodi could disagree, the panda sneezed.

A glob of slime landed nearby.

"Okay, that was somehow both adorable and disgusting at the same time," said Po.

Harper grinned, and she picked up the slimeball. "You never know," she said. "This might come in handy."

"Harper!" said Po, **looking grossed out**— as much as an avatar in a wolf-sheep skin could. "I hope you know how to craft a sink, because you need to wash your hands. Like, right away!"

"A little slime never hurt anybody," said Harper, and she waved her blocky hands in Po's face.

While Po squealed and laughed, Morgan appeared lost in thought. After a long moment, he said, "It's a zoo. But who would make this, and why?"

"IT'S NOT A ZOO," said Jodi. "It's a prison! And whoever built it is obviously the same person who was trapping animals in a pit." She hopped in anger. "It isn't right. It isn't fair. And I'm going to set them all free."

"Now, hold on a minute," said Morgan.

But Jodi didn't listen. She flung open a gate. A goat stepped out, leaving the gravelly, mountainous landscape of its cage. **"BE FREE!"** said Jodi. "Get out of here. Hurry!" The goat bleated once, then hurried past them into the swamp.

Jodi didn't stop there. She ran down the line of cages, throwing open one door after another.

"JODI, STOP!" said Morgan. "We need to talk about this."

Just then, an eerie giggle rang out. Jodi froze, confused. The sound was coming from the cage that she had just opened. Inside it, a colorful bird sat atop a log.

"Dude," said Po. **"DID THAT PARROT JUST LAUGH AT US?"**

Jodi saw the worry on her brother's face. "What is it?" she asked. "What's wrong?"

"Well . . . parrots make different sounds depending on what other mobs are nearby," Morgan explained. "They hiss when a creeper is close. They groan when a zombie's around. And that giggle . . . it sounded like . . ."

"Like what?" asked Jodi.

Morgan answered: **"LIKE A WITCH."**

Jodi turned to look at the nearby hut. A menacing figure loomed in its open doorway. It wore a pointed hat and a dark cloak. And it was watching them with bright green eyes.

It was a witch. It laughed—a wicked, haunting cackle that sent a chill through Jodi's avatar.

And then it attacked.

Po was the first one to be hit. He didn't even have time to draw his sword. A potion struck him square in the back. He flashed red and fell to his knees.

Just one hit, and he was out of the fight.

"WE'RE UNDER ATTACK!" cried Harper, and she fired an arrow. It struck the wood hut with a *thunk*.

"Where did the witch go?" said Theo, and he gripped his sword. "It was right there a second ago."

"Behind you!" yelled Morgan. But his warning came too late. The witch leapt from the shadows, hurling potions at Theo and Harper. As they fell to their knees, **the witch disappeared again, fading into the gloomy darkness of the swamp.**

"THE WITCH IS TOO FAST," said Morgan. "It shouldn't be able to *move* like that—or that fast. That's no normal mob."

Jodi pressed her back against his. "Just keep your eyes open, big brother," she said. **"THE WITCH CAN'T SNEAK UP ON BOTH OF US."**

Morgan and Jodi turned in a slow circle, back to back. They gazed out into the swamp and down the aisles of the strange, swampy zoo.

But when Jodi heard the witch's cackle, it wasn't coming from either of those directions. The sound was coming from *above* them.

Jodi looked up in time to see the witch peering down from atop the nearest cage. The mob hurled a flask at them. It shattered against Morgan, **splashing him with its foul liquid.**

And now Jodi stood alone. She held her sword in one hand and her shield in the other. "I'm not afraid of you," said Jodi. "I'm going to save these animals you've captured. You can't stop me."

"Stop you, hrm," said the witch. The voice was strange and shrill. The mob took a step back, fading into the darkness.

Jodi turned to her brother. **"ARE YOU OKAY?"** she asked him.

And then the witch's shrill voice sounded just behind her. "Stop you, hah!" said the mob.

Jodi felt a splash potion shatter against her back. It didn't hurt . . . but it had a strange and immediate effect on her. Jodi felt suddenly weak— weak, and so, so tired. She dropped to her knees. She couldn't even summon the strength to stand.

"What . . . what is this?" she asked.

"SOME KIND OF SICKNESS," Morgan said

beside her.

Standing above them, the witch cackled in triumph. "Cursed, you are," said the mob. Its speech was odd, full of pauses and purring sounds. "Fix you, hah, I can."

"Do it, then," said Harper. "Lift this . . . this spell or curse or whatever it is you've done to us."

"A PRICE, HRM, YOU MUST PAY," said the witch. It leaned in closer. This mob moved her arm as she talked. That definitely wasn't like any normal Minecraft witch. "A mooshroom of brown. You bring one, hah, to me."

"You want us to bring you . . . a brown cow?"

asked Po. "That's your price?"

"We won't do it," said Jodi. "We won't help you hunt any more animals!"

"Help me, hah, you will," said the witch. "For the cure you seek, hrm, is the *stew* that, hah, **THE MOOSHROOM MAKES.**"

Silence fell over the group. Jodi wanted to argue—she wanted to *fight.* But she could barely crawl.

"QUEST FOR ME, YOU WILL," said the witch. "Over land, hah, and sea, hrm." She opened the gate of a nearby cage. Inside it was a row of neat beds. "But first . . . heh. You rest." She cackled, then added, "Hah-hah-hrm. Rest well . . . **MY PETS.**"

Chapter 5

SUSPICIOUS STEW: IS THE CURE WORSE THAN THE DISEASE?

Theo felt a chill as he removed his VR goggles. Was it the library's air-conditioning? Or . . . could it be the curse of the witch?

He shook his head. **Surely the witch's magic couldn't affect them here, in the real world.** Even so, Theo was thoroughly creeped out. The witch was an adversary unlike any they had faced before.

Although . . . that was only half true. **The witch was faster, more menacing, and much more talkative than a typical Minecraft witch.** There was only one explanation for that. Just like the monstrous Enderman and the mind-controlling cave spider before her, this unique mob *must* be one of the Evoker King fragments. And that meant, even if they *could* fight it . . . they probably shouldn't. They would need a unique approach to the problem.

"I think we have to do what the witch says," Theo said to his friends. **"We need to find a mooshroom and bring it back to her."**

Po sighed. "That sounds like a lot of work. But we definitely need the cure."

"It's not just about the cure, though," said Theo. "If that witch is one of the Evoker Spawn, then we need to show her that we aren't her enemies."

Jodi gripped her goggles tightly. "There has to be another way. We can't do her dirty work for her. Not if it means capturing another poor animal. **Who knows what's she's up to?!"**

"We don't have a lot of choices," said Morgan.
"We're her prisoners . . . because *somebody* ran into
danger without a plan."

Jodi scowled at him. "*You're* the one who runs
off every time a butterfly floats by!"

"Blaming each other won't help us right now," said Harper. **"Instead of pointing fingers, we should focus on what we can do next."**

Po scratched the top of his head. "Maybe we can figure out the cure by ourselves," he suggested. "What did the witch say about soup?"

"Stew," Theo corrected him.

"And not just any stew," said Morgan. **"Suspicious stew.** Believe it or not, you can get it from mooshrooms."

"That does not sound delicious," said Po. "But does it mean we could cure ourselves? Could we get this . . . suspicious stew . . . and not give her the mooshroom?"

"Or could we make the stew ourselves?" suggested Harper. **"I'm certain it can be crafted."**

"We don't have enough information," Morgan said, shaking his head. "Suspicious stew is unpredictable. It can have all sorts of different effects on a player. And when you get it from a mooshroom, the stew's exact effects depend on what the mooshroom has eaten." He shrugged. "So the witch only told us *part* of the cure. **We know it's suspicious stew, but we don't know what kind."**

"We're really trapped, then," said Harper. "We have to do what the witch says."

"Easier said than done," Theo said. "Brown mooshrooms are **extremely rare**. They're even rarer than the red variety."

"What about breeding one?" Morgan suggested. "If you pair two red mooshrooms together and they have a baby, there's a chance the baby will be brown."

"Yeah," Theo said, scoffing. "A one-in-1,024 chance, to be specific."

"Never tell me the odds!" Po replied, having no idea exactly how good or bad those odds were.

Theo dragged his feet as they all walked up to the front of the library and turned in their headsets. He was a programmer, so he couldn't help but think of the odds. And the odds really were not in their favor this time.

As they left the library and stepped out into the

sunshine, Jodi said, "I still don't like it. **I wish we knew why she wants a mooshroom.** Does she really just want to keep it in a cage?"

"Does it matter?" Theo said. "It's not a real animal."

"But they *seem* real," said Jodi. "They eat food, and they have babies, and they run away from you if you hurt them."

"They do those things because they're programmed to do them," said Theo. **"They're just little bits of code.** They don't have feelings."

"Well, you could say the same thing about the Evoker King," said Po. "But we care about him, right?"

"Sounds like a very serious discussion," said a voice. **Theo turned to see Mr. Malory, the library's media specialist, sitting beneath the library's famous sculpture of a sword.** He was on a break, and enjoying a snack.

"What do you think, Mr. Malory?" asked Theo. "Do NPCs and virtual animals have feelings?"

Mr. Malory thought about it for a moment.

"They don't have feelings, no. Not as we understand them."

"See?" Theo said to Jodi.

"However!" said the librarian, holding up a finger. "That doesn't mean we should treat them as if they don't matter. **It's a fine idea to show compassion to all creatures, whether they can appreciate it or not.**"

"Even if that slows down your progress in a game?" Po asked. **"Or makes it harder to win?"**

"That's what I was thinking," said Morgan. "Isn't it sort of a waste of time to be nice to creatures that aren't even real?"

"I don't think compassion is ever a waste of time," Mr. Malory answered. "Positivity, kindness, patience . . . these are all crucial skills to develop. Not just because of what they do for the people or animals around you. You benefit, too. **Put positivity out into the world, and good things happen.**"

"I agree with Mr. Malory," said Jodi. And then she stuck her tongue out at Theo, which did *not*

feel especially compassionate.

Theo sighed. He didn't have the energy for a larger argument. But in his heart, he was worried.

Jodi's compassion had already gotten them into a very difficult situation. If she cared more about digital mushroom-covered cows than about being cured . . . **would the witch's curse ever be broken?**

Chapter 6

AN ITSY-BITSY SPIDER CAUSED A GREAT BIG PROBLEM!

It was several days later when Harper and her friends finally had time to put on the VR goggles and enter Minecraft again.

They had expected to appear in the cage where the witch had left them. **Instead, their beds and their spawn point had been moved to the edge of the swamp.** A nearby chest contained a single item: a map, marked with the location of an island.

The kids knew immediately that the island must be the nearest mushroom field—the only biome where mooshrooms could spawn. Clearly, the witch was eager for their quest to begin.

All things considered . . . it didn't get off to a great start.

They had only been walking a short while before they were attacked. **It was a spider, lunging at them from the shadows.** At first, Harper wasn't worried. They had fought—and defeated—more spiders than they could count.

"I've got it," Morgan said, and he swung his sword in a wide arc.

The spider leapt, easily avoiding his attack. Then it sprang at Po, biting him.

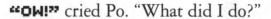

"OW!" cried Po. "What did I do?"

Harper saw her opening, and she took it. Running forward, she attacked the spider while it was still facing Po.

Her sword attack hurt the spider. She could tell by the way it flashed red.

But it didn't hurt the spider as much as it should have.

"We are in so much trouble," she said as the spider turned its angry red eyes in her direction.

It was just a normal, everyday spider. It should have been an easy battle for any one of them.

But the witch's curse had changed everything.

The spider lunged for Harper. She stepped back, striking it again with her sword. At that same instant, Theo shot it with an arrow. Finally, it fell, disappearing in a pixelated puff of dust.

"Whew. That was *much* tougher than it should have been," said Harper, verbalizing her earlier observation.

"IT'S LIKE WE'RE NOOBS ALL OVER AGAIN," said Po. He bit into an apple so that he could regain his lost health.

"It's worse than that," Theo said. "This 'curse' . . . I think it's a **DEBUFF**."

"A what, now?" asked Jodi.

"A debuff," Theo repeated. **"IN A VIDEO GAME, AN ADVANTAGE IS CALLED A BUFF.** Like . . . when a potion makes you stronger, or a blessing makes you faster. That's a buff."

"So a debuff is the opposite," Harper said.

"Correct," Theo continued. **"IT'S A DISADVANTAGE.** Something that makes you less powerful."

"There are plenty of buffs and debuffs in Minecraft," Morgan added. "Like Weakness, which makes your attacks less powerful."

"I CERTAINLY FELT WEAK AGAINST THAT SPIDER," said Harper, and she picked up the string and eyeball left behind by the defeated mob. "We had to hit it a lot more times than we usually would."

"That's why I'm wearing my special 'chicken pox' skin," said Po. "In real life, I feel fine. But here, I feel totally under the weather. And my pox shows it."

Everyone looked at Po, **whose avatar today was a chicken covered in polka dots**. "Oh, *now* I get it," said Morgan.

"You know chickens don't actually get chicken pox, right?" said Theo. "That virus only affects humans. And apes, I think."

Po flapped his feathered arms. "Well, a spotted gorilla would just look ridiculous," he said. "Ba-kaw!"

"I like this look on you," said Harper, and she patted his head.

"Careful," Po clucked. **"I MIGHT BE CONTAGIOUS."**

Theo sighed. *"Anyway,"* he said, eager to get back on topic. "I don't think there's anything magical—or even that mysterious—about this so-called witch's curse. It's a debuff—a way of messing with the code."

"Then we'd better be careful," said Morgan, and he held up the map for all to see. "Because we've got a long way to go. **AND I'M SURE THAT SPIDER ISN'T THE LAST HOSTILE MOB WE'LL HAVE TO FIGHT."**

Morgan's words proved true. Over the days-long voyage, the group encountered an endless series of dangers. They stayed out of the shadows and tried to avoid fighting whenever they could. When a fight was unavoidable, they tried to attack from a distance. **It took a lot of arrows to defeat a zombie,** but it felt safer than getting close enough to swing a sword.

They went over or around mountains instead of cutting through them. When they spotted an Enderman in the distance, **they quickly looked away.** When they saw an illager tower, they crossed a lake to avoid it.

At first, they stopped only to gather apples and other food items. Keeping their health up was more important than ever, and that meant keeping their bellies full. But on the third night of their voyage, phantoms appeared in the night sky. **Morgan panicked.** He knew how deadly the flying mobs could be, so he had insisted that the group stop and rest rather than pushing ahead through a night full of dangers. Despite their hurry, nobody had disagreed with him.

When they finally saw the mushroom island in the distance, they let out a cheer. But it was a small, weak cheer. They didn't have much energy to spare, and it was too soon to celebrate.

"We could swim," said Morgan. **"BUT CROSSING ON BOATS WILL BE SAFER."**

Theo started digging up the grass at the water's edge. "While you all build boats, I'll grow some wheat. We'll need it, so that the mooshroom will follow us."

"Follow us to its *doom*," said Jodi glumly.

Jodi couldn't stay too gloomy for long. Under the light of the full moon, the mushroom fields biome was strange and wonderful, with a ground made of some spongy purple material—her brother called it *mycelium*—**and towering toadstools the size of trees.** But by far the most amazing part of the biome was the mooshrooms themselves. The peaceful mobs roamed around the small island, munching on grass and giving the kids curious looks.

"There are a lot of mooshrooms here," said Po. "But they're all red."

"I had an idea about that," said Morgan. **"RED MOOSHROOMS CHANGE TO BROWN WHEN THEY'RE STRUCK BY LIGHTNING.** So if we can lead one into a storm . . ."

Po looked up at the sky. Other than the Fault, it was totally clear. "I'd ask what the odds are of that plan working," he said, "but I'm afraid Theo would actually tell me the answer."

"I don't know *everything,*" said Theo. "Although I could run some calculations. . . ."

Morgan sighed. "I'll admit: it's a long shot. **BUT IT'S EITHER THAT OR WE ROAM THE OVERWORLD LOOKING FOR ANOTHER MUSHROOM BIOME. THAT COULD TAKE MONTHS."**

"And in our current condition, it's dangerous to go roaming around," added Theo. "I think Morgan's idea is the best we've got. Let's grab a red mooshroom and get out of here."

Harper turned to Jodi. "You could choose which mooshroom will go with us," Harper suggested.

"You're good with animals, after all."

Jodi nodded solemnly. "Let me talk to them," she said. "I'll figure out which one is bravest."

As Jodi went from one mooshroom to the next, whispering into their ears and patting their backs, Theo turned to Harper. "She knows they're all identical, right? **I MEAN, THE CODE IS EXACTLY THE SAME FOR EVERY RED MOOSHROOM.**"

Harper shrugged. "Maybe Jodi sees something we don't."

"I've got a question," said Po. "How do you get a mooshroom onto a boat?" He paused for a moment. "That sounds like the setup to a joke, but I'm really asking."

"I've got that figured out," answered Harper. She pulled the slimeball from her inventory. "I'm awfully glad I held on to this."

"Gross," said Po, but he laughed as he said it.

Chapter 7

INTRODUCING: MICHAEL G! NOT TO BE CONFUSED WITH MICHAEL C OR MICHAEL P.

odi had made her selection. She didn't feel *good* about it. **But she'd chosen the poor mooshroom they would take away from this island paradise and hand over to an obviously up-to-no-good witch.**

Now she only had to make introductions.

"Morgan. Po. Harper and Theo," she said, drawing their attention. "I'd like you to meet the newest member of our team. This is Michael G."

Michael G mooed, as if saying hello. Or maybe he was asking what in the world was happening.

"Hello, uh, Michael," said Morgan.

"Welcome to the team!" said Po, and then he whispered, "I'm not *really* a chicken."

"Michael G," said Harper. **"THAT'S AN INTERESTING NAME."**

"It doesn't seem very fitting," said Theo. "Are there a lot of other Michaels here?"

Jodi crossed her arms. "It's a pun, smart guy. Don't you get it?"

Harper laughed, obviously the first one to get the joke. Everyone else looked at her expectantly. "The scientific study of mushrooms is called mycology," she explained. "Say it fast, and it sort of sounds like, well . . ." She turned to the mooshroom. **"IT'S NICE TO MEET YOU, MICHAEL G. DO YOU MIND IF WE PUT THIS ON YOU?"**

Harper held up a short rope, tied like a lasso. "Where'd you get that?" asked Jodi.

"I made it out of strings and slime," said Harper. **"IT'S CALLED A LEAD,** and it will let us bring Michael G with us wherever we go. Even onto a boat."

"I just thought of something," said Theo.

"Maybe we should bring more than one of the mooshrooms with us. In case anything happens to this one along the way."

Jodi's jaw dropped. "Nothing's going to happen to Michael G. I promised him that!"

Theo frowned. "I'm not sure I'd have made that promise," he said. "We're debuffed, and we have a long way to walk. The cow could be attacked by any number of hostile mobs, or even struck with an arrow or a fireball meant for one of us."

Jodi put her hands to Michael G's head, as if blocking the mooshroom's ears. "Theo!" she protested. "He can hear you."

"All I'm trying to say is we might have trouble protecting him," Theo replied.

"In that case, we're better off with just one mooshroom," said Harper. **"SO WE CAN ALL**

FOCUS ON PROTECTING HIM. Right?"

Theo scratched his head. "Yeah, actually, that does make sense."

Jodi let out a sigh of relief. She sometimes forgot that arguing with Theo usually lead to a dead end. It was much easier to get him to see the logic behind their choices than to appeal to his emotions. Fortunately, Harper was there to act as a translator when they needed it.

Jodi took the lead from Harper. **She placed it around Michael G and used it to guide him onto her small boat.**

Seconds later, they were all speeding across the water back to the mainland.

It was night, and the low moon was nearly touching the calm water. Jodi smiled. In a weird way, she realized, she had gotten her wish. **For the moment, she had a pet.**

Everything was going really well . . .

. . . until the underwater zombie attacked.

It was called a drowned, and they never saw it coming. One second, everything was calm. The next, a trident burst from the water. It smashed into Morgan, knocking him off his boat.

"Morgan!" Jodi cried as her brother disappeared beneath the surface.

"I'LL HELP YOUR BROTHER," Po told her. "You stay here and protect Michael!"

Po dove beneath the waves, and Jodi thought: *That is one brave chicken.* She stayed close to Michael, holding his lead tight with one hand as she gripped her shield with the other.

Nearby, Harper and Theo equipped their bows, aiming arrows at the water. But all was still and quiet.

Suddenly there was a great splash of water beside Jodi's boat. She held up her shield just in time. **The drowned was right in front of her.** It had hopped into her boat and started pounding its fists against her shield.

Harper and Theo launched arrows at the enemy, but they hardly did any damage at all. Jodi wanted to flee, but she didn't dare leave the mooshroom to fend for itself.

Just then, the sun peeked above the horizon. Jodi could see her enemy more clearly in the early-morning light. She saw its tattered clothing. **She saw its eerie blue-green eyes.**

Then it burst into flame!

Jodi had momentarily forgotten that zombies—even underwater zombies—couldn't bear the light of the sun.

Between the fire and the arrows, the mob fell quickly. It croaked out a final moan; then it was gone.

Morgan and Po poked their heads out of the water.

"Is everyone okay?" Morgan asked. "The drowned gave us the slip."

Jodi realized she was still holding her breath. She exhaled and said, "We took care of it. With a little help from the sunlight." She looked at where the drowned had stood just a moment before. **"ALL THAT'S LEFT OF THAT ZOMBIE IS SOME ROTTEN FLESH AND A TRIDENT."**

"That's great news," Harper said from her boat. "Hold on to that trident. We'll need it later."

"If you say so," said Jodi, and she scooped up the weapon. "Can I leave the icky flesh behind?"

"Actually," said Harper, and she broke into a huge grin, "I think I've got a use for that, too." She looked around at her friends. **"ANYBODY UP FOR A LITTLE DETOUR?"**

Chapter 8

PUT YOUR PAWS TOGETHER FOR JODI'S ALL-PURPOSE PET SERVICE!

Back in the real world, it had been several days since Jodi had shown her presentation to her parents. Several days since they had told her "We'll see." And in that time, Jodi had begun to worry that Morgan was right. **Maybe she had gotten her hopes up too soon.**

That was when Jodi decided she needed to prove herself. She needed a *plan.*

She had started with their next-door neighbor. Miss Maribelle was a small woman with two large dogs. **Beefy, a muscular German shepherd,** liked to tug at his leash. **Bo, an energetic Labrador,** tried to chase

everything that moved. Miss Maribelle had to
walk them one at a time so they wouldn't drag her
all over town.

Jodi offered to walk Beefy and Bo in the
mornings, to give her neighbor a break.

At the dog park, Jodi had met other dog owners.

Some of them asked Jodi if she would walk their dogs from time to time. Some of them even offered to pay!

It was a dream come true. Getting paid *money* to spend time with animals? She said yes to everyone who asked.

Including one very familiar face.

"I can't believe you're going to walk Doc's dog," Po told her as they moved along the sidewalk. "In fact, I can't believe Doc is a dog person! **Are you sure she isn't paying you to walk a killer robot?**"

"I'm sure," Jodi said, and she tugged on Bo's leash to keep him on the sidewalk. "I met her dog at the park just the other day."

Po narrowed his eyes. "So it's a very *convincing* killer robot," he said. "With a fur suit and everything."

Jodi shrugged. **"Only if killer robots love to eat Vegan pepperoni,"** she said.

It was early in the morning, but there was no school for the entire week—and that meant no basketball practice for Po. He had offered to tag along, just so he had something to do.

The others were also coming along, simply out of curiosity. **They'd never seen a teacher's house before!**

"I bet Doc has a smart home," said Harper. "With all the latest gadgets."

"In that case, look out for stray lasers," said Theo. "Doc can be a real menace around technology, if you haven't noticed."

"We've noticed," said Morgan. "Believe me, we've noticed." **Doc wasn't just responsible for their special VR goggles.** It had been her experiments with AI, or artificial intelligence, that had led to the unintended creation of the Evoker King.

But if they were expecting a high-tech wonderland, they were disappointed. From the outside, Doc's house looked just like any other—with the exception of a souped-up antenna on the roof. Harper grinned at the sight of the device. **"She probably gets channels from Alpha Centauri on that thing!"** she said happily.

As soon as Doc answered the door, a poodle

bounded out onto the porch. The dog shook its pom-pom tail at the sight of Jodi.

"Hello, Nicolaus Pupernicus!" Jodi cooed. "I'm happy to see you, too. Yes, I am!"

"Students! Greetings," Doc said brightly. "I hope you're enjoying your time off."

"We are now," said Po as he scratched the poodle behind its ears. "What a cutie!"

"He *is* cute," agreed Doc. "He's also crafty! He takes after his mama." Doc chuckled to herself. "He's even found a way to slip out of his collar once or twice. If he gets away from you, call him back with this, and he'll come running."

Doc handed Jodi a strange piece of high-tech equipment. It looked a little like a flute . . . mixed with a spaceship.

"What is it?" asked Jodi.

The teacher bounced on the tips of her toes. **"Why, it's a dog whistle of my own design!"** said Doc.

"I guess now we know what Doc does with her time off," Morgan whispered, and Harper quickly shushed him.

"I've heard about dog whistles," said Jodi. She turned to her friends. "Dogs have very sensitive ears. They can hear sounds that are too high-pitched for human ears. That's what a dog whistle does. It makes a sound that only dogs can hear." She turned back to Doc. **"But why is this one so, um . . . complicated?"**

"I've made great improvements to it," said Doc. "Think about it: Why make a *single* silent note when you can play an entire silent *symphony*? I think you'll agree that dogs deserve to enjoy music that is more sophisticated than a simple whistle can deliver." **Doc handed Jodi a thick instruction manual.** "It looks complicated, but it's really quite simple once you get the hang of it. Play 'Claire de Lune' to get him to sit, Beethoven's Fifth to get him to come to you, and

'Mary Had a Little Lamb' to get him to play dead."

"Got it," said Po. "I think."

As Jodi led the dogs away from Doc's porch, Po reached for the whistle. "This I've got to try," he said.

But Jodi pulled back, keeping the whistle out

of his grasp. **"Po, this isn't a toy!"** She shoved the instruction manual into his hands instead. "If you really want to use it, you'll have to make sure you're doing it right. Otherwise you could scare the poor things."

"Blargh," said Po. "Reading? On my day off? Forget it!"

"Wow," said Morgan. "Normally you go along with Po's mischief, Jodi."

"Well." Jodi lifted her chin defiantly. "I happen to take my responsibilities very seriously, if you didn't know."

Morgan surrendered. "Point taken."

"Can I at least give them treats?" asked Po.

"Yes, but you'll have to be careful. Nicolaus is lactose intolerant, and we have to wrap Beefy's vitamins in cheese. You do not *want* to get them mixed up. Oh! And Bo sometimes eats his treats

too fast, so you have to cut them up into little pieces first."

As Jodi dug through her bag of treats, she caught Morgan giving her a weird look. "What?" she asked him.

"It's nothing," he said. "It's just that I'm starting to think that maybe I was . . . I was . . ."

Morgan couldn't finish his sentence. He sneezed so loudly, it made the dogs howl.

"Gesundheit," said Po. "Hey, are you feeling all right?"

"Now that you mention it, I feel a little . . . debuffed at the moment." He chuckled at his own joke. "I hope I'm not getting sick while we're

on break. Wouldn't that be typical?"

"**No getting sick!**" said Harper. "We have to play Minecraft later."

"Yeah, Michael G is depending on us," said Po.

"That's not actually true," said Theo. "But I'm anxious to get back to our quest, too."

"Count on it," said Morgan, and he sniffled. "**Nothing's going to stop us from getting that cure.**"

Chapter 9

ONE MOB'S ROTTEN FLESH IS ANOTHER MOB'S TREASURE. (BUT SERIOUSLY, I'D RATHER HAVE THE EMERALDS!)

Theo recognized the Minecraft village immediately.

"We've been here before," he said. "THESE ARE THE VILLAGERS WE SAVED FROM THE GIANT CAVE SPIDER."

"That's right," said Harper. "And one of them is a cleric, remember? Help me find that one."

Now Theo was *really* curious. "What do you need a cleric for?" he asked.

"It's a surprise," Harper said. Her avatar smiled. "TRUST ME. I'VE GOT A PLAN!"

That was good enough for Theo. He *did* trust Harper, and her plans tended to be good ones, so he set out in search of a cleric.

As Theo looked around the village, he saw that the square Minecraft sun was low in the sky. That made him anxious. **Theo had grown to fear the night,** because that was when it was hardest to avoid hostile mobs.

Working together, the kids were still more than a match for any danger in Minecraft. Theo knew that. But they were running low on supplies. They were eating through their apples and bread too quickly. And they had used almost all of their arrows.

They were nearly back to the swamp, though. **Once they got there, they could trade the mooshroom for a cure.** And this whole nightmare would be behind them.

As Theo stepped onto a cobblestone pathway, he felt something nudge him from behind. He turned to see Michael G close behind him.

"AW, HE LIKES YOU!" said Jodi. "I dropped his lead to let him graze for a while, and he went right to you."

Theo sighed. "He doesn't *like* me," he argued.

"He doesn't like *anything*. He's incapable of it. HE'S JUST COMPUTER CODE WEARING A COW SUIT."

Jodi harumphed. "Well, he's not going to like you for much longer if you keep saying things like that!"

Just then, the sun dipped below the horizon. Theo felt his anxiety grow. "Keep a grip on Bessie's lead, okay?" he said. "THE TOWN'S TORCHES SHOULD KEEP ANY HOSTILE MOBS FROM SPAWNING, BUT MONSTERS COULD ALWAYS CREEP IN FROM OUTSIDE."

"Don't listen to him, Michael," Jodi said, taking the lead. "He knows your name. He's just being silly."

Theo watched the villagers as they started returning to their homes for the night. **He saw that Harper had found the cleric,** and he walked over to see if she needed any help.

"I traded a stack of rotten flesh for emeralds," she told him. "And now I'll use the emeralds to buy some lapis."

"Lapis?" Theo echoed. "You must be enchanting something."

"You guessed it. Check it out!" Harper held up her brand-new piece of lapis lazuli. It shone bright blue in the torchlight. **"HEY, JODI, CAN I HAVE THAT TRIDENT?"**

With the trident and the lapis in her inventory, Harper dropped an enchantment table right in the middle of town. Next, she placed a series of bookshelves around it.

"I love libraries, too," Jodi said. "But are you sure you want to build one in the middle of a sidewalk?"

"THE BOOKSHELVES WILL MAKE MY ENCHANTMENT MORE POWERFUL," Harper said. "And get me the enchantment I want."

"What enchantment do you want?" Jodi asked.

"I've been trying to guess," Theo said. "But I'm stumped."

"Channeling," Harper answered. "We'll still need to wait for a thunderstorm," she explained further. "But with a trident that's enchanted with Channeling, we won't have to rely on luck for lightning to strike. **WE'LL BE ABLE TO CALL DOWN A BOLT OF ELECTRICITY FROM A THUNDERCLOUD.**"

Theo wished he had fingers that he could snap. He settled for a little hop. "And the lightning will change Michael G from red to brown. Brilliant!"

"I just hope this works," said Harper. She bent over the enchanting table. "I might not get Channeling **ON MY FIRST TRY.** You should get a grindstone ready, in case we need to start over."

But she was worried for no reason. Theo could tell by the way she smiled. **The enchanting had worked perfectly.**

Harper whooped in triumph, and she held up the enchanted trident for all to see. It glittered purple in the night. The kids fell silent as they looked at it in awe.

And in the momentary silence . . . **Theo heard a hiss.**

Theo whirled around in alarm. His fears were true. He saw the creeper sneaking up behind Jodi and Michael. He saw it . . .

Too late.

With a sudden burst of light and sound, the creeper exploded. Jodi and the mooshroom both flashed red as **they were knocked forward by the force of the blast.**

Theo held his breath. Would the mooshroom survive? It couldn't possibly have much health, could it? If only there were something he could do!

That's when Theo remembered: he had one precious **splash Potion of Healing** in his inventory. He'd been saving it for an emergency.

He figured this fit the bill.

Acting quickly, he hurled the potion at the mooshroom. The flask shattered, and the life-restoring liquid washed over the animal.

"Ow," said Jodi, rubbing her head. "What hit us?"

"IT WAS A CREEPER," said Harper. "It came out of nowhere! Are you okay?"

"And is Michael G okay?" asked Theo.

A smile broke across Jodi's square face. "Aw, you care about him."

Theo cleared his throat. "No, I don't. I just don't want to have to go all the way back to that island to find another one."

"Sure, that's it," said Jodi, but she didn't sound convinced. "Did you hear, Michael G? He even got your name right!"

Harper and Jodi laughed as Morgan and Po hurried over to check on them. **They all doted on the mooshroom, who mooed with**

pleasure at the attention.

When Michael G turned its big, bovine eyes to Theo, he couldn't help himself.

He gave the mooshroom a little pat on the head.

For a string of computer code . . . this cow was pretty cute.

Chapter 10

SMALL BUSINESS OWNERSHIP! IT'S LIKE PUTTING THE WHOLE WORLD ON A LEASH AND HAVING IT DRAG YOU AROUND.

In the real world, Morgan was feeling sicker with each passing day. He was almost paranoid enough to believe it had something to do with the witch's curse. But if that was true, shouldn't his friends be sick, too?

Jodi, for one, seemed healthier than ever. **As her pet-walking service got more popular, she seemed to have more and more energy.**

The one thing she seemed unable to do . . . was to say no.

"I thought you were a *dog*

walker," said Po. "What's that guy doing here?" And he pointed at an iguana on a leash.

"The iguana makes more sense than the fish," said Theo, **and he tapped at the goldfish bowl in Po's lap.**

"You leave Bubbles out of this!" said Po. "She just wanted some fresh air."

Theo rolled his eyes. "I think fresh air is the *last* thing a water-breather wants."

"Are you sure we can't take some of those leashes for you?" asked Harper.

Jodi shot her brother a quick look before answering. "No, no," she said. "I'm fine. I'm good! **Super responsible, that's me."**

Morgan could only sneeze in reply.

Jodi was holding leashes for no fewer than six dogs, one iguana, and a birdcage on wheels. Somehow, she managed to keep all the animals on the path. Even Baron Sweetcheeks, in his plastic exercise ball, was careful to stay close to her. Morgan and Jodi had volunteered to care for the hamster during the school break, and **Jodi hadn't wanted to leave him home alone.**

Suddenly, the hamster squeaked as if excited. **He rolled ahead of the group.** It seemed like he recognized a woman on the path ahead of them. She was pushing a baby stroller and wearing large sunglasses.

When she took off her sunglasses and smiled at them, Morgan recognized her, too. **It was Ms. Minerva, their homeroom teacher.**

"Baron Sweetcheeks, is that you?" she said. "And my favorite students are all here! I almost couldn't see you past all those . . . dogs."

The way she said the word, Morgan figured something out right away: Ms. Minerva was *not* a dog person.

"Hi, Ms. Minerva!" said Harper. "I didn't know you had a baby."

Ms. Minerva laughed. "Just my fur baby. This is Dewey." She pulled the cover of the stroller back, revealing an orange-striped cat, crooked whiskers, and a very annoyed expression. **"He's an indoor cat,"** she said by way of explanation.

Morgan had never seen a cat in a baby stroller before. But he had learned a long time ago that adults did some very strange things.

Suddenly, Jodi lurched forward. One of the dogs had taken an interest in Ms. Minerva's cat, and now he tugged against his leash.

"Wait, is that . . . is that Doc's dog?" asked Ms. Minerva, suddenly alarmed. **"Oh, no. There's bad blood between these two. . . ."**

Time seemed to freeze. Morgan held his breath as dog and cat locked eyes. He saw Jodi's grip

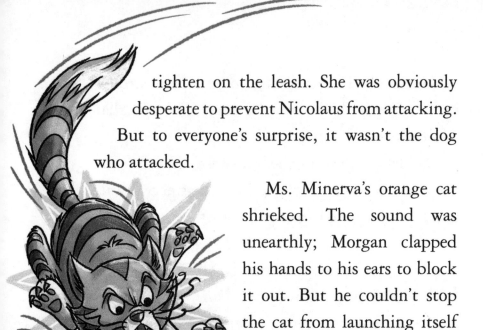

tighten on the leash. She was obviously desperate to prevent Nicolaus from attacking. But to everyone's surprise, it wasn't the dog who attacked.

Ms. Minerva's orange cat shrieked. The sound was unearthly; Morgan clapped his hands to his ears to block it out. But he couldn't stop the cat from launching itself out of the stroller and onto the dog's back. The dog **howled**, the cat **hissed**, and **Jodi cried out in surprise.**

The animals all panicked, pulling in eight different directions at once.

Jodi fell. She lost her grip on the leashes. **And the pets went wild.**

Chapter 11

WHO LET THE DOGS OUT? AND COULD THAT PERSON PLEASE COME GET THEM?

Jodi couldn't believe this was happening.

All she'd wanted was to show her brother that she could be responsible. That she could take care of animals. Every sort of animal!

And now those animals were scattered all over a public park. They were people's beloved pets . . . and they were lost. All lost.

All her fault.

"Dewey!" cried Ms. Minerva, and she ran off after the cat. "Dewey Decimal, come back here!"

Jodi fought back tears. "I lost them. I can't believe I lost them."

"Uh, well, not *all* of them," Po said. He held up the fishbowl. "Bubbles here stuck around."

Jodi couldn't fight the tears anymore. She stood there in the middle of the park, her knees skinned and her fingers sore, and she cried.

Then she felt her brother's arms around her. **He gave her a good long hug**—then he gripped her by her shoulders and he looked her in the eyes.

"We can fix this, Jodi," he said. "But we can't do it without you."

"M-me?" Jodi said.

"you know these animals," he said. "You know them extremely well. And you can tell us what we need to do to get them back." He smiled. "You just have to believe in yourself. Like I believe in you."

Jodi almost wanted to cry again, hearing that. But there was no more time for tears.

Those animals needed her.

"Okay," she said, wiping her cheeks. "Here's what we're going to do. Polly always wants a cracker. Theo, get the parrot back by giving her as many treats as it takes. Harper, same idea for the iguana—but give him fruit, not crackers." Theo and Harper grabbed the treats from Jodi, saluted, and ran off.

She rubbed her chin. "We could round up the dogs if we knew how to use Doc's whistle. . . ."

"Oh!" said Po. "I know how to use it. **I read the instruction manual last night!"**

Morgan gave him a suspicious look. "Really?"

"Why is that so hard to believe?" Po asked. "I'm a reluctant reader, sure. But Doc is an absolute

poet." He turned to Jodi. "I can do it. I know I can. Beethoven's Fifth Symphony, right? Consider it done-done-done-*donnne*."

"I trust you, Po," said Jodi. "And Pupernicus is a natural-born leader. If he comes running, the others will follow." She paused. "That just leaves Ms. Minerva's cat."

"So what do cats like?" asked Morgan. He thought about it for a moment, and his eyes went to the goldfish.

Po covered Bubbles with his body. **"Don't even think about it!"** he cried.

Jodi snapped her fingers. "I've got it!" She dug around in her bag until she found the laser pointer she'd used for her presentation. "Cats love to chase laser pointers. We'll get him back in no time."

Morgan grinned. "I knew you'd think of something."

"Thinking is only half the battle," said Jodi. "Go, go, go!"

It took nearly an hour. Po blew the whistle until he was out of breath—and surrounded by a captive canine audience. Theo had to climb a tree to reach the parrot. And to her embarrassment, **Harper captured the wrong lizard on her first attempt.** She had to go back and find the right one all over again.

But as Jodi used the laser pointer to lure Dewey back into Ms. Minerva's waiting stroller, they all breathed big sighs of relief.

"Ms. Minerva, I am so sorry," Jodi said. "I take full responsibility for that."

"Nonsense," said Ms. Minerva. She was wiping grass stains from her clothes. **"I should have**

recognized that
dog of Doc's in time to keep
things from getting out of hand.

Or maybe I should put a seat belt in this thing."
She patted the stroller. "But in the end, no harm
was done."

For a moment, Jodi believed that. She thought
everything was fine.

But then she saw shattered plastic in the grass.
She recognized it right away. Somehow, in all the
commotion, Baron Sweetcheeks's ball had broken
into pieces.

The hamster was lying unconscious
atop the wreckage.

"Baron Sweetcheeks!"
cried Jodi. "He's hurt!"

Chapter 12

SWEET OF CHEEKS.
STRONG OF SPIRIT.
INJURED OF PAW.

Jodi was so nervous in the waiting room of the vet, she thought she would shake apart into a million tiny bits.

Morgan held her hand, and **Ms. Minerva promised that everything would be okay.** But Jodi felt sick to know that Baron Sweetcheeks had been injured. And it had happened when she was supposed to be taking care of him!

"Your hamster will be fine," promised the veterinarian. She was a young woman with a kind voice. "It's only a sprained paw."

"I didn't know hamsters could get sprains," said Ms. Minerva.

"It's actually very common," said the vet. **"I love hamsters, but they tend to get underfoot."**

"What's the treatment?" Morgan asked.

"He just needs rest," said the vet. "The injury will heal on its own. In a few weeks, he'll be as good as new."

A few weeks? Jodi wanted to sink into her seat. **It was good news, mostly.** But she felt bad

that he would need so long to recover.

"**I gave him a little medicine to calm him down,**" said the vet. "So he's sleeping now, if you'd like to see him?"

The veterinarian led Jodi and Morgan into the back room, where Baron Sweetcheeks lay sleeping on a pillow. His adorable, super-pinchable cheeks puffed in and out with each little breath.

"It's all my fault," Jodi said. "You were right all along, Morgan. **I . . . I'm not ready for a pet of my own.**"

Morgan shook his head. His nose twitched. "That's not what I—I—"

He covered his nose and mouth just before letting out a tremendous sneeze.

"Bless you!" said the vet.

"Thanks," said Morgan. "I think I'm getting a cold."

"Think again," said the vet. "I can see exactly what's going on. **You're highly allergic.**"

"Allergic?" echoed Morgan.

The vet nodded. "To dogs and cats, yes." She smiled. "I'm assuming you don't have any at home."

Jodi swallowed hard. "No, we don't," she said. She looked at her brother as he wiped his nose. "And now . . . we never will."

Chapter 13

THEY SAY LIGHTNING NEVER STRIKES TWICE. BUT "THEY" DON'T HAVE A TRIDENT OF CHANNELING.

Hhen they returned to Minecraft, Po and the others had just a short way to go until they would arrive at the witch's hut. And the brown mooshroom she was expecting . . . **was still red.**

Po had other things on his mind, though.

"YOU GUYS . . . I THINK I WANT A GOLDFISH," he said.

Morgan glared at him. **"NOT NOW, PO."**

"But—"

Morgan cleared his throat and inclined his head in Jodi's direction. She had been quiet ever since the incident in the park. Obviously, her own plan to get a pet was not going well.

"Sorry," said Po, realizing that he hadn't been thinking of Jodi's feelings. He moved to her side and pushed his blocky shoulder against hers. "Hey, cheer up, kid," he said. **"I'M SURE YOU'LL GET A PET EVENTUALLY."**

Jodi frowned. "Baron Sweetcheeks is limping. And my brother sneezes every time he even looks at a dog." She shook her head sadly. "I think this is one dream I have to let go."

"Well, Morgan's older than you, so he has to move out one day, right?" Po snickered, but Jodi didn't respond to his joke.

"Seriously, though," said Po. "What happened to the Baron wasn't your fault." As soon as Po said that word, he realized something. **"HEY. THE FAULT,"** he said. **"I CAN'T SEE IT."**

"It's the storm clouds," said Jodi. "They sort of suit my mood today."

Rain had already begun to fall. "Yeah, normally I hate stormy weather," Po said. "But today, it's just what we need."

"This is perfect!" said Harper. **"IT'S TIME TO CALL DOWN SOME LIGHTNING.** Jodi, you shouldn't stand too close to Michael."

"Can I do it, Harper?" asked Po. **"CAN I THROW THE TRIDENT?"**

Harper didn't seem too sure about that. "You know how important this is, right?"

"Yes!" said Po. "I can be serious. You've seen me play basketball, right?" He crossed his chicken-wing arms. "I've got great aim, and I don't choke under pressure."

Harper handed over the trident. **It still glowed with magic.** "Just don't throw it directly at the mooshroom," said Harper. "A block or two away from him will work fine."

"Got it," said Po. "More like a lightning rod, less like a steak fork."

As the rain fell harder, Po gripped the trident tight.

He lined up the shot.

He threw it . . .

. . . and he missed his target by several yards.

"What was that?!" asked Morgan.

"Sorry!" said Po. "I was distracted by that pig."

They all turned to look. Po was right—a pig

had wandered up to them. It saw the trident stuck in the ground nearby, and, curious, it approached the enchanted weapon and gave it a sniff.

Just then, **a great bolt of lightning shot down** from the heavens.

Po turned away from the searing brightness.

And when he turned back . . . the pig had

been transformed. Standing where the cute little animal had been, there was now a strange creature that appeared half pig and half human . . . with its face partially melted away to reveal a gleaming skull.

"**PIGLIN!**" he cried. He pulled his sword from his inventory. "It's a zombified piglin!"

"I thought they only spawned in the Nether," said Jodi. She hurried back to Michael's side, raising her shield.

"Let's everybody stay calm," whispered Morgan. "They aren't hostile, remember? **IF WE DON'T ATTACK IT, THEN IT WON'T ATTACK US.**"

Po found that hard to believe. The mob looked dangerous. **It was even holding a sword**

made of solid gold! But the zombified piglin sniffed again at the trident, looked around at the kids, and shuffled off into the storm.

Po had a funny feeling they hadn't seen the last of it.

"Let's try this again," said Jodi. She led the mooshroom over to the trident, gave him a quick kiss on the nose for luck, and then dropped the lead and ran clear.

It was only a few seconds before lightning struck again.

This time, it found its target. Michael G stood transformed . . . a brown mooshroom at last.

"MOO?" he said, and he looked at them with big questioning eyes.

"Look at that face!" said Theo, and he giggled. Everybody else joined in.

Chapter 14

WHICH WITCH ORDERED
THE MOOSHROOM?

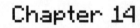

The witch cackled from the door of the hut, utterly gleeful at the sight of Michael G. The mob came down from the porch, skipping happily to a specially prepared cage. **The cage had a floor of mycelium, and tiny mushrooms grew around its edges.** For a moment, Jodi thought that perhaps Michael would be happy here.

She hesitated, though, when the witch opened the gate to the cage. The witch reached impatiently for Michael's leash, and Jodi knew she didn't have a choice. "Sorry, buddy," she said to the cow. **Then she handed the lead to the witch,** who

locked the mooshroom in his new cage.

"HIS NAME IS MICHAEL G," said Theo. "He likes wheat and gentle pats on the head. You'd better treat him right."

"Treat, hrm," said the witch. "Trick, hah."

And then the witch drew a gleaming **netherite sword**.

Jodi took a step back. "What is that for?" she asked.

"A powerful spell, heh, will I cast," said the witch. "Many, hrm, *ingredients,* has it. Chicken feather. Wool of,

hah, sheep. Horn of, hrm, goat." **The witch grinned maliciously.** "And leather . . . from a brown mooshroom . . . **SLAIN BY SWORD.**"

"Slain?!" said Jodi.

"The witch is going to destroy Michael G for his leather!" said Morgan.

"No," said Theo. **"THAT IS NOT GOING TO HAPPEN."** And he readied his sword.

The witch still smiled. "Weak, you are."

"You're right," said Harper. "We're still weakened."

"That's why we phoned a friend," said Po.

The kids stepped aside . . . **and Ash leaped forward, swinging her sword.**

It was a direct hit. The witch fell back, screeching and flashing red. Ash—who hadn't been debuffed like the others—had clearly done a lot of damage with that attack.

"Are you sure about this, everybody?" Ash asked. "If we defeat the witch . . . you might never be cured."

"We're sure," said Jodi.

"WE CAN'T LET THE WITCH HURT THAT MOOSHROOM," said Theo. "It just . . . it isn't right."

"In that case, everybody, start opening cages!" said Ash. She gripped her sword. "I'll keep the witch busy."

"Hah!" said the witch, throwing a splash potion at the group.

"Scatter!" said Morgan, and they all dove in different directions.

Theo was too slow.

The potion hit him square in the back. **"YEOW!"** he said.

"LEAVE THEM ALONE!" cried Ash, and she took another swing.

Jodi hurried to Theo's side. "Are you all right?" she asked him.

"I'm fine," Theo insisted. "Get Michael out of here!"

Jodi waited for her moment to act. She watched as Ash swung her sword again, and the witch melted into the shadows. Then Jodi sprang into action, running to Michael's cage and throwing open the door.

"GET OUT OF HERE, BUDDY!" she cried.

As a parrot flew overhead and a fox rushed past her, Jodi realized her friends were hard at work all the way down the line of cages. She saw her brother hurrying toward the baby panda's cell.

But then the witch slipped from the shadows just beside him.

"Morgan!" Jodi cried in warning, but it was too late. **The witch hurled a potion.** By the time it had shattered against him, the mob was already gone again.

"I can't keep up!" said Ash, running past Jodi and swinging her sword at every shadow. "How is that witch moving so quickly?"

Strangely, the witch showed little interest in Ash. The mob stayed clear of Ash's sword. Instead of fighting back, **the witch hurled potion after potion over Ash's head.**

Theo and Morgan had already been hit.

Harper was next.

And then Jodi was struck.

But to her surprise . . . it didn't hurt.

In fact . . . it felt good.

"What was in that splash potion?" Jodi asked.

Theo and Harper exchanged a look. **"I FEEL STRONGER,"** said Harper.

"The witch buffed us back to our normal stats," said Theo.

"I don't know what that means!" said Ash as she swung her sword.

"Ash, stop!" said Morgan. "It means . . . it means the witch cured us!"

Ash was just about to bring her sword down on

the witch. She stopped her swing just in time.

The witch cackled. This time, instead of sounding menacing, the laughter had a friendly tone to it.

"I don't understand," said Ash, poised for action. She didn't dare take her eyes off the mob. "What's going on here?"

"A, HRM, TEST," said the witch. "To see . . . see if you care. If beings of flesh and blood . . . can care about *them*." The witch waved an arm at the animal mobs around them.

Ash put down her sword. "Of course we care."

Jodi nodded. "All of us do," she agreed. "Right, guys?"

Theo stepped forward. He put a hand on Jodi's shoulder. "That's right."

The witch nodded, cackling again, but more quietly. "Hrm . . . be good to them. Be good, heh, to each other." With bright green eyes, the witch looked at them all, one at a time. "Your compassion, hah. You will need it. Need it, hrm, for what comes next." Those green eyes sparkled. **"SAVE THE BEES."**

"Save the bees?" Harper echoed. "What does that mean?"

The witch didn't answer. The strange mob just lifted an arm and waved at the animals, as if telling them good-bye. Slowly, that arm began to glow . . . and then it shattered, transforming into a swirling mass of butterflies. They swept over Ash, swirled around Jodi, **and then soared into the sky.**

And there, in the murky swamp water where the witch had stood, was the right arm of the Evoker King.

"I PROMISE. We do care about them," Jodi said to the night sky. "We care about this whole world. Even if it *is* digital . . . it's real to us."

"Hear, hear," Theo agreed.

The clouds parted, and **Jodi felt her heart surge with new hope.**

But then she saw the Fault. It was even larger than before.

And she couldn't help wondering if this digital world they loved . . . might be in terrible danger.

Chapter 15

WITH GREAT HAMSTERS THERE MUST COME . . . GREAT RESPONSIBILITY!

Jodi spent the rest of the week nursing Baron Sweetcheeks back to health. She also continued to walk her neighbors' dogs . . . but she had learned not to walk them all at once. **Taking one or two at a time took her longer, but she was happy to spend her vacation in the company of so many animals.**

She had surprised her parents when she'd told them that she had changed her mind about having a pet. She wasn't certain that she was ready yet for that much responsibility. And even if she was, she couldn't stand to see Morgan suffer. His allergies were pretty severe (and he didn't always cover his mouth when he sneezed, either).

But Jodi had no idea what awaited her when she returned to Stonesword Library the following weekend. All her friends had gathered in the meeting room, along with Mr. Malory, Ms. Minerva, and Doc. **Even Baron Sweetcheeks was there,** and Ash had once again dialed in on Theo's laptop.

And best of all, right on top of the meeting room's central table, there was a large gift with a big bow on it.

"It was your brother's idea," Mr. Malory explained. "And your teachers convinced me that you're ready for it." He slid the box across the table. **"Go ahead and open it."**

Jodi tore away the gift wrap, and she was stunned by what she saw.

It was a brand-new hamster cage . . . with a brand-new hamster inside.

"It only seems fair," said Mr. Malory.

"Woodsword has a class hamster. Shouldn't Stonesword have one as well?"

"We thought you could care for her, Jodi," said Doc. "So that you can get practice caring for a pet, with help from your friends and under adult supervision."

"She'll stay here at the library," Ms. Minerva explained. **"But she'll be your responsibility. You even get to name her."**

Jodi's eyes filled with tears. **The hamster's cheeks . . . her cute little tail . . . it was like a dream come true.**

"I promise I'll take care of you," Jodi told the hamster.

Morgan put a hand on her shoulder. "I know you'll do a great job," he said. "And one day, when you're ready for a puppy or a kitten of your own . . . I promise I'll get an allergy shot."

Jodi gasped. **"But you're so afraid of needles!"**

"Well, yeah, I am," said Morgan, blushing. "But I won't let that stand in the way of your happiness."

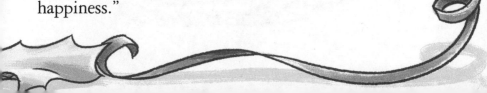

Jodi gave him a big hug. Then she went around the room and gave everyone else a hug, fist bump, or high five. She "booped" Ash's nose on the laptop screen and patted Baron Sweetcheeks on his fuzzy head.

Then she cuddled Stonesword Library's new addition and said, "Welcome to the family, **Duchess Dimples.** I love you already!"

Everyone crowded around to give Duchess Dimples a proper welcome. It was a joyful moment that Jodi would remember forever.

But she saw a hint of worry in Harper's eyes. She noticed that Morgan was scratching his ear, like he sometimes did when he was nervous.

Save the bees. That's what the witch had said. And whatever that meant, they would have to figure it out soon.

They still had three more pieces of the Evoker King to find. Jodi knew in her heart that helping their digital friend— that putting him back together again—was one responsibility they couldn't put off any longer.

And to do that, they were going to have to go deeper into Minecraft than ever before....

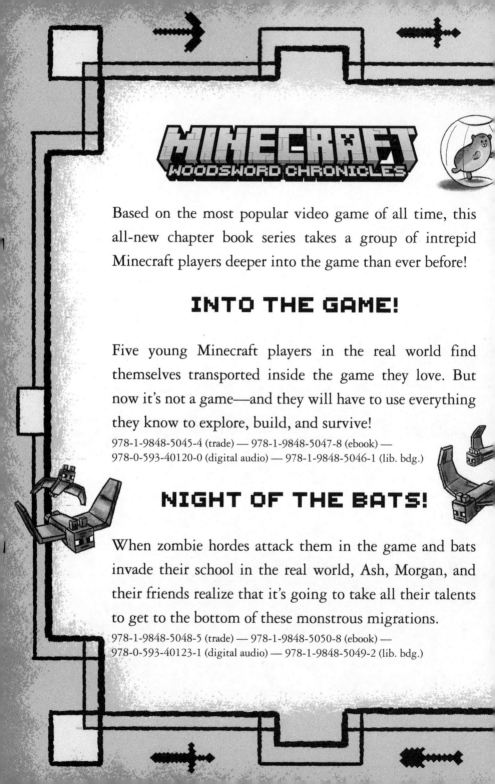

MINECRAFT
WOODSWORD CHRONICLES

Based on the most popular video game of all time, this all-new chapter book series takes a group of intrepid Minecraft players deeper into the game than ever before!

INTO THE GAME!

Five young Minecraft players in the real world find themselves transported inside the game they love. But now it's not a game—and they will have to use everything they know to explore, build, and survive!

978-1-9848-5045-4 (trade) — 978-1-9848-5047-8 (ebook) — 978-0-593-40120-0 (digital audio) — 978-1-9848-5046-1 (lib. bdg.)

NIGHT OF THE BATS!

When zombie hordes attack them in the game and bats invade their school in the real world, Ash, Morgan, and their friends realize that it's going to take all their talents to get to the bottom of these monstrous migrations.

978-1-9848-5048-5 (trade) — 978-1-9848-5050-8 (ebook) — 978-0-593-40123-1 (digital audio) — 978-1-9848-5049-2 (lib. bdg.)

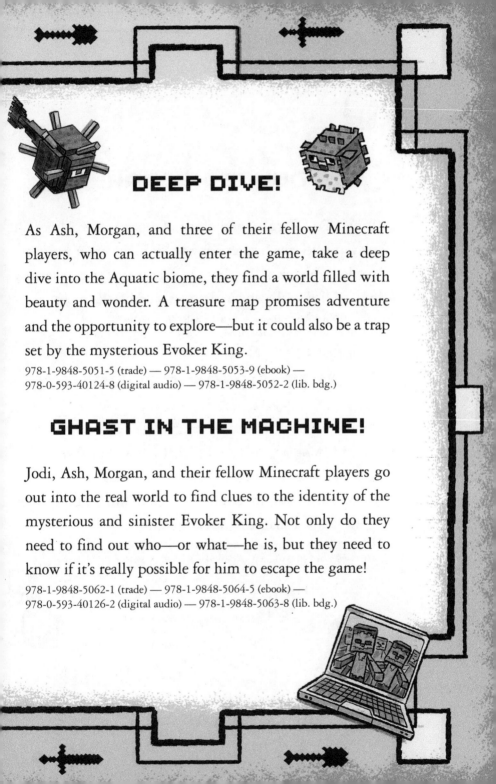

DEEP DIVE!

As Ash, Morgan, and three of their fellow Minecraft players, who can actually enter the game, take a deep dive into the Aquatic biome, they find a world filled with beauty and wonder. A treasure map promises adventure and the opportunity to explore—but it could also be a trap set by the mysterious Evoker King.

978-1-9848-5051-5 (trade) — 978-1-9848-5053-9 (ebook) —
978-0-593-40124-8 (digital audio) — 978-1-9848-5052-2 (lib. bdg.)

GHAST IN THE MACHINE!

Jodi, Ash, Morgan, and their fellow Minecraft players go out into the real world to find clues to the identity of the mysterious and sinister Evoker King. Not only do they need to find out who—or what—he is, but they need to know if it's really possible for him to escape the game!

978-1-9848-5062-1 (trade) — 978-1-9848-5064-5 (ebook) —
978-0-593-40126-2 (digital audio) — 978-1-9848-5063-8 (lib. bdg.)

DUNGEON CRAWL!

When Po, Morgan, and three of their fellow Minecraft players track the Evoker King to his home in the heart of a perilous dungeon, they have to gear up for an epic fantasy quest filled with danger, dragons, and hostile mobs.

978-1-9848-5065-2 (trade) — 978-1-9848-5067-6 (ebook) —
978-0-593-40128-6 (digital audio) — 978-1-9848-5066-9 (lib. bdg.)

LAST BLOCK STANDING!

As the world of Minecraft falls under the Evoker King's control, Morgan, Ash, and their friends get ready for the final showdown. But with their enemy now in possession of the most powerful building block in Minecraft, do they really stand a chance of defeating him?

978-1-9848-5069-0 (trade) — 978-1-9848-5071-3 (ebook) —
978-0-593-40130-9 (digital audio) — 978-1-9848-5070-6 (lib. bdg.)

THE ADVENTURES CONTINUE IN

MINECRAFT
STONESWORD SAGA

CRACK IN THE CODE!

Someone—or something—has turned the Evoker King to stone. And now a new player, Theo, has joined the team on their quest to return their former enemy to normal. Theo has modding skills that could come in handy, but does he have what it takes to be part of the team, or will his meddling put a crack in the game code that none of them will survive?

978-0-593-37298-2 (trade) — 978-0-593-37300-2 (ebook) — 978-0-593-40132-3 (digital audio) — 978-0-593-37299-9 (lib. bdg.)

MOBS RULE!

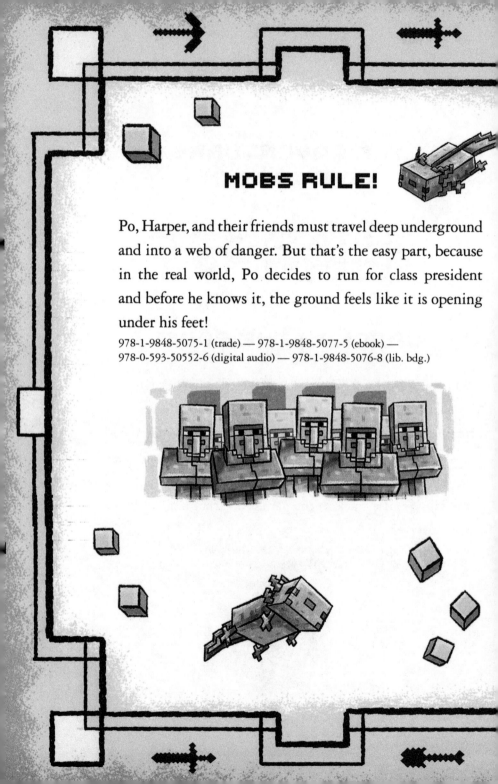

Po, Harper, and their friends must travel deep underground and into a web of danger. But that's the easy part, because in the real world, Po decides to run for class president and before he knows it, the ground feels like it is opening under his feet!

978-1-9848-5075-1 (trade) — 978-1-9848-5077-5 (ebook) — 978-0-593-50552-6 (digital audio) — 978-1-9848-5076-8 (lib. bdg.)

MORE MINECRAFT ADVENTURES COMING SOON . . . !

MINECRAFT is a game about placing blocks and going on adventures. Build, play, and explore across infinitely generated worlds of mountains, caverns, oceans, jungles, and deserts. Defeat hordes of zombies, bake the cake of your dreams, venture to new dimensions, or build a skyscraper. What you do in Minecraft is up to you.

Nick Eliopulos is a writer who lives in Brooklyn (as many writers do). He likes to spend half his free time reading and the other half gaming. He cowrote the Adventurers Guild series with his best friend and works as a narrative designer for a small video game studio. After all these years, endermen still give him the creeps.

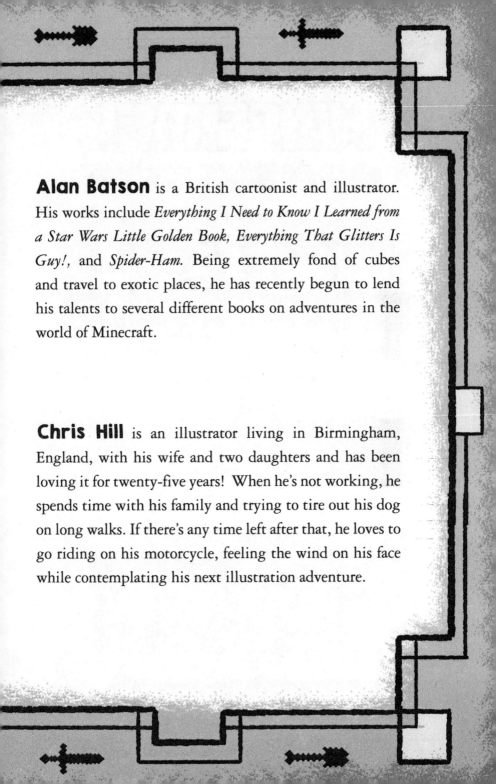

Alan Batson is a British cartoonist and illustrator. His works include *Everything I Need to Know I Learned from a Star Wars Little Golden Book, Everything That Glitters Is Guy!,* and *Spider-Ham.* Being extremely fond of cubes and travel to exotic places, he has recently begun to lend his talents to several different books on adventures in the world of Minecraft.

Chris Hill is an illustrator living in Birmingham, England, with his wife and two daughters and has been loving it for twenty-five years! When he's not working, he spends time with his family and trying to tire out his dog on long walks. If there's any time left after that, he loves to go riding on his motorcycle, feeling the wind on his face while contemplating his next illustration adventure.

JOURNEY INTO THE WORLD OF

MINECRAFT™

—BOOKS FOR EVERY READING LEVEL—

OFFICIAL NOVELS:

FOR YOUNGER READERS:

OFFICIAL GUIDES:

DISCOVER MORE AT READMINECRAFT.COM

MOBS RULE!

Published in the United States by Random House Children's Books, a division of Penguin Random House LLC, 1745 Broadway, New York, NY 10019, and in Canada by Penguin Random House Canada Limited, Toronto. Random House and the colophon are registered trademarks of Penguin Random House LLC.

rhcbooks.com
minecraft.net

Library of Congress Cataloging-in-Publication Data is available upon request.
ISBN 978-1-9848-5075-1 (trade)
ISBN 978-1-9848-5076-8 (library binding)—ISBN 978-1-9848-5077-5 (ebook)

Cover design by Diane Choi

Printed in the United States of America
10 9 8 7

MOBS RULE!

By Nick Eliopulos
Illustrated by Alan Batson and Chris Hill

Random House New York

MORGAN

ASH

HARPER

LAYERS!

PO

JODI

THEO

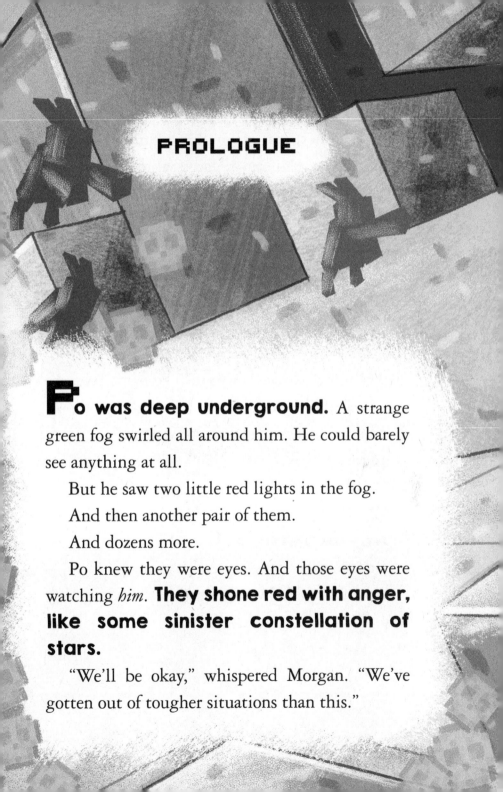

PROLOGUE

Po was deep underground. A strange green fog swirled all around him. He could barely see anything at all.

But he saw two little red lights in the fog.

And then another pair of them.

And dozens more.

Po knew they were eyes. And those eyes were watching *him*. **They shone red with anger, like some sinister constellation of stars.**

"We'll be okay," whispered Morgan. "We've gotten out of tougher situations than this."

But Po wasn't so sure.

They'd never seen anything quite like this before. They had never faced a mighty *swarm* of angry, vicious Minecraft mobs all working together as if they shared a single brain. A *hive mind* controlled these mobs, and its instructions were simple: **Destroy Po and his friends.**

It was hard not to be worried. Even if the mobs *were* awfully cute.

"Here they come," warned Morgan.

The mobs bounced forward. Their small, square eyes flashed like rubies in the torchlight. And now Po could see what they were up against.

It was a *tidal wave* of dangerous . . . *adorable* **bunnies**.

"Run away!" cried Po. **"RUN AWAY, RUN AWAY, RUN AWAY!"**

But his friends were already fleeing.

And the rabbits were gaining with each passing second.

Chapter 1

WHEN THINGS SPLIT APART, WHOSE FAULT IS IT ANYWAY?

Po Chen tried his best to ignore the strange hole in the Minecraft sky.

His friends had recently started calling it **the Fault.** Though it was small, it was easy to see in the daytime. Against the light blue color of the sky, the blacked-out pixels were hard to miss.

But Minecraft was Po's happy place.
He was not going to stress out over a little thing
like a hole in the sky. Strange and wonderful things
happened here all the time. Why worry about it?

"Well, *I'm* worried," said Po's friend Morgan
Mercado. Morgan was a Minecraft expert, and he
didn't like it when the game acted unpredictably.

**"I'D LIKE TO GET A CLOSER LOOK AT
IT,"** said Harper Houston. While Morgan tended
to react to situations quickly, Harper liked to
gather facts before coming to conclusions.

"If we want answers, the best place to find them
is in the game's code," said Theo Grayson. Everyone
shot him a look. His would-be programming and
modding skills had gotten them into trouble
before. Theo shrugged and added sheepishly, "It's
just a suggestion."

"WHATEVER THE FAULT IS . . . it's
definitely not cute," said Jodi Mercado. She was
Morgan's little sister, and she enjoyed meeting
cute animal mobs and adding artistic flair to the
things they built. **Wild adventures, epic
mob battles, and eerie holes in the sky**

were not her idea of a great Minecraft session.

"La la la," said Po, putting his blocky hands to his ears. "Can't hear you."

Morgan scowled. "Be serious, Po," he said. "Aren't you even a little bit curious about what the Fault is? Or about what caused it?"

"OF COURSE I'M CURIOUS," said Po. "But just because it's *weird* doesn't mean it's a problem. I mean, this version of Minecraft has always been weird."

Po knew Morgan was making a good point. After all, he and his friends weren't just playing Minecraft—they were *living* it. Thanks to their science teacher's experimental VR technology, they were able to visit a digital landscape that looked and acted almost exactly like their favorite game. *Almost* exactly. There were occasional exceptions . . . like the artificial intelligence named the Evoker King who called this place home.

But the Evoker King had turned out to be a pretty cool guy. So maybe the black spot in the blue sky would turn out to

be pretty cool, too?

They had been walking across the Overworld for days, stopping occasionally to gather resources or fight a zombie or chase a chicken around just for fun. It To outsiders it might have looked like aimless wandering, but the kids were on a mission.

They were hunting butterflies.

Butterflies—like Faults and artificial intelligences—didn't belong in a normal game of Minecraft. The small, colorful mobs had only appeared recently, and they had something to do with the Evoker

King's dramatic transformation.

"I saw one!" said Theo. He peered into the distance. "I can't see it anymore. **BUT IT WENT THAT WAY.**"

Po looked in the direction Theo was pointing. Across the plain, there was a mountain, and at the base of that mountain, he saw a small collection of homes. "Hey, there's a village over there."

"We might as well check it out," said Harper. **"MAYBE WE CAN PICK UP SOME SUPPLIES . . . OR SOME CLUES."**

Po agreed. He hoped they were on the right track, and that they would soon find a way to help the Evoker King. Shortly after the kids had become friends with the Evoker King, their AI ally had turned to stone—or so it had appeared. It was more accurate to say that the Evoker King had been *cocooned* in stone. And when that cocoon had split open, several mysterious mobs had emerged. **Those mysterious mobs were all made from pieces of the Evoker King's programming.** If they wanted to put their friend back together, they needed to find each piece. And the unusual digital butterflies that had appeared when the cocoon first split open seemed to appear near those mysterious mobs. It was almost like the game was leaving a path for the kids to follow.

And right now, that path was leading them to a village.

The village was a small one, with only a few houses. Its residents were all going about their usual business.

"See?" said Po. "They're not worried about the Fault, either." **He chuckled, remembering that he was using an alien skin for his**

avatar today. "Hey, Earthling," he said to the nearest villager. "Take us to your leader!"

The villager only honked in reply and kept walking.

Theo frowned. "I was actually *hoping* there'd be something unusual about this place," he said. "I don't think we're going to find the next piece of the Evoker King in a normal village."

A farmer held out an emerald for Harper to see. "Oh!" said Harper. **"THE FARMER WANTS TO TRADE AN EMERALD FOR SOME HAY THAT'S IN MY INVENTORY.** I think we can spare it. . . ."

"Hey, look over there!" said Jodi. She pointed up

the nearby extreme hills biome and the mountain that loomed over the village.

"What is it?" asked Morgan. "Another butterfly?"

"Even better," said Jodi. **"IT'S A LLAMA!"**

"Wow," said Po. "Good eyes, Jodi." The llama was some distance away. It looked tiny! But now that Jodi had pointed it out, Po could see it walking around about halfway up the mountain.

"I haven't seen a llama in *weeks*," said Jodi. "Can we go visit? **I WANT TO PET IT!"**

Morgan shook his head. "We need to focus on the mission," he said.

"Aw, come on, Morgan," said Po. "I want to help the Evoker King as much as you do, but this village is a dead end. I don't see any butterflies."

He shrugged. "And llamas *are* pretty cute."

"Besides," added Harper, **"CLIMBING THE MOUNTAIN MIGHT BE A GOOD STRATEGY.** We'll be able to see for miles in every direction. Maybe that will help us figure out where to go next."

"Yeah, okay," said Morgan. "That makes sense." **Jodi gave Po a fist bump** and a smile.

The mountain was tall, but it wasn't too steep. Po and the others were able to take it one block at a time. And in Minecraft, they didn't have to worry about altitude sickness or landslides or any of the other dangers of real-life mountain climbing.

They did have to worry about falling, though. **Falling from such a great height was as dangerous in Minecraft as it was in real life.**

Po decided not to look down.

But when he looked up, he saw the Fault, too close to ignore.

By the time they reached the llama, the sun was getting lower. It dipped behind the mountain, casting everything on their side in shadow.

"Be careful," said Morgan. "Even though it's daytime . . . monsters can spawn in the shadows."

"HOW CAN YOU THINK OF MONSTERS AT A TIME LIKE THIS?" said Jodi, and she held out her blocky hands toward the llama. It was facing away from them and hadn't noticed them yet. "Hello, my precious! What's your name?"

"Hm," said Po, deciding to guess the llama's name. "I think it looks like a *Winifred.*"

Jodi chuckled, and she placed a hand on the llama's back. **The animal spun around to look at her and its eyes shone red.**

There was something sinister and unnatural about those red eyes.

"Okay," said Po. "Definitely not Winifred!"

Jodi just had time to gasp before the llama spat at her. She flashed red as she took damage from the projectile spit. She was also knocked back— dangerously close to the edge.

"CAREFUL!" said Morgan, and he quickly

pulled his sister to his side.

"I don't understand," she said. "Why did it attack me?"

"It's *still* attacking," warned Theo. **"LOOK OUT!"**

Theo was right. The llama appeared to be furious. It reared up and kicked at them, spitting again, and all the while, it bleated angrily.

Po pulled a sword from his inventory, but he hesitated. "I don't really want to hurt it!" he said.

"THEN GET AWAY FROM IT!" said Morgan. "Everybody, retreat!"

Po didn't need to be told twice. He put his

sword away and followed the others as they fled the angry animal.

A glob of spit passed by his head, narrowly missing him. Bleating sounded from just behind him. The llama was actually *chasing* them.

"This is too weird!" Theo cried.

Harper was in the lead, and as she headed down the mountain, she curved around it to the other side. "This way!" she said. "We have to get out of its view."

PO FOLLOWED. As he rounded the bend, he saw a small fissure in the ground, just past the foot of the mountain. It looked like an earthquake had left a narrow crack right in the grassy dirt of the

plains. Harper ran into the fissure, followed by the others.

Po was the last one to enter. The others all stood with their backs pressed against the stone wall, hiding in the dark. He joined them.

There were sounds of bleating from outside, and shuffling hooves. But the llama didn't follow them inside.

"I think we lost it," whispered Harper.

"WHY WAS IT SO AGGRESSIVE?" asked Jodi. "Did I do something wrong?"

Po turned to Morgan, expecting him to have something to say about what was normal and abnormal llama behavior. But Morgan had stepped

a little farther into the fissure. **He looked astonished.**

"Check it out, everybody," he said. "It's a lush cave biome."

Po joined Morgan and peered deeper into the cave. He was surprised to see so much color beneath the stone-gray mountain. He saw green moss, pink flowers, brown roots, and bright blue water.

"I've never seen this biome before," said Theo.

"Me neither," said Harper. **"I'D LIKE TO EXPLORE IT!"**

"It's better than going back out *there*," said Jodi, hugging herself.

"Let's set up our beds," said Morgan. "This is as good a spot as any. Tomorrow, we can take our time exploring the cave."

It sounded like a good plan to Po. He had homework waiting for him back in the real world ... **and something else on his mind, as well.**

Soon, Woodsword Middle School would be holding an election.

And Po didn't intend to miss out on that.

Chapter 2

A SPOONFUL OF COMPETITION NEVER HURT ANYBODY—BUT A FORKFUL OF BAD IDEAS WILL POKE YOU IN THE EYE EVERY TIME!

The next day at school, Jodi was still thinking about the llama.

"You should have seen it, **Baron Sweetcheeks**," she said to the class hamster. "It was the *meanest* llama of all time. **Eight feet tall ... with red eyes, and fangs ...**"

Baron Sweetcheeks trembled in her hands. At first, she worried that she had frightened the hamster. But then she realized he was just excited to be surrounded by so much food. (It was lunchtime, and Jodi had brought him to the cafeteria.)

"You're exaggerating," said Theo. **"The llama did not have fangs."**

"She's right about the eyes, though," said Harper. "They were as red as rubies."

Morgan was clearly troubled. "I don't know what it means," he said. "But I wonder if it has something to do with the Evoker King. And I also wonder . . . is it sanitary to have Baron Sweetcheeks at our lunch table?"

Po gasped. "How dare you!" he said. "The Baron is *immaculately* clean. He bathes more often than you do!"

"And I *need* him here for emotional support," said Jodi, hugging the hamster close. "I see that llama's mean old face every time I close my eyes!"

Harper shrugged. "To be honest, I'm glad he's here, too," she said. "Because I've got bologna for lunch, and there's no way I can eat it all."

"Ooh," said Theo. **"I love bologna."**

"Well, now I've heard everything," said Harper, and she handed him half her sandwich. **The hamster squeaked with envy.**

"I'm glad you could join us today, Baron Sweetcheeks," said Po, suddenly sounding gravely serious.

Jodi giggled. Po only sounded *gravely serious* when he was being silly.

"You're a hamster," Po continued, "but you're also part of our team. So it's only fitting that you're here for my big announcement. I, Po Chen . . . have decided to run for class president!"

Baron Sweetcheeks didn't seem especially impressed by this news. He was fixated on Theo's gelatin dessert. But everyone else around the table gave a little cheer.

"That's exciting news!" said Jodi.

"Totally," said Theo. **"YOU'VE GOT MY VOTE."**

"How can we help?" asked Harper.

Morgan scratched his chin. "Po . . . are you sure you have time for this?" he asked.

Jodi elbowed her brother.

"What?" he said. "Class president is a lot of responsibility! And Po has a lot going on, between schoolwork, basketball, drama club, and, you know . . ." He lowered his voice. **"Searching the Overworld for the missing fragments of a sentient artificial intelligence so that we can put him back together again."**

In response, Po waved around a homemade "Vote for Po" pennant. "It's fine," he said. "Drama club is on break for a little while. And as class president, I'll be able to set the schedule for the whole student government. **That means no** meetings on days we play Minecraft."

"All right then," said Morgan, and he smiled. "I'm in. And I'm impressed. I heard you have to fill out a *lot* of paperwork to get your name on the ballot. I don't know when you had time to do that."

"Paperwork, you say?" Po gulped. "Sounds like . . . I should get on that."

"Po!" said Harper. **"That paperwork is due this week!"**

"Well, how was I supposed to know that?" asked Po.

"The student council mentioned it on the morning announcements," answered Theo. "Every morning. For the last three weeks."

Po just shrugged. "Maybe the paperwork can get done quickly if we all pitch in," he suggested.

Jodi reached across the table to pat him on the shoulder. **"We'll help you, Po,"** she said. "Don't worry. I've got a good feeling about—"

Before Jodi could finish her sentence, an amplified voice boomed across the cafeteria. "Good afternoon, fellow students!"

Everyone turned in their seats. At the front of

the room was a girl holding a megaphone. Jodi had never met her, but she recognized her outfit. The girl was wearing a Wildling Scout uniform similar to the one their friend Ash used to wear, and a sash full of merit badges.

"**I'm Shelly Silver**," said the girl. "And I'd like to announce my candidacy for president of student government!"

Everyone in the cafeteria applauded. Even Jodi felt it was the polite thing to do. But Po just glared and gripped his pennant tighter.

"**Thanks, everybody**," said Shelly. "I have a small—but sweet—treat for you all today." Her smile flashed white, even at this distance. "So remember me when it's time to cast your ballot. **Vote for Shelly!**"

As soon as Shelly had finished speaking, a dozen Wildling Scouts emerged from the kitchen. They each carried a tray piled high with little ice cream cups, and they circulated through the cafeteria, giving each student a free ice cream and spoon.

Jodi felt a little guilty accepting the dessert. But she would have felt worse turning it down.

She could feel Po's eyes burning into her as she took her first bite. It was *really* good ice cream. But she tried not to show it.

"Check it out, Po," said Theo, and he held up the spoon he'd been given. "There are words printed on it."

Jodi looked at her own spoon. Theo was right. The spoons had a simple slogan: "Vote for Shelly."

"Looks like you've got some competition, buddy," said Morgan.

Po nodded grimly, his pennant drooping as if in defeat.

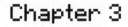

Chapter 3

THREE HINTS ABOUT WHAT'S IN THE WATER: IT'S AN AMPHIBIAN. IT'S A PASSIVE MOB. AND IT'S DIFFICULT TO SPELL!

Po wasn't happy to learn that Shelly Silver wanted to be class president, too. He had hoped to be the only person on the ballot. **Now he would have to plan a real campaign.** He had to convince everybody to vote for him . . . somehow.

He expected to be grumpy about it for the rest of the day. But that afternoon, when he and his friends reconnected to their shared Minecraft server, he forgot his irritation almost immediately. **The lush cave biome was just too awe-inspiring for his rotten mood to last.**

He had spent a lot of time underground. Usually that meant being surrounded by gray diorite, gray

andesite, gray deepslate . . . **and occasionally some bright-orange lava.**

But this cave had plants. Flowers! Faintly glowing berries grew upon long, hanging vines, and tree roots hung from the stony ceiling, like fingers reaching down for him.

"Should we take some of the roots with us?" asked Theo. **He had removed a pair of iron shears from his inventory.**

"Sure," said Harper. "Let's take a little of everything! You never know what we might be able to use later. Po, grab that flower!"

"On it," said Po, but before he had a chance, he heard Jodi call for him.

"Po!" squealed Jodi. "Harper! **COME HERE, QUICK! YOU'VE GOT TO SEE THIS!**"

Po and Harper shared a grin. Then they rushed

over to see what had made Jodi so excited.

"LOOK!" she said. **"IN THE WATER!"**

Po stepped right up to the edge of the underground lake. He bent over and peered into the water.

Nothing could have prepared him for the strange creature that peered back at him.

THERE IN THE WATER WAS A LONG, SKINNY ANIMAL WITH BRIGHT PINK COLORING. At first Po thought it must be a fish—maybe an eel—but that wasn't right. Unlike a fish, it had limbs. Its face almost reminded him of a puppy's.

Jodi gripped his arm. "It . . . it . . ." She took a steadying breath, then bellowed, *"It's even cuter than a llama!"*

Before Po could stop her, Jodi dove into the water. Luckily, the mob appeared to be friendly.

It swam right up to Jodi as if curious, and she chased it, laughing.

"WHAT'S THAT THING?" Po asked.

"It's an axolotl," answered Harper. "It's an amphibian—a type of salamander. Some people call it a 'walking fish' because, well, that's sort of what it looks like."

"I don't think I've seen an axolotl in Minecraft before," said Theo. He and Morgan had joined them at the edge of the water. "Are they safe to be around?"

"Sure," said Morgan. **"THEY'LL ATTACK SOME UNDERWATER MOBS,** but they're passive toward players. And fun fact: they can heal when they get damaged."

"Just like in real life!" said Harper. "Axolotls can regrow lost limbs—or even organs. They're like little miracles. Unfortunately, they're endangered. . . ."

As fascinating as all this was to hear Po found himself increasingly jealous of the good time Jodi was having. "Sorry, everybody," he said. "I've got to see it up close for myself!"

And he dove into the water.

There were two axolotls now, swimming in

circles around Jodi. One was
pink, and one was gold.

**Po joined the swimming, petting
the axolotls when they got close.** They
were weirdly adorable, and Po wished he could
just stay down there and never come up for air. All
his problems were above the water's surface. Down
here, it was a party.

But then he caught sight of Jodi. She looked
worried—*panicked*. She was flapping her
arms madly, trying to tell him

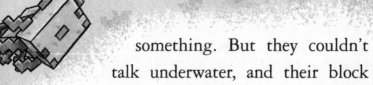

something. But they couldn't talk underwater, and their block hands made it difficult to communicate with gestures. What was she trying to warn him about?

THEN, SUDDENLY, PO WAS FALLING THROUGH OPEN AIR.

Oh, he thought. *Waterfall.* That was what she'd been trying to tell him.

That underground lake had been more of an underground *river,* and he'd been swept up in the current without even realizing it!

Po flipped head over rump, and before he had a chance to worry about where he would land, he splashed down into a *true* underground lake. He swam to the surface, but it was hard to see anything. **He was really deep underground now,** and except for the light of the glow berries high above him, it was dark.

"Po!" came Morgan's voice from above. "Are you okay?"

"Yeah!" Po shouted back. **"COME ON DOWN, YOU GUYS. THE WATER'S FINE!"**

He thought they might all dive into the lake,

but they took a safer route. He could see them clearly by the light of the torches Harper was leaving behind as they walked carefully down a rocky slope.

Once they reached the bottom, the whole cavern slowly revealed itself to Po, the light peeling away the darkness a little bit at a time. It was a huge subterranean space, with multiple lakes, a giant waterfall, and dozens of dark tunnel openings.

There was a splash nearby, and Po saw that the axolotls had followed him down the waterfall. The mobs twisted and turned playfully in the water.

"This is so cool," said Theo as he reached ground level. He and Jodi and Harper and Morgan all walked in different directions, poking their heads into side tunnels and **placing torches all around the cavern.**

Morgan stepped up to where Po was swimming. "I was worried when you went over the edge," he said.

"IT WAS A BIG DROP, but you didn't need to worry," said Po. "I've got luck on my side."

Morgan grinned—and then he noticed the green mist gathering at his feet.

"Uh," said Morgan, his smile dropping away. "What's *that* about?"

He looked around for answers. He looked left and right. Up and down.

But he didn't look behind him. **So he didn't see what Po saw.**

And what Po saw was a monster. It skittered out of the dark tunnel, right at Morgan's back.

Chapter 4

AXOLOTLS: SUPER CUTE! TERRIBLE JUDGES OF CHARACTER!

Morgan could tell by the look on Po's face that **something was terribly wrong.**

Po seemed to be warning him about something. Still floating in the underground lake, he opened and closed his mouth, looking like a fish, making no sound. Morgan had been playing Minecraft a long time, so experience quickly translated Po's expression: *Behind you!*

It was a cave spider.

But it was far larger than any cave spider Morgan had ever seen. Its eight legs were as thick as tree trunks. Its ten ruby-red eyes shone with eerie intelligence. Its fangs dripped with green venom.

And on its abdomen . . . **was the frightening image of a skull.**

Morgan didn't hesitate. He quickly swapped his torch for a weapon. He chose a diamond sword that had been enchanted with sharpness.

He had never fought a mob quite like this one. But no mob could survive for long against such a powerful sword.

Morgan leaped forward and slashed.

He was fast—but the spider was faster. It jumped back, much farther and higher than he expected. In an instant, it was up on the edge of a looming cliff, too far away to hit with a sword.

"Careful," said Theo. He was gripping his own sword as he came to stand beside Morgan. "Cave spiders are venomous."

Morgan didn't like it when Theo acted like he knew more about Minecraft than anybody else. "I know cave spiders are venomous," he said, a little less politely than he meant to. "But it can't poison me from way up there."

"Uh," said Theo, "are you sure? Look—"

Morgan looked. **And he saw the spider doing something strange. . . .**

The hostile mob reared back, lifting its front legs and spreading its jaws wide. It made a hissing noise . . . and green mist poured from its mouth. Morgan and Theo were covered in the mist within seconds.

Judging by the mist's sickly green color, Morgan thought it must be a

poisonous fog of some kind. But he didn't feel any effects from it. He looked at Theo, who also seemed uninjured.

Po, however, shrieked in pain and surprise.

Morgan whirled around to see Po splashing around in the lake. "Get them off!" Po cried. "Get them off me!"

It was hard to see much through the fog. But as the water all around Po swirled and splashed, Morgan realized what was wrong. It was the axolotls. They'd become hostile, and they were attacking Po.

"PO, GET OUT OF THERE!" cried Harper.

Jodi didn't wait. She dove into the water in order to drag Po to solid ground. Morgan and Theo ran around the edge of the lake to join the group just as

Jodi and Po hopped out of the water.

"What's happening?" asked Harper. "Where did that green fog come from?"

"There's a spider over there," said Morgan. **"A BIG ONE. DO YOU HAVE A BOW AND ARROWS?"**

"Forget about the spider," said Po. "The axle-what-alls are out to get me!"

The axolotls hopped out of the water. **Their small eyes glowed red in the dark.** Morgan had almost forgotten—unlike fish, amphibians can survive on land for a time.

As the pink one lunged for them, Morgan yelled, "Follow me!"

He led them into the nearest tunnel. He didn't

know where it would take them. He only hoped it would put some distance between them and the spider . . . and the strangely hostile axolotls.

The tunnel twisted and turned. Morgan placed torches down as he ran, but he had to use them sparingly. The darkness was always looming just ahead. **He only hoped he wouldn't lead his friends right over a cliff.** Or what if the tunnel circled back to the cavern, and they ran right into the clutches of that eerie spider?

When Morgan ran out of torches, he stopped, and the others stopped right behind him. The tunnel was narrow, but he could see past his friends. **The axolotls were no longer following them.**

"I THINK WE'RE SAFE," said Morgan. "But let's not take any chances." He placed cobblestone blocks on either side of them, turning the tunnel into a small stone room.

"That was so weird," whispered Po. **"I WAS SO FREAKED OUT BY THE BIG MOB.** When the cute little ones attacked, it caught me by surprise!"

Jodi spoke up. "When I jumped into the water to help you . . . I saw them." She shivered. "Their eyes were red."

"Just like the llama!" said Theo.

"I'll repeat my question from before," said Harper. "*What* is happening here?"

Morgan didn't have an answer. "We should talk about it in the real world, where it's safe. Let's set up our beds." He looked at the torch on the wall. It had been the very last torch in his inventory. He knew they would need more—a *lot* more—if they were to have any hope of surviving down here in the dark.

Chapter 5

WE ALL SCREAM FOR ICE CREAM, BUT MAYBE WE SHOULD USE OUR INSIDE VOICES.

The giant spider was a creepy foe, to be sure. And Po had not *loved* being a target for the axolotls.

But in the bright lights and open spaces of the real world, it was easy to let that stuff go. Besides, Po had a real-world hostile mob to worry about, and her name was Shelly Silver.

And it was time to fight ice cream with ice cream.

"I can't believe you brought a whole ice cream truck to school!" said Theo after the lunch bell rang the next day. He was clearly impressed.

One down, thought Po. *About four hundred more students to go.*

"It's my cousin's truck," explained Po. "She's in high school, and she sells ice cream on the weekends. And she owed me a favor."

"That's a pretty big favor," said Theo. "What did you do, save her cat or something?"

"I fainted," said Po. "Or I pretended to." He smiled at the memory. "We were at a family wedding, and she was desperate to leave early. So I pretended to have a little fainting spell. She rushed to my 'rescue' and drove me home, which got her out of there—and made her look like a hero at the same time."

He put his hand to his head and groaned as he slumped in his wheelchair. After a pausing a moment for dramatic effect, he added, "See. I told you guys I'm a good actor."

"But what kind of *politician* are you?" asked Harper, giving him a quick eye roll before getting down to business. "Giving out ice cream to the whole student body is a good way to get everyone's attention. But what are your policies, your ideas?"

Theo added, "You should use this opportunity to actually inform everybody about your platform."

"**Platform?**" echoed Po.

"You know," said Harper. "What kind of changes will you make if you're elected? What promises are you making? **Why are you a better candidate than Shelly Silver?**"

"Um . . . ," said Po. "Well, *my* ice cream is soft serve, which is way better than those little cups."

Harper frowned. "You need to give some thought to this, Po."

"**She has a point,**" said Theo, nodding in agreement with Harper. "If you don't have a plan for being president . . . if you don't have a reason *why* people should vote for you . . . **then all of this is just a popularity contest.**"

"I love popularity contests!" said Po. He saw Theo and Harper exchange a worried look. "Don't worry," he said. "I'll think about what you just said. Consider *that* my first campaign promise."

He pressed the button for the automatic door that led out of the school.

"But right now, I need to make sure my cousin does her part."

Po's cousin, Hope, was in position and ready to go. **She had parked her ice cream truck right across the street, outside Stonesword Library.**

Po wheeled up to the truck and greeted his cousin with a high five.

"Hey, Hope," he said. "Thanks for doing this."

"Anything for you, little cousin," said Hope. "Especially since you'll owe me big-time."

"I figured we'd be *even*," said Po.

Hope chuckled. "That's cute," she said. "But this is a lot of ice cream, we've got *two* family weddings coming up, and I've had enough Chen family country line dances for this lifetime."

Po couldn't argue with that. His grandparents really liked to get down. **It could be weird.**

"Hey, Po!" said a voice. It was Morgan, wearing a bright orange vest over his T-shirt. Despite the sunny outfit, he looked deeply tired.

"Everything's all approved," said Morgan. "It took me most of the night, but I finished the paperwork to get you on the ballot *and* the paperwork that allows you to give out ice cream." He stifled a yawn. "The only catch is that we need a crossing guard to make sure students can safely cross the street between the school and the library."

"And you volunteered?" asked Po, understanding now why Morgan was wearing the vest. "Thanks, Morgan. You're the best! When I'm president, I'm totally making you my second-in-command."

"You know that's not how it works, right?"

Morgan said, pinching the bridge of his nose. "There's a whole separate election for vice president. And for class secretary, and treasurer . . ."

"**So many rules**," said Po. "You can tell me all about it later. Right now, I've got an announcement to make."

Po pulled a brand-new megaphone from his backpack, and he held it to his lips. "Free ice cream for all Woodsword students!" he bellowed. "**Come and get it. And vote for me, Po!**"

Morgan winced at the noise, then hurried to stand at the crosswalk.

The school lawn was full of students who had taken their lunches outside. They all perked up at Po's announcement. Most of them stood and stepped forward, drawn by the promise of free dessert.

"Here they come, Hope," said Po. And then, into the megaphone again: "**Vote for Po! Vote for Po!**"

Within seconds, there was a line of students winding halfway down the sidewalk.

Jodi stepped from the crowd. "Hey, Po!" she

said. "I made an announcement in the cafeteria, like you asked. There are a lot more students coming your way." SHE LOOKED OVER AT MORGAN, WHO HAD CAUSED A MINOR TRAFFIC JAM. Cars had begun honking, but with students in the road, there was nothing he could do but hold up his stop sign.

"Maybe I should go help Morgan," she said, and Po just nodded. Into the megaphone, he said, **"Vote for PO! VOTE for Po.** VOTE for me . . . PO!"

The students in line all cheered.

And there were *a lot* of students in line. Po smiled at the turnout.

And then he frowned. Why wasn't the line moving faster? It was growing longer, and paper

airplanes were taking flight.

Po wheeled to the truck and stuck his head inside. "How's it going, cousin?" he asked.

He was able to guess the answer just by looking at Hope. **His cousin always appeared calm, cool, and collected.** But now, there was a hint of panic in her eyes, and a single drop of sweat running slowly down her cheek.

"All good, cousin!" she said. "It's just . . . you didn't tell me there would be *quite* so many kids."

"Don't think of them as kids," said Po. "Think of them as *votes*. And make sure they're happy. **Extra sprinkles!"**

Hope jabbed a thumbs-up in his direction. But

she did *not* look happy.

"Hey, uh, Po," said Theo. **"Kids are getting a little restless."** A paper airplane hit him in the side of the head. He didn't even bother to try to figure out who threw it. Half the kids in line were throwing things.

"Maybe you should talk to them?" Theo said. "Give a little speech. Something to keep everyone occupied."

Harper checked the time on her phone. "Only, make it quick. Lunch period is over in a few minutes."

Po brought the megaphone up to his mouth. He licked his lips. "Uh, hey, everyone," he said. "I just want to say . . ."

What *did* he want to say? Po's mind went blank. What did politicians talk about?

"Uh, vote for Po!" he said at last.

That didn't seem to do the trick. **This time, he got more jeers than cheers.** The students were rowdier than ever, and the line was still moving far too slowly. Cars and trucks continued to honk from the street.

"What is all this racket?" said a voice. "What's going on out here?"

Po spun his wheelchair around to see Mr. Malory, Stonesword's media specialist. **He looked . . . grumpy.**

"Mr. Malory!" said Po. "I'd offer you an ice cream, sir, but I don't think you get to vote in the student election. . . ."

"This noise level is unacceptable," said Mr. Malory. "The media center is for quiet study, and all these voices are coming right through the windows." He looked around the library's courtyard. **"And look at this mess!"**

Po hadn't even noticed, but the trash receptacles were overflowing with garbage. There was recycling in the trash, and trash in the recycling, and extra cups and spoons had been left right on the ground, along with paper airplanes and rubber bands.

"I trust you'll pick this mess up?" said

Mr. Malory. "And see that it's sorted properly?"

"I . . . I'm sure we can make time for that," said Po.

"I have a perfect suggestion," said Mr. Malory. "You and your friends can clean up instead of playing Minecraft in the library today."

Po's heart sank. He could feel the disappointment coming off Theo and the others in waves. And those waves felt like they were crashing right into him.

"Yes, sir," Po said. And just because he thought it couldn't hurt, he added, "Sorry, sir."

Then the bell rang, and the students who hadn't gotten ice cream yet all grumbled and moaned with disappointment.

"I was promised ice cream!" cried a voice from the back of the line. It was Doc Culpepper, their science teacher.

Suddenly, Po felt like he had *a lot* of apologizing to do.

Chapter 6

GETTING OVER THE UNDERGROUND IS HARD TO DO. SURVIVING THE UNDERGROUND MIGHT BE EVEN HARDER!

With everyone working together, Harper knew the after-school cleanup wouldn't take too long. Jodi complained that the job was "icky," Po was upset that his ice cream event had been so chaotic, and **Morgan and Theo were clearly impatient to get back to Minecraft.** But Harper took recycling very seriously, and she made sure that everybody stayed focused on their shared task.

It was a reminder that they made a great team, both in and out of Minecraft.

"Nicely done, kids," said Mr. Malory. He nudged a recycling bin with his foot, checking that everything had been sorted correctly. "You still have time to use the computers before your parents arrive, if you want. **I set aside the VR goggles, just in case.**"

"Thanks, Mr. Malory," said Harper, and Morgan and the others whooped with excitement and hurried into the library.

Mr. Malory shushed them, but he was laughing as he did it.

As soon as the kids spawned in Minecraft, Po twirled around to show off his new avatar skin. **"I'M READY FOR ADVENTURE . . . AND DRESSED FOR SUCCESS!"** he said. He looked like a politician, with a suit and tie and slicked-back hair.

"Nice!" said Jodi. "Maybe we should build a

replica White House for you. Ooh! Except we'll make it out of wool!"

"That sounds . . . interesting. And highly flammable," said Theo. **"BUT LET'S NOT FORGET THERE COULD BE A GIANT CAVE SPIDER PROWLING AROUND DOWN HERE."**

Harper nodded. "Morgan and Po said they saw that green mist before the spider appeared last time," she said. "That information could help us avoid the spider while we find a way back to the surface."

"We *could* do that," said Morgan. "But I think we want to do the opposite. **I THINK WE WANT TO FIND THE SPIDER."**

Jodi put her cube hand to his head, as if checking his temperature. "Are you feeling all right, big brother? Because you are *not* making sense."

"Hear me out," said Morgan. "We were all excited to explore these caves, so we got distracted. But we're *supposed* to be looking for strange mobs. The mobs that used to be the Evoker King."

"YOU THINK THAT TERROR-ANTULA IS ONE OF THOSE MOBS?" asked Po.

"We are *not* calling it that," said Theo.

Morgan nodded. "Whatever we call it, it has to be what we're looking for," he said. "We've all seen dozens of cave spiders, but we've never encountered one like that. And it didn't just *look* unique . . . **IT HAD SOME KIND OF SPECIAL POWER.** I'm pretty sure it was the reason those axolotls attacked Po."

"I've already forgiven the sweet little things," said Po, pretending to wipe away a tear.

"So my big brother isn't as fevered as we thought," Jodi said. "But what do we do next?"

"We need a plan," Theo agreed.

"I think we need more information first," said Harper. "Let's try to find this spider. If we're quiet enough, maybe we can observe it from a safe distance. Then we can learn whether it really is doing things a normal spider can't do."

"That works for me," said Morgan. "We'll know if we're getting close when we see the green mist, so it shouldn't be able to catch us by surprise."

"And we can explore the caves in the meantime!" said Po. **"SCORE!"**

Harper had to hand it to Po: he was right to be excited about the caves. **There was more to see underground than she had ever expected.**

"Wow," said Po as they stepped out of a tunnel and entered another large cavern. **"LOOK OUT FOR SPIKES!"**

"Those aren't spikes," said Harper. She looked at the icicle-like cones of stone that filled the cavern. "That's dripstone. The spiky shapes it makes are called stalactites and stalagmites," she said.

"I always forget which is which," said Morgan.

"I have a trick for remembering," said Harper.

"Stalactites hang down from the ceiling—like a capital letter T. Stalagmites, on the other hand, jut out from the ground—like a capital M."

Theo grinned. **"THAT'S A REALLY CLEVER TRICK, HARPER,"** he said.

Harper was glad her avatar couldn't blush. "Thanks," she said.

"DOES ANYBODY ELSE HEAR THAT SOUND?" asked Po. "It's almost like music. . . ."

Harper listened intently. Po was right. There was a faint tinkling noise nearby. "I think it's coming from the other side of this wall," she said, pressing her ear to a wall of dark gray stone.

Theo examined the wall. "That looks like basalt," he said. "But I've only ever seen basalt in the Nether before now."

"NOT QUITE!" said Morgan, and his eyes went wide. "If that's smooth basalt, then I know exactly what's making that sound." He pulled a pickaxe from his inventory. "Stand back!"

Morgan struck the smooth basalt wall with his pickaxe. "Smooth basalt is normally found in the Nether, **BUT WHEN YOU DO FIND IT IN THE OVERWORLD, YOU FIND THIS. . . ."** He dug a few blocks deep, then stepped aside to let everyone see what he'd uncovered. It looked like a hidden room made of glittering purple gemstones.

"Is that amethyst?" asked Harper.

Morgan nodded. **"IT'S A WHOLE GEODE OF AMETHYST."**

Jodi gasped. "It's so pretty!" She ran through the opening Morgan had made. Harper watched as Jodi spun around in joy, surrounded by gems. "Just think of the artwork we could make with this," she said.

Morgan hefted his pickaxe. **"THEN LET'S GET MINING,"** he said.

Chapter 7

THANK YOU FOR YOUR HOSPITALITY, VILLAGERS! I ESPECIALLY ENJOYED IT WHEN YOU STOPPED HITTING ME.

Theo led the way back to the surface.

While Morgan and Jodi had mined the amethyst, Theo and Harper had done some exploring. They'd found iron, copper, lapis lazuli **. . . and even a few emeralds.**

It had been Theo's idea to head back to the village they had seen before. There, they would be able to trade their emeralds for something useful.

It took longer than he expected to reach the top. **They were deep belowground,** and they couldn't dig straight up, since they couldn't fly. (Theo wondered if he could come up with a mod to change that.) He had to cut a zigzagging diagonal path up through countless earthen blocks, while Harper placed torches behind him.

He was cutting blind, and that was always risky, because you could accidentally open a hole right into a raging river of water—or worse, lava. Theo kept some cobblestone handy just in case he needed to quickly plug a hole. But he was lucky. He cut through stone, and then through dirt, and finally, the night sky appeared just overhead.

As they emerged onto the surface, it took a moment for everyone to get their bearings. There was the mountain—and there, at its base, was the village. **They walked quickly across the plain, eager to avoid any unnecessary fights with the hostile mobs that prowled the Overworld at night.**

As they reached the outskirts of the village,

Harper bounced on her blocky feet. "What should we buy?" she asked. "I had a few emeralds already, so we should have enough for something good. **MAYBE AN ENCHANTED BOOK? OR REDSTONE DUST!** We don't have much of it."

Morgan nodded. "Let's see what the villagers have," he said. "I didn't see a librarian when we were here before. But their cleric might have redstone dust for sale."

As the others spread out among the villagers, **Theo saw Po placing a sign in the dirt.** In glowing letters, it read VOTE FOR PO!

"Where in the world did you get that?" Theo asked.

"I crafted it myself," said Po. "While you guys were mining for ores and amethyst, **I FOUND SOME GLOW SQUID. THEY DROPPED GLOWING INK!**"

"I don't think these villagers get a vote," Theo said, but Po didn't seem to be listening.

Harper had already found the cleric, a serious-looking mob with green eyes and a purple robe. While they haggled, Theo looked around for a librarian.

It was difficult to see anything, though. **The fog was partially blocking the light of the torches.**

"Wait a minute," said Theo. **"WHERE DID THIS FOG COME FROM?"**

Suddenly, the cleric's green eyes turned red. The villager lunged at Harper, bashing into her with a blocky shoulder.

"Hey!" said Harper. "What gives?"

"Oh no," said Jodi. She backed away from a red-eyed farmer. "Not this again!"

Theo pulled a sword from his inventory. "Should we fight them?" he asked. "It feels wrong."

Harper stood her ground as the cleric made another lunge at her. "They're . . . super weak, actually," she said. "I don't think this cleric is even doing any damage to my health."

The farmer was joined by a fisherman, and several other angry villagers were leaving their homes to join the crowd.

"I'm almost afraid they're going to hurt *themselves*," said Po. "They're all worked up!"

"I agree," said Morgan. "There's no point fighting them. Let's retreat and see what happens."

THEO FOLLOWED THE OTHERS AS THEY FLED PAST THE OUTSKIRTS OF THE VILLAGE. Some of the villagers gave chase, but they soon gave up. Their eyes still glowed red in the night, but they didn't seem interested in pursuing the kids.

"I wonder what they'll do now," said Theo. He couldn't help but imagine the programming that determined how villagers would act. **And he tried to imagine how that program had been warped and rewritten by the spider's mind-poisoning fog.**

As they watched from a distance, they saw the villagers form a single-file line and leave their village. It looked as if they were hypnotized and following the commands of some unheard voice.

"Where are they going?" whispered Po.

"MAYBE THEY HEARD SOMEONE WAS GIVING OUT FREE ICE CREAM?" teased Jodi.

"I think I know where they're going," said Harper. "Look! They're headed right for the hole. The one we climbed out of a few minutes ago."

As usual, Harper was right. Theo watched as the villagers descended into the darkness, one after another.

"THAT IS AN EERIE SIGHT," said Morgan. "I hope they'll be okay. . . ."

"It's the spider," said Po. "It has to be. **IT'S CAUGHT THEM IN ITS PSYCHIC WEB!**"

"But what does it want with all those villagers?" asked Jodi. "Should we follow them?"

Harper shook her head. "We got a late start today, remember? We don't have time to follow them now. We'll have to try to track them down tomorrow."

"I GUESS WE HAVE A WHOLE EMPTY VILLAGE TO OURSELVES," said Morgan. **"PLENTY OF SPACE TO SET UP OUR BEDS."**

Theo felt uneasy, but he knew this problem would simply have to wait.

"Let's make sure we come back as soon as we can tomorrow," he said.

Po nodded. "I'm with Theo. Because I think I know why the spider wants those villagers." He gave his friends a long, serious look. "It seems to me . . . **LIKE THE SPIDER IS BUILDING AN ARMY!**"

Chapter 8

IF YOU LOVE YOUR JOB, YOU'LL NEVER WORK A DAY IN YOUR LIFE. IF YOU HATE YOUR JOB . . . TOUGH!

"**ALL RIGHT,** Block Headz. Face front! Your assignments . . . are ready!"

Po put *energy* into his words. The ice cream truck had not been the grand slam he'd hoped for. But there was plenty of time to get his campaign in shape. **He could still win all the votes he needed to become class president!**

And his friends had said they wanted to help any way they could, right? So he'd take them up on that.

The good news: They all looked excited and ready to begin. **The bad news:** They had a lot of their *own* ideas already.

"I've already been sketching some posters," said Jodi. "And I'm going to do the graphics for the website that Theo is building."

"I'm putting together polls so we can have accurate models to make predictions," said Harper. **"And I've got Ash on the phone, like you asked.** She said she'll help however she can."

Harper propped her smartphone up against a juice box. Their friend and fellow Minecraft fanatic, Ash Kapoor, waved at them from the screen.

"It's good to see you, Ash," said Po. "But everybody . . . slow your roll! I'm glad you're all eager to help, but I already came up with everyone's assignments."

Morgan gave him a suspicious look. "Really?"

"Posters and websites and that stuff—it's all kind of basic," said Po. "We need to think bigger. Bolder. We need a campaign that's truly one-of-a-kind!"

74

"Okay," Harper said, crossing her arms. "What do you have in mind?"

"Well, let's start with you, Harper," he said. "You know how our morning announcements are all automated with Doc's technology? **I want you to hack into the system and replace the normal announcements with pro-Po slogans.**"

Harper frowned. "I'm pretty sure that's against the rules . . . like, *all* the rules," she said. "And anyway, that sounds like a programming job, and

that's Theo's area of expertise, not mine."

"Unfortunately, Theo will be busy," said Po. "I need him to link up with my basketball teammates and lead them in a flash mob. I'm imagining coordinated dancing through the halls of the school! Music, fireworks, go wild!"

"Me? Dance?" said Theo, going pale. "In *public*?"

"And fireworks indoors?" said Morgan.

"I haven't forgotten about you, Morgan," said Po. "You did such a good job on all that paperwork, and I want you to know how much I appreciate it. Now I need you to put those skills to use and bake some cookies! If everyone in school gets a cookie, they'll forget all about that ice cream disaster."

"Wait a minute," said Morgan. "What does paperwork have to do with baking?"

"And what does baking have to do with Morgan?" asked Jodi. **"The last time he tried to bake something, he set our kitchen on fire.** And somehow the cake was *still* undercooked."

Po turned to Jodi. "You're good at noticing details like that, Jodi. You're a master spy, after all." He grinned. "So I want you to spy on Shelly

Silver. I need to know every move she makes. If she puts up ten posters, I'll put twenty ads in the paper. If she hands out candy, I'll give away whole chocolate bars. Name-brand chocolate bars. Whatever it takes!"

Jodi frowned and said under her breath, "I *spy* someone who is being *ridiculous.*"

"I'm almost afraid to ask what you have in mind for me, Po," Ash said.

Po shrugged. "Easy. You're here for emotional support," he said. **"You're good at it!"**

Ash breathed an immediate sigh of relief and said, "I can handle that."

Just then, a gleam of reflected light caught Po's eye. Morgan was eating gelatin with a shiny spoon. **Po recognized that spoon.**

"Morgan!" he said. "How could you?"

Morgan froze, a spoonful of gelatin halfway to his mouth. "How could I what?"

"How could you use one of *her* spoons?"

Morgan looked down at the spoon, then back at Po. The gelatin quivered.

"It's just a spoon," he said. "It doesn't mean anything."

Po harrumphed. *Just a spoon!*

"Wow, Po," said Harper. **"I feel like you have a lot in common with that spider mob we're after.** If only you could fill the hallways with a mind-altering gas. Then you could just hypnotize everyone into voting for you."

Po had to admit . . . he didn't hate that idea. "How does the science on that work, exactly? Would Doc have something we could use?"

"Po!" exclaimed Harper. **"I was only joking!"**

Ash cleared her throat. "As the emotional support expert," she said, "I'm feeling like your campaign is getting . . . a little out of hand, Po. Can we talk about this?"

"It'll have to wait," said Po. "I've got to head

to homeroom and get Baron Sweetcheeks ready for his photo op." **He held up the cutest little "Vote for Po!" T-shirt in the world.**

"He's the campaign mascot, and I want his image on everything—stickers, mugs, water bottles, you name it. Because who wouldn't want to vote with the Baron?"

"There's no way Baron Sweetcheeks agreed to that," Jodi said under her breath.

"When will it end?" Morgan muttered.

"When I'm president," said Po, **and he waved the tiny T-shirt like a flag.** "And not a minute before!"

Chapter 9

STRAIGHT INTO THE SPIDER'S WEB! WHAT COULD GO WRONG? PROBABLY NOTHING—EXCEPT A GIANT SPIDER!

Despite the unresolved disagreements from their lunchtime meeting, Theo and the others all agreed to return to Minecraft as soon as possible. **The moment the end-of-day bell rang, they hurried to the library and put on their VR headsets.**

They spawned in the village. Theo had hoped to find the villagers back where they belonged. But the houses remained empty. The streets were silent.

That meant the villagers were still underground. And the kids had no choice but to follow them.

"Let's cut down some trees first," said Harper.

"We're going through a lot of torches down there."

As they climbed back down the hole that Theo had cut through the earth, **he readied his sword and thought back to the last major foe they'd faced.** They'd called it the Endermonster, and they had not been able to defeat it by fighting it. Instead, they'd trapped the mob in a pit, and then Theo had talked to it— *connected* with it. He'd made it understand that they meant no harm.

Would their conflict with this strange spider work similarly?

"I THINK WE SHOULD TRY TO TRAP THE SPIDER," he said. "Like we did with the Endermonster. That way, we can maybe find out what it wants . . . *without* hurting it." Theo remembered the other lesson he'd learned on that adventure: how to be a team player. "That's just my idea," he added. "What do you all think?"

"It makes sense to me," said Harper.

"Do you want to get it to chase us?" asked Jodi.

Theo nodded. "AND WE'LL LEAD THE MOB RIGHT INTO A WAITING PIT."

"I bet it'll be even easier with the spider," said Po. "At least it can't teleport!"

"But we'll be running through the fog, if it's chasing us," Morgan reminded them. "I think it's a good plan, Theo. We'll just need to be careful."

They descended to the dripstone cavern where they'd mined for materials the day before. "The villagers must have come through here," said Theo. "I didn't see any other paths the entire way down."

"We came from that direction the other day,"

said Harper, pointing. **"AND WE KNOW THAT'S A DEAD END, SINCE WE BLOCKED THE TUNNEL WITH COBBLESTONE."**

"So it's that way," said Morgan, pointing at the only other exit from the cavern. "They had to have gone through there."

Theo gulped. It was easy to be brave when they were just talking about a plan. But now, as the dark pressed closer to them and their encounter with the spider drew near . . . he felt a trickle of fear run through his avatar.

HARPER STEPPED INTO THE MIDDLE OF THE CAVERN, AND SHE PULLED A PICKAXE FROM HER INVENTORY. "Spiders can jump, so we need a pretty deep hole this time," she said.

"I'd better free some space in my inventory for all the dirt we're going to kick up," said Po. He jabbed a couple of glowing "Vote for Po" signs into the ground.

"How many of those things did he make?" asked Theo to no one in particular.

Harper sighed, then forced a smile. **"LET'S START DIGGING,"** she said.

The pit had been dug, and Theo crept along a tunnel toward the spider. The tunnel was two blocks wide, so there was just enough room for two of them to walk side by side. Theo was in the lead with Harper.

They'd agreed not to use too many torches. **They didn't want the spider to see them coming. But it was dark.** Theo walked with one hand in front of him so he wouldn't bump into anything.

He didn't even realize that the tunnel had begun to fill with mist until Harper pointed it out. "We must be getting close," she whispered. And then, suddenly, she gripped him and pulled him back.

The spider was directly ahead of them, standing in the middle of a large cavern. The only light came from the slight bluish glow of two small ponds. **Theo guessed there were glow squids in those pools.** He squinted and saw axolotls swimming alongside them.

Those aquatic creatures were not the only mobs

present. The spider was surrounded by red-eyed villagers, sheep, rabbits, and more. Theo saw a llama, and he was pretty sure it was the same llama that had attacked Jodi. **As for the villagers, they seemed to be treating the spider like a king.** They offered it fresh-baked bread and emeralds. Theo half expected to see them massage the mob's eight big block feet next!

"Po was right. **IT IS BUILDING AN ARMY,**" Theo whispered.

"I don't know," whispered Harper. "They all seem sort of . . . peaceful. They look more like worshippers or servants than soldiers."

"This doesn't change anything," whispered Morgan. "Our plan's still a good one. **PO, DO YOU**

WANT TO DO THE HONORS?"

Po smiled. "You know I do."

"Then make some noise," said Morgan.

Po stepped in front of Theo and cleared his throat. Then he yelled at the top of his lungs: "VOTE FOR PO!!"

The spider snapped to attention. The large mob hissed, lifting one of its long legs and pointing right at them.

"Here it comes," said Theo. "RUN!"

They dove back into the tunnel, this time with Jodi at the front and Po bringing up the rear. Theo was right in the middle. He glanced back, and he could see Morgan and Po right behind him, but through the swirling mist it was impossible to see if the spider was near or far.

They ran through the thickening fog.

They turned left. Then they turned right.

Then Theo thought: Wait. That's wrong.

"Are we lost?" he said.

"I think I took a wrong turn!" cried Jodi from ahead of him.

"Well, we can't go back now," said Harper.

"JUST KEEP GOING!"

As soon as they stopped talking, Theo heard the unmistakable sounds of pursuit. There was definitely something following them. It sounds like a whole *lot* of somethings, in fact.

"HERE THEY COME," warned Morgan.

"Run away!" Po cried frantically. "Run away, run away, run away!"

"Forget this!" said Theo. Sometimes being a team player just wasn't worth the trouble. He took a quick glance at the compass he carried, which gave him his bearings. Then he took out a diamond pickaxe, which would allow him to cut through stone in no time at all. **"I'M MAKING A NEW TUNNEL,"** he said. "Everybody follow me!"

Theo's sense of direction proved true. He only had to hack through five layers of stone before he cut right through to the chamber where they'd begun. Their pit was nearby.

"Hurry!" he said.

Out of the tunnel, they were able to spread out at last, and they ran side by side toward the pit. **They leaped and their pursuers fell**

into the deep hole in the ground, just as they'd planned.

Only it wasn't the horrible spider who had pursued them. **It was dozens of bunny rabbits.**

"It didn't even follow us, did it?" said Theo. "It sent these rabbits to do its dirty work!"

"And you, bunnies?" said Jodi, heartbroken. "The spider turned *you* against us, too?"

Harper leaned over the pit. "Look at their eyes, though," she said. "They're back to normal." She stood again. "That's good news. It means the

spider's control wears off at a distance. Probably as soon as there's none of that mist around."

Jodi eyed the bunnies with suspicion. "I don't know. **I JUST DON'T KNOW IF I CAN TRUST THEIR CUTE LITTLE FACES.**"

Po patted her on the head. She'd been through a lot this week.

"You know, the bunnies *are* awfully cute," said Theo. "Maybe the spider isn't such a bad mob if it's gathering fuzzy animals and villagers instead of bats and zombies." He rubbed the top of his head. **"MAYBE PO'S ARMY THEORY DOESN'T HOLD UP AFTER ALL."**

And then a sound erupted from the tunnels. It was a sound of sadness and desperation, and it sent a shiver across Theo's digital skin.

"It's . . . *wailing*," said Harper.

"It sounds sad," said Jodi. **"DO YOU THINK IT MISSES THE BUNNIES?"**

"Sad or not, it sounds awfully creepy to me," said Po.

"Me too," said Theo. "I think we should retreat to the village."

Morgan nodded. "This plan was a bust," he said. "We have to come up with something else."

Chapter 10

IF YOUR RIVAL REACHES ACROSS THE AISLE ... GIVE HER A COOKIE.

It was a beautiful morning outside in the real world. Jodi, Harper, and Theo were together, **sitting beneath a tree. Jodi was sketching Minecraft rabbits on graph paper.** She wouldn't let some creepy, kooky Minecraft mob ruin her love of bunnies. Or llamas. **Or axolotls!** She'd never known how cute amphibians could be. She'd looked them up online and confirmed that they were just as adorable in

real life as they were in pixels.

Jodi glanced at Harper. She was drawing, too, and Theo was looking over her shoulder. They were putting their heads together on a new plan to deal with the spider.

Morgan was nearby, rushing to finish his homework. He'd spent all night making cookies. They were unappetizing, but at least he hadn't set the kitchen on fire. To Jodi, that was progress.

"Hi, everybody," said a voice, **and Jodi looked up to see Shelly Silver standing over them.** "Can I join you for a minute?"

Jodi was surprised. She'd never talked with Shelly—and despite Po, she'd certainly never spied on

her. So what was Shelly doing here?

"Uh... sure, you can join us," said Morgan. He obviously felt awkward. Jodi even saw him look around to make sure Po wasn't nearby. But there was still twenty minutes before the first bell, and Po usually didn't get to school this early.

Harper set aside her notebook. "Have a seat, Shelly," she said. "What's on your mind?"

Shelly smiled. She had a nice smile, Jodi thought. Friendly.

"Thanks," Shelly said, and she folded her legs to sit on the grass. "I know you're all friends with Po, so I won't try to convince you to vote for me. But I'm trying to speak with *every* student before the election." She took out a pocket-sized spiral

notepad and a glitter pen with a big pink pompom on the end. "That way, if I *am* elected, I'll have an idea what everyone cares about."

"What we care about?" echoed Theo.

"Yeah," said Shelly. "You know. **What's your number-one issue?** What would you like to see change around here?"

Theo thought about it. "I'd like the computer lab back," he said.

"Ditto," said Morgan. "Our computer equipment should be in the school, where we can keep an eye on it."

Jodi knew they were worried that keeping their VR headsets in the library meant that someone else would use them.

"I care about recycling," said Harper. "And other sustainable practices."

"Oh, me too, actually!" said Shelly. "Woodsword is pretty good about all that, but it could be better. I have a lot of ideas."

That got a big smile from Harper.

"What do you think about the upcoming block party?" she asked.

Jodi understood immediately why Shelly was asking. The block party was an annual event—an after-school party for all the students and their families. But some students had decided the party was a big waste of money. They argued that the money could be spent on important improvements around the school.

"I think it's a waste," said Harper, and Theo nodded in agreement.

"No, I love the block party!" said Morgan. "I've been looking forward to it all year."

Jodi noticed Shelly writing their responses in her notebook. She was really paying attention to what they cared about.

And she had a sudden, sinking feeling . . . that Po might not win the election.

"Oh!" said Shelly. Her eyes had landed on Morgan's containers full of cookies. **"Are you selling cookies?"**

"Yeah," said Morgan. He squirmed a little. "Uh, they're for Po's campaign, though. Sorry."

Shelly shrugged. "That's okay."

She'd been so nice, though, that Morgan let

her have her choice of cookie anyway. She chose one and bit into it immediately. Jodi watched as Shelly's expression went from excitement . . . to confusion . . . to mild disgust. She chewed for several seconds, then winced as she swallowed. "That is . . . an *interesting* cookie," she said.

"I'm sorry!" said Morgan, knowing the cookies were terrible. "I think I mixed up the baking powder and the baking soda. *But why is baking soda a powder?* It's so confusing!"

They all laughed, Shelly the loudest of all. She didn't eat the rest of the cookie, but she politely wrapped it in a napkin and placed it in her purse, as if she might get back to it later.

Po saw it all. Hidden behind a large oak tree, he watched in silence as Shelly approached his friends. He saw them invite her to sit down. He saw them laugh and smile with her like they were having the best time in the world.

What was Shelly Silver up to?

And why were his friends going along with it?

Po never would have believed it if he hadn't seen it with his own eyes. But there could be only one explanation: *Shelly Silver was turning Po's own friends against him.*

Chapter 11

A CHIP OFF THE OLD BLOCK HEADZ. LET'S JUST HOPE THESE CHIPS DON'T END UP IN A BATCH OF MORGAN'S COOKIES!

After school, the kids met up in Minecraft. Everything was just as usual.

Except for one big difference. **This time, Po watched his teammates with anger and suspicion.**

They were standing in one of the village's many abandoned houses, where they'd set up their beds in a neat row. "Theo and I have a new plan," said Harper. "Or a new version of the old plan."

"We're still going to trap the spider," said Theo. "But not in a pit this time. We're going to build a trap . . . **USING REDSTONE.**"

Po scoffed. "Redstone is too complicated,"

he said. "Here's my plan: Let's go to the Nether. Let's get some netherite. Let's craft some powerful weapons and armor and defeat the spider in a direct attack!"

"But we don't want to hurt it," said Theo. "Remember, it contains a piece of the Evoker King's code. **WE NEED THAT CODE TO PUT OUR FRIEND BACK TOGETHER.**"

"If we trap it, we can find a way to communicate

with it," said Harper. "Maybe we can convince it to give us what we need, like we did with the Endermonster."

"BESIDES, THE SPIDER HASN'T ACTUALLY HURT US," Jodi added. "It keeps using its mobs to chase us away when we get too close. Maybe it isn't so bad, really."

Po felt hurt that nobody was listening to him. "Did you guys ask *Shelly Silver* what she thought about your plan?" he asked.

MORGAN'S JAW DROPPED IN SURPRISE.

"Yeah, that's right," said Po. "I saw you all talking this morning. She was even taking notes! What did you tell her?"

"It wasn't like that," Morgan said. "She was just asking us some questions about the school. About our opinions . . ."

"Sounds like she's spying on my campaign," said Po. He looked at Jodi. "Speaking of spying, have you learned anything I can use, Jodi?"

Jodi put her blocky fists on her hips. **"I REFUSE TO USE MY DETECTIVE POWERS FOR EVIL!"** she said. "Shelly is a nice person."

"SHE'S MY COMPETITOR," said Po.

"She can be both of those things!" argued Jodi.

"That's enough, everybody," said Harper, and she stepped between them. "Let's remember we're all on the same team."

"Are we, though?" said Po. He frowned at Morgan. "Or were those inedible cookies part of your plan to sabotage me?"

"THEY'RE NOT INEDIBLE!" Morgan argued. "They're even pretty good if you dip them in mustard."

"What's going on here?" said a voice from the doorway.

They all turned to see a familiar avatar. "Ash!" said Jodi. "Thank goodness you're here!"

Ash smiled. "It's always good to see you guys." Then her smile fell away. "But I hate to see you like *this*. You'll never topple that tyrant if you don't work together."

Theo chuckled. **"WHEN YOU SAY 'TYRANT,' ARE YOU TALKING ABOUT THE SPIDER? OR PO?"**

Po felt a rush of anger. "I'm not a tyrant!" he

said. "I just want things to go my way for once!"

Everyone was quiet after that. Po was normally such a happy guy. **His anger had caught everyone by surprise.**

"I think we all need to take a time out," said Ash. "There's no way we should be going up against a hostile boss mob in this state."

"I'll make it easy for you guys," said Po, and he disconnected without another word.

Po exited the library before his friends could disconnect and follow him. He knew Ash was right—he needed a time-out. He needed to *breathe,* before he said something he would regret.

And then, suddenly, he had a microphone shoved right into his face.

"I'm Ned Brant with the *Woodsword Chronicler,*" said the student on the holding the microphone. "I'm doing profiles on our candidates. What can you tell me about your platform?"

"Wait, what?" said Po. His mind was still reeling

from the argument. He wasn't at all prepared to talk to a student reporter. "I don't know."

"You don't know anything about your platform?" said the reporter.

"I mean, yeah, of course I do," said Po. **"look, I'm just trying to have a good time. you can print that! Call me the happy fun-time candidate."**

The reporter frowned. "But what about the issues? Where do you stand?"

Po nodded as if he took the question very

seriously. "I have a lot of opinions about a lot of different issues. Pretty much all the issues, actually."

Nailed it, thought Po.

"What about the block party?" said Ned.

"Sure," said Po. "That sounds fun. Let's do it!"

Ned shook his head. "No, I mean where do you stand on the debate? A growing number of students believe it's a waste of the school's money."

"They do?" said Po. "Then we'll just cancel it."

"Cancel it?" echoed the reporter. "You're saying that if you're elected class president . . . the block party will be canceled?"

Po hesitated for a moment. **He felt that maybe he'd said the wrong thing.** But this reporter had just said that students weren't happy about the block party. So his was obviously the right answer. Right?

"Yes," said Po. "Consider it a campaign promise. Now get out there and spread the word, Ned." As Po wheeled away, he shouted over his shoulder, **"Vote for Po!"**

Chapter 12

EXTRA! EXTRA! READ ALL ABOUT IT . . . SO YOU'LL KNOW WHAT EVERYBODY'S YELLING ABOUT!

Po couldn't wait to arrive at school the next morning. He was pretty sure he had nailed that interview with the student reporter. **His whole campaign was about to turn around.**

In a way, he was right. But not at all in the way he expected.

He noticed the looks and the whispers as soon as he approached the school. Po was generally a popular guy. People tended to say hello to him in the hallways. Today, it was the opposite. Nobody seemed to want to talk to him.

They all seemed to be talking *about* him instead.

Finally, Po's teammate Ricky approached him.

"Dude," said Ricky, "is it true?"

"Is what true?" asked Po. "What's going on around here?"

"The newspaper ran a story," said Ricky. He held up his phone to show Po the digital edition of that morning's *Woodsword Chronicler.* "They're saying you want to cancel the block party!"

"That's not true," said Po. He thought about it for a second. "Well, it's *kind of* true. But I just said that because that's what people want me to do!"

"Which people?" said Ricky. "I was looking forward to that party." **He waved around the hallway at all the glaring, eavesdropping students.** "And I'm not the only one."

"Fine," said Po. "Okay. No problem. I can fix this." He pulled his megaphone from his backpack and held it to his mouth. "Attention, everybody! There's no need to panic! I'm reversing my position on the block party. **Po is the pro-party candidate!**" He lowered the megaphone, then quickly raised it once more. "Vote for Po!" he added.

"Are you serious?" said a student. "We need that money for repairs around here. The door to my locker just fell off!"

"That's because you're always slamming it shut, *Megan,*" said another girl.

"We should spend the money on repairs!" someone shouted.

"No!" said Ricky. "We study hard all year long. **We deserve a party!**"

"I'm with Ricky," said Doc Culpepper, stepping

out of her lab. "Things are too tense around here. A fête is just the thing."

Ms. Minerva, Po's homeroom teacher, crossed her arms. For some reason, she was soaking wet. "Don't be foolish, Doc," she said. "You know better than anyone that we need new equipment around here."

"Bah," said Doc. **"I can just fix the old equipment."**

"Like you fixed the sprinkler system on the lawn?" said Minerva. She wrung water out of her blouse. "Because I think it's still got a few bugs."

Doc turned to Po. "Well, Po?" she asked. "What do *you* say?"

All eyes were back on Po. Everyone disagreed . . . but they *all* wanted him to be on their side.

Po had absolutely no idea what to do. He hated to admit it—**but if he had the spider's mind-zap mist power right now, he just might use it.**

Suddenly, a clear voice cut through the silence. "Give Po some space!"

To Po's surprise, his defender was none other than Shelly Silver.

"It isn't fair to catch him off guard like this," she said. **"A politician needs time to consider their position on complicated issues."** She waved her notebook in the air. "I've been thinking about it all week, and I'm *still* considering where I stand."

Po felt miserable. He liked making people *happy*. And here he was, making them angry and frustrated instead. And who came to his defense? Not Ricky. Not the Minecraft crew. No, it was his political rival speaking up for him.

That made him want to lash out.

"You sound awfully indecisive, Shelly," he said, loud enough that everyone would hear him. "Don't you think we need a class president who's daring and *decisive*?"

Shelly didn't seem to know what to say to that. Her mouth dropped open.

Po saw his chance. **This was his opportunity,** at last, to prove to everyone that he was the right man for the job.

"Shelly Silver," he said. **"I challenge you to a debate!"**

Chapter 13

BE CAREFUL WHAT YOU TRAP FOR. YOU JUST MIGHT CATCH IT!

"A DEBATE?!" said Morgan. "Po, are you sure that's the best idea?"

"No, I'm not," Po admitted. "But I panicked. I wasn't thinking!" It was after school, and Morgan and Po were in the library, waiting for the others to join them. "I've been doing that a lot lately, haven't I?" he said after a moment. "Speaking without thinking first, I mean. I'm sorry I lost my temper yesterday."

Morgan sighed. "Yeah, well. I'm sorry I pretended my cookies weren't terrible. They really are inedible."

Po laughed. "I appreciate that you made the

effort. And I appreciate their obsidian-like quality."

Morgan smiled. It felt like everything was back to normal. Po was being his old, fun self again. "But seriously, Po," he said. "What's been going on with you? Are you, you know . . . all

right?"

Po took another moment to think before answering. "I want to win the election," he said. "I want it really badly. I don't even know why—**I just hate the thought of losing.**"

"Everybody likes to win," said Morgan. "But sometimes that makes us fight the wrong battles."

Po blinked. "Morgan, that sounded seriously wise!"

Morgan blushed and confessed, "I'm actually just quoting something Ash said yesterday."

"Well, if you're going to steal," said Po, "steal from the best."

Theo, Harper, and Jodi arrived. **The five of them all put their headsets on at the same time—as a team.**

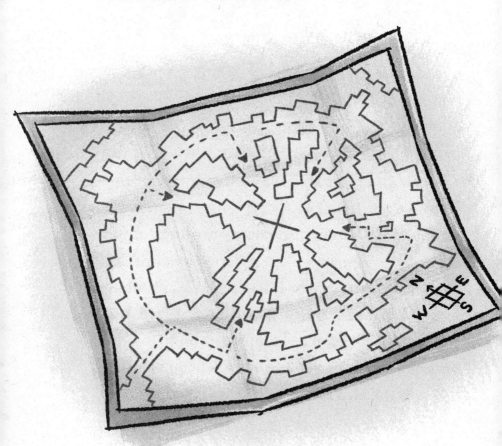

In the caverns beneath the Overworld, the trap had been set. Now they needed to lure the spider out of its hiding place. Po followed his friends through the dark tunnel that led to the spider's den.

"I can't believe we're going *toward* the creepy-crawly," said Jodi.

"It's okay," said Ash. **"WE'VE GOT EACH OTHER BACKS."**

"Yeah," said Morgan. "Except for the part of the plan where we're all alone . . ."

Po was nervous about that, too. But he trusted Harper and Theo, who had come up with this whole idea. They had figured out where to dig the tunnels and where to place the redstone dust. The blueprint that showed where everything should go looked a little bit like a spider's web. **That had made Po giggle . . . nervously.**

They were going to catch the spider in a web of their own. But it was a very big spider.

They all walked slowly as they approached the

den. The strange green mist swirled all around them.

And there, surrounded by its loyal mobs, was the spider.

Po whispered, "Okay, there he is. Lucky us! Now what?"

Harper grinned. "Now we make a mess. **EVERYBODY, THROW YOUR POTIONS!**"

Po didn't need to be told twice. He threw the Splash Potion that Harper had given him, and the other kids did the same. The potions glowed purple as they spun through the air. **When the bottles shattered, the liquid splashed the spider, the villagers, the axolotls, and all the other mobs with Slowness.**

Now the mobs would be easy to outrun for the next ninety seconds.

They needed to make those ninety seconds matter.

"Come and get us!" Theo said, and the spider turned its red eyes on them and hissed. It was the sound of paper being torn to shreds in anger. In seconds, the entire group of mobs stepped forward. Their eyes, too, flashed red as they gave chase.

"HERE THEY COME," said Ash.

"Be careful what you wish for, I guess," said Jodi.

"Let's go," said Harper. "Follow me!"

As a group, they turned and ran down the tunnel. But then Morgan turned right down a side path.

And a little farther up, Jodi turned left.

Po felt a little rush of nervousness as he took a

different side path of his own. He knew their plan relied on this. They needed to separate that big crowd of mobs, and the best way to do that was to split up. Still, he was anxious about being alone in the dark.

He looked back and saw that several of the villagers had turned to follow him. **They were moving slowly because of the potion, so it was easy for Po to stay out of their reach.** In fact, he slowed down a little bit. He didn't want to lose them.

He let them get closer. **Closer . . .**

And then he hit a lever, and an iron door swung closed behind him.

The villagers threw themselves against the iron door—*thump-thump-thump*—but there was nothing they could do. They were trapped . . . and now the spider's army was a little bit smaller than before.

"SEE YOU LATER!" Po said, cackling. He was starting to feel good about the plan.

Po followed his tunnel back to the central cavern. Harper, Theo, and Jodi were already there.

"How'd it go?" Harper asked.

"I trapped some villagers," Po answered.

Harper nodded. "Great. So working together, we trapped villagers, axolotls, sheep, a few cows . . ."

"AND I JUST TRAPPED ONE VERY AGGRESSIVE LLAMA," Ash said as she came running into the cavern.

Morgan appeared next. He entered the cavern at full speed, and he didn't stop. Mist swirled all

around him. "The spider's on my tail!" he cried.
"And I think the Slowness just wore off!"

Morgan was right. The spider appeared mere
seconds later, leaping into the cavern and hissing.
Theo pulled a lever, and a set of doors swung closed.
Now every tunnel was blocked with an iron door.
The spider was trapped.

And the kids were trapped with it.

Chapter 14

HOW CAN YOU TELL SPIDERS HATE TO BE TRAPPED? BECAUSE THEY'RE ALWAYS CLIMBING THE WALLS!

Po selected a sword from his inventory. The spider was big and scary. Its fangs were sharp, and its skin looked hairy. But it was also alone, without its army of mobs to protect it. This finally felt like a fight they could win.

The real question was did they *want* to fight it?

"LET'S TRY TALKING FIRST," Theo insisted. "The Evoker King is inside that spider somewhere. Or at least, a part of him is . . ."

"What if it's the part of

him that wanted to destroy us?" asked Po. "I think I'll hold on to my sword, just in case."

The spider looked at Po's sword and hissed. It skittered onto the wall.

"Wait!" said Ash. **"WE COME IN PEACE."**

"Don't you recognize us?" asked Jodi, hoping to appeal to some part of her friend the Evoker King.

Theo said quickly, "What do you know about the Fault? Can you tell us more about it?"

Morgan raised an eyebrow at Theo's question, but any discussion about that would have to come later.

The spider didn't speak. But it didn't attack, either. **It skittered along the wall, retreating into the mist and shadows at the far corner of the cavern.**

"Don't let it get away," warned Morgan.

"It can't get far," said Harper.

"Well, let's keep our eyes on it anyway," said Ash, peering into the darkness.

They all moved forward together.

And none of them saw the spider's trap in time to avoid it.

"Hey!" said Jodi. **"I'M SINKING!"**

Po realized she was right. They were *all* sinking. What had happened to the floor?

"It's the pit!" said Theo. "The one we dug for our first plan. It's full of cobwebs!"

"Then . . . we're helpless!" said Morgan, pulling against the sticky stuff. "It will take forever to get out of this."

Po had his sword out, but his arm was caught up in the sticky web. He couldn't quite get enough movement out of his arm to effectively swing the weapon. Everyone was in the same predicament. Only Morgan seemed to have any real mobility.

"I can move one hand. Do we have shears to cut through it?" said Ash. "Harper?"

"We left our shears in a chest aboveground," Harper said. "We didn't think we'd need them. . . ."

And then Po saw the red eyes shining above them.

"Our original trap worked after all," he said. "I mean, it worked out great for the spider!"

"WE DON'T HAVE ANY CHOICE," said Morgan. He took a bow from his inventory. "We're sitting ducks. We have to destroy the spider before it destroys us."

As if responding to Morgan's threat, the spider showed its fangs and hissed. Soupy green mist rolled down into the pit, making everything hazy.

"THAT WON'T SAVE YOU," said Morgan. He took aim with his bow. "And none of your friends can help you now, either."

Friends. The word triggered something in Po. Visions of mobs danced through his head: villagers and bunnies, llamas and sheep.

"Wait!" he cried. **"MORGAN, DON'T HURT IT."**

Morgan gave Po a strange look. But he lowered his bow. "Why not?" he asked.

"I think . . . I think I know what it wants," said Po. "It isn't attacking us. See? We're helpless, and it's only spitting that gas at us."

"Which is pretty rude!" said Jodi.

"Maybe." Po shrugged. "But the gas doesn't work on us. It only works on mobs. And it doesn't hurt mobs, right?"

"Right," said Ash. She smiled with understanding. "The gas makes mobs into its friends!"

"You mean . . ." Theo rubbed his blocky chin. "The spider is trying to *befriend* us right now?"

"IT'S A GOOD THEORY," said Harper. **"BUT HOW DO WE TEST IT?"**

"By extending our hands in friendship," said Po, trying to sound like the politicians he'd heard on TV. He turned his face up toward the spider. "Um, hello? **TERROR-ANTULA?** Is it okay if I call you that?"

The spider hissed.

"Yeah, okay, bad idea," said Po. "I just wanted to let you know that I understand where you're

coming from. It feels nice to surround yourself with friends. It feels really good to be popular."

The spider tilted its head. It seemed to be listening.

"ME? I LOVE BEING POPULAR," Po continued. "Being the center of attention is the best. But . . . I would never mind-zap anybody into following me around or force them to do what I wanted." He thought about Morgan's cookies and Jodi's refusal to spy for him. "Well, maybe I *have* tried to force people to do stuff. But that was wrong, and I regret it." He felt his friends' eyes on him, and he got a little nervous. But when he looked back, they were all smiling at him. There was no judgment in their eyes, only encouragement.

Po felt a new surge of confidence.

"THE ENDERMONSTER WAS THE PART OF THE EVOKER KING that was afraid to be seen," he said. "I think you're the opposite. You're the part of him that desperately wants friends. I think that's why you surround yourself with villagers and bunnies and any other mob you can find." Po shook his head sadly. **"BUT FORCING THEM . . .**

MANIPULATING THEM . . . CONTROLLING THEM? That's the wrong way to do it. You have to be honest, and open, and let your friends *choose* you." He smiled. "And we will choose you. We *want* to be your friends. I mean, you're kind of, sort of the Evoker King—which means we're kind of, sort of friends *already*."

The spider stood totally still, as if it was thinking about what Po had said. Po wondered if he should say or do more. But then, after a long pause, the spider nodded, just once. The mob then erupted in a burst of light, pixels . . . and digital butterflies.

The butterflies swarmed over Po's head, briefly blocking his view. As the butterflies flew off, the

eerie green mist dissipated. Gone, too, was the spider. In its place . . . was a long, blocky leg.

Po recognized it as the second leg of the Evoker King. He whooped for joy, and the others echoed his cry of excitement.

They were one step closer to putting their friend back together.

Or they would be . . . just as soon as they were able to cut themselves out of the massive tangle of cobwebs.

Chapter 15

THE BIG DEBATE! THE MOMENT OF TRUTH! ... AND THE REASON GYM IS CANCELED TODAY!

PO LIKED TO WIN. Often, that was a good quality. When he was on the basketball court . . . or rehearsing for a play . . . or studying for a test? That drive to succeed was hugely important.

But it was possible to be too competitive. To take things too far. To put just winning ahead of how you win.

He tried to remember that as he adjusted his microphone in the moments before his debate with Shelly Silver. The entire class had packed into the cafeteria to witness it. And Po found himself craving their applause.

But he reminded himself that he wasn't here

for applause. He was here to discuss important subjects that his fellow students cared deeply about. And he needed to take that seriously.

Mr. Malory stepped to the center of the stage and addressed the assembled students. "Greetings, Woodsword," he said. "As a neutral party, I've been asked to moderate this debate over my lunch hour. **Normally I'd be sad to miss lunch ...** but I was going to eat a bologna sandwich today, so I'd rather be here with all of you."

Mr. Malory paused, as if waiting for laughter. But no one made a sound. He turned to Po and Shelly. **"Tough crowd,"** he whispered to them.

Shelly was at her own lectern, which was set up a few feet away from Po's. She didn't look nervous. In fact, she looked eager to begin.

"Let's start with you, Shelly," said Mr. Malory.

"Why do you want to be class president?"

Shelly didn't hesitate. **"I want to make a difference at Woodsword,"** she answered. "I want to help make our school the very best it can be. I have a plan to expand our after-school activities by twenty percent, and to reduce our carbon footprint by twice that percentage. That's why I gave out reusable spoons when I announced my campaign—the disposable plasticware that the cafeteria provides us is wasteful and unnecessary, and it has to go."

Po was stunned. It hadn't even occurred to him that her handouts were part of a waste-reduction plan. He'd thought she was just trying to be flashy!

"And I had to stay up late doing the math, but . . . **I think I may have a solution to the block party dilemma,**" said Shelly. "If we change the event into a ticketed fundraiser, we have the opportunity to keep the party fun . . . while actually *making* money instead of spending it. I think that might satisfy everybody!"

The students all applauded for Shelly, and Po found he couldn't blame them. He almost wanted to join them!

"Same question for you, Po," said Mr. Malory. **"Why do you want to be president?"**

Po thought for a moment about his answer. And he decided to be honest.

"I *don't* really want to be president," he said. He heard gasps from the crowd, but he didn't let that stop him. "What I *want* is to win the election, because winning feels good. And winning a *vote* makes you feel like people really like you." He sighed. "I like being the center of attention. But that's the *only* thing I would like about being president. I'm not actually ready for the responsibility. I mean, nobody told me there'd be *math* involved." He grinned. "And that's why . . . **I've decided to endorse Shelly Silver for class president.**"

Now Shelly herself gasped. Everyone else seemed to be stunned into silence. Po looked into the crowd and saw that every student was sitting absolutely frozen in place.

Then he saw Morgan begin to clap.

And Jodi. And Harper and Theo and Ricky.

And then everybody else.

A huge cacophony of cheering and applause swept over Po like a wave. It was so loud that it almost felt like it could knock him backward.

He soaked it in. Being the center of attention really *did* feel good.

Especially when you were getting attention . . . for making the right choice.

He nodded to Shelly, then rolled away from the lectern.

Chapter 16

THE RESULTS ARE IN! EVERYBODY'S A WINNER! BUT THERE'S STILL ONE LITTLE PROBLEM....

Jodi swung a pickaxe, and the "Vote for Po" sign was destroyed.

Po laughed. **"THAT LOOKED LIKE FUN."**

"It really was!" said Jodi, smiling.

Po and his friends had returned to the caverns of Minecraft. Back at school, the votes were in. Shelly had won by a landslide . . . and Po could not have been happier about that.

Woodsword's students had chosen the right candidate for the job.

It wasn't totally necessary to remove the glowing signs he'd placed throughout the caves. It wasn't as if anybody but the five of them would ever see them. But Po hoped that getting rid of the signs would help them put the whole experience behind them.

Especially the parts where he'd behaved badly.

The sooner they forgot about all that, the better he'd feel.

"For what it's worth," said Morgan, "I voted for you, Po."

"You did?" Po couldn't help it: he smiled.

"I think we all did," said Jodi, and Harper nodded.

"NOT BECAUSE YOU'RE OUR FRIEND," said Harper. **"BUT BECAUSE WE BELIEVE IN YOU."**

"You would have been a great president, Po," said Morgan. "Even if you weren't totally prepared . . . **YOU ALWAYS RISE TO MEET WHATEVER CHALLENGE YOU'RE FACED WITH."**

"Aw, you guys," Po said dramatically. "Careful, or my high-tech VR goggles are gonna end up full of salt water."

As Morgan demolished another sign, Jodi reached down into a pond where a blue axolotl was swimming. **"I'M JUST GLAD EVERYTHING'S BACK TO NORMAL,"** she said, patting the mob's head with affection.

With the last sign taken down, the five friends prepared to return to the surface. But Theo pointed into the darkness. "What's that?" he asked.

Po saw what Theo meant. There was a faint glow coming from around the corner. "Did we miss one of the signs?" he asked.

But when he turned the corner, **he was met with a shock.**

Big, blocky letters were shining on the cavern wall. Someone had written a message in glowing ink.

Po read the message out loud: "Come to the zoo . . . **if you dare.**"

"What does it mean?" asked Harper.

"Who could have written it?" asked Theo.

"We'll have to find out somehow," said Morgan.

"I hope we can pet the animals!" said Jodi.

Beneath the words was the image of a butterfly. **But somehow, that was not very comforting. . . .**

MINECRAFT is a game about placing blocks and going on adventures. Build, play, and explore across infinitely generated worlds of mountains, caverns, oceans, jungles, and deserts. Defeat hordes of zombies, bake the cake of your dreams, venture to new dimensions, or build a skyscraper. What you do in Minecraft is up to you.

Nick Eliopulos is a writer who lives in Brooklyn (as many writers do). He likes to spend half his free time reading and the other half gaming. He cowrote the Adventurers Guild series with his best friend and works as a narrative designer for a small video game studio. After all these years, endermen still give him the creeps.

Alan Batson is a British cartoonist and illustrator. His works include *Everything I Need to Know I Learned from a Star Wars Little Golden Book, Everything That Glitters is Guy!,* and *Spider-Ham.* Being extremely fond of cubes and travel to exotic places, he has recently begun to lend his talents to several different books on adventures in the world of Minecraft.

Chris Hill is an illustrator living in Birmingham, England, with his wife and two daughters and has been loving it for twenty-five years! When he's not working, he spends time with his family and trying to tire out his dog on long walks. If there's any time left after that, he loves to go riding on his motorcycle, feeling the wind on his face while contemplating his next illustration adventure.

FROM BLOCKS TO PANELS,

MINECRAFT™

COMES TO COMICS

MINECRAFT: WITHER WITHOUT YOU VOLUME 1

After an intense battle with an enchanted Wither, Cahira and Orion's mentor is eaten and they are now alone! The two monster hunters go on a mission to get their mentor back, and meet an unlikely ally along the way!

978-1-50670-835-5 • $10.99 US/$14.99 CA
88 Pages Trade Paperback

MINECRAFT: WITHER WITHOUT YOU VOLUME 2

After saving their mentor from the belly of a Wither, twin monster hunters turn their sights on solving the mystery of their new friend's curse and set off a chain of events leading to the zombie apocalypse!

978-1-50671-886-6 • $10.99 US/$14.99 CA
88 Pages Trade Paperback

MINECRAFT

Tyler's family has to move but thankfully, he has a strong group of friends forever linked in the world of *Minecraft*! They go on the ultimate quest and face off against the Ender Dragon!

978-1-50670-834-8 • $10.99 US/$14.99 CA
88 Pages Trade Paperback

MINECRAFT VOLUME 2

When Evan and the gang find themselves assaulted by pirates, and then by an even bigger threat, all the players realize they must learn to rely on each other to overcome adversity.

978-1-506780-836-2 • $10.99 US/$14.99 CA
88 Pages Trade Paperback

MINECRAFT VOLUME 3

Candace, Evan, Grace, Tobi, and Tyler continue their adventures in the world of *Minecraft* and find themselves stumbling upon a mysterious ruined portal. Arriving to a strange and wonderful corner of the Nether that they've never seen, the group turn to their Nether expert, Grace, for help.

978-1-50672-580-2 • $10.99 US/$14.99 CA
88 Pages Trade Paperback

MINECRAFT: STORIES FROM THE OVERWORLD

With tales of rivals finding common ground and valiant heroes new (or not!) to the Overworld, this collection brings together stories from all realms, leaving no block unturned!

978-1-50670-833-1 • $14.99 US/$19.99 CA
88 Pages Hardcover

Minecraft.net
DarkHorse.com